THE WOLF ROAD

THE WOLF ROAD

BETH LEWIS

b

THE BOROUGH PRESS

The Borough Press
An imprint of HarperCollins*Publishers*
1 London Bridge Street
London SE1 9GF

www.harpercollins.co.uk

Published by HarperCollins*Publishers* 2016

1

A catalogue record for this book
is available from the British Library

ISBN: 978-0-00-814545-3

This novel is entirely a work of fiction.
The names, characters and incidents portrayed in it,
while at times based on historical events and figures,
are the work of the author's imagination.

Set in ITC New Baskerville

Printed and bound in Great Britain by
Clays Ltd, St Ives plc

MIX

FSC is a
to promote
Products
to assure con
to m

Find out

For my mum and her red pen.

THE END A' OLD ME

I sat up high, oak branch 'tween my knees, and watched the tattooed man stride about in the snow. Pictures all over his face, no skin left no more, just ink and blood. Looking for me, he was. Always looking for me. He left red drops in the white, fallen from his fish knife. Not fish blood though. Man blood. Boy blood. Lad from Tucket lost his scalp to that knife. Scrap of hair and pink hung from the man's belt. That was dripping too, hot and fresh. He'd left the body in the thicket for the wolves to find.

I blew smoky breath into my hands.

'You're a long way from home, Kreagar,' I called down.

The trees took my voice and scattered it to pieces. Winter made skeletons of the forest, see, made camouflage tricky 'less you know what you're doing, and I know exactly what I'm doing. He weren't going to find no tracks nor footprints nowhere in this forest what weren't his, I know better'n that. Kreagar looked all around, up high and 'neath brushes, but I've always been good at hiding.

'Who's that talkin' at me out in the trees?' he shouted. His voice was like rubbing bone on bark. Something raw in it when he raged but when he was kind it was soft rumbling that cut through a chill night. I didn't want to think about him being kind no more. His kindness was lies and masks.

'Saw what you did to that boy,' I said, 'saw where you put him. See his curly hair on your belt.'

Kreagar sniffed hard. Cold making his nose run into his beard. Teeth bared like one of them mountain bears. Didn't even have a shirt on, never did when he did his killing. Blood splashed all over his chest, mingling with the tattoos and wiry black hair.

'That you, Elka girl? That my Elka playing squirrel in the trees?' he shouted.

'I ain't yours,' I said, 'never was, never gonna be.'

I took out my knife. Long blade, barbed saw teeth on the back, and stag-horn handle.

Kreagar stamped around the forest, showing all the critters where he was, trailing blood like a damn invitation.

'Come down, give ole Kreag a hug. I've missed you.'

'I don't think so. Think I'll stay right where I am.'

His eyes searched the trees. Black as pitch them eyes, black as disease and disorder and hate and lies. He grinned, flat white teeth like gravestones, and twirled his little fish gutter in his fingers, flinging blood everywhere, rolling out the red carpet.

'Elka, you know I don't mean you no harm.' His voice turned friendly. 'I'd never hurt my Elka.'

He wandered around like a blind man, trudging through the snow, steam lifting off his body. Always hot after a killing. He was lean, carved out of wood some say and, but for the tattoos, had a face you'd take home to your mother. He leant up against a cottonwood tree, panting to keep the cold out, getting sick of hide-and-seek.

'Could a' killed you a hundred times, girlie,' he said, slow. 'Could a' taken my pig-sticker and cut you neck to navel while you slept. Could a' peeled your skin off easy as boiled trout.'

I remembered all those years calling him Daddy and felt sick.

'Could a' made my winter boots out of your back,' he carried on, voice getting more excited, smile getting bigger, like he was reeling off courses at a feast. 'New belt out of your arms. Could a' stuffed my mattress with your silky brown hair.'

He laughed and I felt sicker. He raised his knife, pointed it into the trees, right at my face though he didn't know it.

'You'd make a fine pair of boots, Elka girl.'

Heard it all before but it didn't stop the cold creeping up my back, cold that weren't snow. Cold that weren't ice and winter. I heard him say worse but never to me. I was still afraid of him, the things he'd done, the things he made me do. But damn if I wasn't trying to turn it to good.

'All these months you been looking for me, Kreagar, and I found you first.'

I raised up my own knife. Weighted right nice for throwing. I told him in my head to stay there against the tree, told him don't you move a muscle.

'I been worried something rotten for you, Elka. This world ain't no place for a kid like you on your own. There are worse things than wolves in the dark. Worse things than me.'

But for the blood he could have been a normal Joe out on a stroll. But for the kid's scalp swinging in the breeze, he could've been anyone. But he wasn't. He was Kreagar

Hallet. Murdering, kid-killing bastard Kreagar Hallet. Took me far too long to figure that out and no prettied-up words would change it now.

I stood up on the branch without making more'n a snowflake shudder and wound back my arm. Breathed out. Pictured him like a deer. Threw my knife with all the force I had, straight and true and hit him in that soft spot just below the collarbone. That metal went through his shoulder into that tree, pinned him hard, heard that wood-thud you get during target practice. And I'd done a lot of target practice. Damn if that weren't a perfect shot.

Hollered and howled he did, more out of shock than pain. Didn't think his little Elka could throw that hard I'll bet. Kreagar shouted some things I daren't repeat, some threats that shouldn't see light of day. His own blood met the boy's. The fat black lines on his chest now coated red, hot and steaming fresh in the cold.

He tried to pull it out but I cut them barbs deep. He screamed like a dying sow when he tried.

'Get here, girl, I'm gonna rip you up!'

Still looking around for me, screaming up something fierce. He roared at me, filling the forest, making birds flee their nests, rabbits scrabble into their warrens, but he still couldn't see me. Ghost I was in those woods. He'd taught me well.

'I'm gonna find you! I'm gonna kill you slow, Elka!'

I couldn't help but laugh. I had him. Finally. Sprung the trap and caught me a rabid bear.

'Magistrate Lyon's gonna find you first,' I said. 'Told her where you is and where the boy is too. She'll see what you did to him. She's been hunting you a long time, across mountains she's gone, looking for you.'

That shut him up. Colour drained right out of him. Nobody wants Lyon and her six-shooter on their tail and Kreagar had for months. But then, so had I.

He started pleading, trying the friendly on me, but I wasn't hearing it. Strands of spit hung off his beard, flaring out with every breath. I watched him until I heard the clomping horse hooves, kicking up snow and soil. Steam rising off hard-ridden flanks. I smiled. Magistrate Lyon and her lieutenants, here to bring in the bad guy. Another life and that bad guy could a' been me.

No reward a' course, gold don't mean nothing to me no more, only life got value in my mind.

I saw them coming through the trees, Kreagar still stuck and hollering, panicking and pulling on the handle, that blood trail leading them right to his feet.

Lyon's smarter than Kreagar, got eyes like a sparrow hawk, she'd see me in half a breath and she'd take me too, for what I done. She'd have questions. Big ones I didn't feel much like answering.

Kreagar heard them hooves, heard them whinnying mares. His eyes went wide like a buck about to be shot and that's when I got to leave it up to the law. Shame about the knife, that skinned me many a rabbit and marten, saved my life more'n once too. A good knife is hard to come by, about as hard as finding a good person in this damned country. When your life is your only currency and you got debts to pay, a good knife can make all the difference. I might've lost my blade but I paid my debt. Lyon shouldn't come looking for me no more. 'Less a' course, Kreagar tells her the truth.

THE BEGINNING
OR CLOSE AS YOU GONNA GET

When the thunderhead comes, drumming through the sky, you take cover, you lock your doors and you find a place to pray because if it finds you, there ain't no going back. When the thunderhead came to Ridgeway, my clapboard town, I had nowhere to hide. Seven years old I was and screaming up something fierce at my nana. She wanted me to go collect pine resin for the lamps. Said it made 'em burn with a pretty smell. I told her pretty is for fools and I didn't want no pine smelling up my house.

'My house, girl,' she said, 'you just a guest here till your parents come back. Pray that it be soon.'

I think I had a different name back then. Don't remember Nana ever calling me Elka.

I told her to go spit seeds and started howling.

'That mouth of yours is black as the goddamn devil's,' she shouted in that tone what meant I was in for a beating. Saw her reaching for her walking stick. Had me welts the shape a' that stick fresh on my back.

'My mouth ain't nothin', you ain't my momma, you can't tell me nothin'.' I was wailing and trying my damnedest to push over the eating table, to send all them plates and three types a' fork scattering all over. That'd show her, I figured, show her good.

Nana let out one a' her big sighs. Seen other old folk in Ridgeway sigh like that, like they weren't just sick a' the person giving them ire but sick a' the world what was full a' them. All them years, Nana must a' been hundreds, all them wrinkles creasing up her face, that sigh is what them years sound like, wheezing, long, and dog-tired.

'Your momma,' Nana said, 'my fool of a daughter, running off with that man.' She looked at me like I was Momma for a minute, kindness in her eye, then must a' seen that Daddy half a' me and got mad again. She clenched up all her teeth so hard I wondered brief if they was going to crack and fly out her head.

'They coming back to get me,' I said, whining voice full a' tears. 'Daddy gonna show you the back a' his hand for beating me.'

Nana laughed, high-pitched and trilling like a shrike bird. 'Your daddy's too busy hunting gold up in the North and your momma's too busy shining his boots to think of you, girl. You're stuck with me and I'm stuck with you so you better go out and get that resin or so help me child I'll beat you blue.'

Nana's fists was tight and her body was shaking. She was a rake of a woman but she was Mussa valley born, built head to toe out a' grit and stubborn. She had strength in her what you'd never credit behind that paper skin. Broke my arm once, she did, with just them hands a' hers.

I crossed my arms over my chest and I huffed and I said

I didn't want no pine and I hated pine 'bout as much as I hated her.

Then she threw up her arms, sick of me, and said she was going walking.

'Don't you follow me,' she said. 'I don't even want to look at you no more.'

She'd been gone not half an hour when the sky boomed black, cut out the sun. Sounded like a mountain splitting apart. No matter how many times I've heard that since, I get the fear. Cold runs up my bones from my toes to my skull. I shake. I sweat like a snow fox in summer. All because of that day. All because my nana left me alone when the thunderhead came.

Our little two-room shack, far out in the forest, didn't stand a chance against that weather. Nana said her and Grandpa, afore he died in the Second Conflict some twenty years past, rebuilt that shack a hundred times and she'd rebuild it a hundred more no doubt. Nana and me was like butting rams most days but not all my thoughts a' that shack were dark. When that thunderhead came, I sure as shit wanted that woman and them iron arms round my shoulders.

I saw the thunderhead coming down from the north, rolling 'tween the hills at the top of our valley. Our idiot valley. Acted like a corral, funnelled all that raging storm right toward our forest, our front door, and to Ridgeway a few miles down the way. It kicked up rocks and broken branches and mashed them all together with ice and rain. I saw it out the window, roaring down the hill like a grizzly in heat.

Ground shook. My toes went cold. The roof ripped off and smashed against the cedars. I don't remember screaming but I'm sure I was. Felt like all hell was coming down on my seven-year-old shoulders. Cracking thunder all but deafened me. Hail and rain all but froze me solid. I hid under the eating table, arms and legs wrapped tight around its leg, and shouted at it all to go away, leave me be. Shouted for my nana to come back. Cursed her name more'n once.

Then I was in the air. Table lifted up like a dry leaf and afore I knew it, I was too high to let go. I dug my nails into the wood and scrunched up my eyes. Rocks and twigs snagged at me, cut up my arms and legs, pulled out my hair in clumps. Tiny balls of ice hit my face and felt like hot metal filings. That wind threw me and the table around like we was nothing. Only existing for the fun of the thunder. Table got ripped away or I let go, I don't know. Spinning and careening and screaming. No idea if sky was up, rock was down or if I was already dead.

I don't know much a' what happened next. The storm must a' let me go, had enough of playing. Next thing I knew I was falling, rushing air pulling at me, storm passing off to the east. Head-first into the Thick Woods. I fell through close branches, smells of cedar and alder and cypress. Cradled me, slowed me, till one a' them branches didn't want to let me go. My vest ripped and snagged and I was swinging ten feet up from the dirt. Felt blood on me and cuts stinging and my lungs was stripped from screaming. Then my vest ripped and I dropped. Landed with a thud on the moss, a pain shooting right up my back.

Dazed, I was. I remember that clear as spring. The thunderhead blew itself out over the ridge. They never last long though they make sure you never forget them. I sat in that same spot in the Thick Wood, swaying, gathering up all that had just happened in my baby head. Trying to make some kind a' sense of it all. Could a' been ten minutes. Could a' been half a day. Think it was when I started to get hungry that I snapped out of it.

Everything was green and brown. Couldn't see the sky for the branches. Couldn't see more'n a few feet in front of me. Lucky I was small and could squeeze 'tween the trunks.

'Nana,' I shouted. 'Nana, where you at?'

But the forest didn't answer. Didn't take me long to realise Nana weren't coming.

She said we lived south in the valley. Ridgeway town was souther still. Showed it me on a map one time. I figured the thunderhead came from the north so that's where it took me back to. My young head said go south. South was down on the map so that's the way I went. Down any hill I could find.

Got lost quick.

I tried picturing all those places on that map of BeeCee. That's what we call our country now, just letters of its real name what most people have forgot or don't care to remember. The map said that old name behind all the scribblings, all the new borders and territories my nana drawn on, but I could only read letters then, not whole words. All I know is that one day all the maps became useless and we had to make our own. The old'uns called that day the Fall or the Reformation. Nana said some down in the far south called it Rapture. Nana was a babe when it happened, said her momma called it the Big Damn Stupid. Set everything back to zero. I never asked why, never much cared. Life is life and you got to live it in the here-now not the back-then. And the here-now for little me was the Thick Woods with night coming fast.

I had these little boots on, cute things stitched from

marten pelt, soft and warm but no good for travelling. They tore up in a few hours. The thunderhead torn a swatch out a' the knee of my denims and them trees had chewed up my vest so's it was barely hanging onto me. Seven-year-old me walked till it got dark. Belly rumbling worse than the storm. I started crying proper then, big fat tears, blubbering and wailing. I huddled myself inside a hollowed-out log as the darkness crept through the trees. Bugs and grubs crawled all over me. I shivered so hard it shook rotten wood dust into my hair.

Never been alone before. Always had Nana close by and afore her, though I barely remember them, my momma and dad. Nana said they'd gone north, far far up the world to find their fortune and bring it home to me. That was a few years ago. They sent a letter 'bout a year after they went, brought to the Ridgeway general store by some kind traveller heading that way. I couldn't read it course but I made Nana read it to me till I knew all them words like I know my own name. Words like gold and sluice and them what sounded foreign and exciting: Halveston, the Great YK, Carmacks, Martinsville. My momma and daddy's names. I made Nana read them over and over. Made the world and them sound close and far all at one time, that letter did. I kept it 'neath my pillow, ink fading with readings and years. Put an ache in my chest thinking the thunderhead took it.

I sniffed hard, sucked up all my fears, and tried to sleep. Worst night of my life that was. No matter all them nights that came after. No matter all those cold, dark things that happened. That one night was the worst. It was the first time I realised that you're all you've got in this world. One moment you can be in your home, fire in the grate, clothes on your back, your kin nattering beside you, the next moment you're lost. Taken up by the thunderhead and dropped into nowhere. No point fixating on all those other things. My nana weren't here, that letter weren't here. My parents sure as shit weren't here. I had me and I had this log and, though I would've loved some hot stew right then, I couldn't much complain. I wriggled about, got somewhere close to comfort and shut my eyes.

Something scratched at the side of the log. Claws running down bark. My eyes sprung open.

My heart damn-near stopped. Night was full, I must a' been sleeping. Moonlight cut through the branches. Sky's always crystal after a storm, almost brighter'n day sometimes. But these woods were thick and old and I couldn't see further than the swaying fern tips an arm's reach outside the log.

Fern twitched. Heart raced.

Scrabbling got louder. Came closer.

I stopped breathing, hoping it wouldn't find me. I thought I saw bear claws, heard big grizzly sniffling. Forest was playing tricks. I burst out that log quicker than a rabbit down a hole and ran. Ran and ran and ran. Didn't look back once. Not a clue how long I ran for, how far. Then I smelt smoke and saw a light.

'Nana,' I shouted. 'Nana! I found you!'

The hut sat square in a small clearing. This weren't Nana's shack. This place was smaller. A pipe out the roof puffed smoke and the light spilling out the window showed the fire inside was burning hot. A wooden awning came off the front, propped up with two thick trunks and below it, close to the door, two A-frames stretching deer hide. Dozen or so metal traps clinked together, hung over a branch. Wire snares, broken and not, littered all over the ground and hanging from trees. Thin strips of red meat dried on racks. Sight of them made my belly grumble and filled up my mouth with water. Nana always told me not to steal from good folks but I figured there were so many the trapper wouldn't miss just one strip. 'Sides I didn't know if he was good folks and Nana never said nothing 'bout stealing from the bad'uns.

I snuck up, quiet as a wolf on the hunt, listening all around for trouble. The racks were just under the awning and I had to pass by one of the windows. I told myself I was a shadow, invisible in the dark and I could run so fast no fat old trapper could catch me. The smell of that meat was a drug. That metallic tang, that sting of salt and smoke. I thought I could smell juniper in it, maybe even some apple wood. Sweet and salty and close enough to touch. I yanked a wide strip of that jerky and a high-pitched bell rang at the door. Smart trapper. Alarmed his dinner in case of bears and hungry girls.

Big boots stomped inside. I shoved the jerky in my mouth and ran. Couldn't tell what meat it was, deer or moose or something else, but it tasted as good as it smelt. The hut door flung open. The trapper didn't shout but I looked back anyway. Hat on his head, just a black shape, but he had a shotgun. Wasn't no law out in those parts and he had every right to shoot a thief on his land. I forced my tired legs to run.

Then I heard him coming after me.

I was a hare darting quick and low and quiet. He was a lumbering ox, crashing through.

My heart thundered. I didn't want to die in that forest, shot for taking a mouthful of meat I didn't even get to enjoy. Curse that thunderhead for dropping me here. I cried and bawled. Must a' been screaming. That trapper followed me close. He never shouted for me to stop, same as you don't shout for a buck to stop afore you pull the trigger.

He's going to kill me, I thought. Shoot me to shreds.

A trailing scrap of fur on my boots caught on a branch, tripped me. Don't know how I kept that jerky in my mouth but I did, even as I fell ass over face into a dry creek bed. Landed face-first in the dirt and everything went quiet. No more ox crashing. No more footsteps.

I'd lost him. I got the better of that trapper. Got his jerky and got away. I sat up on my knees and ripped off a chunk of that meat, swallowed it whole.

Something made me look over my shoulder. That feeling you get in your bones when someone is watching you. A shadow stood over me.

Big and black and breathing. I didn't even see the butt of the shotgun.

Woke up in the trapper's hut with a sore head wrapped in bandage. He sat on a chair by the door, staring at me with eyes like the devil. Shotgun rested against his leg, his hat on his knee. He must a' fallen too, his face was all covered in streaks of black dirt.

'Where'd you come from?' he said. His voice had a breath of kindness to it.

Nana told me not to speak to strangers, and this man, living far out in the woods all by himself, was the strangest I'd met.

'Where you going to?' he said. Didn't seem all that surprised I weren't talking. 'You got a momma and daddy? Where they at?'

I blinked then, shook my head. 'Just my nana.'

He smiled, showed off a row of flat white teeth.

'Now we gettin' somewhere,' he said. 'Where you and your nana live? Dalston? Ridgeway?'

Something in my face must have gave me away.

'Ridgeway then,' he said. He rubbed his cheek but none of the mud came off. 'You a long way from home, girl.'

He put his hand on the shotgun barrel and relaxed in his chair.

'You can just point me the right way,' I said, 'and I'll be gone afore you know it.'

'There are beasts in these woods would eat you up quicker'n you can scream. Couldn't let you do that.'

I shuffled a bit on the bed, felt my cheeks get hot and red. I couldn't tell much about the trapper, other than he wore old denims like me and his shirt was ripped like mine. A coat made of fur and skins hung next to the door with a pair of snowshoes propped up under. His shirt, once white, had spots and smears of something dark brown on it, maybe dried blood from the animals. He stared at me long and hard and my belly started growling again.

'I ain't got no real way of telling if you're speaking true or false,' he said. 'You could be a trouble maker on the run from the law. You could be a thief and stolen worse than a bite of jerky. You could be anyone.'

My nana would a' said I was a troublemaker but I weren't telling him that.

'I'm headin' down to Ridgeway in the morning to trade some pelts, two-day round trip mind.' He stopped, rubbed his face again, mud stayed put and by then I weren't sure if it was really mud.

'Your business is your own, girlie, but I'll do some asking and see if I can find your nana. If I do and she wants you back, I'll take you to her.'

'I'll help you find her quicker,' I said, scooting off the edge of the bed. I got dizzy then and fell down, landed hard on my hands and knees.

The trapper didn't move to help me, just said, 'You couldn't walk more'n a mile in that state. You're just a baby, no more than a few winters on you. You're dead weight until you can carry a rifle.

'Go to sleep,' he said and picked up his hat. 'I'll be gone when you wake up. Keep the fire lit and don't touch nothing.'

He put his hat over his face and leant his head back against the door.

I climbed back onto the bed and pulled up the blanket. 'You got a name?' I asked.

'I got a few,' he said, without moving his hat.

Something in the way he said that put a seed of fear in me. I pulled the blanket up close to my chin and hunkered down. There was no chance of me sleeping that night. I didn't take my eyes off him. He didn't make a sound all night. Not a snore. Not a sniff. Didn't move, didn't even let go of the shotgun. Even my nana slept louder than that. He was like one of them statues carved out of stone. Nana took me down to Couver City to see them last summer. She said I needed *culturing*, whatever that meant. Couver was hit hard in the Damn Stupid, says Nana, and only a few of them statues are left in the ruins. Three-day ride up and down that was. After six days in the saddle, sitting awkward 'tween Nana and the horse's neck, I told her I didn't care for culturing.

I must've slept because one moment I was fixing my eyes on the trapper and the next it was dawn and the chair was empty. Shotgun and him were gone. Keep the fire lit, he said, and don't touch nothing. I never been much good at following the say-so of grown-ups, not even now I'm grown-up myself.

First thing I did was get another strip of jerky from the rack outside. Then I stoked up the fire and roasted up that jerk so it was crispy and charred at the edges, and I had me a fine breakfast. Then I went through the trapper's things. Found a few coins no one uses no more, bowls carved out a' cherry wood, a little wooden box locked up tight, and a knife sharp enough to skin a boar in three seconds flat. It had a long bone handle, probably deer or moose leg, and the blade was longer'n my forearm. Beautiful thing, I remember thinking, and I sliced up my jerky just to feel it in action. I told myself then that I would have a knife like this. Maybe I could get the trapper to make me one.

I got bored quick. Two-day trip to Ridgeway and back he said. Meant I was further from Nana than I'd ever been and I didn't know north or south or up or down or which way would take me back to Nana. Shit, by then, that knife in my hands and no grown-up telling me what for, I weren't even sure I wanted to go back.

Trapper didn't have much of anything and, once I had a full belly, I didn't have nothing to occupy me. I went outside, kicked dirt, climbed trees, watched the sun reach noon and start falling into dusk. I wondered if he'd reached Ridgeway yet. If he'd asked around about me. Strange that he didn't ask for my name. Strange that he didn't ask where'bouts in Ridgeway I lived. Because, strictly, I didn't live in Ridgeway. Nana's shack was up the valley. Enough people in town knew about us that I thought he wouldn't have no problem finding her.

I kept the fire hot and twirled that bone-handle knife in my little hands. Thinking of all the things I could do with it. How thin I could slice jerky, how neat and quick I could kill a rabbit. Night came fast with those thoughts swimming inside me and I fell asleep on the floor by the fire.

Woke up to spring dawn singing through the trees and spent that day much as I had the last, exploring the land, finding rabbit runs. I even reset one a' the trapper's squirrel poles what must a' fallen in the thunderhead.

Sun was dipping and I was sucking on another piece of meat, knife in hand, when the trapper came back. He came in the door with a sack over his shoulder. He stared at me, jerky hanging out my mouth and blade in my hands, and he didn't say nothing. Something in his head ticked over and he stopped a beat, then dropped the sack with a sound like logs tumbling off a pile.

'Found your nana,' he said and hung up his coat.

Felt a sting in me, like my fun was cut short and I'd be back to beatings and her schooling tomorrow. I set down the knife on the floor and I stared at that blade like I was giving up my favourite toy.

'You takin' me back tomorrow?' I said. Part a' me wanted to see my nana, but I knew soon as she saw me she'd have me hauling planks to fix the shack or learning letters at that whiteboard a' hers.

Then he said, 'Your nana got caught out in the thunderhead, tree fell on her.'

'She dead?'

Trapper nodded once and kept his eyes on me.

Shame on me that my first thinking was hot damn, I don't got to go back to schooling. Shame on me twice that my second was serves her right for treating me rough. Then came the aching like my insides was full a' river mud, thick and sucking me down, a deep place a' sorrow I didn't

want no part of. I weren't all that sure how to feel in them
moments. Should I be crying? But I didn't feel nothing like
crying. Should I be whooping for joy? But I didn't feel like
doing that neither. I stared at that knife, chewing on that
jerky, quiet-like for an age. Trapper didn't say nothing, he
just watched me, waiting to see what I'd do, what kind a'
person I was.

He shifted his foot, floorboard creaked. My eyes was
locked on that blade and my head and my heart came
together and told me how to feel. I reached for the knife.

Soon as I touched that white bone handle I realised
quick I chose right. I didn't much want to go back to Nana's
shack, she never let me eat jerky and play with knives. Her
ways were learning letters and sums, clean hands and clean
clothes. Them ways weren't mine and, much as she'd tried
to force it, they never would be.

The trapper nodded to the meat 'tween my teeth.

'You like that?' he asked.

I nodded.

'You know how to use that knife?'

I weren't quite sure what he meant but I nodded again.

'You ever skinned a hare?'

I flinched then. I had, year or two ago, but when Nana
caught me she whipped my back bloody. Second time she
caught me she broke my arm.

'You ever skinned a hare, girl?' he asked again, something
raw in his voice.

'Yes, sir, I have.'

'If you can skin a hare you can 'bout skin anything,' he
said and pointed to the sack. 'Traded my furs for a pig. I
already jointed it for easy carryin'. Take off the skin and fat,
take off the meat, and cut it thin for smokin'. Got it?'

I nodded and stepped forward. The trapper lifted up the sack and poured out the chunks of pig. Pink skin and pale flesh, it would work fine with apple wood, I could almost taste it already. Even though I was just seven, I always knew I was born to work a knife. Took me most of the night but I did it, and all while the trapper watched over me, sipping on a flask. He didn't once tell me to be careful. Didn't say much 'cept 'other way', when I got to separating the knuckle.

Come dawn we both laid the strips on racks and hung them up in the tiny smokehouse outside.

The trapper put a hand on my shoulder then and said, 'You got a gift with a blade, girlie, I'll teach you to use it right. Names don't mean nothing in these woods but I got to call you something.'

Then he looked at me, pulled at my scruffy hair.

'Rougher'n elk's fur, this,' he said.

So he called me Elka, 'stead of Elk, on account of me being a girl. I stopped asking for his name after a few weeks and just called him Trapper in my head. He taught me to tie a snare, taught me to set a deadfall trap and shoot a squirrel from fifty yards. All I had to do was help him clean the kills, prep the traps, stretch and scrape the furs, and tend to the hut. I slept on the floor by the fire and him in his bed. Though, thinking about it, I don't think he slept much. He hunted a lot at night, said the wolves come out at night but he never brought back a wolf pelt.

That was my life then and damn if it weren't fun. I was a new person, I forgot my old name quick, and I was Elka from then on. I could make a bow and arrow from sticks and shoot me a marten. I forgot my sums and my letters. I forgot my nana and near forgot my folks, though them words in the letter never went out my head. All them skills

Trapper taught me I remember to this day but there are big ole patches a' them years that are fuzzy and dark, whole months a' winter what went in a blink. Much as I tried, I couldn't fill up them gaps.

But hell, I was an idiot kid. Trapper was my family even though I didn't know a sure thing about him but I figured quick I didn't know much more 'bout my parents and they was kin. Trapper was the kind a' family you choose for yourself, the kind that gets closer'n blood. He was my daddy from then, I just needed to find myself a momma.

MOMMA IN THE FOREST

Three winters I spent with Trapper afore I found her. Ten years old and my skinny arms and back was strong with hard living. Trapper weren't the friendly sort but him and me quick found our rhythms. Shit, I think he even started to like me.

We had rules a' living but thinking on 'em now, they was mostly for me to follow. Don't ask no questions. Don't wander out a' sight a' the hut. Don't talk to no people 'bout him. Last one weren't no trouble, I ain't seen another face 'cept Trapper's in three years. The rage I had in me when I was with my nana, what made me scream and shout and tantrum, weren't there no more. Trapper saw the wild in me and didn't try to tame it and cage it like my nana done. I didn't have no bars to rage 'gainst no more. You trap a wolf and he's going to snarl and rip you up till he can get free but once he's out there, treading his own path in the snow, you ain't got much to fear 'less you provoke him. Trapper knew that and I saw that same fierce in him.

We was closing in to winter, just a few weeks we figured till the white blanket would come smothering. Winters were eight months a' harsh. Snow up to your eyebrows, winds what'll rip your skin right off your bones, trees hunkered over with the weight a' the season, like crooked old men at a whisky parlour. Trapper said winters got colder since the Damn Stupid, snow deeper and ice thicker, summers got sweltering like them tropics far down south. Any animal or man what could survive the whiteout would come out the other side fiercer and that much harder to kill. Made living long a rare thing indeed. Folks now are wrinkled up and wizened where the same years would a' looked fresh-faced afore the Damn Stupid. People round here get killed by hailstorms and drought, 'stead a' invisible diseases and bombings. Nature ain't friendly no more but least nowadays it's honest 'bout it.

Trapper had me chopping logs to kindling in the rain, stocking up for the freeze. Chopping wood weren't no fun and our axe was blunter'n a river rock.

'Shit,' I said when the rain made my hands slip and the axe stuck hard in the wood. I threw the whole thing, log and axe, into the woodpile. 'I might as well chop down an oak with a dead rabbit all the good that blade is.'

Trapper was cleaning his rifle 'neath the awning, prepping for a hunt.

'Why don't you never let me come with you?' I shouted so he could hear me over the weather. 'I could help dressin' them deer, hauling meat.'

He didn't even look up from the barrel. 'You want to freeze up solid in the night?'

I wiped wet, stuck-down hair off my face but the rain just started falling heavier. Ground was turning quick to mud 'neath my boots. Trapper got me them boots early that spring, said they came off a barrow, some boy in Dalston died that winter. When I asked 'bout the blood on 'em he said the boy had a sickness a' the lungs what made him cough red. I washed them boots in the river till my hands was numb and raw. Trapper said the boy got too cold and the devil got in him 'tween the shivering.

'No,' I said, less I end up like that boy, 'I don't want to freeze up.'

He screwed the scope back on the rifle. 'We all got our jobs, Elka. Even this rifle got a job.'

Always liked that gun I did, it was black and sleek and the barrel was longer'n my arm. I could just 'bout hold it right but Trapper never let me fire it. Said the kickback would knock my whole shoulder out a' joint.

He put the rifle bolt back in the stock and tested it a few times. That bolt slid back and forth smooth as butter over a hot plate.

'Where'd you get that gun?' I said. I winced soon as them words left me. Don't ask no questions was one a' our rules.

But Trapper didn't growl at me like he normal did. 'Stead he set down the rifle and started loading up one a' the magazines with bullets. Homemade bullets a' course.

'Took it off some ruski fella in the Second Conflict,' he said, looking at the gun not me. 'I gave him my rotten M-16 as payment. Gun what I just shot him with. This here is a Dragunov. Got to take the best a' what's in front a' you, girl.'

I picked up the axe, still stuck in that log, and tried to pull it free. It was the best axe we had and it was better'n splitting logs with a knife and hammer.

'You was in that fight?' I said. 'My nana said my grand-daddy was too.'

'Everyone was in that fight,' he said, 'only not all of us was wearing uniforms.'

He watched me struggle with that log but didn't make no moves to help. He put the last bullet in the magazine and loaded the rifle. Then he picked up his hat and wax jacket from inside the hut.

'I'll be back tomorrow,' he said, slinging that rain gear on and striding out into the mud. He'd been gone all last night and now it weren't all that much past noon. It weren't normal for him to be gone so frequent and so early, but I figured he must a' had his reasons and I'd already pushed my luck with the questioning.

He stopped at the edge a' the trees.

'Hold the axe at the end a' the handle, not the head,' he said, 'and put your foot on the log.'

I did, and the axe popped out easy.

'Keep the fire lit, Elka girl,' he said and stalked off into the trees.

I always kept the fire lit and he knew it but he said it every time he left no matter what. Figured maybe it was his way a' saying a kindness without having to. Stead a' I love you, you keep the fire lit.

Not sure why I thought a' them I love you words then, I don't remember no one ever telling me that. Trapper never did, that's for damn sure, and I can't even imagine them sneaking out 'tween my nana's gnarly lips. But them words was stuck up in my head.

Tell my little girl, I love you.

Momma's letter. The paper they was on was lost or rotted or stolen by the thunderhead but them words was still there. Quick realised I hadn't thought a' them the whole winter past, since the middle a' last year.

Suddenly had me a longing to see Trapper. Didn't want no girly cuddle off him or nothing soppy like that but I wanted him close, not gone all night on a hunt. Never felt as safe in this world as when he was round.

I set my head firm and figured he can't a' got far. It weren't often I went 'gainst Trapper's words but some deepdown feelings got the better a' me and I was decided afore my senses got a say in it. I set down the axe on the porch and went inside for my coat and hat as well as a hunk a' bread and strip a' jerk for dinner. Thought twice afore I left and grabbed two more pieces a' meat. Trapper's always got a fierce hunger on him when he's been hunting.

When I came out the hut the rain had eased off to a weak drizzle, like it weren't even trying no more, and I figured I was no more'n ten minutes behind Trapper. I went after him, right where he'd gone through the trees. I thought I'd paid attention when he taught me 'bout tracking but I couldn't see shit in all that mud and wet. His footprints had turned to sludge pools and the path quick turned to moss and mulch. I didn't call out, that was another a' them rules. When you in the forest, when you on a hunt, you don't speak. Even if a grizzly takes a swing at you, keep that mouth sewn up tight.

I walked for god knows how long, till the rain clouds cleared and the sky turned deep blue, maybe five hours, but my legs was short and I was slow back then so I don't know how far I got in truth. Summer meant long evenings a' sunlight what can play tricks on you. I sure broke Trapper's rule though. Don't go out a' sight a' the hut. But I figured I knew my way back so he couldn't go raging at me too hard, 'sides, I was grown up to ten now, weren't a kid no more.

I came to a clearing with meadow grass near tall as me

and I froze. Straight across the other side, brown eyes was staring back at me. Wide and terrified and belonging to a woman. A human woman. Wondered brief if it was the late light confusing my brain but she raised her hand, waved, and started limping toward me. Thought about running. My hands was shaking. My head was racing through all kinds a' options. Hide. Help. Run. But it was a woman. Hell, I hadn't seen no woman for years.

Don't talk to no one, Trapper said. But my curious got the better a' me and I figured I'd already broke one rule, might as well break two.

Strange as it was to see a person out in the forest, I couldn't stop staring at her. I had hair down to my chin and I thought that was longer'n was strictly practical but she had black silk reaching her waist. I thought my eyes was pretty brown enough but hers was damn near golden. I thought I was tall enough but she was half my height again. Only woman I ever remember seeing was my nana and I can tell you now, she was a shrivelled shrew compared to this one. Realised quick I was smiling. Grinning like a clown watching her walk at me.

'Hey,' she said, voice weak and raw. She had one hand held tight at her chest, holding the corners of her shirt together. When she got closer I saw it weren't a shirt but a nightgown, lacy thing fit for nothing.

'What you doing out here dressed in that?' I said, 'cause that, not who in the hell are you, was the first question that came into my ten-year-old head.

She kept looking round and kept down low in the grass, like someone was chasing her or they was playing hide and go seek and I was 'bout to give her away. Don't think she heard my question 'cause she didn't answer it.

'What are you doing out here all on your own? Are you lost?' she said and came up right beside me. She didn't have no shoes on her feet and I wondered brief if she might be simple. She didn't sound it though, didn't look it neither. Her voice was new to me and all the more pretty for it. So many years a' harsh Trapper tones had hardened up my ears but her voice melted all that away.

'I ain't lost,' I said.

She knelt down and put her hands on my shoulders like she was checking I was real. 'Do you live nearby?'

I said yes and she smiled and when she did that all my doubts went skipping off. I'd found me a momma, gone off into the woods by myself and I caught me one, same as Trapper catches rabbits. He'd be right proud a' me. I smiled wide, showing her all my teeth, what I always kept clean. Trapper always said clean teeth meant good health and his was always white and sparkling.

I took the bread out my pocket and offered it to her. She looked at me a minute, trembling, eyes darting every which way, then she snatched it out my hands and ripped off a chunk 'tween her teeth. She murmured thanks 'tween mouthfuls and I didn't right know what to do.

'We have to get out of here,' she said, barely whispering. 'Do you know the way to town?'

Cold air was floating down from the mountains and she weren't even close to dressed for it. Wouldn't make it to no town, that's for sure.

'Fire's lit in my hut,' I said. 'You can come but you can't touch nothing.'

She nodded, finished off the bread and started following me.

'How old are you?' she said once we got into the trees.

'Ten winters,' I said.

'What are you doing out here?'

I didn't tell her 'bout Trapper. Figured I'd surprise her once we got back home and I'd had a chance to get her cleaned up and fed. By the look a' this woman, Trapper'd be a fool to say no to having her as his wife and my momma.

'Could ask the same 'bout you. You got a name?' I said.

She kept looking 'bout like she was expecting something to jump out the trees any minute. 'Missy,' she said.

Didn't think much a' the name but Trapper could always change it, like he'd done with mine. I said, 'What you fearing? Ain't nothing out here gonna hurt you.'

'What makes you so sure?'

I puffed out my chest and said, 'I know these woods like I know my own skin. Lived out here all my life with my daddy.'

I never called Trapper 'Daddy' to his face but sometimes, when he weren't around, I tried it out, enjoyed the sound of it on my tongue.

'I woke up,' she said, 'out here in the woods this morning. I went to bed last night. Then a. . . a shadow, I saw a shadow in my window,' she shook her head and I saw a line a' blood trickling down her forehead out that pretty black hair, '. . . then I was here. I've been out here all day.'

I didn't pay no mind to what she was saying, people babble 'bout all kinds a' stuff when they been out and cold all day. I told her we should stay quiet 'case a' bears. She stayed close to me, bent over, arms wrapped around herself and we didn't talk much for the rest a' the walk. Trapper liked people who could be hushed.

We got back to the hut when the sky was dark and stars was poking through the black. Missy was shivering and soon as I opened the door, she was in by that fire. I grabbed a pile a' logs from outside and stoked up the fire. Maybe it was having company that turned me into a dunce but as I was putting one a' them logs in the burner, I caught the back a' my hand on the iron door. Red hot pain went through me and my skin blistered up in one fat line.

I hissed and swore and Missy jumped up quick, with a soft gasp, and grabbed my hand. I was 'bout to slap her away with my good one till I figured she was helping. She blew cool air over my skin while I squirmed and whined and I couldn't help it. This weren't pain I knew, ain't never been burned to blisters afore.

'It's OK,' she cooed, 'it's not that bad, we'll get you fixed up.'

And she smiled so sweet that it close took the heat away. She led me outside to the water butt, where Trapper and me catch rain and melt water for drinking, with her arm round my waist. I don't never remember my nana holding me like that and sure as shit Trapper never did. Felt a warming in me that didn't hurt none.

Missy gentle dipped my hand into the cold water. Made me wince and grit my teeth but soon the cold did its job.

'A lot of fuss for nothing,' Missy said, smiling and letting my hand go. She ripped off a strip a' her nightdress, showed off her knees all goose-skinned from the chill, and soaked it in the water. Then she wrapped it all gentle-like around my hand.

'Keep this cold and wrapped up until the pain stops. Don't pop the blister, OK?' She said it like she was talking to a kid she'd known since birthing. She was the momma I was meant to have, all kind and beautiful and sweet as honey.

'Thank you,' I said and in truth, my hand didn't hurt all that much no more.

'My mother used to do the same for me when I was careless around the kitchen,' Missy said. 'Come on, let's get back inside before you catch your death of cold.'

We did and Missy dropped a few more logs on the burner and lit the lamps, told me just to sit quiet, draped a blanket round my shoulders. I let her. Weren't every day I was the one tended to. With the light high in the room I spotted a smear a' blood 'cross the front a' her nightgown but figured she must a' just scratched herself in the forest. Her hair was full a' twigs and strands a' moss and it looked like she'd been dragged backwards right 'cross the Mussa valley.

'You got to clean yourself up,' I said and got up to fetch a bowl a' water and a comb what Trapper brought me back from a trip to Ridgeway. Tame that rats' nest head a' yours, he'd said.

Missy looked at me strange and slowly picked up the comb. With my help, pulling out the twigs and worst a' the moss, we got all that hair smooth in no time.

Then Trapper came through the door.

It shocked me worse'n seeing Missy in the first place. He weren't due back, he was hunting, he'd be gone all night. But there he was, standing in the doorway, hat covering his face, rifle in his hand. Missy tensed up and shuffled closer to the fire, her hand closed round a log.

'Who you brought home, Elka girl?' he said in a voice I couldn't right read.

'This is Missy,' I said. 'She's gonna be my new momma.'

'What?' Missy said and I heard more'n horror in her tone. She looked from me to Trapper and back. 'Please,' she said over and over, shaking her head, 'please.'

Trapper took off his hat and hung it on the peg and he
rested his rifle by the door frame. Then his face changed.
Where normal times it'd be hard as stone, it turned soft
and smiling.

'Oh, honey,' he said to me and my eyebrows raised up
so high they was in danger a' coming right off my head.
Then he turned to Missy. 'I'm so sorry about all this, she gets
carried away, since her mother passed.'

My mouth fell open and I just watched him. I didn't have
no sense a' who this man was. He had Trapper's face but it
was like it was some stranger in his skin. Missy's grip on the
log relaxed a little.

'Are you hungry?' he said, and darted 'bout the place
looking for that hunk a' bread she'd already ate. 'Where do
you live? I can take you home.'

'But—' I started but he quick cut me off.

'Hush, Elka, you done enough.'

'D-Dalston,' Missy said.

Trapper nodded and held out his hand to help her to her
feet. She took it and gave me a look like I was the one to be
fearing.

'It's not far,' Trapper said. 'I'll take you back, make sure
you get home safe. But it's late, you're welcome to stay
the night.'

She said she just wanted to go home, please thanks.

He took off his coat and wrapped it round her shoulders
and if my eyes could a' bugged out my head they would.

'Elka, you stay here while I take Missy back,' he said, then
he opened the door for her. What in the good goddamn!
Trapper don't open doors for people. Trapper don't never
speak to people.

'Sorry, Elka,' Missy said, 'but thank you for the bread.'

I was 'bout to say no, don't you take my new momma away, when Trapper turned round to go out the door.

Trapper was gone all that night and all the next day. I never saw Missy again a' course.

When he came back, we didn't speak 'bout her nor 'bout me getting a' momma. He didn't whip me, didn't shout at me, acted like it never happened. He was Trapper again, none a' that honey in his voice, none a' that sweetness no more and not never again.

Week after Missy, when my hand was healing up nicely, I came to the woodpile and found the axe sharp enough to shave a leg off a cricket afore it'd even notice.

'People – *women* – are dangerous, Elka girl. Some are fierce as wolves, some are meek as deer, but you don't figure out which till they're in too close.'

Never asked him right what he meant, Trapper didn't take kind to back talk. He came and stood next to me at the woodpile.

'Just you and me, Elka girl,' Trapper said to me, 'it can only be you and me.'

I never went searching for a momma again 'cause I knew he was right. He'd never let me have no one else and for another seven winters that's how we stayed. He showed me how to shoot that rifle a' his and how to break it down for cleaning. Every year we stocked up for winter and he kept that axe sharp for me. We built a bigger smokehouse as I was growing and we needed the space for more food and he got us a pressure cooker so we could can the meat in case a' leaner times. That burn scar faded to silver then to nothing you'd notice if you didn't know it was there. I forgot all 'bout the pain what put the scar on my arm but the kindness that soothed it stuck with me. Missy didn't have nothing but she gave me a piece a' herself and she did it gladly. That's something I kept inside me, secret from Trapper and anything else what might go looking.

When I was tall as his shoulder he figured I was grown enough and took me on hunts. First it was just for skinning and hauling but as the years went on, he let me shoot all kinds a' game like rabbits, bear and even a moose. All 'cept deer. I turned seventeen few months past and less'n a week ago, Trapper let me take first shot at a buck, not more'n a few years old but enough to feed us for days with some left to trade for bullets and salt for curing. Deer was Trapper's chocolate and he was precious 'bout it. That's when I knew he trusted me all the way, that's when we was closer'n we'd ever been. That's when I weren't afraid to call him Daddy out loud.

DALSTON AND THAT WOMAN

In Dalston, a scrap-and-shit mining town, one deerskin and three rabbit pelts got me a box of shotgun shells and bed and board in the Stonecutter's Inn. Trapper had no worries in sending me to town by myself, not now I was grown. Ten years in the woods grows you quick. I never stayed long, never traded for drink or company and he knew I could handle a blade should any of the miners take a more'n passing interest.

Dalston was one of them places that god and man both forgot at the same time. Two rows of buildings, half-wood, half-stone, all half-finished. Everyone in Dalston got a look of coal-soot fury on 'em. I don't like people at the best of times, give me trees and wild things any day, but in Dalston they were a special breed. They were full of grim luck them boys, 'specially then, coming to the end of summer when the air outside is chill but the mines are no more'n stone ovens. Like chipping stone in hell. Every time I came back from that pit town I washed twice.

One hand on my deer-horn knife, other clutching the ammo, I stopped dead when I saw Trapper's face tacked up outside the Stonecutter's. Someone had drawn him in charcoal and written some kind of letters and numbers around him. They got his tattoos just right.

'You know this man?' a woman asked me. Clean, sharp voice, cold like water lapped right out a frozen lake.

Funny thing was, I didn't hear her come near me, didn't hear her stepping on the boards, didn't catch her scent on the air. I can hear a bear farting on the other side of the mountain. Can smell it too, and follow it back to its den afore the beast has time to scratch.

This woman crept up on me and that set my bones shaking. I looked at her. All in black with a black ribbon tied tight around her neck and a silver chain dangling. Six-shooter on her belt. No need to hide it, best not to in a town like Dalston. Taller'n me and I was no short stack, Trapper said I was tall as a big grey wolf was long, tail an' all, and just as skinny. The woman had a straight back and blue eyes cold as her voice. Made me feel right uncivilised, that straight back. Never seen a woman like her before nor since.

'Do you know him?' she said, slower, like she was trying to get answers out of stubborn cattle.

'Never seen him afore,' I said.

Don't think she believed it 'cause she kept talking at me. Trapper's first rule he told me was don't tell no one 'bout him. He wanted a quiet life in the forest and I couldn't argue with that.

'His name is Kreagar Hallet and he is wanted for the murders of eight women and one child.'

At that word *child*, she shifted slight. Gave herself away.

'We think he lives out in the forest. The women,' she raised them perfect eyebrows at me like she was looking for a lie, 'were abducted from their homes and hunted, like animals.'

'What's it to you?' I asked. Didn't want to be around her. There was something about her. Felt like she could look right into me, see my soul and my sins. Feeling like ants crawling all up inside my skin. Trapper's face. Talk a' killing. Them things didn't add up in my head.

'Murder is against the law.'

I had to laugh. 'Ain't no law here, lady, never has been.'

She put her hand on her gun and mine went to my knife. 'There is now,' she said and her voice went from cold to steaming.

'Who in hell are you?'

'Jennifer Lyon, Magistrate of Dalston, Ridgeway, Erminton. Hell, all south BeeCee is in my jurisdiction.'

'Fancy name, fancy words. Don't mean nothing to real folk out here,' I said.

'And what about you?' she said. Didn't seem put out by my laughing. 'Do you have a name?'

I smiled wide, showed off all my teeth at her and said, 'I got a few. Now if you'll 'scuse me, lady Jennifer Lyon, Magistrate, I'll be on my way.'

I waved my hand in circles and bowed low and grand. I started walking, suddenly didn't want to stay the night in the same town as her. Cold went through my bones. That charcoal picture was Trapper, no doubt in my head, but she'd called him Kreagar. Said he killed women. Said he killed a kid. Something froze in me. Hunted women, she said, out in the forest, but there's a lot a' hunters in BeeCee. A lot a' men out there in the woods, living away from people. Maybe they had my Trapper mixed up with one a' them. Must be that. Figured I should warn him, least I could do.

I weren't thinking all that straight, that Lyon woman put some kind a' fear in me and it made my feet clumsy. My boot caught on the edge a' the step down to the street and I shot out my hand 'gainst a post to stop falling. Silver scar. Old burn. Missy. Seven years passed without so much as a thought 'bout her and now her face was right there in the front a' my head. That long black hair. That look a' terror in her eyes. Was she running from this Kreagar fella? Lyon said them poor women was taken from they houses. All them memories a' Missy came back like a smack upside the head. What she say? Went to bed, saw a shadow at her window.

That Lyon woman didn't seem like the type to get things wrong. I stopped and looked back at her.

'When these killings happen?'

She took a few steps closer to me. 'The most recent was four nights ago, a few hours before dawn, another was a few days before that, but we believe they go back as far as ten years, probably even longer. He could have killed dozens,' she said. Hand came off her gun and she started fiddling with whatever was on the end of that silver chain.

Week ago, me an' Trapper had gone deer stalking. First time he let me be on point. Bagged a buck on my first shot. Few days later Trapper had gone wolf hunting by himself. He didn't come back with a pelt but he came back with blood on his shirt. I reckon now, looking back, that's why he started killing in his skin, less evidence as Lyon would say.

'And you say you've never met him?' she said.

I shook my head. 'Never met no one called Kreagar Hallet,' I said, plain truth it was. Them ants was burrowing deep in my skin and scratching on my bones. I wanted away from that woman and that town fast as I could.

I got back to the forest and got back to my home. Seeing

my hut, place what I ate and slept and lived so many years a' my life, made me think that Lyon woman was wrong, had to be. It weren't the same fella. Anyone can have tattoos on they face, not anyone can go murdering. No ma'am, I thought, ain't my Trapper on them posters.

Trapper weren't home so I stoked up the fire and went out to check the trapline. That's when it all went to crap. Trapline came up empty save for a few rotten wood pigeons. Trapper sometimes set the snares too loose and open, let them critters sneak right through. I baited them and reset them, hid 'em better in the brush.

I got back to the hut and saw someone moving around inside. It weren't Trapper and they weren't alone. Three of 'em, and three horses tied up outside. They were banging up something fierce, throwing over the table, smashing the cups. Trapper's chair crashed through the window, spooked the horses. Then that woman came out the door. Holding something. Trapper's box, a wooden thing I weren't allowed to touch no matter what. I seen him, after he came back from his wolf hunts, sometimes after a deer hunt, putting something in that box and hiding it 'neath the floorboards where he thought I wouldn't go looking. I didn't, out of respect you see, but that's not to say I weren't tempted.

That Magistrate Lyon had followed me home and taken that box. I took out my knife, silent-like, and held it ready to throw. She opened the box and started shaking. Her face and eyes went blood red. She took something out, I tried to see, I wanted to see, but I couldn't risk moving.

Lyon held up a scrap of skin.

I know all types of skin, see. I know moose, deer, hare, pig, boar, even grouse and goose 'neath the feathers. But that weren't any skin I'd cut before. That was human, that was a scalp of bloody hair. Lyon dropped the box and them hard little lumps went skittering about. One a' them still had long, silky black hair attached.

Silky black hair I'd combed, felt 'tween my fingers, all them years ago. Felt sick down deep. Felt that silver scar on my hand burn and itch.

'It's not his,' Lyon said and two men, one tall and bony, other stocky like he was made out a' packed meat, came out the hut. 'But this one matches the other recent victim.'

I never figured out who she was talking about. Chittering somewhere in the tree above me said squirrels were coming out. I couldn't see them, but I had squirrel poles up in all sorts a' places so I'd catch some no doubt. Trouble was, thought a' eating anything set my stomach churning.

Faster'n I could blink, Lyon drew her gun and fired. The sound near deafened me and a squirrel, or what was left of it, fell right at my feet. Right then I figured I wouldn't get the best of that woman, least not in a fair fight.

I held my breath, felt my heart raging up in my chest. Didn't move. That woman's eyes, like hawk eyes, scanned the trees, trying to pick out her prey.

'No doubt,' she said, 'this is the place.' She threw the scalp on the deck. It slapped and stuck. 'Hallet won't come back now we've been here,' she said, then mounted her horse in one quick move. 'Burn it down.'

One of the men flung kerosene about like it was holy water and my home for ten years was kindling. I watched it burn for a while after they left. All in one go I'd lost my hut and, when I saw that scrap a' Missy's hair fizzle and twist in the flames, like my heart was doing, burning and ripping apart inside me, I knew I'd lost a man I thought of as daddy. Trapper weren't Trapper. I didn't know what he was in truth.

Lyon said he was Kreagar Hallet. Murdering, kid-killer. I couldn't figure it. I couldn't unravel all them strands, all them lies and feelings what got knotted up over the years. Any lie can turn to truth if you believe it long enough and I knew, right in the dark part a' me, that Trapper didn't take Missy home that night. I'd been telling myself lies all along to make his lies all the more convincing.

Tears came pouring down my cheeks. My daddy killed the woman I wanted as my momma, only woman what was ever kind to me, and he acted all friendly about it. Course he did. Trapper always said it's kinder to kill a calm animal, kinder to kill one what ain't fearful. Trapper took the fear right out a' Missy afore he did what he did.

That ain't what a daddy's supposed to do. But he weren't blood, he weren't kin, he was what I chose and I chose wrong.

Words came crawling over my eyes like spiders. *Tell my little girl, I love you.* Blood parents say that, even in a letter, even when they miles and miles up in the far North. Trapper – Kreagar – never said that, not once. I wiped my eyes, told myself them tears was from the heat a' the fire, the burning down of an old life. I left my nana and didn't look back, didn't have no choice after that thunderhead. Figured I could do the same with Trapper. Least till I got my head and my heart right, then maybe I could come back and hear him out, figure his side, let him tell me his truth. Then we'd see. Part a' me said my head was thicker'n a redwood, that he done all them things Lyon said, all them scraps a' skin told his truth. But another part a' me, getting smaller the more my cabin was eaten up by them flames, wanted to think best a' him.

I needed to be away, get myself some distance, figure it all through.

I had my knife and I had a few strips of jerky from that young buck I shot last week. Didn't need much more'n that.

Can't go living in the back-then, I always say. Back then was Trapper. And I weren't at all ready for Kreagar to be my here-now.

Whoever he was, he'd killed people. For fun, for sport. That weren't right by any measure. He killed women and at least one kid. He'd killed Missy. I didn't remember all that much from my years with that man, my head had put memories behind doors and locked them tight. But I remembered her and now, seeing that box a' scalps and hair, I know what he done.

'Damn it,' I said loud, watching the fire. 'Kreagar Hallet. Kid-killin', lyin', murderin', Kreagar Hallet.'

I knew that bastard had a name. All this time he had a name.

'You was my Trapper!' I shouted. 'You taught me fire lighting and snares and how to clean a rifle barrel. Goddamn you for tending my cuts and bruises when all this time. . . all this damn time. . .' I dropped down right on my knees in the dirt and I cried all the fiercer.

The heat off that fire made my tears hiss and steam, like the world was telling me he weren't worth the water. And he weren't. He was what Lyon said. He was what was in that box and I was done with it.

Any happy feeling I had with him these last ten years burned up with my house and tears. I knew the truth, really down deep maybe I always had, and knowing Trapper, he'd kill me quick as I could say *promise I won't tell no one.*

Wolf hunting, my eye. Worst damn wolf hunter in BeeCee and this country's full of 'em. I was a fool not to see it. I ran to the woodpile and threw logs onto the flames. I picked up that axe and threw that on too. Feed it. Burn it all to ash and shit. All them lies go up in smoke.

There are some lines you just don't go crossing. Rules of life. Killing for fun is one of them. It does no one any good. You kill for meat, you kill for survival, you don't go killing for sport. Forest'll eat you whole if you do and spit out the grit.

I walked in circles. Out into the trees, back toward the hut, again and again. I didn't have nowhere nearby to go to. Didn't have nothing to trade. Didn't know a soul to lean on for help. Thought 'bout running to Ridgeway, begging in the street to any stranger who'd take me in. Thought 'bout going to Dalston, finding Lyon and saying, I do know him, he killed all them women so you go kill him.

I don't know if it was pure fear a' that woman or damn idiot loyalty to Trapper but the thought a' him at the end of her six-shooter made me sick. That feeling mixed up with smoke and fire got in my lungs and sent me coughing on my knees. I had to get gone afore he came back and took my scalp for his little box. Had to get as far away from that place and that Kreagar as my legs would take me. But after my screaming and shouting and cursing I was empty. All I had left inside my head was words from some years-ago letter. *Tell my little girl, I love you.*

Trapper asked me once about my momma and daddy and I told him they went to find their fortune. He laughed and said they must a' been simple folk, probably dead by now. But I bet they did find it, bet they living the life of luxury, covered in gold up there in the far far north, just waiting for they little girl to come join 'em. I'd have a real momma and a real daddy and they'd be so rich they'd have one a' them indoor outhouses my nana always wanted.

They'd have a room just for me what I could call my own and a bed so's I wouldn't have to sleep on the floor. They'd have people what would tidy up after them and work their mines for them so's they could spend their days with me. I'd have arms round me what was loving arms and they'd say them I love you words right to my face and mean it.

Soon as I figured it out the thunder came, hammering through the sky. My toes went cold, the wind whipped up the fire so's it ate the wood quicker. Even with my house burning down right in front of me, heating me up to boiling, my bones shook. Shook worse when I realised I had to go right into that storm. I had to walk into the thunderhead if I was going to get clear of Kreagar and find my parents. I took out my knife, deep barbs cut in the blade, and held it up at the storm.

Sky went dark and fierce. Lightning flashed and thunder cracked stone. Fire lit up my face and I yelled, for all to hear, 'You ain't getting me today, thunderhead! I'm comin' for you first!'

I ran at it, screaming like a wild thing, screaming out all my angry and tears at what my Trapper was 'neath the skin. That storm saw me, saw into my eyes and down deep into the heart of me. It saw what I was intending for it when I caught it, punishment for leaving me with Kreagar, and that cowardly storm blew itself out. Skies went calm quicker'n you could draw a pistol. It left the clouds white and split down the middle, showing off a thin blue line of sky. That blue line pointed due north. That blue line pointed to my momma and daddy, to their fortune and my new home.

The thunderhead was giving me safe passage, for now. I didn't say thank you or nothing, didn't sacrifice a goat like some folks would a'. It was the least the damn thing could do after dropping me in the lap of that murdering, kid-killing Kreagar Hallet. I had so much anger in me it killed any speck a' sensible thinking. I didn't bother to cover my tracks or take a zig-zagging path. It never crossed my idiot head that he'd come looking for me.

MUSSA COME BACK

Ten days straight north I went. Sometimes when I looked back I saw the smoke a' the hut curling up into the blue. After four days it turned white meaning the fire was out and, after six, I couldn't a' spotted it for anything. Couldn't a' spotted my home no more and I figured that was the wild telling me I didn't have one. If all that was true 'bout Trapper then I weren't even close to being far enough away from him. There was still some nagging bit a' me what said Lyon was wrong but every time I thought 'bout turning back and finding that man I called Daddy, a picture a' them shrivelled-up scalps flashed up inside my head. Weren't nothing wrong in that. Weren't no lies there. So I kept walking.

Trees started changing the further I went. Thinned out, got taller and broader. It was lighter and brighter in those dying summer days, cool enough not to sweat through your shirts and warm enough to not lose your toes to the bite. All that made for easier walking. I was following the Mussa River, sleeping rough and hunting hand-to-mouth. Sick of squirrels by day three, sick a' nights on stones and tree roots. Seemed all the other critters were hiding so's even I couldn't find them. My snares were coming up empty. My deadfalls triggered but when I went rushing to check them, something bigger had taken my prize. Forest was working against me in those days.

I missed him. I'll confess that right now without no shame. I missed Trapper in them days. Thought 'bout turning round more'n once and seeking him out. But without no hut to go back to I didn't know where to start. Wondered brief if he'd come looking for me but I figured he'd be too busy keeping clear a' Lyon and that six-shooter a' hers.

But then I saw that dead black hair burning. Saw his charcoal face on that poster and I told myself another lie. Trapper's dead. Kreagar Hallet killed him. Murdering bastard Kreagar Hallet killed my daddy. Then I didn't miss him so much no more.

Day ten the ground sloped up steep and I figured I'd got to the top of the valley. River narrowed and I lost it over a high rock face. Never been this far up the world afore. Never seen the Mussa go thin, turning more a stream, trickling over boulders and sand, than the big ole snake of the valley.

I had no chance of climbing that rock wall and much as I didn't want to leave the river and the only water for miles, I didn't see no other way. Kreagar always taught me to keep the water close. Water is life and death in the wild. You're dead in three weeks without meat but only three days without water. Cruel way to die that is. You get head pain something rotten, it sucks the water out your mouth till you feel you're eating dust, then you start to see things. That's the worst. Most a' the time it ain't the desiccation that kills you, it's thinking your sweetheart is just over the ridge and running to get to her, arms open, legs flailing. You lose all your senses, all your smarts go flying out your head and you trip and fall off a damn cliff. Seen more'n a few smiling bodies at the bottom of Coats Canyon. Cruel a' the forest to let that happen but anyone stupid enough to go out in the trees with nothing in their head and nothing in their hands got it coming.

I filled up the old Conflict flask Kreagar gave me years ago. Wondered brief if he'd got it off a soldier he killed, like that rifle a' his. I had enough water for a day if I was careful and I knew I'd get up the hill and back to skinny Mussa in half that.

But I didn't.

That rock wall curved, long and wide and far away from the river. The trees were the same everywhere I looked. I realised, quick and with a big stone falling in my stomach, that I was in one of them False Forests. One of them that they cut down and regrew in straight, soulless rows. Every tree the same size, ground flat as a calm lake, same sickly smell of pine, and nothing in the world to navigate by. Fat green leaves blocked the sky and I only figured it was getting dark when the sundown crickets came chirping. I kept the wall to my right side, made sure I could always see it, always reach out and touch if I needed. Always got to keep your heading straight and true when you're stuck in a False Forest.

Mussa is just over this rise, I kept saying. Just over this rise.

But it weren't. Mussa was nowhere. I had an inkling that it went 'neath the rock, hiding from the sun and bears. A fluttering went through my chest. Night was coming quick and I was nowhere close to where I needed to be. I had two fingers of water left and the cold was setting down roots.

Then I saw something that put the fear in me. Some
twenty feet north I saw a tree that weren't like the others. It
weren't uniform and plain. This one had a great gash taken
out of the bark. Whole bottom of the tree, from more'n a
head higher'n me down to my knees, was stripped of rough
brown and taken right back to yellow flesh. I went up to that
tree, trembling like a babe. Ground all around was rucked
up, muddied even though it hadn't rained in a week, grasses
and moss dead and gone.

I reached out my hand to that tree and prayed I wouldn't
feel what I knew I would.

Warm wood. My blood went colder'n snow melt. I pulled
a tuft of brown hair out a snag. Rubbed it 'tween my fingers.
Knew it like a kid knows its momma.

This was a brown bear's rubbing tree. Big bear too, probably close to eight feet on two legs. Tracks led off to the
north-east, same way I was going. I hunted bears afore, killed
one too, but damn if that weren't with a rifle and Trapper by
my side. On my own, with just a knife? Shit.

I turned tail then. Looked south, back where I came.
Figured there might be another way round the rock. Maybe
I could cross the Mussa, find a way up the other side. But I'd
walked a day north and was near out of water. I was *invested*
as Trapper would a' said. The bear tracks, wide paws, claws
longer'n my fingers, led up a rise. Mussa could be over
that rise. Bear wouldn't go too far out of his way just for a
rubbing tree.

As I stood there trying to figure out what to do, night was
settling down. Tracks quick disappeared and all a sudden I
couldn't see my hand in front my face. Bears can see a whole
lot better in no light than I can. I cursed myself. I was in
bear country and I didn't have no fire. No shelter. No hope.

'Shit,' I said and spooked something small on the ground.

Owl started hooting from somewhere up high, starting his dusk hunt. Everything in these woods was out to kill something else. Normal times I was right at the top but that night I could a' been a lame rabbit for all the chance I had 'gainst a hungry grizzly. Out in the open like that I was fair game for anything. My eyes woke up to the dark and I could see outlines and that was worse'n not seeing. Everything looked like death to me, a bush was a hunched-over grizzly, a skinny tree stump was a wolf staring right at me. My heart was thumping and kicking in me like it was trying to get free a' my stupid.

Then I spotted an outcrop near the base of the rock wall. With stone at my back at least I wouldn't be surprised.

I snapped a few loose branches and a slab of bark off the rubbing tree and went for the wall, hoping there were nothing that already made its home there. No rain for a week had dried up all the leaves and grass to fine tinder. I made me a bundle, scrabbling about in the dark, probably looking a fool, groping blind for leaves.

Panic set deep in my bones. I didn't have no time left. First rule if you find yourself out in the woods, come dusk you better have a fire or you're just meat waiting to be ate.

I pulled out my shoelace and tied it tight to one of the branches, curving it right nice. I dug a rut in the bark with my knife, sharpened the end of the other branch and got ready. Made me a quick and dirty bow drill and worked it hard, foot on the end of the bark, till smoke started rising. Smell of burning wood lifted my heart. I caught the ember in the tinder and blew me up some flames.

I had stone and fire 'tween me and anything wanting to take a bite. If a critter got past that I had my knife. Damn good knife that. Deer-horn handle. Blade sharper than any bear claw. Good knife is hard to come by.

Didn't even try to sleep, not so close to a grizzly trail. I kept shouting loud, into the trees, letting any bears or wolves know they had a fight coming if they were stupid enough to try it. Trapper would a' called me an idiot if he'd caught me out in this state. No shelter. No water. And now I was holed up on the Kodiak Highway. He would a' slapped me silly and made me gut trout for a month.

Worst job I can think of. I never had much time for fish, you see. Too wet. Too hard to catch. Maybe I just ain't got the patience. I heard folk used to do it for fun, sitting by the river for days hoping for a nibble. The Fall stopped all that nonsense and I can't say I'm cut up about it. One fish for a whole day? That ain't a good return no matter how you weigh it. I heard half the time they put the slimy suckers back in the river. Fish get smarter see, catch 'em once then they're trouble to catch again. All them idiots was doing was breeding the stupid out, putting themselves out of dinner.

Trapper took me fishing once when I was 'bout twelve, he said we was going for sockeye salmon in a fat part a' the Mussa. Said it was they golden pond, place what they came back to every year for egg laying. Trapper had himself a net and he said I had to learn to catch 'em with my bare hands like his daddy taught him when he was a boy. I was up to my belly in that freezing river for nigh on four hours. Didn't catch a single damn fish while Trapper was pulling 'em out that net like they wanted to be roasting on our fire. I couldn't even stay on my feet, all them slippery stones 'neath me. Didn't speak a single word to him all that day till he gave me the first salmon eye, cooked to milky. Delicacy he said, best part to the best hunter and I felt a swell a' warm in me.

Ain't never tasted anything so rotten. Ain't never heard Trapper laugh so long and so loud neither. So rare to hear that sound though that I couldn't stay sore at him. Won't never eat no fish eye 'gain though, no matter some man says it's delicate.

No way, never had time for fish. You catch a rabbit and that rabbit ain't gonna learn not to be caught again. That rabbit is going in my pot.

I didn't see no bear that night. Heard them close though, snoring, snuffling for grubs and roots. They was fattening up, eating everything they could afore the big winter sleep. They'd be extra ornery and wouldn't think twice 'bout charging anything they thought would take their food. That meant me.

Dawn came up, songbirds tweeted their good mornings. I stamped out the fire and covered it in dirt. Last thing I needed was a blaze chasing me down. 'Sides, you always leave a forest as you found it. That's just common decency.

I laced up my boot and kept my knife handy. Drank up the last of the water and I prayed something fierce the Mussa would be over that rise. I started walking and a few hours later I crested that hill, heart in my mouth with excitement.

Heart sank like stone in soup.

Just more damn rock.

No river. No water. And the last summer heat was rising, turning the forest into a steam trap, agitating the beetles, and pulling sweat out my skin.

The bear tracks led close, skirting the wall and I had a shaking, fist-in-the-belly feeling. I weren't exactly lost but I was getting there. The rock blinded me to the land. My

world was false trees, grey rock and a bear trail. Nothing to
guide me 'cept my wits and, without water, those would soon
be playing tricks.

I didn't have no choice no more. Going back was wasting
time and I hated few things worse than wasting time. Mussa
was somewhere close and if I couldn't find it myself, a big
ole bear sure as shit could. I felt sick for it but I put one boot
in front the other, put my steps in the bear's and trusted two
things. First, that this bear knew what in hell he was doing.
I hoped to high heaven I wouldn't find a dead Kody at the
end of this trail, searching out for water he never found.
Second and most pressing on my mind, I sure prayed I
weren't gonna meet a live one.

Noon came and went and my throat burned for water.
My head filled up with hot irons. Like god was cattle-
branding on my brain. No water for most a day, wrapped
in my heavy coat, sweating out what I got, felt myself drying
up inside. Couldn't hear no trickling, just mice and birds
making a nuisance. Just bugs and flies buzzing about,
asking to be stamped and slapped. Then the False Forest
started changing. Neat rows swallowed up by creepers and
twisting trunks. Bushes sprung up like fat feather pillows
and I confess I rushed head and heart first into that proper
woodland.

I kept following that bear trail, walking and running
quick as my legs would let me. But the trail started fading or
my eyes just stopped seeing it. My mouth was sucking sand,
my head was fighting fire. Desiccation was coming.

The forest turned thick and nasty. Thorns snagged at
me, roots and vines saw me coming and tripped me. Lost
the bear trail in the mess. Birds crowed up in the branches,
mocking me harsh every time I stumbled. Ferns up to my

chest hid ruts and fallen logs and I figured I mustn't have gone more'n a handful of miles that whole morning.

Then I heard the voices.

Trapper. Kreagar. He snuck up on me and now he was announcing his presence like he'd already won the fight.

'You betrayed me, Elka girl,' he said. 'Led 'em right to me.' Trees cut up his voice and I couldn't tell if it was coming from behind me, above me, hell, he could a' been crawling in the dirt for all I could figure.

'I didn't do nothing,' I said and held my knife tight, slashing at the ferns.

'There ain't no names in the forest, girl, no one knows who you are, no one going to miss you.' All that rumble, that heat in his voice was gone. He was talking like a hunter talks to his prey.

'I didn't tell her nothing, Trapper,' I shouted. I stumbled through them woods, waving my arms around, knocking down phantoms.

'Don't talk to no one,' he said. 'You broke the rules, Elka girl.'

Desiccation got me. Got me good and quick. Trapper always said I didn't drink enough on the best a' days. Soon as I found it, I'd drink the Mussa dry and show him how much I learned.

Twig snapped.

Real one. Not no phantom making noises. Snapped me back to the here-now in two seconds flat.

Yellow eyes stared at me out a clump of ferns. No more'n ten strides away. A flash of grey fur 'tween the green. Them eyes blinked quick. It moved through the brush, keeping its gaze right on me and I gripped that knife so tight my skin turned ghost pale.

Wolves ain't no joke and one had me in his sights.

Everyone knows that once you seen a wolf, its pack already carved you up for dinner. My heart would a' drummed right out my chest if my coat weren't buttoned.

Trapper never taught me to hunt wolves. Every time he went out on a night hunt, I'd ask to come. Never know, I'd said, when I might need to kill a wolf, be a shame if I didn't know the ways. He always said no, course. I figured it was too dangerous and he was protecting me. Fool I was.

Damn him straight to the fire. Bears I know, bears are simple beasts. Wolves have smarts to rival most the folk in Dalston.

Yellow eyes got higher in the ferns, then ears came visible. He was walking up a fallen tree to get himself a better view of me. He jumped and my heart near stopped.

Then I all but laughed.

Just a cub, probably only a few months old, all fluff and fat paws. He had a black line of fur on his forehead, like someone streaked soot on him.

'You scared the living shit out a' me, what you doing out here?' I said. Course I knew the beast couldn't answer but, hell, I was still shaking and my head was pounding and I didn't know what to do.

Skittish little pup he was. At the sound of me he cowered on the log, yelped, and that sound near softened my heart. I looked around, didn't see no sign of his pack. Didn't hear no growling, no movement in the ferns, no stalking paws. This little cub was alone in this forest, just like me.

I went closer, hand out in one of them gestures of peace. I didn't have no meat to offer and to tell the truth, I felt rude about that.

He bounded off that log away from me, sent wood dust

and moss showering all over the ground. He was gone, into the forest, quick as a jackrabbit. Then I noticed something lifted my heart so high, I thought I might just float away. That log had paw prints on it. Fat, fluffy wet ones.

I leapt over the log and ran and ran. That pup weren't breathing hard, he weren't skin and bones, he found water close.

Just over another rise I heard the most amazing sound. Don't think I ever heard anything so beautiful since. Fast, rushing, magnificent water.

I whooped and hollered and ran all the harder, I didn't pay no mind to the forest then, didn't care what was stalking me. I could a' kicked a bear in the face for all the attention I was paying.

There it was, the stupid, hiding, skinny Mussa. I fell onto my knees and I sucked up that crystal cool river, much as I could fit in. Then I lay on my back on the bank and laughed and laughed.

I said, thank you little cub, thank you bear trail, thank you forest. The head pain dulled and my wits turned sharp and fierce. Across the shallow river, on the other bank, young yellow eyes stared at me out a' the reeds. Pup came to the edge and started lapping, black soot smudge on his head. I watched him for a minute, had a wonder where his momma was. Not often you see a pup on his own. Not often they survive. Forest got rules for wolves that are even harsher than rules for humans. A wolf needs a pack. Wolf without a family is as good as dead and this cub, for whatever reason, broke that rule and the forest don't take kindly to that. Damn though, I thought, I hope the forest forgives him.

He drank his fill and scrambled up the other bank, all gangly and flopping about, none of the skill and grace of a grown wolf. He looked back at the top, then something that weren't me spooked him and he ran off into the woods. I didn't expect I'd see that pup again, though I hoped I might. I went to fill up my flask, when I stopped. I looked where the pup had disappeared. I figured I could follow him, make sure he was safe, hell maybe he knew something I didn't and could lead me to dinner if he weren't so easy to spook.

But I quick put him out my head when I saw what did the spooking.

TOP OF THE RIDGE

I always figured I could run faster'n any fella in the Mussa valley, sure as hell could outrun Trapper, but no matter how fast your legs can carry you, there ain't no way you're outrunning a six-hundred-pound brown bear. I put everything I had into my legs, making 'em hurt, making 'em jump over logs and slip 'tween close trees. Guess that bear didn't like me touching his rubbing tree or drinking out his river.

I know I shouldn't have run. I know it like I know the sky is blue and snow is cold. You run, bear gonna chase you. But shit, that bear was big and it came up on me quick. White foam poured out a' his mouth and I felt his breath on my back, hot and heavy and too damn near. All that water I just drank came out my skin in sweat and panic and I felt my blood drying up and slowing down.

Dense trees and brush slowed that lumbering beast and I gained a bit of ground on him. My lungs burnt like smelting fire. Hottest you can get. Turned all that water straight to vapour. I couldn't see nothing but strokes of mushed-up green and brown. All I knew was the thundering bear. I felt every footstep shake the earth and send critters dashing for cover. Felt every roar vibrating in my chest but I just kept running.

Then I saw something up ahead that scared the spit out a' me.

A clearing.

No way I was outrunning a bear on open ground. I wanted to scream and curl up in the dirt and hope he got bored of me quick. One swipe of a paw and no more Elka. Death put his hand on my shoulder and laughed.

But I weren't that easy to kill.

Afore the trees stopped, I found my way out. I darted off to the left, heard a roar behind me. Bears, for all their power, are big animals and don't do well with corners. He crashed into a trunk and I heard that wood split like kindling. Took him a few seconds to recover and that was all I needed.

Three running strides up a fallen tree leaning 'gainst his neighbour, and a leap of stupid. I caught a branch and swung on it, let go right at the right moment and flew like a hawk to one higher. The bear swiped at the fallen tree, smashed it to splinters. I climbed up on my high branch as the bear stood up. I'd figured eight feet from the rubbing tree but, shit, my numbers always been bad. This boy was closer to twelve.

I weren't high enough. He started leaning on the tree, rocking it, trying to knock it down and me with it. He growled and the wood started cracking. He reached up with those blade claws and took a chunk out my branch, near took my foot with it.

I was screaming, shouting up a storm. Telling that beast to go back to fishing.

'You don't want to eat me, bear! I'm all grit and string! Wouldn't put no fat on you for the sleep.'

I caught the bear's eyes, like he'd heard my words. Eyes like black marbles stared up at me. Saw the life of the forest in those eyes. Bear reached up one big paw and rested it, nice and gently like, on my branch, just a finger-length away from my toes. He huffed, gave some kind of low yowl like he was sad and just wanting someone to play with.

Then he dropped down, back to all fours. All that rage and fight drained right out of him. He clawed about in the dirt for a bit, like he was waiting for me to change my mind, then wandered off. Either he figured I weren't worth the fight, he was already plump and glossy, or he understood my words, saw something in me that he didn't much fancy eating. We're both children of the forest, after all, almost be rude to take a bite at me.

I was breathing hard, chest burning, heart thundering. I settled down careful on that branch and got some kind of comfort. Next I opened my eyes it was dark, moon was high and filled that clearing with cool, white light. Near beautiful it was but I knew the beasts that lurked just outside the light, no beauty in them, just teeth, just hunger. Forest was silent but for a few scratching insects. Didn't hear or see no bears or wolves but that didn't mean much, could a' been one sitting 'neath my tree for all I knew.

I grabbed my flask but felt it empty afore I brought it to my mouth. I didn't fill it at the Mussa. That bear got to me first.

My belly gurgled and ached. No food for days sent pains through me. Never been that long without a good meal. Even on the week-long hunting trips with Trapper, we could always catch enough to keep us fed. Maybe he shot a few more geese but then, he never did let me go it alone. Afraid I'd show him up no doubt. Afraid I'd come back ten geese and a deer richer and he'd be left scratching his head thinking, shit that girl's the best damn hunter in BeeCee and she knows ten times what I ever did.

I'd been eleven days in that forest by myself but I wasn't even close to living. I was surviving and I weren't even doing it well. Think I was just a little out of sorts then, see, little bit in shock maybe after discovering the man I called Daddy was... well... Kreagar Hallet. That kind of thing has an effect, it can knock down the smarts, make simple snares and baiting seem like constructing a cathedral out a' matchsticks. It can knock down other parts of you too. I sat up in that tree and saw everything in my head. All my days with kind Trapper, all my nights with fierce Kreagar, all the hunts and skinning, all the cuts and scrapes he patched up when I was a young'un. All the laughs. All the teachings. What else had he taught me that I didn't see as true back then?

Felt a tear on my cheek. A tear for all those times, wrecked and ruined now. A tear for Missy and all them other people he'd taken the knife to. I had fear for him when I saw him that first time, running after seven-year-old me but that went quick. Missy and them other women and that kid he killed, they must a' had fear for him right till they died. Couldn't imagine knowing your death's coming at the hands of a real beast. That bear could a' killed me, true, but a bear don't have no malice in his heart. A man like Kreagar, well, seems that's all he got.

I left them tears right where they was and climbed down the tree. I stepped quiet and slow to the edge of the clearing. All moonlight and floating motes and midges. Little piece of beauty in a world gone to shit. Sky was quiet, no storms threatening to tear it all up though this wood was full a' felled trees and split trunks what said the thunderhead don't spare it. Moonlight edged the top of the ridge in silver. That ridge marked the true end of the Mussa and my second life. Right then I didn't care I hadn't eaten and didn't have no water, I just wanted out a' that valley.

I got to the top of the ridge at sunrise.

The world stretched out 'neath me, ripe and ready and all mine. Land was flat and dry, grass and prairie 'stead of trees and ferns. This prairie weren't like none I'd seen on my trips south. This was hard land, grass was pale brown 'stead a' the green it should a' been this time a' year. Seen this in some a' the places hit by the Damn Stupid. Trapper said poison leaked out a' some a' them bombs and seeded the land, turned it all to scrabble and scratch and sucked out all the goodness. Weren't like this was dead land, but it weren't happy and didn't give up its fruits easy no more. Had a fear that the more north I went, the more a' this unhappy land I'd see. The Damn Stupid had turned forest to mud and mountains to rubble and put ice in the hearts a' those what lived through it, and there weren't no place hit worse than the North.

Line of mountains, high and ragged, dusted with snow, ran crossways straight ahead, bigger'n any hill, any ridge, I'd ever seen. My true momma and daddy were waiting beyond those mountains, living it up, surrounded by coin and salt beef. A piece of that soon to be mine.

I quick found north and spied, lit up by the new dawn, a line of smoke trailing up to the sky. Sat out a little ways west, far across the brush and close to a copse of pine, was a sprawling homestead. Herd of cattle penned up, few horses maybe and one of them veranda porches ringing the house.

Looked like whoever made a life in that place made it well and bountiful. Maybe they'd have a mouthful or two and a cup a' water to share. What set my head firmer was the thought that my parents might a' passed up this way. The big north road weren't far from the homestead and I figured all them years ago they might at least a' stopped for directions.

The ridge sloped nice and easy down to the flat and I kept that smoke in eyeline. It went out of my way, few miles west, but the promise of a good meal and warm fire, maybe news a' my folks, was worth it.

MATTHEWS HOMESTEAD

Men got a lot more rules for living than the forest. Some of them are simple and most folk stick to 'em without question: no killing, no stealing, and the like. Then they got the strange ones. No talking while chewing on food. No hunting a deer on someone else's land, though hell, I broke that one more'n once. There's a rule for meeting new folks too. No sneaking. Come up on their door like a friend coming for tea and wisdom. Show your weapons open, don't go hiding. Though I broke that one too and made sure to tuck my knife 'neath my coat. Rules is one thing but if I don't follow 'em I can't trust no one else to neither.

Wooden sign above the gate swung on one chain, struck through with a bullet hole. That should a' been my first clue that something weren't right in the place. Cattle penned when they should a' been out on the plain, getting the last of the summer grazing should a' been my second. Lot a' houses in BeeCee had metal shutters over the windows in case a' bad thunderheads and this one weren't no different, but half them shutters were closed, locked that way with heavy chains. Sun was shining up there and there weren't no scent in the air what said a thunderhead was near, weren't no reason for them shutters to be closed. But my belly rumbled and my hands started shaking for want of a meal and I ignored all them clues. More fool me.

I walked slow up the track to the house, arms up to show I weren't carrying no gun. I was halfway to the door when it opened and a man, older'n a willow tree and just as thin, stepped out, double-barrel by his side.

'What's your business here, miss?' he said.

Another rule a' men is not to say what you want up front, then you got nothing left up your sleeve.

'I got myself turned around in that forest back there,' I told him and he looked at me sideways, like I was lying, 'and I'm in need a' directions up north.'

He didn't have a hair on his head and I remember thinking, I ain't never seen no one afflicted like that. In the woods, you see a bobcat or a bear without fur, it means he's sick as a dog and likely to die that winter. Looked like this fella had seen more winters'n I could count so I couldn't right reconcile the two.

'Where you headed?' he said.

'Halveston,' I said 'cause that was one a' them magic words from my momma's letter.

The man looked at me strange for a few more seconds then his face cracked into a smile.

'What business has a girl your age got in Halveston?'

One a' them Trapper rules came into my head. Don't go asking questions.

'My business is mine. All I need's to be pointed the right way.'

He nodded slow. 'You've got a long road ahead and you look no more than skin and bones,' he said and quick I thought he was a fine one to talk 'bout that.

'You hungry?' he said.

He put the gun inside the door and pushed the door open wide.

My good sense jumbled up. I was asking for directions but he was offering a place at his table. Sure I'd hoped he would but I didn't think it'd be that easy. People in this country ain't that easy.

My stomach let out one a' them angry gurgles and he must a' heard it 'cause he said, 'I've got a pot of chilli on the stove.'

Felt the knife in my belt and I figured if he tried anything, I'd have a fine chance a' beating them stick-bones a' his afore he got to his gun. Belly rumbled like a damn thunderhead.

'Yes, sir, I am hungry,' I said.

'Then please, come in. I can draw you a map while you eat.'

His voice was calm and friendly and he smiled right through his eyes, something Trapper never did. His smiles were on the surface, this man's were down deep. Once you seen 'em both, you can tell the difference quick enough.

I thanked him and went closer though those were the hardest steps my body ever took. My legs were lead and my joints seemed close to giving up on me if I pushed them much further.

'You own this place?' I asked, worrying over the bullet hole in the sign.

He kept smiling. 'You read the name on the gate?'

I shook my head.

'Gate reads *Matthews*,' he said.

My patience weren't waiting around for him to make sense. 'So you Matthews?'

'I'll claim that,' he said, 'unless I owe you money.'

Then he winked at me and laughed loud. I weren't sure what to make of him, this Matthews fella, but I could smell that chilli simmering on the stove and he was stick-thin and older'n god.

Seems he could sense my worry. He put a face on like he knew my thinking and said, 'I've got chilli to check on, miss, so you just come in when you like. Door's open for you.'

Then he went inside. Turned his back on a stranger and left his door swinging in the wind. I could a' been a killer for all he knew. Maybe he figured being a girl I wouldn't be no danger to him. I hated that my head went to these dark places on first meeting someone new. I don't got any trust left in me no more but it seemed Matthews had enough for the both of us.

I went in the house, slow and steady like I was stalking through deer country but I soon gave that up. Walking in that homestead was like stumbling right onto the pages of one of them glossy magazines. Nana kept a stack 'neath her mattress in some plastic wraps so's they didn't rot. If I was good, what weren't all that often, she'd let me look through before bedtime. Said it kept her head on all them things we lost in the Damn Stupid and the Second Conflict, that's why she kept pictures a' my granddaddy right 'neath her pillow. Maybe that's why she was so sore all the time, she was living in the back-then, not the here-now. But them magazines was what told me I'd done good by her so I paid attention. Seemed like all them pages had their pictures took in Matthews' homestead. Holidays in the Wild. See bears up close and personal. Come home to a warm fire and hot cocoa. That kind of thing. He had a grizzly-skin rug on the floor, claws an' all, leather couches, cooking-place with a double range and more pots and pans and ladles and plates than any right-minded folk would need in ten lifetimes. All you truly need is a big iron pot, a skillet and a damn good knife. Seemed like fancy for fancy's sake. Made my ten-year home with Trapper look like a flea-pit.

Matthews was at the stove, stirring the chilli with a long wooden spoon. He didn't say or do nothing when I came in but I saw a chair been pulled out from the eating table. He picked up another spoon, a little silver one what didn't seem much use for anything, and dipped it in the pot, took a taste of the sauce. He puckered up his lips like a goat about to bleat and chucked in some salt, some pepper and something I couldn't place, some herb or something.

'Coffee?' he said then tasted the sauce again.

Trapper never let me have coffee. He said it frightened the mind and made it misfire. I didn't want nothing interfering with my senses.

'Thank you kindly but no,' I said, 'though I'd be glad of a drink of water.'

Keep your manners friendly, Trapper always told me, but keep your wits sharp, ain't no telling what kind of folk live in these woods. I never figured he was talking about himself.

Matthews set down a small glass of crystal cool water and said, 'This is mineral water, it'll set you right.'

I weren't right sure what *mineral water* was and why it was different to the normal stuff out the river but it was cold and it hit my throat like rain on dust. I drank it all in one long breath and quick forgot my manners. I slammed that glass on the table and belched hearty, loud enough to rival any man.

Matthews didn't do nothing 'cept smile at me and nod.

'I apologise, fella,' I said, 'I didn't mean nothin' by that, I just ain't had no water all day and sometimes you just can't control your urges. Damn, that chilli sure smells good.'

He took the glass off the table, holding it real delicate 'tween two fingers and said, 'I know how that is, young lady, and I take no offence. In fact, I take it as a compliment.'

I smiled a bit at him but I confess I felt heat in my cheeks and I'm sure they went red as cherries. Matthews pulled out a chair opposite and sat down.

'Have you been to Halveston before?'

'No,' I said. 'I'm travellin' north, lookin' to find some folks I ain't seen in a few years. Wondered if they might a' passed this way.' I weren't quite sure what to tell him, he seemed kind enough, seemed friendly and sweet, but I didn't know him from a hole in the ground.

Wafting smell of that chilli sent shivers through me.

He nodded again. Did that a lot, I was noticing. 'I don't get many visitors.'

'This would a' been summer 'bout fifteen years back. Lady and her fella heading up to them gold fields.'

Part a' me hated giving out so much but the part a' me what still played my momma's letter in my head when I was trying to sleep, hoped to high heaven he'd a' seen 'em. Least so's maybe he could tell me what they looked like. Nana kept magazines like they was sacred but didn't keep no photographs a' her own daughter.

Matthews leaned back in his chair and puffed out his cheeks, then he scratched at the back a' his head. 'Fifteen years. That's a long time to remember strangers. But you say they went for gold?'

I nodded.

'That was the summer we finished building the church over in Martinsville. We had a few travellers pass through our doors in those months.'

Felt a swell a' hope in me. Martinsville was one a' them words in the letter.

When he spoke again he spoke slower, kept his eyes on me when before he'd been staring at the ceiling like it had all them memories stored in its rafters.

'We had mostly men, groups of four or five friends who pooled their time and resources. Had a few on their own, idealistic, foolish. Then, yes, I do remember a couple now I think on it. Can't remember their names but they were looking for Halveston too. She was pretty, the wife,' then he laughed a bit and said, 'that's right. I remember her because she called it the Great YK. Never heard the old Yukon called great before.'

More words out my momma's letter. Must a' been grinning 'cause Matthews shut up and stared at me.

Then he said, in a strange flat voice, 'Were they your parents?'

Something in his tone made me not want to answer but he must a' read my face. He was quiet, looked at me with a mix a' pity and pleasure. Weren't at all sure what to make of him.

Then he got up and went to a tall bookshelf on the other side of the room. From the gap 'tween shelf and wall, he pulled out a roll of paper and spread it on the eating table. A map of BeeCee and the North and a bunch of other places I couldn't figure. It didn't have no scribblings on it like Nana's.

'We're here,' he said and poked his spindle finger at a black dot surrounded by a whole lot a' nothing.

I picked out the ridge I climbed down and the Mussa and further south another dot I guessed was Dalston, though it could a' been Ridgeway. On that map, I hadn't travelled more'n a knuckle-length and when I looked at the North, big and vast and more nothing, that put the fear in me.

'That Martinsville?' I said, pointing to a dot with a little black cross on the top.

Another nod and smile. I wondered brief if he could do anything different with his face.

'Your parents, they went to cash in on the second rush?'

I said yes, sir, they did. 'I heard that durin' the Damn Stupid, them fools dropped a heap of bombs in the wrong place, cut up the land something nasty and unearthed a bunch more of that yellow metal.'

Matthews sat back down and stroked his chin like he was stroking a cat. 'That's right. That's a long way. That dot there, that's Halveston.' That one was way, way up in the empty part a' the map. 'How are you going to get there by yourself? That's a good few hundred miles.'

I scrunched up my face. What kind of asking was that? 'Sides, that mention a' hundreds a' miles worried me down deep but I weren't 'bout to let it show. Walking is walking, one mile or a hundred, it ain't no different. Least that's what I told myself.

'I got two legs ain't I? Don't need nothin' more.'

Nod nod nod, like a dunce watching a ball of string.

'Except food,' he said, looking at his pot of chilli, 'and water.' Then he looked at the empty glass. Then he looked at me.

I felt squirmy then. My chair didn't offer comfort no more. 'I'm just caught in a bad run of luck is all, I can fend fine. I just, well. . . I just had a bad run is all.'

Matthews smiled, right through his eyes again, and tapped the table. 'Say your thanks to the Lord that you found me then.'

Then he got up and went to the bubbling chilli pot. My belly gurgled loud enough for him to turn and raise an eyebrow.

He ladled a bowlful and set it steaming down right in front of me with a one of them silvery spoons. Didn't take none for himself.

'Eat up, don't let it go cold,' he said.

I didn't need to be told twice. I burned my mouth quick but I didn't care. That chilli, spicy and meaty and full of black beans, was like heaven came down on me and said Elka, you're gonna be fine. Get used to this luxury, you got it waiting for you in the North.

Then I heard a horse galloping down the track. More'n one horse. My stomach tightened up. Matthews' face turned dark and stormy. With not one word he got up, got his gun, and went to the door. I kept chewing. No matter what was about to happen, I'd eat as much as I could afore shots fired.

'Ho, there,' Matthews whooped and flung open the door, set his gun down. Horses was still clomping up the track.

I was side-on with the entrance, could see a bit outside without seeming like I was looking. Matthews stood on the threshold then looked back at me. His face, caught in that half-light 'tween out and in, took on a demon's grin. I felt a tremble up in my chest and went back to my chilli.

Matthews had one of them crucifixes above the door, like god was blessing him every time he took a step outside. Cowardly was what I thought of that, god ain't going to protect you if you can't do it yourself. Then I squinted against the light, gave a little chuckle. Crucifix was upside down. God ain't going to bless no one what can't even nail a bit of wood straight.

I shook my head, ate my chilli, and checked over that map. Little towns marked by red dots, bigger ones marked by black squares. Didn't see too many black squares 'tween me and the North. Just a handful of red dots and a whole bunch of wild. I was grateful for that, didn't much like towns, didn't much like people. Can never tell what a person's thinking you see. They could be meaning to kill or kiss you and you'd never know till they gone and done it.

Near the top of the map, Matthews had shaded out a big section of the old territory. I figured that was where the Damn Stupid bombs went off. There was one red dot near that but I didn't know the letters, couldn't name the town.

Horses stopped.

I finished up my food, scraping the bowl for every bit. Then I let out a rolling belch. That was some fine food and my stomach said its thanks.

I heard talking outside. Woman's voice what I knew. What in the good goddamn was Lyon doing here? She follow me here? She track me all this way? Or was it just this was the only place 'tween Mussa and them big mountains? Had Lady Chance brought this pale demon to me or was Lyon better'n I ever thought? All them questions but no answers in my thick head. Suddenly all that food wanted to come right back up into the bowl. I got up quick and pressed my back 'gainst the wall behind the door.

'Reverend Matthews?' Magistrate Lyon said. That voice sent shivers through me. Ice-cold woman with an ice-cold voice.

Stomach churned up that chilli with a big ole gutful a' fear.

Didn't hear Matthews answer, figured he must a' nodded.

Heard the creak of a saddle what said the rider was dismounting.

'Do you know who I am, Reverend?' Lyon said.

'Yes, ma'am, I do.'

'I'm looking for two people,' she said and it felt like a big rock hit the side a' my head. Two people.

'This man,' she said, heard the crumple a' paper and figured she was showing Matthews that charcoal face a' Kreagar. 'Have you seen him?'

'My word, that's a face I'd remember,' Matthews said. 'I sure haven't seen anyone like that.'

'What about a girl?' she said and all my muscles tensed up.

Matthews didn't say nothing for a few seconds too long. Was he gonna give me up? Had he done it already? My eyes went frantic round that room for a back door or window but them storm shutters turned the place into a rat trap.

Then I heard footsteps, clink a' spurs, then a heavy thud on the wooden step. 'Mind if I take a look around?' Lyon said, so much closer now.

My hand went to my knife and I moved right behind the door. Them other two horses didn't move, just heard them huffing. Their riders, I figured her two lieutenants, didn't say nothing. This woman had her men trained like dogs and I didn't expect nothing less.

'Ma'am,' Matthews said, quick in his voice, quick in his step. 'I think a lone goat like me would remember if he'd seen a girl.' Then he laughed.

A mite a' relief crawled up in me. Matthews weren't selling me out. Not yet.

Lyon moved and I could see her side-on through the skinny gap 'tween door and frame. Till that second I saw her, I didn't right believe she was there. There's miles a' wild out there and she turns up here? That just said to me stay away from people, they draw in other people, it ain't never safe. But she was here now. White skin like a china cup, all in black, not a hair out a' place. She was taller'n Matthews and weren't no hint of a slouch in her back. My back straightened up just seeing her again.

She didn't say nothing else to him, just stared with them cold eyes a' hers. Then she was at the door, half a step over the threshold. Close enough that I could smell the horse's sweat on her. Heard her breathing. Slow and measured just like everything else. I reckoned that even if a bear chased her up and down a mountain, she wouldn't breathe heavier than a whisper the whole time.

My hands got hot. My head got hot. She took a step inside and I couldn't see her no more and that was worse.

'What does this girl look like?' Matthews said.

Floorboard the other side a' the door creaked. 'About so high, brown hair to her chin, brown eyes. Feral thing.'

My heart hammered and I prayed she wouldn't hear it.

'Wearing a dark green coat?' Matthews said and that heart a' mine near stopped.

'Likely,' Lyon said and came back so's I could see her through the gap. 'You've seen her?'

'Oh yeah, I've seen her,' he said and I wondered brief if I could get the other side a' this door and wring that scrawny neck afore Lyon shot me.

'What's she done?' Matthews said.

Lyon smiled on one side of her mouth and that chilled me worse'n a mid-winter blizzard. 'She's wanted in connection with several murders.'

Hell, *that* chilled me worse. I ain't done nothing and it

took all I had in me not to burst out from behind the door and shout that right in her smirking face.

'Oh dear, oh my,' Matthews was repeating, 'and I fed her and gave her directions. I can't believe it. She seemed uncivilised but harmless. God forgive me if she hurt anyone.'

'Where is she?' Lyon said and there was a harder edge in her voice. It weren't ice in there no more, it was iron.

'I sent her on her way not two days ago with mine and the good Lord's blessing,' Matthews said and I could a' collapsed right then. 'She said she was going to take the road west. To the coast she said.'

Lyon's eyes narrowed and I suddenly weren't sure if she was believing all this.

'If you're planning on sticking around,' Matthews said, 'I'd love to see you in church this Sunday. Our services are rousing indeed. This week we'll be bleeding a lamb for our Lord in exchange for a mild winter.'

I rolled my eyes. People what kill animals thinking God's got control over the winds and the snow are more fools than any other in these lands.

Lyon gave a nod but it weren't to Matthews. I guessed she was telling her lieutenants they was done. Then she strode off, down the steps, and quick mounted her horse.

'Keep your god,' Lyon said, all iron in them words. 'The law has no place for god.'

She shouted 'Yah!' at her horse and the three a' them galloped off.

Matthews, no matter how much of a fool his god made him, had saved my skin and when he came back inside I could a' hugged him. I quick stowed my knife so's he wouldn't see it, then sat back down at the table.

'Hot damn,' I said, my heart still thudding in me, 'I appreciate your words, sending Lyon on her way like that.'

Matthews stood in the middle a' the room for a minute, not moving nothing 'cept his lips. Was like he was quiet praying for something. Then he filled up my empty glass and set it down in front a' me. I drank it up while he stared, hard face on him. Expected him to ask me 'bout Kreagar or why Lyon was looking for me but he didn't. Was like it didn't matter. 'Stead he sat down at the table and asked me for my name. Lyon didn't know it so I didn't see no harm.

'Elka,' I said. Figured I owed him a speck a' truth after what he did.

'Strange name.'

'My daddy said I came out my momma with antlers big as a ruttin' stag. Damn near killed her. Cut them off when I was a yearling,' I said smiling wide. 'They left for the North soon after.'

Nod. Nod. All that bobbing was churning my belly.

He wouldn't look at me no more, kept wringing his hands like he was itching for something. He put my teeth on edge and I figured my welcome was just about used up.

'Thank you kindly for lettin' me share your table,' I said, standing. 'But I best be on my way now.'

The deer horn on my knife dug into my side and I felt my toughness come back.

Matthews' half smile fell right off his face. 'Lyon won't have got far. You'd best wait a bit longer,' he said, then all quiet and wistful like added, 'it won't be long now.'

All at once my head fuzzed up, turned me dizzy and I slumped back down on the chair. Figured I'd stood up too quick, but the bright spots weren't going away.

'Good idea,' I said.

The world was swimming round me.

'Not long now. . .' he murmured, all sweet like he was cooing a baby to sleep.

Everything went dark and I woke up face down on a cold table.

I couldn't move no more'n to breathe. My arms and legs were spread wide, held tight with iron chains. My knife weren't digging into my side no more. My flask weren't knocking 'gainst my leg no more.

I quick realised, with shaking in my bones and ice growing to a blizzard in my gut, that I weren't wearing a stitch of clothing. Blurring filled my eyes but I saw Matthews knelt on the floor beside the table, praying with something, maybe a knife, 'tween his palms.

'Dear Lord, bless this child, your lamb,' he said to the blade but his words sounded like they was spoken through cotton wool, 'bless this home and all who contribute and may this sacrifice ensure a mild and safe winter for us all.'

Crazier than a three-peckered mountain goat.

'Goddamn son of a bitch!' I shouted with all the voice I had but he just prayed harder.

I raged against those chains but they weren't giving an inch. I couldn't figure how I'd get out of this. I couldn't see nothing but Matthews. Couldn't hear nothing but Matthews. Couldn't feel nothing but cold steel on my skin.

MIXIN' BLOOD

I figured I was in the basement but whatever that dog Matthews put in my water made my eyes swim and my head fuzz up and down, my ears throbbed and rushed and I couldn't hear or see right. The bit of wall I could make out was stone 'stead a' wood and the ground was dirt. Shelf in my eyeline, all skewed and blurred in my eyes, stood behind kneeling Matthews and was full to brimming of canned meat and fish, boxes of greens and potatoes 'side it. Devil been good to this fella, filled his stores but stole his hair, and all it took was a bit of killing. Least he had a reason, selfish and skunk-shit crazy as it was. Kreagar didn't have no reason. Kreagar didn't have nothing.

I kept hollering and cursing at the good Reverend but my words were slurred up and I can't be sure I was even speaking 'em right. He didn't move nor even blink till he finished his praying. Talking to god or the devil 'bout spilling blood and making friendly winter. Praying so the snow didn't freeze his damn toes off.

'Ain't no reason I got to die,' I shouted but my words muddled up in my mouth and I didn't reckon what was coming out was what was meant to. 'What in hell I done to you?'

'Hush now. The lamb must be bled and its sins must flow from the vessel as commanded by our Lord.' Every word was buzzing like he was made a' flies.

'I ain't. . . lamb,' I think I said, felt sick rising up in me.

'You, Elka, are full of sin. I see it in you like a taint. The lamb we had picked for the service on Sunday, well, she was guilty of lusting after several men but if Lyon is to be believed, and her honesty is unfaltering, then you are guilty of murder. The worst sin.'

'I. . . killed no one. She didn't, said I. . . I. . .' I tried but my brain weren't playing fair. I strained at them chains, trying to ignore the pain throbbing in my head.

'Whether you took the life or stood by as someone else did, you are guilty and your hot, devil blood will thaw our winter.'

Them words, or what I thought I heard a' them, stuck in me. Was I guilty if someone else did the killing?

'May you guide my hand and my blade to bring glory to your name, oh Lord,' Matthews said then stood up and came close to my head. He held the knife, the bastard, *my* knife, in one hand and I swore blind I would rip his heart out and feed it to the devil myself.

Steady hand. Not a tremble. He'd done this plenty no doubt.

'Best if you're relaxed, young lady,' he said, soft like he was offering another bowl of chilli. 'Now, you'll feel a little sting.'

He stroked my hair and I wanted to bite his damn hand off.

With my own knife he cut me. Starting from my left elbow he dragged the blade up my arm, 'cross my back and down to my other elbow. I didn't scream or nothing. It didn't hurt that much though I reckoned it went pretty deep. I'd had a worse whipping from Trapper in my time but it was the principle that stung more'n the blade. Felt warm blood run down my spine.

'First you will be marked with the cross so the Lord knows you are for Him,' Matthews said and cut me from neck to nethers.

Heard a floorboard creaking up in the homestead. Least I think I did. Maybe them drugs was telling my head what it wanted to hear. Or maybe Lyon had come back.

'Get this crazy bastard off me!' I might a' shouted. 'He's got a knife! Hurry it up!'

'No one can hear your foul language here,' Matthews said, then he went off somewhere I couldn't see and I heard a sack dragging on the dirt.

Nobody came rushing to my rescue, no one yelled back and I didn't hear no more creaking. Fear started settling deep in my bones, putting a coldness in me that I thought would never leave.

'Second,' Matthews said, 'the evil must be cleansed.'

Heard something strange then, like he was shoving his hand into snow, that crunching, gravelly noise that didn't make no sense in this place.

Then I screamed. Then my sight went from blur to stark to black in half a second.

Matthews slapped handfuls of salt on my back, in those cuts, ground 'em deep into the blood. I screamed loud and fierce and with everything I had in me. My head went to mush and my eyes couldn't see or hear or speak no more. I just kept on screaming, it was all I could do. Kept hearing him dig for more salt and the clanging of iron chains on iron table.

Didn't hear the footsteps.

Didn't hear Matthews shouting.

My head was swimming in mud, struggling through pain and a thundering heart, struggling 'gainst death itself. This crazy son bitch was seconds from killing me. Cutting me open and draining me dry.

Thought I saw my knife, covered in my own blood, fall on the floor. Could a' been just wishful thinking. Then a wave of hot water crashed over my back, soaked up all that salt, cut off the sting but didn't do nothing to clear my head. I didn't even know where I was no more. I figured it was a dream or I'd wake up in the forest, next to the Mussa River, wet from swimming. This was a desiccation dream. I was dying.

Matthews gurgled and sputtered something then fell heavy on the ground right 'neath my head, blood spurting out a gash 'cross his neck. Weren't no dreaming that. It weren't water what rushed over me. Different pair of legs walked around the table. Smell a' woodland on 'em. Quiet as a wolf on the hunt. I was in the forest. I must a' been.

'Morning,' I said, my voice all slur, felt the wet, gravelly earth in my fingers. Don't know if I even said the word or just thought it. Whatever god there was watching was punishing me something awful. I was gonna die. I was gonna die on that table or by that river, wherever the hell I was. I kept saying it to myself, it's killing me, it's killing me, and I can't do a goddamn thing about it. I opened up my eyes but I didn't know they'd been closed and I saw Matthews on the floor. Terror cut the tongue out my mouth.

My head weren't swimming no more, it was drowning and sputtering and gasping for air. It spun the whole room till I couldn't hold my eyes open no more. Couldn't see nothing for certain, couldn't make no sense of what I was seeing neither.

Someone was in the room with me. Part a' me hoped it was Trapper come to take me home. No. Weren't no chance of that in truth. Must be some Samaritan or someone what hated the Reverend. Only figured after a minute that the man was speaking. Words floated round above me but didn't have no meaning to my ears, words like 'killing' and 'fire and flames'. Sounded right biblical, just like the Reverend. The voice was muffled by them drugs and the salt and I couldn't see nothing but blurred-up legs. Hell, you ever tried picking out a man by just his legs? Ain't easy even when you ain't half-addled by bad water.

Whoever it was unchained one a' my hands and one a' my feet but I didn't dare move.

Then he bent over me. I felt his shadow heavy on my back. He kissed me on the top a' my bloody head and shivers went all down me. Some stranger doing that felt wrong but there was a softness to it what mushed up my head even more. Time was I'd a' stripped birch bark with my teeth to get that kindness off my Trapper. Don't know if it was the pain, the blood, the salt, the smell or Matthews' dead eyes staring up at me, but that kiss set my stomach kicking and my whole body shaking.

Then whoever he was spoke, close to my ear, words what came clear and cold as lake ice. They was of a tone I ain't never heard, full a' venom and grit-tooth rage.

'Think on why I ain't killin' you.'

Then he was up the stairs, footsteps through the homestead and gone. Tears and crying and blubbering came out a' me like I was a babe what stubbed its toe. Stayed lying out like that, shaking and fearful, for what felt like forever. There weren't no creaking up in the homestead, no doors opening or closing, no horse hooves clapping on the dirt. Everything turned quiet as a feather-fall on snow.

I bent my free arm, tried to push myself up. The cuts ripped, salt burned through the blood and set my teeth hissing. Funny feeling being buck-naked in a stranger's basement, sticky head to toe in his blood. But all that barely touched my head. Alls I could think was who in the hell just let me go? Some crazy fella what just happened to be passing? Someone what knew what Matthews was and what he did and didn't like it none? Hurt my head just thinking on it. All them words the stranger spoke were fog and smoke in my head 'cept those last few. *Think on why I ain't killin' you.*

Hell if I knew. Told myself it weren't worth caring 'bout or dwelling on. You don't stop to ask a bear why he ain't chasing you. You don't go questioning your fortunes or you ain't going to get none.

Told myself all that. But that dark place inside me, what held all them things I ain't supposed to remember, didn't believe it for one second.

I twisted myself up on my knees, felt like a hawk what broke its wing, not being able to move my hand none. I shook all over though I couldn't figure if it was from pain and fear or being naked this close to winter.

The chain around my hand was held with nought but a steel clip and I quick set myself rest of the way free. The dirt floor was turning to bloody mud what squeezed warm 'tween my toes like I was stepping on summer moss. Then I saw something what made me turn around and kick dead Matthews in the gut.

The wall at the foot of the table was a mirror. That crazy

bastard wanted to watch himself killing in the name of his god. Like just doing it weren't enough, he had to see his hand raise that knife and slice me up. Could see my own slicing in that mirror and my back, red with all kinds of blood and lumps of salt, was a cut-up mess. I kicked him again for good measure.

Every time I moved the salt stung deeper, sucking out my water like it was trying to cure pork. I thought about putting my clothes back on and getting shot of that place quick as flies off dung but I didn't much fancy scrubbing Matthews' blood out a' my shirts for a week. There weren't no well in the basement so I picked up my knife. I knew somewhere deep that the stranger weren't there no more, weren't hiding in the closet. Weren't no sense in killing me upstairs 'stead a' downstairs.

I realised then, holding my knife, how bad my hands were shaking. I felt the tremble through all my bones and heard the flutter in my breathing. I didn't hear nothing in the homestead. Nothing outside, save a cow lowing in the pen.

Came out the basement into a corridor the other side of the eating table. Naked, bleeding and stinging up something fierce, I went quick to the cooking-place looking for that water for rinsing. Pot of cold chilli sat on the stove. Time was I would a' eaten it to spite him but my appetite was sucked out a' me by the salt.

I wandered about in my skin, an angry stinging in my back in need a' soothing. Didn't see no tub for bathing and figured Matthews must have a well or stream round back to get water that cold.

One of the best things 'bout living close to the wild is you get to walk out your door in whatever you want and ain't nobody around to say nothing. I was sure thankful for that then when

I walked out Matthews' front door naked and painted red. Didn't see no fella hightailing it across the plains, didn't see no tracks neither but I didn't care to look too hard.

It was getting close to sundown and I wanted shot of the homestead afore dark. I'd much rather be sleeping in the dirt of the forest than spending a second more'n I had to in that godless hole. No telling what demons might get woken by all that blood.

I went around back and saw a clutch of cattle cosying up for the night. Cattle trough is good for a bath as any tub. Big steel thing, longer and wider'n me and waist-deep standing, sat on the other side of the gate. I climbed over, flinching like a kid walking barefoot on gravel, leaving bloody smears all over the railings.

I lowered myself into that cold water and didn't even try to quiet my screaming. A skittish cow bucked and hid itself on the other side of the herd but I didn't pay it no mind. My back burned and goddamn I wish I'd killed Matthews myself.

All gentle-like I ran my shaking fingers up my arms, trying to fight the hurt. I washed off the blood and salt, cleaned up the cuts. The stinging eased slow and I ducked my head under to get the blood out my hair. I couldn't right tell you the last time I had a bath. Didn't much like 'em, seemed to take too long when I could a' been setting traps or chopping wood. Quick rinse in the river once a fortnight was all I needed, though I confess I did take a few minutes more in that trough than was strictly necessary. When I got out, dripping and shivering, the water was red and I said my apologies to the cattle.

'Though it is most your rancher's blood,' I said after thinking 'bout it for a second, 'and he done killed a whole lot of you in his time. Drink him up and piss him out.'

Felt fresh blood trickling down my back, mixing up with the water, as I went back into the homestead. I found that crazy fucker's bedroom and tore up one a' his soft linen sheets. Made rough bandages and had a hell of a time getting them to fix. Ever tried to wrap up your back with trembling hands? It's a crapshoot. Once I got them to stay, the pain eased up and I weren't worried no more 'bout getting blood all in my coats. Left that room red as the basement and didn't give two shits 'bout it.

I got my clothes and a few cans out the basement, quick saw boot prints in the red mud, making circles round the table and I didn't fancy staying down there with them and dead Matthews any longer'n I had to. Found a backpack and filled it with them cans, few carrots and a bunch of them nice silver spoons. Found myself a tinder box gathering dust and let out a whoop a' joy. It had one of them nice metal rods with a flat striker, few bits a' wool and a fat strip a' wax paper. All kinds a' useful. I know stealing is one of them human rules you don't break but then so is murdering and Matthews was fixing to break that first.

I got out that homestead just as night was falling. I'd been in them walls half a day but my life had changed so much in them few hours. Lyon weren't just after Kreagar, she had me in her sights and she was closing in. Them words, *Think on why I ain't killing you,* swirled round in my head, mixing up with pictures a' Lyon and Matthews and Kreagar, confusing me and putting cold fear in my chest the whole walk to the forest. Soon as I got in them trees the swirling stopped. Smell a' mulch and bark and pine and dirt filled me up and calmed me down. I was in the wild and there weren't no way Lyon or Kreagar or no one else was going to find me again.

SOMETHIN' LIKE PARADISE

For a month, I didn't see hide nor hair of any other person. My life in them days leading to winter was walking, hunting, sleeping, walking. To tell the truth I was getting sick a' walking. The snow was crawling down from the mountains in fat drifts and some mornings I woke up with a dusting a' white around me. I kept the Reverend's cuts clean when I could, last thing I needed was my blood going rotten, but the sticky itching was burning up my back something awful and I weren't nowhere close to a doctor. Not that I put much stock in their potions and tonics. Trapper said doctors were crooks ready to fleece you for a cup of whisky. He said they made you sicker so they could keep you coming back lining their pockets with coin. But when Trapper cut his hand and it went all yellow and wet and puffed up like a mushroom 'bout to spore, he was crying and whining like a weakling child. He was begging for the doctor to cure him and at the same time roaring at me for taking him to town in the first place.

Sickness makes babes and bastards of us all. I had no intention of letting my back go bad but it was headed that way. You can cut off a sickly hand, or least cut out the bad meat, but you can't be cutting off your arms and back. I figured I had to stop all the walking and make myself a proper situation.

I knew where the road was but weren't going close to it for fear a' Lyon and her hawk eyes spotting me. But I stuck close enough to it, thinking that if my back did get bad, I could risk being found by a kindly soul.

From the road I went a mile or two west and came out the thick woods next to a pretty lake, water still as a pigeon full a' shot. Trees around were good hazel and alder and elder, even a big old oak reaching his branches south to the sun. He told me where I was at, made sure I kept my heading true. Round the lake I spied a stand of lush firs and, bit further, a whole damn *field* of ferns. Trees was full of scrabbling and chattering critters and I spotted nigh on ten rabbit runs without even proper looking.

I went to the edge of the lake and what I saw near took my breath away. The water was clear as glass, like it weren't really there. The shale and rocks 'neath it were white and caught every bit a' light the sun could throw on 'em. Near the middle, the water got dark and I guessed that's where it got deep. I didn't see no fishes in the shallows nor nothing what would say there was fish in there anywhere. On the far side a crag of rocks stood twice-me high and dribbled fresh water into the lake so soft the ripples didn't make it all the way over to me. It was a perfect circle this lake.

The air round here was warm too, when I breathed there weren't no smoke and my skin didn't go goosey when I took my coat off. No wonder them woods was full of birdsong and scratchings, I must a' hit one of them hotspots Trapper was always rambling about.

'Them's where you want to be, girl,' he'd say. 'Never winter in them crater lakes. You could live the life of Riley all year round. Heat off them ruski bombs stays warm for a hundred years.'

I never asked who Riley was but he sounded like one of them freeloading types. Didn't matter though, I found myself standing on the shores of a goddamn paradise and I said to myself, Elka, this is where you got to stay for a spell and fix yourself up. You got water, you got food and you got heat 'neath your feet.

BeeCee had taken some big hits in the Damn Stupid a' course and this place was one a' them what people talked about. The trees were huge but I could tell they weren't old, like whatever bomb was sitting in that lake was making the water rich so's everything grew up super quick. I didn't care none for the bomb, it couldn't do nothing to me now, but it made the brush thick and green and ripe for hunting.

I did a quick bit of scouting and I found me a spot close to the crag, 'tween a stand of hazel and alder. Golden rule of outdoor living is go where the goods are, don't be traipsing around bringing it all to you. That wastes everyone's time and ain't many things I hate more'n wasting time. In that spot I had me running water, trees for shelter and brush for comfort. I figured I had a few hours afore sundown so I dumped the Reverend's pack and pulled out my knife. I found two trees just longer'n me apart, each with branches growing out the trunk about waist height. Perfect set up that were.

I found a hazel trunk fat as my arm and, with my knife and a rock, chopped it down to use as my cross beam. Set that up 'tween the trees, nestled nice and tight in the crooks of them branches. I kept my head on making me a little hut so's I didn't think much on my back and that sticky burning. Every time I hefted a bundle of branches, the cuts on my arms opened up fresh and sent aching through me. Could a' screamed every time if I weren't so damn determined to get this shelter built. Once I put my thoughts to it, ain't no amount of suffering or sorrow going to stop me from getting a roof above me afore nightfall.

I stacked up skinny branches along the beam like a deer's rib bones after boiling. All white and smooth and a hand's thickness apart. Nice and close to keep me warm. I covered the whole thing in ferns and bracken and leaf litter, didn't pay no mind to ticks and spiders, they don't bother me if I don't bother them. Maybe I'm using their home as roofing but they get a warm sleep and I don't get rained on. Win–win and when you're eking out a life in the forests you make the most a' them little victories.

Found some nice dry tinder and a flint rock and set me a spark. Set that close to the entrance of my hut and built it up right nice into a crackling blaze.

Night fell quick but the moon came out smiling and turned that lake into a mirror. It lit up my glade and I sat 'neath my roof, watching glowbugs dancing on the other side of the water. I ate some canned deer, care of the good Reverend, and settled myself down. Something right serene about it and to tell the truth, I ain't slept better'n that night in a long while.

Soon as sunup woke me, I set a dozen snares and decided it would be a fine time to bathe my back. Trapper hated bathing. Said it made him smell too human and told the animals right where he was. I recall only one time he came back to our little home not stinking of sweat and dried blood. Said he did it to smell *more* human and fit in with them other animals. I didn't pay no mind to what he was saying back then, he oftentimes talked in riddles but now I think back on it, knowing he's a murdering son bitch, them words weren't no riddle, they was instructions.

I stopped counting the weeks I stayed by that lake. There was magic in that water and my back healed up quick, leaving nought more'n thin scars crossing my skin. I did some exploring in them woods and found the edge a' the warm. A small clearing 'tween the lake and the road was criss-crossed in tracks what looked human. One time I heard voices what I didn't recognise as Kreagar or Lyon, but whoever they was they never came close. I never saw no one and I sure didn't go looking.

Most days my snares caught a rabbit and I ate fancy. One day I checked my squirrel poles and found me a pigeon hanging by the foot, flapping about and squawking. He'd near ripped off that foot by the time I found him and I tell you, he wouldn't have lasted a day out in the wild, hopping about. I did him a kindness.

He was a bit small and the only good eating on a small bird like that is the breast. Trapper taught me a trick when I was eight for getting in and getting out quicker'n a fox after your chickens. First I broke the poor devil's neck, nice and quick-like so the meat didn't have no time to tense up with fear. Couple a' twists and a few sharp tugs and I had his head and wings on the grass in a neat pile. No point being messy. Killing can be clean and neat if you don't put no fury in it.

Pigeons are clever birds see, no matter what the town folk say, and they keep seeds and nuts and whatever they been eating that day stored up in their necks for tougher times. This guy had a couple plump acorns and I figured I ain't letting these go to waste. Acorns is good eating if you cook 'em up right. I put them in my pocket and dug both my thumbs deep in the bird's neck. I always loved this part when I was a babe, feeling how the bird's put together, all that fresh, bright blood telling me there's goodness to be had. Hell, it was like touching god and seeing his thoughts when he decided on the design. Fact that it was so easy told me we was meant to be doing it. Even my young'un hands had enough strength to pull apart breast and back and turn that pigeon inside out. I opened it up like a juicy orange. Scraped out them guts and set 'em close and neat 'side the wings, then just peeled them breasts away in one clean chunk. Dark, purple, heart-shaped goodness it was, still warm and ready for roasting.

I took it back to camp and skewered it over the fire then cleaned myself up in the lake. Now, it's just good manners and sense to clean up your kill site so's it don't bring bears and such right to your front door. Rules say you got to dig a hole and put them remains back where they came from. Bury 'em deep and say your thanks.

I waited too long afore going back.

Pigeon cooks perfect pink in just a few minutes and when I smelled that meat, all them sugars in there browning, turning sticky-sweet, that fine alder wood smoking it up to a crisp char, I didn't want to leave it for a second. Two bites a breast and gone. Better'n rabbit any day. I weren't going to let that crown burn or dry out, no sir. But I sure should a' cleaned up them guts and wings quicker.

As I got close to the site, I heard crunching. Sharp teeth on weak bone. I froze. Felt cold for the first time since getting to that lake. I stuck close to a fat trunk and peered round the bark. White downy feathers puffed and scattered about the grass, like they was trying to get flying again though their owner was in pieces. It was all crunch, crunch, puff puff.

It weren't a bear, that's for sure, didn't make enough noise and wouldn't be bothering itself with something so scrawny as pigeon guts.

Felt the wind on my cheek and my stomach dropped out my shoes. That wind picked up my scent and took it right to the beast.

Crunching stopped. Feathers settled.

My heartbeat bounced up inside my ears, thundering worse than any storm. I went to pull my knife out my belt and my heart damn near exploded. I'd left my knife at camp. I could see the blade glinting in the sun further round the lake, like it were laughing at me, saying, Elka, you're a fool'n a half.

Brush leaves rustled and a few feathers landed close to my tree, flown by breath 'stead a' wind.

I could run, I thought, I could run and get my knife. Might be quicker'n whatever was eating my tailings. I could jump out and spook the beast, shock it to scarpering. Or piss it off something rotten. I moved, quiet-like, and looked further round the tree.

Yellow eyes staring at me.

Big goddamn timber wolf, not fifteen strides away.

I kept my eyes on it. Once you look away from a wolf, next and last thing you know will be their jaws round your neck. All other noise ran away scared from that forest. No birds, no scratching critters, not even the wind rustling branches. All I heard was that wolf breathing in time with me. Yellow eyes held mine. It weren't attacking, weren't raging at me, just stood there, head low, feathers all round his mouth.

'Spose he was just trying to have some dinner and I interrupted him.

'OK, fella,' I said and moved out from 'hind that tree so's he could see all my intentions.

He bared his teeth. He didn't seem all that old, hadn't grown into his ears yet. Maybe three-four months but he was a big'un and skinny, what meant hungry. Didn't look like he'd had a good meal in all his life. Had snow all over his fur and I figured winter was coming down hard other side them trees. No wonder he wandered to my lake, temperature had barely dropped in all the weeks I been here. I backed up a step, arms up in a sign a' calm. He growled, showed off all his pearly whites and my heart damn near backflipped it wanted to get away so bad. A hungry wolf is a whole new type a' danger.

Snow on his head shook off and 'neath it I saw a black smudge a' fur right down 'tween his eyes. One of them gods, whoever the wolves hold to, had taken his thumb and drawn soot down this one.

'Damn. You're that pup what lead me to the Mussa. . .' I said though I didn't much believe it. Never seen another wolf with markings like that afore. Never since. I wondered brief if it was for me, so I'd know this guy on second sight and wouldn't take my knife to him. That floppy little fuzzer by the river was no more'n a handful of weeks old and this guy was getting on months. 'Spose I'd been by the lake longer'n I thought.

He didn't seem to have no rage in him. He weren't coiled up ready to strike or nothing, he was just telling me all polite-like to leave him to his pigeon.

'All right, Wolf, you go have yourself a feast,' I said and I backed away one big step at a time. When I was out of sight of him, I heard that crunching again and knew, somewhere down deep in me, that I weren't in no danger from him. As a pup he had saved my skin and I was more'n happy to return the favour.

Time went strange by that lake. Winter let loose on the world, I saw the storms and blizzards and I hunkered down best I could in my shelter but nothing hit too hard. The snow quick melted when it hit the grass and the ice at the edges of the lake barely stayed past the morning. Wondered brief with a smirk if bleeding out that Reverend had given us all a mild winter.

Wolf stuck around, skirting my camp, keeping his distance for the most part. I weren't afraid of him same as he didn't see much to fear in me. I'd catch a squirrel or rabbit and I'd leave the guts and heads in a pile. Couple minutes later I'd hear slurping and crunching. Funny kind of comfort that. I'd been on my own so long and I didn't much realise how sad it made me. Afore Wolf turned up, I figured I hadn't spoken out loud for nigh on three weeks. Wondered if Wolf hadn't turned up, I'd a' forgotten how to speak altogether. Now I was talking loud, shouting dinner's ready, come and get it.

Carried on like this for a while till one day I stuck around at his eating spot. Everything felt slow by that lake, like I had all the time in the world. I sat quiet-like a good ten foot from his table and waited, nice pile of rabbit guts for him. Don't know what made me do it, think it might a' been a cry out for something closer. Wolves are pack animals see, they live best with company and us humans do too. I spent my life so far with a companion, no matter if he was a bastard, and to tell the truth, I felt something missing deep in my gut.

Wolf came up as normal but when he spotted me so close he growled low and rumbling. I figured that was more a hey, what you want? Rather than a I'm gonna have your head. This was new territory for us both and I weren't in the mood to get bit. When he figured I weren't after his dinner and I weren't about to skin him for bedding, he started crunching that rabbit head. He didn't take his yellow eyes off me, his big tongue lapped up all them guts and brain like it was separate from the rest of him. Weren't no growl in them eyes. Weren't no ferocity. Think he was curious about me. Maybe saw me less as one of them human hunters wanting his fur and more as a missing member of his pack.

Soon as he was done eating he scarpered back into the forest and I didn't see him again that night. Next day I did the same, just sat an inch or two closer. And the next, and the next, till he didn't growl no more when he saw me and didn't pay me no mind when he was crunching through skulls. Once he had comfort with me, I chucked a rabbit leg to him, made sure it landed halfway 'tween us.

Wolf didn't move. Stared from me to the meat. Then tiny, shaking steps forward. He was no more'n two foot away from me now. I could smell his fur, kind a' musty, sour scent, something familiar about it. He sniffed at the rabbit, fresh killed and still warm, then looked up at me. Thought for a second he weren't going to take it.

Finally, he picked it up in his teeth and lay himself flat on the grass to eat. My heart and my joy swelled up, filled up my chest like a flower 'bout to bloom. But them wolf teeth and claws weren't no pretty petals, they kept me grounded they did, one false or quick move and they could rip right through me. Didn't think Wolf would do that, course, but he was still a wild'un and you can't be too careful with them. Joy makes wits dull and slow and I weren't in the business of letting it get the best a' me.

Wolf finished the leg and sniffed the air up and down looking for more. I had the other leg in my hands and I set it down 'bout halfway 'tween us. He was laying like that Sphinx rock I'd seen in the old picture books. Front legs out straight, ready to lever himself up without no warning. He gave me a little snarl but I paid him no mind, just sat still and quiet and waited.

Wolf shuffled forward. Bit more. Bit more. Then snapped up that rabbit.

My life, he was close to me. I could a' reached out and touched him, could see specks of dirt and leaf stuck in his coat, could smell his breath. Don't know what idiot god possessed me but next thing I knew I was reaching out my hand.

Wolf snarled proper then and backed up an inch.

My heart went drumming through every bit a' me. Every muscle tingled like I'd sat funny on it and it was coming back to life. I tried just thinking of my breathing, in out over and over but, damn me, I didn't put my hand down.

Thinking back on it now, I could a' lost that hand in a second. Could a' lost my life a second after. It was stupid. One of the worse stupids I done. But hell, it was worth it.

Wolf stopped growling and got curious. He stretched out his neck, all thick grey fur, and sniffed my hand. I was trembling. My head was yelling at me to put my arm down.

'It's a goddamn *wolf*,' my head shouted at me but I told it to shut up, told it I knew what I was doing and butt out.

Wolf sniffed at me again, closer, then closer, then he nuzzled his nose right into my palm. I tell you, I thought I might shout and holler and dance a jig. Felt tears in my eyes as this wild thing, this old-world creature, decided I was good enough to be friends. Wolf rubbed his face on my hands and I started scratching him 'neath the chin.

My face hurt I was smiling so wide.

He made a few deep rumbling sounds that said he was relaxed and liked what I was doing so to hell with it, I kept on scratching.

Then something spooked him. Don't know what. Maybe a rabbit dashing through the brush or he caught sight of one of them garter snakes or something, or maybe he'd just had enough a' my attention. He bolted up, stood tall and king-like, towering above me. Felt like I'd lost a piece of me in that moment, like that wolf had stolen something and I had to stick with him always to make sure I'd get it back.

Then he turned round and ran into the trees, bushy grey tail swinging behind him.

I didn't see Wolf for days, don't even know how many, I had an ache in my chest from it. The pile of guts was getting higher and insects were buzzing about it, turning it rotten. I thought I'd lost him and I ain't too proud to say I cried for him. He'd become my friend by this strange lake where time slowed and seasons stayed firm. He was the only thing that changed and when he didn't come crunching on them squirrel skulls, day after day after day, I felt chills of fear inside me I hadn't felt in months.

DEMON IN THEM TREES

In them weeks without Wolf, I felt strange. Like I was walking about in a dream. Soon I stopped hearing them words from Matthews' basement, *Think on why I ain't killin' you.* Then I stopped worrying over Lyon and her six-shooter on my tail. Soon after that, I stopped thinking on my parents, stopped checking my traps, stopped stoking my fire, I just lay in my shelter, waiting. Guess a kind a' sadness had come about me. Something dark swaddled me up and held me tight like a babe to her momma's teat and I let it and I wanted it. My body was heavy and my head full a' buzzing flies. I didn't sleep much no more.

The lake and forest were warmer'n ever, I didn't need no coat and I was living just in my linens. The sky kept on being white and blue. Nothing was changing and something *wrong* was taking root inside me.

When I weren't lying down, staring, I was sat out by the lake watching the water. Started to see things in that water. Colours I ain't never seen afore swirled 'bout, turning into shapes of bears and eagles, into human faces and kids running around, playing. Thought I was going loon. Don't know if it was Wolf not being there no more that sent my head off in a spin or it was just being by that lake with sorrow in my heart 'stead a' joy. I always said that lake had something of a magic about it, something that dulls the senses and turns a wily whip of a girl into a thick-headed dolt.

Felt like I was dosed with nightshade or valerian all the time. I knew that feeling. Trapper had used them herbs to calm a frantic deer once. He said you eat meat full a' terror you might as well be eating shit off the ground. Got to keep them quiet and friendly. I told him once, though, that I saw a doe eating nightshade berries like they was treats. They didn't work on deer.

'They don't work on them deer, they work on some a' the other types,' he said and that seemed like a fine answer to me.

I started seeing faces in the trees and could a' sworn up and down I heard footsteps, human boots on twigs, stomping through the night. I checked that clearing near the road but never saw no one. I sat up all night, twitching and shaking, knife in my hands.

'Come at me, demons,' I whispered over and over. I figured they would stop messing about out in the woods and attack me tooth and claw. I'd fight them right till they sucked the soul out my body.

Shadow passed by the end of my shelter. Smell of rot and iron followed it. Smell of hell and devils. I weren't waiting for it to get me sitting down in my bed. I weren't going to die that way. I'd go out slashing my knife 'gainst its throat. I gritted my teeth and rushed outside. No moon showed my way, night was deep and full, but I saw that shadow stalking through the trees. Ain't no hiding true evil, not even in the dark.

I followed it, knife held tight, right out to the edge of the water. Big black shape, something like a man, something like a beast, stood there casting looks out in all directions. Looking for me. Saw its head swinging left to right like an owl searching for vermin. Hands sharp like eagle talons hung by its side and I felt my heart raging inside me. My eyes blurred and everything shook but I was ready for it.

I screeched worse than anything the demon would a' heard in hell and run at it. Must a' took it by surprise. It snapped round, hissed and said words in some kind a' devil language. I blocked my ears of it, didn't want no evil putting a spell on me, dulling my mind even more. The demon raised his claws but I was quick as a hazel switch. I ducked his swiping arms and sliced my knife into his belly.

The beast roared and I heard something in that roar that sent my mind back a few years. That roar, I heard it when a buckhorn gored a hole in Trapper's gut. It weren't bad, not even deep, but he raged for days. I heard that sound sunup to sundown for near a week and I'd know it anywhere.

But this demon weren't Trapper, weren't Kreagar. Couldn't a' been. Kreagar couldn't find me, I said so, I said he ain't never finding me and I ain't seen no sign a' him since afore Dalston, 'less it really was his legs I seen in Matthews' basement. Ain't no matter, Lyon must a' caught up with him by now. I twisted away and I saw nothing but darkness in that *thing*. I didn't know what it was. My brain hurt and ached and I couldn't think in straight lines. The demon said something, words what didn't make sense to me, words like 'you learning, you learning'.

He was gone fast as I could blink. Woods fell quick silent

and I didn't hear no more footsteps. I figured it had to a' been a demon or a ghost to disappear like that. I didn't know much a' what happened next 'cept I woke up on the shore a' that lake, knife still in my hand and a pool of dark blood next to me.

I slept all night and almost all through the next day after that. Body was drained and empty. Didn't remember last time I ate. A heavy cloud weighed on my head and no amount of sleep seemed to lift it. But hell, my heart swelled when I went down to the water one morning and I saw Wolf standing, tight and tense, halfway round the lake.

'Hey, Wolf!' I said loud, saw his ears prick at the sound a' me. Forgot all 'bout that demon.

Wolf came round the lake on them fat pad paws. Didn't have no snow on him so he couldn't a' gone far. He was a hell of a sight, that's for sure, all muscle and claws and teeth, and that fur, mixes of white and grey and that brown you get just when the leaves are turning. That black line down his head, 'tween his eyes. I tell you, that feeling is something no number a' pretty words can make real. That's ancient, old-time respect 'tween beasts. We could both kill each other quicker'n you could snap your fingers and maybe one day we will, but by that lake and in them forests, I felt more kinship with that wolf than I ever did with a human.

He came close to me and sniffed, still a bit a' nerves running through him. I knelt down and held out my hand.

'Got no rabbit heads for you no more,' I said and he came up, nuzzled his nose 'gainst my hand.

Then he clamped his jaws right round my arm.

I fell onto my backside and tried to pull away. Cursed myself for leaving my knife in my hut. Felt his teeth pressing into my skin but he weren't biting me. He was just holding my arm in his mouth. Right gentle, like he was carrying a pup by the scruff.

My shock went away slow but I kept looking in his eyes and there weren't no hate there, no snarling. But he weren't letting go neither. He started tugging me. Pulling me away from the water and toward my hut. I was so confused by it I went along, bending down all awkward to keep my arm straight.

He let me go when we got to my shelter. Then he started jumping about, running away into the trees and then coming rushing back at me. He wanted me to follow him, that was plain.

'I got all I need here, Wolf,' I said, dizzy for straightening up. 'I got water and heat and food, I ain't goin' nowhere.'

I turned away then heard a mighty growl behind me. Wolf weren't playing games. Soon as I turned back he started dashing about again.

'Where you want me to go, huh?' I said to him.

I folded my arms and shook my head at him.

He growled again, fiercer.

'Where you been?' I said, fiercer too. 'You just up and leave me then come back like nothin' happened, tellin' me to leave my cushy set up? What you thinkin', Wolf?'

I knew he didn't know my words, I weren't touched in the head like that. I figured he might get my meaning though, wolves ain't stupid, they're meant to be part of a pack and all packs got their issues.

Wolf yapped and run quicker into the forest and back. His eyes was full of something close to worry. Maybe he'd seen something while I was away, some kind a' danger that was headed this way. Maybe he'd seen the demon and knew I was in trouble. Something was wrong in that lake.

Something in the deep dark part that put this whole area into a fog a' forget. The North weren't no more'n a compass point to me no more.

Maybe whatever bomb was in that lake was leaching out something nasty. Maybe it was drinking that water, eating meat what lapped it, bathing in it, letting it in my blood. No wonder them rabbits and squirrels were so easy to catch, they were all drunk and stupid.

Wolf was right. Time to go.

'Should call you Wise Wolf from now on,' I said, and nodded firm to him. I quick gathered up my stuff, still had a can or two left from the Reverend, and figured filling up my flask from that water was a fool's idea of a good time.

He didn't growl at me. I suppose he knew us humans weren't well equipped for outdoors in just our skins. Once my pack was strapped to my back, I followed Wolf away from the lake. Maybe he had some kind of plan told to him by the wolf god, maybe he just wanted a change of scene or to punish me for not giving him better cuts of rabbit, but damn that beast, he took me straight to Lyon's front door.

TOWN A' GENESIS

There weren't no snow.

Least not big drifts of it I expected from a winter in these parts. There were a few branches still laden with white but that was old fall. It hadn't snowed in days. Ground was wet and muddy with melt and my heart dropped right out my stomach. It was spring. I'd been by that lake near half a year.

That first night away from the water I wished I was dead. Had shakes and shivers and they weren't from the cold. I screamed at high heaven to strike me down and I must a' told all them hungry woken-up bears just where to find me. Wolf stayed close, kept me warm with his fur, kept me still with his weight. Woke up the next morning breathing him in, my face right up in his neck.

Took me two days away from that poison lake but I soon started to feel more like old Elka. I was a bit slower, bit quieter, but I felt my wits coming back. Felt my tongue sharpening up. Felt all them things I forgot coming back to me. *Tell my little girl, I love you.* Them words hit me first and hardest. I was getting

closer to my momma and daddy. I was looking forward 'stead
a' looking back. I didn't want no life with Trapper no more.
Trapper weren't really Trapper after all. But my parents, they
was real and they was waiting in the far North.

Their words came back to me but so did pictures a'
Matthews' basement. Them legs I saw walking round, they
came clearer in my head, saw stitching and red stains. Seen
the stranger's hand on the table next to my head. Scar on it.
More a' them words spoke in my head, like they was struggling through a snowdrift. *Ain't no sport in killin' something
caught in someone else's snare.* There was more. More words
what was still buried, more smells and sights what my brain
couldn't pull out. Could a' just been some crazy-ass bastard
what hated the Reverend. Could a' been Kreagar. But shit,
Lyon must a' caught him by now. All that ice and bluster in
her, all that law she got on her side.

When I saw a town from the top of a rise, I dropped flat
onto my stomach and cursed the wolf. I weren't in no mood
for humans. He lay flat beside me and didn't say a word. Felt
like he was rolling his eyes at me like my nana did when I
said something stupid. But when I thought about it more,
I said all right then, Wolf.

I needed to know where I was and how far it was to
Halveston. Trapper told me stories of fools rushing up
there hundred years afore the Damn Stupid and they all
went through Dawson city. Dawson weren't there no more.
It got hit nasty in the Second Conflict when them over the
ocean tried their luck few years after the Damn Stupid but
from a different direction, down 'stead a' up. Shit, them
ruski folks Trapper spat about, they tried it every which way
but the Mussa valley men cut 'em off at the knees, so says
the old'uns in Ridgeway anyways. They said with an actor

running our show and a woman in charge 'cross the ocean, it weren't no surprise that them ruskis got as far as they did. It was the Mussa men what single-handed won the Second Conflict if you believe the talk. Hard to put too much stock in what them sodden men say. Damn Stupid and Second Conflict, hell, they was what they was and they both done and dead now, ain't no sense in dwelling.

Dawson was gone but I figured another town must a' sprung up in its place, figured that might be Halveston. Just like the Reverend said, the north is big and I admit I didn't know what road was leading me where.

This town was built up at a crossroads. One road ran east–west, the other north–south and the north–south was wider and more travelled. Wooden arches over each road marked the boundaries. Even saw a few folks heading north, dragging sleds and bulky packs. This was one of them 'gateway' towns. It was maybe twice the size of Dalston and mostly acted as a trading post for them passing through.

'You go in that town,' I said to the wolf, 'and they're going to string you up and skin you.'

Wolf huffed and crawled forward.

I put my hand firm on the back of his neck and said, 'They'd kill you soon as look at you. Stay here.'

I think he got my meaning 'cause when I stood up, he didn't. Looked right forlorn he did, gave me a few yaps, few little howls, but it was for the best. He knew it same as me.

I turned up my collar as I went 'neath the town's south arch. Few folks milled about, old timers sat outside stores and chewed on 'bacco, a rifle resting on their bony knees. Nobody paid me much attention. Streets were quieter than I expected and the buildings, all wood boards, were bigger'n they looked from the rise. Never been in a town this big and it sent prickles running up my neck. Kept my knife close to hand. Kept my wits. Get in, get out, and get back to Wolf.

I came to a general store. Usually them shopkeepers are gossips a' the worst kind. They know everything and everyone what has passed through their town and if anyone was going to point me in the right direction, it'd be them.

Stuck up in the window was one a' them charcoal posters a' Kreagar. Strange seeing his face after so long away from him. Made me miss him but that passed quick like gas. Couldn't tell if the poster was an old'un and he was caught already or if he was still running. I sure as shit weren't 'bout to ask no questions to find out.

A tin bell tinkled when I pushed open the door. Two free-standing shelves stood taller'n me, running down the centre of the shop. Walls was covered in goods and produce and, on the far side, a thickset woman sat behind a counter, scraping at her nails with a file.

'Morning, love,' she said as I got to the counter, 'help you?'

'Wonderin' if you can tell me what this town calls itself?' I said.

Woman put the file down and looked at me, caterpillar eyebrows meeting in the middle of her head. 'Can't read the name on the arches?'

Shook my head.

'This here is Genesis and this is Maud's General Store. I'm titular Maud,' she chuckled though I didn't get the joke. My eyes went to her chest and she sure was titular, didn't do much to hide it neither.

'Where are you headed?' she said.

Weren't no point in lying. Don't get no fruit out a' good folks when all you feed them is lies. I could tell by this woman's voice she was a good'un. Had kindness deep in her though I wouldn't want to push it too far.

'Halveston. Heard about a yellow metal makin' men rich. Figured I'd get mine.'

Maud smiled, showed off teeth black from 'bacco.

'Ha!' she laughed like a donkey braying. 'You and the rest of the world, darlin'.'

I turned my face meek, like her words had hurt my delicate feelings.

'Aw, hell, child, I didn't mean nothing by it,' she said, and put a meaty hand over mine. With her other she took a map out the rack and spread it 'cross the counter. Was 'bout the same as Matthews' map.

'All those guys who are looking for the gold and stones got to pass through Halveston so be mindful. You take the road north through the mountain pass, cross the lake, careful though, only a handful of towns from here to there. Just follow the trail of fools.' She winked at me and I felt a mite of discomfort at how familiar she was.

Found the lake, skinny and long, and north of that by a fair way, 'neath her finger, was Halveston. Felt good to have firm points what meant I didn't have to go on that road. Mountain pass. Long, narrow lake. Long as I kept that road close, I weren't getting lost.

'Thank you, ma'am,' I said and went to leave.

'Hold up,' Maud shouted, didn't stand up, didn't think she could easy lift all that bulk. 'Hope you're going to stick around town, we got a hanging today, whole town will be in the square for the celebration.'

'Who you hangin'?'

'A woman who kept quiet about her kid shooting up a store.'

Big cold rock sat in my throat. 'They hang people for that?'

'Hang them for less than that around here.'

'Is that right?' I said and I tried my damnedest to keep the tremble out my voice.

Maud nodded. 'The kid turned the gun on himself when the law caught up. He got his, now the one who helped him hide is going to get hers.'

'Damn awful,' I said but I couldn't bring myself to feel like it was right. Sounded like the momma didn't do nothing bad. Sure not bad enough to be hung for it.

'You ain't wrong,' she said. 'Magistrate Lyon arrested her herself and brought her here for justice. After all, we've got the best hanging tree north of Couver City,' she laughed and all her flesh bubbled like a stewpot on coals.

That rock in my throat dropped hard into my gut. Lyon. Here. Right now. She knew my face and I didn't much want a second meeting with her. But hell, something in me, some dark part, wanted to see her again, like I had an urging in me to face down a bear. I wanted to see if she could find me, if she still remembered my face after a winter a' darkness. There was something about Lyon that scared me right to the core, but damn it all, she made me curious. She made me wonder how anyone could get that cold.

'You all right, darlin'?' Maud asked.

I'd been standing still for too long.

'Never seen a hangin' before,' I said, 'think I'll stick around a bit longer.'

'She's swinging at sunset,' she said and I thanked her and left the store.

Sunset was near and I followed the crowd to the town square. A big oak grew in the middle and they'd slung a rope over the fattest limb and tied it off to a pair of horses ready to run. Rest of the tree had been lopped off. No leaves, no other branches. They'd turned the king of the wood into a death-bringer. Like they'd taken a great proud grizzly, shaved off all his fur and made him dance. Made me sick to see it. Didn't care much for the woman going to die but that poor oak didn't deserve to be the gallows.

Spotted Lyon right away. She stood by the tree, all in black, her lieutenants either side, and a gleaming six-shooter on her belt for all to see. She was all ice. Wouldn't surprise me if you cut her open you'd find glaciers 'stead of blood and icicles 'stead a' bones.

Crowd started cheering and I soon saw why. Pair of deputies brought out the devoted mother. Skinny woman, looked like she'd had a hard winter. She'd tried to do right by her son and I found it hard to see the bad in that. Hell, maybe she didn't even know what he done.

Saw her eyes, that woman, and they didn't have no fear in them. Then I saw Lyon's and they may as well a' been black holes for all the feelings they gave away.

I bet my blade that Lyon had gone round questioning folk 'bout her same as she did 'bout me. Wanted in connection with murder. Connection's all it takes in this godforsaken country. You stand in the same room as someone what done bad and Lyon'll string you up. Weren't all that much hope for me, living so long with Kreagar.

Saw myself in that woman, defiant of her fate. She done right by her kid, best she could, and no one, not even Lyon, could take that away.

One a' the lieutenants looped the rope round the woman's neck. The horses stamped and blew. They were ready. The crowd was baying. Weren't no stopping this train now.

I closed my eyes when the whip crack set the horses to

bolt. Cheer of the crowd silenced the snapping neck. I'd never seen no one hang before and a loving mother weren't going to be my first.

I opened my eyes when I heard the body hit the ground. Lyon hadn't moved. Didn't seem affected none by a woman dying beside her.

A kid brushed past me and I felt tiny fingers in my pocket. Thieving beast. I snatched the arm and pulled the kid round to face me. Mask of mud and grime but it was a boy no more'n ten.

'Let me go,' he wailed but the crowd drowned him out.

I dropped to my knees and came nose-to-nose with him.

'Give it back,' I said and my eyes told him not to play games.

He opened up his hand and one of my old snares fell into the mud. Must a' kept it in my pocket and forgot 'bout it. I didn't have no coin to steal anyways.

'You tryin' to steal with all these lawmen around?' I said.

Kid didn't say nothing.

'Do somethin' for me and I'll give you silver worth a hundred of them snares.'

His baby eyes lit up at that and he nodded.

I whispered my instructions in his ear.

'You understand?'

'Yes ma'am, I do,' he said and tried to pull his arm free but I held on.

'You cross me,' I said, and slid my knife out its sheath, 'and I'll slit you neck to navel, get it?'

His body tensed and he nodded again, proper this time, none of that frantic kid-like excitement no more. There was fear in them eyes and fear, when used right, is better'n all the coin in the world.

I let him go and he run off in the crowd. I stood up and

watched him push through and walk right up to Lyon. She knelt down to greet him, muddied up her black pants and didn't seem to think nothing of it. The boy passed on my message and I held my breath waiting for her reaction.

Lyon's head snapped round to her lieutenants and she said something I couldn't hear. Then she smiled at the kid, gave him a coin, and sent him away. She quick stood up, said something to her stocky lieutenant, and strode off, both men right behind her.

The kid arrived back to me a few seconds later.

'I told her what you said.'

'You sure? Tell me exactly what words,' I said.

Boy took a deep breath and said, 'My cousin saw a man with tattoos all over his face down in Martinsville not two days ago, he was saying the law burnt down his house. I told her that the man was hollerin' about how he was going to kill all the lawmen he sees. I said I thought you should know, Miss Lyon.'

'Good,' I said and felt a swelling a' pride at my plan. It weren't a total lie after all, Kreagar could a' been near Martinsville and the Reverend, but that would a' been six months ago 'stead a' two days. I wanted to know for damn sure he weren't in one a' Lyon's cells or hung already from that poor oak.

'What she do?' I said.

'Do I get my silver now?' he said, holding out his hand, skinny eyebrows crossed up like I'd swindled him already.

I growled like Wolf and said, 'What did she do?'

He huffed and finally said, 'She asked if there was a girl with him.'

Lump grew hard in my throat. 'What you say?'

'I said I don't know nothing about a girl.'

A flutter of relief went through my chest but did nothing to break up the lump.

'Then what?' I asked.

'She shouted at them men to saddle the horses. She said "I'll watch that bastard swing for what he did to my boy" then she run off.'

Shivers went all through me.

I gave the kid one of them spoons and sent him on his way. My head was dazing worse than it was by the lake. Kreagar weren't caught yet and Lyon's boy had been one of his kills. No wonder she was so fierce about him. She'd ride clean across the country to find Kreagar, that was clear as day and I bet whoever stood in her way would get a bullet and all. I felt cold. I had stood in her way and now I was in her sights. I hadn't told her the truth in Dalston and I felt sick for it knowing what Kreagar'd taken from her. Maybe she figured me and him was in it together. Maybe she thought I'd known all about his wolf hunts. Maybe she was right. There was so much I didn't remember from my life with that man. But the longer I was away from him, the more and quicker it was returning to me.

BOATS ARE FOR SPITTIN' AT

I don't much like roads. Roads is some other man's path that people follow no question. All my life I lived by rules of the forest and rules of myself. One of them rules is don't go trusting another man's path. No matter if that's a real one trodden into dirt or all them twists and turns his life has taken. People do it, they do what their mommys and daddys did, they make them same mistakes, they have them same joys and hurts, they just repeating. Trees don't grow exactly where their momma is, ain't no room, ain't enough light and water so they end up wilting and dying off. It's the same with us humans, though you wouldn't know it to look at them most a' the time. Ranches and stores are passed father to son, momma to girl, but there ain't no room for it. Son tries to run things like he wants, father ain't having none of it, they start feuding and soon that family ain't no more.

I weren't following no one up through life. Sure Kreagar taught me skills but I weren't going to walk his line, 'specially knowing now where that line took him. Certain things I did when I was with him, certain steps I took along his path, are things I'd rather be forgetting. When I was staring into the flames of his hut I swore I'd never walk in another man's steps ever again and I just hoped all them gods out there would forgive me for 'em afore too long.

Weren't no telling what was along that road going north out a' Genesis. A road is a draw to thieves and unsavoury types. They go where the fools go and I weren't no fool.

I went back up the hill to where I left the wolf. He weren't there a' course. Can't be expecting a wild thing to stay in one place for too long. He knew my scent, he'd find me when he wanted feeding or comfort. I was fixing to walk when my eye caught something that sent mid-winter chills all through me.

Boot prints in the dirt.

Right where I'd left Wolf. Right where, not a few hours past, I'd been lying on my belly staring out over the ridge. They was half a foot bigger'n mine. The right had a chunk taken out the tread and the left was worn down smooth on the inside. I knew them boots. I'd cleaned them boots and set 'em to dry by the stove after rain. Running prints, walking prints, they ain't that clear. These been made on purpose, these were a message made special for me.

The forest turned silent. Every sound turned mute by my heart beating in my ears. Kreagar was coming up right behind me, snapping at my heels. He had stood here, looking down at Genesis, knowing right where I was. Was he still here, behind that log, over that rise, just waiting for me to come back? I spun on my heel, looked for sign a' him on every branch, every twig, then I saw it. Brown smear a' blood on a tree. I wondered brief if it was his or someone he'd killed. My mind went dark and cold. I could smell him in the trees, see him moving 'tween the trunks, hear him whispering my name.

I ran.

Made a path in zig-zags and switch backs. Covered up my tracks best I knew how. I kept the road mostly in sight and picked my way through the woodland. That night I found a shallow cave and made me a rough camp. Tried to forget them boot prints, what they meant, who they meant. I built a big fire in the mouth a' the cave so bears wouldn't be tempted to go cosying up to me. I ate my last can a' Reverend's food and soon as that first bit of meat hit my stomach I realised just how long I'd been without a proper meal. I guzzled all that can like one of them gulls taking a whole fish in its gullet.

Dog-tired by fear and days a' stamping through woods meant I didn't have no trouble sleeping. Next morning I woke to cold sunlight and quick spotted bear tracks, close to my cave, but thankful no boot tracks. Them bears must a' come over for a sniff and didn't fancy taking on the fire. At least it let me know they was awake and roaming. I kept north for two more days, didn't see hide nor hair of Wolf and I got a little worry in me for him. I hoped he weren't hurt or nothing, hoped he was keeping fed and clean, hoped I'd see him again soon.

I didn't see track nor trace a' Kreagar neither. Must a' lost him, must a' run rings round him and sent him following my boot prints over some cliff. He weren't right over there, behind that dead fall, weren't in that cave or hollow, no sir. He was long gone.

Hell if he was.

But that's what I had to tell myself else I'd go mad all alone in them woods, seeing demons and devils in every shadow. I had to keep going because we was sharing this forest and it weren't that big.

Forest trees had turned to spruce and pine. All drooping boughs and thick needles. They gave off a heady smell of sap and resin and I sucked it in. Usually I didn't much care for pretty smells, my nana would a' told you that, but I was learning to look at them things as all part of the forest. Them smells had a purpose. They told critters not to go chewing on the poison leaves and sent signals to bees and other buzzing flies letting them know which flowers to feed off. 'Sides, it was more friendly on the nose than the rotten mulch a' some woods.

I spent three more days walking north. Made sure I covered my tracks and could see that road least twice a day. Saw a horse and cart dawdling like a fat snail trying to slide up a rock and one time I spied a line of men, packs on their backs what looked like they weighed twice their carriers.

On the fourth day I climbed up a slope a' loose rock and shale and came out on the top of a wide flat-top ridge. No trees up this high and some scraps of snow still clung in the shaded parts 'neath boulders. Fresh, cold wind blew right through me and, for the first time in a while, I buttoned my coat right up to my chin. Wished I had a hat then. Trapper had a hat and he never complained a' chilly ears. Once I put on one a' my nana's big-brimmed fancy hats and she said I looked like a toadstool. Didn't wear no hat 'cept in the rain though I wanted one right now. That wind was fierce and pushed ice right in my eyes. Didn't stop me from seeing something that made my stomach churn up like a whirligig.

Big damn lake. More like an ocean to tell the truth, I couldn't see the end of it, even from the top of a mountain. I gulped hard and swallowed sand. I didn't like open water like that. Weren't no trees, weren't no food 'cept slippery fish, weren't no firm ground, just rocking wood. At the southern edge of the water, there was what looked like a dock. People like ants was running about in a line 'tween a square thing on the water, guessing it were some kind a' boat, and a row a' squat buildings. Couldn't tell if they was carrying anything, too far up, but I could see a cart and I wondered if that was the same one I spotted on the road.

That same road stopped dead at the edge of the lake. Mountains rose up either side of the water as far as I could see and the road didn't have no forks or curves nowhere. Road changed into a boat. I hated boats.

'Son of a bitch,' I shouted on that mountaintop. I shouted it loud and over and over and even didn't care if them people on the boat or Kreagar in the trees heard me. Hell, I hoped they did.

I ain't never been on a boat but I seen them down the fat end of the Mussa, carrying lazy folk from Clarks down to White Top, near halfway to Couver, just so's they wouldn't have to walk. Felt like spitting on them and I did more'n once. Trapper and me used to have contests on how far out into the river we could spit. He taught me the right way to do it, hock one up, use your whole body for distance, then let rip. Trapper won till I turned thirteen then I spat one and hit the first mate right in the middle of his forehead. We stopped playing after that. Trapper didn't like to be beat, 'cept when we was last buck hunting. Was just 'bout a week afore I met Lyon in Dalston, and then he liked it when I pulled the trigger first. Said it gave him warm pride feelings in his chest, like he was passing on a legacy. I thought about that buck sometimes, thought about the jerky drying in the smokehouse afore Lyon burned it down. Shame, 'cause that was some fine tasting meat.

I looked out at that boat and figured I'd have to suck it up if I wanted to get to the north, and put some real distance 'tween me and Kreagar. Boats are just like carts but with no horse shit. That's what I told myself anyways. I scrambled down that mountain and by nightfall I'd joined a trail of fools heading to the dock.

There was a line a' buildings running close to the water. Eating houses, boarding houses, even a whisky den. Wooden crates stacked up along the dock with a bunch of spring-heeled boys and hard-set men running them onto the boat. The heavy ones they lifted with a rusting crane and set 'em deep 'neath the deck in the cargo hold. Further along the dock, people were spilling out of the whisky den, sodden and steaming and taking their revelry right onto the streets. Tiny electric lights like glowbugs in glass jars were strung up 'tween tall posts and made that street look like the starry sky. Trapper never trusted the electric, said even afore the Damn Stupid people lived without it and were happier for it. Now it all came out a' generators and most people turned up their noses, but, shit, those lights were magic to me.

Smells of all kinds came at me, sour sweat from them dock-workers, spiky gin and whisky, a woman's flowery perfume laid on thick, and the water, musty smell of lakeweed dried up by the sun and diesel fuel leaking out from the boat engine. Above all that, I smelled something that set my stomach growling like a snared wolverine.

A hut halfway up the street coughed out sweet smoke, cherry wood I think, and was crowded out by hungry fools. I followed my belly, 'tween groups of rowdy men and women, all shouting their joy to anyone who came by.

They was all shouting some version of, 'We're going where the riches are, we'll be back here in six months and buy this whole dock with rubies picked right out the rocks.'

I didn't take no notice. Had me a fierce craving for some of that jerky Trapper and me used to make. He'd bring home a pig he got from town, all cut up to make for easier carrying, and we'd cure it and smoke it right nice. We didn't get pigs too frequent on account a' the cost, but when we had 'em, they made some fine eating. I stared into that hut's barbecue coals, hog-fat dripping in them, making them hiss, and the smell hit me hard. Weren't as good as our pigs but, on an empty stomach, that meat is chocolate.

'You want some or you just staring?' man behind the hog said. He was a willow of a thing, years of standing behind that coal heat must a' melted most a' him away. Think he was a Chinaman but I ain't seen one afore so couldn't be sure. He held a machete in one hand and a two-pronged fork in the other.

The hog was crispy, golden and dripping goodness. It had some kind of red glaze on it which was turning black at the edges. Smelled sweet but it weren't woodsmoke, it was something in that skin. My belly was begging me for a bite.

'What you want for it?' I said and suddenly felt the lack a' coin in my pocket.

'Two dollar a plate or a gram of gold dust,' he snapped like one of them nasty turtles in swamp lakes and served two more customers while he was talking.

'You take silver?'

I held up one of them spoons. The man squinted at it then laughed, all high-pitched and mean.

'Get out of here, I not a charity!'

Elbows and shoulders barged me out the way. I lost my

feet on a slick of hog-grease and fell into the mud. Heard laughing behind me and calls of scrounger. My cheeks went hot and red and my belly ached for want of feeding. Creeping shame came over me and I felt like a fool for even thinking them spoons was worth it. I pulled them out my bag and flung 'em in the dirt.

Rain started. Soft and unsure at first, then when I got up, dusted myself off, it came heavy and fat. Hungry people crowded 'neath the hut and shouted their orders all the louder. The street turned quick to a mud slick but it didn't do much to turn off the drunks. One of 'em took off their shirt and shorts and started dancing naked. I ran, collar turned up, to the other side of the street and took shelter on a store's wide, wraparound porch alongside others who had the same idea. I sat myself down on the wooden floor, back to the wall, and watched the barbecue hut serve plate after hot plate of meat and fried potatoes. My mouth kept filling up with water and I didn't notice the fancy-dressed man coming toward me, smiling like the devil. Didn't notice what was in his hands neither.

THE DANDY MAN

'I've never seen a girl trying to barter with spoons,' he said, voice friendly like warm water, kind you put your feet in on a mid-winter night. 'Especially with Chen and his machete.'

He was a dandy type, grey suit and shiny shoes, and even in the light cast by them strings of glowbugs, I could see a handsome face 'neath his bowler. Had both his hands behind his back and him just coming up and speaking at me made me nervous.

'What's it to you?' I said.

He brought both hands out and both carried stacked-high plates of barbecue. Set my stomach growling.

'Oh nothing,' he said, gave a cough and his tone changed just slight enough for me to notice. 'I was hungry so I got double helping, just being greedy really. You want one?'

'What you want for it?' I said, wary. I was sat with my knees up near my chest, knife was hidden 'neath my coat so pulling it would be awkward but maybe I could do it before he caught on. 'I ain't got no coin.'

He shook his head and sat on the floor beside me. Bit close, I thought, and I shuffled away an inch or two. He offered me the plate. The smell of that meat, all sweet sticky glaze and moist flesh and crisped-up taters. . . I took it off him but it took all I had not to dive my face right into it.

'Coin doesn't mean much, does it?' he said, and now I could see his face proper. Stubble but no beard, brown eyes and square, solid jaw. Fine-looking man. Fluttering nerves went through my chest and I found it hard to keep looking without seeming like I was staring at him. He was a good few years older'n me but didn't have no age lines on his face not any grey wisps.

He took off his hat with his free hand and set it balanced on his knee. Just like Trapper did my first night with him.

'Why you givin' me this?' I said and wondered brief if he'd slipped nightshade into the gravy.

He paused a beat, sighed and said, 'Because once upon a time kindness was valued. You tried it on with Chen, with a spoon no less, you deserve it. Besides, you look like you need it more than me.'

He nodded to the plate and I wondered if he knew my thoughts. He spoke fast, not so much as a breath 'tween words. That change in his tone, that pause, they weren't a way I'd heard no one speak before but his eyes and his voice had kindness and I was damn hungry.

'Thank you then sir, 'preciate it,' I said and dug right into that pork. Spices and flavours the like of which I ain't never tasted coated that meat and sent my tongue into a frenzy. It was all at the same time sweet and sour and spicy like chilli peppers and salty like you licked the ocean. I didn't have no clue how that Chen fella did what he did but that pork was something else and worth them two dollars the dandy paid for sure. Flavour might a' been better but the texture of it weren't a patch on mine and Trapper's pig. Chen's had a mite of toughness through it 'cause he hadn't cured it right. Suppose it could a' just been different breed.

The dandy was picking at his and had barely eaten two mouthfuls by the time I drunk up all my gravy. I looked at him watching me and felt that heat in my cheeks again, that squirmy shame at my actions and how they probably weren't *proper.*

Noticed him staring, smiling, then he handed me his own plate. Found myself looking at that smile a little too long.

I ate all what was left on his plate and I kept my belches to myself.

The dandy tutted and shook his head and raised his arms and said, 'I've lost all my good manners.' He shifted to face me and held out his hand. 'I am James Everett Colby, up from Boston, Mass. I'm glad to meet you.'

He raised up his eyebrows, thin and shaped over his eyes like one of them dressed-up ladies. Ain't never heard of no Bostonmass. Sure weren't in BeeCee, though I suppose it could a' been in the far south. Kreagar always said the south is full a' pretty men with soft hands and I weren't seeing nothing in Colby that made that a lie.

'Name's Elka,' I said, cradling that plate and using my finger to get up the last morsels of pork. Ignored his handshake, that was too familiar for my liking.

'El-ka,' he said, breaking my name in two and rolling it around his mouth. 'German origin I believe, meaning "noble", I think.'

I scrunched up my face and said, 'Ain't nothin' German in my name. My momma said I was raised by wild animals. Said I came stumblin' in from the cold woods into their lives followed by a big cow elk. Momma and Daddy shot that elk and kept me. We had food for the whole winter. That's why I'm called Elka. Nothin' German 'bout it.'

Some folks get funny when you tell 'em their thinking is wrong but this Colby fella just smiled all the wider, showing off sharp white teeth. He had something of a fox in him, same twinkle in his eye that they have.

I set the plate down on top of the other. That hot red came back to my cheeks and I didn't know what to do with my hands.

'You lookin' for your fortune in the north like everyone else?' I said 'cause I didn't know what else to say.

'Something like that,' he said. 'I'm in the import-export business. Half those crates sitting on the dock are mine, supplies for the miners.'

I weren't right sure what import export was and I weren't about to show my ignorance by asking so I just nodded.

'You goin' on the boat?'

'I am. I sail at nine tomorrow morning. Will I see you aboard? Between you and me,' he said and leaned in close, 'I get terrible sea-sickness, it would be nice to have company for the trip. Two nights, three days, can be lonely.'

'I ain't got the coin for a ticket,' I said but my thoughts was on the mention of the time. Two whole nights in a rocking wooden box. Felt queasy just at the thought and glad I weren't the only one.

'That's a shame,' he said, tapping his fingers on the brim of his hat. He looked at me out the corner of his eye then said, 'So where are you laying your pretty head tonight? Out beneath the stars? You seem like the type who enjoys the fresh air.'

Hot red cheeks again. The pouring rain had turned the

air cold but I weren't feeling it. Ain't no one ever called me pretty before. Whippet-built, sure, square jaw, feet like a lumberjack and the armpits to match. Most Trapper ever said was about my hair when he named me Elka and that weren't exactly a flattering comparison.

I didn't right know what to say to him. Colby nudged my arm and grinned, more fox-like than ever, and I couldn't help but smile back. Told him I would be kipping in the boarding house. I may have had me some honey glows in my cheeks but the rest of my senses was still sharp. I weren't about to tell a man I just met where I'd be sleeping, no matter how much I might a' wanted to.

'We'll be neighbours then,' Colby said, flashing his smile. 'I've got myself a room on the top floor, as close to the stars as I can get.'

Then he stood up but quick knelt back down in front of me to take my hand off my knee. He brushed off a bit a' dirt and then did something that made my down-belows tremble.

He damn kissed my hand.

'Early start, I should get to that room. Goodnight Elka,' he said and I felt his breath, all hot and new over my skin. He stroked my palm softly with his fingers and my down-belows skipped a beat.

'Uh. . .' was 'bout all I could say.

Colby stood up and straightened his hat on his head. He went to walk away but turned when he got to the edge of the porch.

'Come find me at dawn,' he said, wagging his finger at me like he was tapping out his thoughts, 'and we'll see what we can do about getting you a ticket.'

I could a' hugged him and I wanted to do that'n a hell of a lot more.

'Yes, sir, I will.'

'James, please,' he said and winked. 'Sweet dreams, Elka.'

I'll have more'n sweet dreams about you, I thought.

He walked off, his shiny shoes clacking 'gainst the boards and soon was gone out my sight. Hot damn, I ain't never seen a man like him. Thought about following him, saying I didn't have nowhere to sleep and if he had a couch in that room maybe I could use it. Thought about getting up during the night while he was sleeping, slipping quiet in the bed and letting my hands go wandering.

I shook my head and told myself off. I didn't know the man from a bull in a field, he could a' been all kinds of wrong. But the way he spoke to me, like I was just another girl, not like I was stupid or not worth his time, hell, that caught me wriggling like a fish on a hook.

My instinct always told me to sleep in the woods. Woods was safe, no people meant no danger, but Kreagar's boot prints outside a' Genesis turned that forest into one giant snare. He was in there, somewhere, I felt it down deep. Them dark trees had eyes and ears and snagging limbs and they was all looking for me. I never thought I'd say it but till I got on that boat and put two days a' diesel-powered distance 'tween us, staying in town would be safer'n any wild place. The rain was coming down hard and no one was bothering me where I was, so I hunkered down on that porch and let the music and revelry and thoughts of Mister James Everett Colby send me off to sleep.

GET IN THAT BOX, GIRL

Woke up afore sunup to some crooked crone kicking my shins, barking at me to stop cluttering up her deck. I waved her off and got up, aching and stiff and sent the bones in my neck cracking back to line. Chen's hut was shut up but smoke still puffed out a tin chimney pot, filling the street with burnt char smell 'stead a' that nice sweet meat. Rain had stopped and the sky was just starting to lighten off to the east, behind the mountains.

I went down close to the dock. No one round, all them deckhands sleeping off the ache and booze. Few crates left to be loaded and that boat, hell, that boat was big, I ain't never seen the like. Must a' been long as a redwood and taller'n ten of me upright. My stomach went hard at the thought of getting on that for a couple a' days. Nowhere to get off. I can swim 'bout as well as a three-legged moose, meaning I can get from one side of a river to the other but I ain't gonna be doing it pretty.

Chill was getting in my bones and the sun weren't going

to be warming me anytime soon. Colby said find him at dawn. That was now. I found the boarding house easy. Young man was cleaning the windows with a rag. He had a greyness round the face what seemed to be common this far north.

'Mornin', sir,' I said, friendly-like.

'Closed,' he said, didn't even turn to look at me, just kept wiping. He weren't so much cleaning them windows, more like just moving the grime around. Then I spotted, with a flash a' shock through me, that the hand what held the cloth had a finger more'n the usual. It didn't move like the others did, just hung off the side a' his thumb like a tree limb 'bout to fall.

'I'm lookin' for a guest a' yours, name a' Colby.'

He stopped wiping but still didn't turn round.

'A lot of girls come here looking for him,' he said, gave a long, rattling sniff, then hocked up a glob a' phlegm onto the boards. Felt me a pang of something new, something sharp in my chest. Colby called me pretty and it made me fierce thinking he'd said it to other girls.

'You know where he is?'

The man sighed, didn't look at me, and pointed his rag up the street. 'Left a while ago. He'll be with the harbour master. Big house. Don't go inside.'

Then he went back to the windows and I didn't pay his tone no mind. He weren't that old, but talked like he been asked every question already, seen every dawn and dusk afore they happen and all types a' people coming and going. I weren't surprised he had that tone, living in a place like this.

I said thank you but I don't know if he heard it or cared much. The harbour master's house was bigger'n all the others in the strip of a town and sat on its own on the other side of the dock. It was tall too, least three levels, and all made a' stone where the rest of the town was wood. I didn't have the first clue what a harbour master was but it must a' been important to get a place like that. It put me in mind a' one of them trees standing alone in the middle of a clearing. Other trees grew up at the edges but no matter how many seeds they dropped, they couldn't get closer. That one in the middle was either king of 'em all, or so full of blight it poisoned the dirt. Weren't sure yet which one this harbour house was.

Light was burning in two a' the lowest level windows and I could see a couple a' shadows moving about inside. I got a bit further up the track and ducked behind a fat tree stump, waiting for Colby to come out.

I didn't have to wait too long. Big wooden door opened, spilling out yellow light and showing Colby step out, just as fine as he ever was. Another man followed him out. He was a head taller'n my man and twice as wide, gut like a sack a' potatoes hanging over his belt, black beard and I could see angry boils in them whiskers, even at this distance. He had one a' them hacking coughs what shook all that fat. Colby waited till the cough was done afore he spoke.

'Do we have a deal?' Colby said. Least I think those were his words, his voice was a bell ringing clear and crisp but I weren't close.

The fat man held out his hand for shaking and said something like, 'Get her on the boat.'

I smiled; Colby had kept his promise. Felt like whooping I did, felt like running up there and kissing Colby smack on them rosy lips a' his and even shaking that fat man's hand in thanks. I was going north. I was getting on that boat and I was going to see my parents. Wondered if Colby might come with me when he was finished with his business. It would be a hell of a thing for me to see my parents for the first time in forever with a fella on my arm. I decided I'd ask him soon as we was sailing.

Colby and the fat man were saying something else but I weren't listening no more, I just kept smiling. Hell, you couldn't a' pulled that smile off my face with ten wild horses. Colby and him finished their talking and parted ways. Fat man closed the door and Colby near disappeared in the dark. My keen eyes and quiet footsteps followed him back to the dock where he started inspecting crates. I watched him a bit longer. Was nice to see him when he thought no one was watching, nice to see the way his hands ran over them boxes, lifted up lids, slammed 'em back down. I could see him doing sums in his head, working through all his smarts. Sun was starting to peek up and I figured it was about time I said good morning.

I spat on my hands and smoothed down my hair, picked out a few sticks and leaves and straightened up my shirts. I took a deep breath and tried to calm down my fluttering belly.

'Mornin',' I said and he jumped clear a foot in the air.

'Damn, Miss Elka,' he said, hand on his chest like he was quieting down his heart, 'you came out of nowhere.'

Fluttering in my belly weren't calming.

'You're more skittish than a momma deer, you got jumpin' beans in your bones or something?' I said, cheeks going hot and red.

He laughed and it weren't *at* me, not like Kreagar did when I said something foolish. Colby was laughing along with me, all rich and full a' sugar.

'Maybe I do, but in my defence, you didn't make a sound.'

'I never do, 'less a' course you want me to,' I said. 'I'll be sure to tread heavy round you.'

He said thank you and then looked down at his shoes. I saw a blush a' pink in them stubbly cheeks.

'You said come find you 'bout gettin' on that boat,' I said as he weren't forthcoming with the news.

He looked all around, smile dropped off him, and he nodded for me to come closer.

'I can get you passage,' he said quiet-like, 'but it won't be too comfortable. All cabins and berths were taken but I have found a way.'

Little flame blazed up in my chest.

'Comfort ain't no worry for me. Spent my life kippin' in trees or on dirt. I can't get no sleep on pillows and mattresses.'

He sighed and wiped along his forehead with the back of his hand. 'Good, I'm glad. I didn't want to put you off.'

He patted his hand on the top of the crate, tall as his waist and coffin-long, and said, 'This is your ticket. *Just* until the boat is far enough away from the dock, then I will come and fetch you and then, my dear, my cabin is yours.'

He smiled wide, fox-flash in his eyes and lifted up the lid.

My belly flutterings turned to sick churning in the gut and I had me some doubts. 'Why you doin' this for me?'

Colby put his hands on the tops of my arms and leaned in close, his voice changed a beat like my nana's did when she read out my parents' letter, like she knew all the words already.

'Because I was you once. Boston, my home town, wasn't that badly hit in the war but it did destroy large areas of housing. My mother, may she rest in peace, said that her father's home was in one of those areas so she had grown up homeless and so did I. I was trying to survive on the streets, living off whatever I could find in the trash. . .'

I was listening to his tale but weren't right understanding it. Didn't know this Boston place, didn't have much idea a' trash and homeless, why wouldn't he just a' built himself a cabin like any man would? But I let him talk no matter if he didn't make no sense, his words was honey after all.

'A kind man, childless, found me and raised me as his own son. I asked him years later why he did it and he said, and I remember it vividly, he said "It was my good deed, son. If you only do one in your life, make it matter. One day you will find yourself faced with the opportunity to help another where it does not benefit you. A good man, as I know you to be, will grab that opportunity with both hands and never look back." I suppose you are my opportunity, Elka.'

If love hearts could a' floated up out a' my eyes, they would a'. He was helping me out a' goodness, honest to god goodness, and I didn't even know him. Lifted my spirits that there was people in this world what still held to kindness for kindness' sake. He weren't asking anything off me, he weren't expecting nothing in return and I felt a kind a' guilt for even thinking he would in the first place. My doubts was melting with the rising sun.

'No one ever been nice to me afore,' I said.

He leaned in to me and kissed me soft right on my cheek and said, 'Then they are missing out on something extraordinary.'

That kiss was a one-two punch in my down-belows and I stuttered and stammered and didn't have the first clue what to say.

Colby smiled and let me go. 'Your ticket,' he said and held out his hand like he wanted to help me in the box.

I took it, not that I needed it, and matter a' fact, found it harder to get into a box one-handed. I seen women take this kind a' help from a man with a look a' relief on their faces. I wondered if these women knew how much easier their lives would be if they did all this stuff for themselves.

I got into that box, empty but for a few scraps a' old newsprint, and made myself something close to comfort. There was hand holes cut on all four sides and I was thankful for it. I wasn't much for tight spaces.

'Try to stay quiet,' Colby said, whispering. 'The dockworkers will be here soon and they will carry this box into the hold. If they find you, I won't be able to help. Stowing away is a crime, you'll be taken to Genesis to stand trial.'

'I know what they do to lawbreakers in Genesis,' I said. 'Don't you worry, I can be quiet when I need to.'

'A trait that will serve you well. I will have to put a few nails in the lid to stop it sliding off.'

I figured as much and nodded to him.

'See you soon, Elka,' he said and closed the lid gentle.

Through them holes I saw his legs moving around. Then heard the hammer blows. Nails spiked through the wood, splintering it and securing it on all four corners. That hammer was the loudest thing I ever heard and I thought my ears would explode if he didn't finish it up quick.

When it stopped, Colby tapped on the lid and said, 'Until tonight.'

I put my eyes to one of them hand holes and saw him walk off toward town, spinning that hammer in his hand and whistling. I pushed on the lid but them nails held it fast. Pushed on the sides, no give at all. My hand went to my knife, hidden 'neath my coat. I took it out and hugged that blade to me like it was a child's comforter.

'Knife is all you need,' I said, which was good 'cause that and a backpack full a' empty cans was all I had.

I stretched out my legs much as I could and my boots hit the wood afore my legs went straight. That box was like one of them echo caves where you shout and god shouts back in your own voice. I heard my heart beat everywhere, felt it through the wood, heard my breathing thick and fast and I feared the air would run out afore Colby came back for me. Feared them dock men would hear my blood rush and hang me up in Genesis.

Heard talking somewhere near. Rowdy, growling men moaning 'bout how early it was, how they hadn't got more'n a few winks, how them crates should a' been loaded the night before.

Fist slammed down on my crate so hard I thought it would go right through.

'Look at this, huh,' a man shouted, so damn close. 'Says "Fragile" on the side.'

Bursts a' laughter from all sides.

'Get it on, *careful*,' same man said and all a' sudden hands stabbed through the holes and I shifted, silent, so they wouldn't touch me.

Don't think I breathed the whole way. They groaned about how heavy the crate was and how nothing that heavy could be fragile. Felt like I was carried miles. At one point the front end of the crate lifted and I feared I would slide right down and smash out the end. I figured we was going up the gangplank onto the boat. Front end soon dipped down and I figured we was going down into the hold. Smell changed from fresh, cold air, to the stagnant smell a' standing water and algae. They set me down rough and knocked my elbow on the bottom a' the crate. Clenched my teeth hard to stop from shouting curses at them clumsy shits and waited till I didn't hear footsteps no more to swear.

Sun was up now and the inside of my box was light enough to see my hand in front a' my face. Not long later, after a few more crates was loaded, the hold doors was closed and everything went murky dark. Took a while for my eyes to take to the dark and, soon as they did, the engines roared and the floor rumbled and my bones felt like they wanted to shake themselves out a' my skin. Couldn't hear no people, no passengers or nothing and I hoped Colby didn't miss the boat.

We started moving, slow, rocking gentle side to side, and quick got up speed. I looked out one of my hand holes and saw, with all kinds of relief, that I was up 'gainst a round window, dirtier than sin but I could see enough. We was sailing close to the side of the lake, mountains grew up high, lit up nice by the sun. If I kept my eyes on them, my stomach didn't want to empty every time the boat rocked.

Took me hours to get used to the movement and by the time I did darkness was coming and I figured I was hungry. I didn't have no food or water, course, but that weren't no problem, I knew how to get both when I needed 'em. I took my knife and dug it into the join 'tween crate and lid, started levering. My knife was stronger'n that wood and it quick started splitting. I weren't 'bout to wait for Colby to come feed me, could be hours and I weren't no prisoner. Hadn't heard no one in the hold since we started moving so I weren't worried 'bout being discovered.

Like them gods was spying on my thoughts, I heard a noise like a hand slapping wood. I hid my knife in my coats and held my breath.

Another slap. No other sound in that hold 'cept scuttling rats and my blood in my ears.

I looked out the hand holes one by one. One at the head a' the box looked on another box. One at the bottom did too. Course one looked out on the window, but when I peered out the other that looked clean across the hold, my heart near stopped. Right in front a' me I saw another crate, another hand hole, and another pair a' wide, glistening eyes staring right at me.

ALL ABOUT WAITIN' FOR
THE RIGHT SHOT

'Can you get out?' the crate said. Girl crate, young too. 'You have to get me out.'

'I don't have to do nothin' for you, I don't know you from a stone in my boot,' I said and I stopped looking at her. 'Fact, I know that stone better'n I know you.'

'Please,' she said, tone a' her voice spoke a' crying, 'before they come.'

'Don't know who you waitin' for, girlie, but I got myself a good man comin' for me.'

I sat back in my crate, got myself settled and thought a' Colby. Still felt his kiss on my cheek. Still heard his words in my ears, calling me pretty. Didn't want to be hearing from no strange girl in a box but she kept talking at me.

'Are you going to stay in his cabin?' she said and her voice went calm, none a' that panic no more.

'Yes I am.'

'Good-looking guy?' she said and I heard something close

to one of them stuck-up tones. Met a few people with them, Lyon a' course and the good Reverend.

'Not that it's your business, but he's damn fine,' I said and pictured Colby's smiling lips.

Girl went quiet for a few and I thanked her in my head for shutting the hell up.

'Cept she didn't for long.

'Are you his opportunity?' she said and that picture in my head cracked.

I shifted close to the hole and found them eyes again. 'Why you say that?'

She laughed, sour as unripe apples, and said, 'Because I'm James' *opportunity* too.'

James. Colby. That lying son bitch. Felt that strange sharp pain in my chest again, the thought a' him looking and talking to other girls, spinning 'em the same lines he used to hook me. Ain't no way I was waiting for him to come get me, I would go find him and make him choose me or her, I wouldn't be no one's seconds.

Gripped my knife tight and dug it into the gap 'tween lid and wood, started twisting hard. Somewhere outside, in the mountains round the edge of the lake, a wolf started howling. The wild part a' me said it was my Wolf, said he was following me along and keeping me safe, ready to come back to me on the other side a' the water. I know wolf howls like I know my own heartbeat, spent so long in the woods with 'em. Some types a' howl were celebrating a kill and the next morning I'd find nought but scraps and blood in the snow. Some types a' howl were for fighting 'tween the pack, keeping 'em all in line, keeping the ladies happy. But this howl weren't none of them. This was a howl a' warning, told a' danger and I knew enough to listen to the wild when it spoke to me.

Scraping clang of metal on metal and a creak as a door opened somewhere in the hold. My toes went cold.

'Hush,' the girl hissed like an angry garter snake.

Heard voices a' two men and I recognised Colby's right away. His was crystal where the other's was rough like leather not scraped right. Wolf howl kept going and I hid my knife where I could grab it quick.

'Which one?' leather voice said.

'That one. The other is paid-for property,' Colby said but he didn't sound like he did on land. That fox in him had turned feral.

Next I know, someone's kicking my box.

'Still alive in there?' leather voice shouted, then laughed like a donkey choking on hay.

I quick caught sight of the other girl's eyes but then I heard an almighty splintering and a crowbar came 'tween lid and wood. My heart went like galloping hooves and I didn't have time to get into a striking pose, didn't have no time to wonder what was coming for me, didn't have no time 'cause the lid got thrown off. Colby stared down at me, crowbar in his milky-white hands. 'Side him stood something 'tween man and hog. A beast I recognised. He was the harbour master, that fat, boil-covered thing. Stood there with his mouth open, dripping grease and sweat, and looking at me like I was a pork chop.

'Twelve for this one,' Colby said, smiling at me. I wanted to rip his pretty face right off his pretty skull.

The hog snorted. 'Twelve? Dog like that ain't worth eight.'

'She's an ugly sort, I'll grant you,' Colby said, 'but you don't have to look at her face.' Then he sneered at me like he was looking at rotten fruit. 'Probably best you don't.'

Felt like crying, felt like shouting, you said I was pretty, but I weren't stupid. It was all lies. All goddamn lies.

'Let me see the other,' the man said.

Colby put his hand on the man's shoulder and I wondered if I could stand up quick and grab that crowbar off him.

'I told you, the other one is bought and paid for by someone you don't want to piss off. They have big plans for her. It's this one or nothing.'

I shifted my feet to get a better spring but Colby heard me, dropped the crowbar out a' reach. Swore at him in my head.

The beast looked back at me then his fat, sweating hand grabbed my hair and yanked me up. Can't tell you that pain, thought he might pull my head clean off. I screamed banshee-like. Pain shot down my neck and I grabbed his hand, trying to get some kind a' relief. He pulled me up to my feet and dragged me awkward out that box. My knees hit the deck with a crack and I screamed up fresh.

'Get your goddamn hands off me,' I shouted, gritting my teeth 'gainst the pain but he kept his hand on my head and pulled me standing again.

I kicked at him and spat and my boot landed square on his shin, my gob on his eye. He growled and his grip loosened and I got free. Colby was laughing and I turned on him. Fire blazing in my eyes. Fires of hate and killing.

But I didn't get a chance to reach for my blade. Colby slammed that crowbar into my gut. All my air rushed out a' me and I was on my knees afore I knew it. Took a second for the pain to come but when it did, I couldn't see straight. Saw only bright spots. Gulped for air like a fish on the dock. Clutched my stomach tight, felt like if I didn't, all my innards would spill out right on Colby's shiny shoes.

'There you go, now she'll be friendly,' Colby said and the other man just growled.

'Fine,' Colby said. 'Ten and you can do whatever you want to her, just as long as you don't kill her. She's going to a dope house in Halveston, they don't need them pretty there.' He laughed and nudged the beast.

The beast grunted and said, 'Ten.'

I couldn't be hearing this right, I thought, I couldn't be.

I couldn't get enough air in my body, felt a spiky pain when I tried. Figured he might a' broken a rib or two.

Heard the clink a' coins and Colby said, his voice turned back to a ringing bell, 'Have a good time, put her back in the box when you're done. I'll be on deck.'

Then Colby left, heard his shoes clacking on the floor and the door creaking open and closed. Bright spots in my eyes were 'bout cleared and I could see the beast staring at me, mouth hooked up at the edge.

'Just you and me,' he said, voice all breathy and rumbling. Hog man let out one a' them wracking coughs and spat a gob on the deck.

He knelt down in front of me and his gut near touched the floor.

'You touch me,' I said, calm as I could, 'and you won't never see the sun again, I promise you that.'

He pulled back his lips to show off cracked, yellow and missing teeth and I got a whiff a' his breath. Give me rabbit guts lying in the sun all day, that was like roses 'gainst his mouth. Rest a' him weren't much better.

I tried to move away but my belly and ribs was raging and I couldn't do nought but stay right where I was and try to look fierce.

'Aw, come now,' he said, shuffled a bit closer, 'I'll be gentle.'

Then he shot out his hand, quicker'n I expected for a man that fat, and grabbed me round the throat. He squeezed tight, forced out all that air I'd just put back in my body. He pushed me backward and my belly sent spasms through me. I couldn't scream out the pain, my eyes started streaming and hot blood rushed to my face. He scuttled on top of me and drove his knee 'tween my legs.

All that weight on me, smell a' him, his breath heaving on my face, bile rose up in my chest. I pushed and fought 'gainst him but no matter how hard I hit, how much I kicked and thrashed, it didn't make a dent in him.

'Stop it,' he said. His hand still on my throat, he lifted my head and slammed it back on the deck.

Blinding white agony. Felt like I was underwater, cold muffling in my ears, blurry nothing in my eyes, arms and legs heavy and useless.

Felt the beast's hands ripping open my coat. Ripping open my shirt. Felt cold air on my skin. Then his tongue was on me. Slobbering all over. Then his hands was 'tween my legs, tugging at my belt and trousers.

That shocked me back out a' the water.

He had my belt open and started pulling down my unders, rough and frantic.

I didn't know right what was happening. Didn't know how it got to this.

'I'm gonna make you hurt for kicking me,' he said, spit dripping off his beard.

Hunting is all about staying still till you got the right shot. This weren't no different. Ain't no way I was letting this hog get any part a' me. I ain't no prey. Never have been and damn well never will be, 'specially not to a lumbering dolt like this.

His breath was racing, his heart was thumping so loud I could hear it. He started moaning threats and calling me a dog. His head was on my neck, licking me like a bear 'bout to take a bite. But I was the one taking the bite.

I whipped my head round and clamped my teeth down on his ear.

He let out a high scream and put his hand on my face, trying to push me off but my teeth was sharp and my jaw strong as a wolverine. When he yanked his head away, he left the best part a' his ear in my mouth.

Sharp metal tang a' blood filled up my throat and I spat it clean across the hold. He roared and sat up on his knees, taking all that weight off my chest. This was my shot. I twisted, pulled my knife out from the back a' my trousers and, trying to ignore my cracking ribs, buried it right up to the hilt into his gut. It went in easy, like cutting butter.

He quick stopped roaring. Blood poured down his neck and out his belly, splashed onto my skin. I ripped my knife out, and he gurgled, spat up some red. I squirmed out from under him.

'You. . . bitch,' he said, and staggered to his feet. 'You're dead.'

One arm round my stomach, other clutching my knife, slick with his blood, I faced him on my feet.

'I told you, you son bitch, I told you,' I said. 'Women ain't yours for coin, 'specially me.'

He bared his teeth and ran at me. I didn't have the strength in my belly or the clearness in my head to move quick out the way. He fell on me hard and got both his hands round my throat. Rage made him stupid and he didn't even notice I still had my knife. He started wringing the life out a' me, put all his weight on it, started grinning like he'd already killed me.

Men got one hell of a weakness, and when it ain't their arrogance, it's their dangling bits. I drove my knee right up into his. He groaned, grip went slack for less'n a second. My eyes were going sparkly 'gain and that water filled up my ears. He'd made a mistake, see, he had both his hands on my neck but I had mine free.

I whipped up my hand and dug my knife deep into the side a' his neck. I looked him right in those beady hog eyes and I saw his life leave him, same as he saw his death coming. Saw that light flicker out like I was snuffing out a candle. He slumped down dead on top of me, so heavy it was like a foul-smelling tree felled right on my chest.

Just like that.

I ain't never killed no one afore.

Seen that light go in deer or moose but never in a man. Weren't that different really, 'cept the man deserved it.

I rolled him off me and lay there for a minute calming my heart. I was bloodied and bruised but breathing and still whole. My hands shaking, I buttoned up my trousers and tightened my belt. Tried to do up my shirt and coat but the bastard had ripped off the buttons. Girl in the crate was calling for me to get her out but I weren't in the right mind for a rescue. I stood up on trembling legs and pulled my knife out the hog's neck. Didn't bother cleaning it. I was gonna be using it again real soon.

I left that hold with one thought in my head and no man or god could a' stopped me.

Found Colby on deck, cigarette 'tween his fingers, standing 'gainst the railing at the back a' the boat. Right where he said he'd be, lit up by the moon. Weren't no one else around and I weren't bothering stepping silent. Colby heard my steps, no doubt, but he didn't turn, just kept staring out into the white water kicked out by the props.

'That was quick, Tony,' he said. 'You must have liked her more than you let on.'

I stood right behind him, knife in a back-side grip, back of the blade running along my arm. Hate burning in me, turning all my sweat to steam, making the fat man's blood sizzle.

'He didn't like me much,' I said and he spun around. Cig fell out his mouth.

I grabbed his scruff and shoved him back against the railing, other arm across his chest, knife to his throat. He put both his hands up high in surrender but I weren't in no mood for mercy. His eyes was wide like he was looking at a devil crawled right out a' hell. Blood streaked down my face, out my mouth, and my eyes was red with tears and rage. My chest was bare but for the blood and in truth I must a' looked like some kind a' monster.

'E-Elka,' he sputtered. 'Shit, Elka, what did he do to you?'

I tilted my head to one side and thought, you really gonna try run this line with me?

'You tell me,' I said.

'I don't. . .' his eyes kept looking round for help or for a lie to pluck out the air, 'I thought you'd like him, thought you two would get along. W-where is he?'

'You wanted to set me up with a husband? Is that right?'

'Elka, please. . . let's talk about this.'

This was goddamn priceless.

'Ten,' I said.

He scrunched up his forehead like I was speaking in a different tongue.

'I don't think he'll be makin' any woman a husband

anytime soon,' I said and pushed the knife hard 'gainst his neck, 'so I want them ten dollars he paid for me and all the rest what you got, you know, for my trouble. Quick.'

His hands fumbled about in his pocket. I held out my other hand and he dropped them coins right into my palm. I put them in my coat and smiled wide, showing off the blood 'tween my teeth. Now I had coin. Nothing else I needed from James Everett Colby.

'Is. . . is he dead?' he asked.

'What do you think?' I said and I took a step back, let the blade off his throat. I let him take a breath, let him think for a second I'd done with him. I spun the knife round in my hand then smacked him square in the side of the head with the horn butt a' my handle. He cried out but weren't no one round to hear him. Dazed, he stumbled 'gainst the railing. I grabbed him by the collar, fished out his cabin key from his pockets, then put my head right close to his ear.

'I hope you can swim,' I said. Using all the strength I had left, I flung that skinny man over the railing, right into the foaming wake. Barely made a splash. No shouts a' 'man overboard', no one come rushing to see what the fuss was over, no one on this boat cared for the loss a' that man.

I could a' stuck him or slit his throat afore sending him to the waves and I thought I might at one point but when I saw him and looked him in the eye, fear stayed my hand. Not fear a' Colby a' course, but fear for me. Fear for what it might do to me to watch that light go out again. Colby no doubt would a' killed me first chance he got but he weren't right that moment. That hog man had been crushing the life out a' me and would a' taken more'n that if I let him. I did what any animal would do. I fought for myself. That's when a kill is lawful in my eyes, when it's him or me. Weren't like that with Colby. If I'd killed him right there on that railing, no weapon in his hand, I'd be no better'n Kreagar.

Little bit a' doubt crept up and sat on my shoulder. Maybe I should a' made sure he was dead. I stared out into that black water, didn't see no flailing arms nor hear no shouts for help. That water was colder'n snow, ain't no way he could a' lived through it.

Water killed him. Not me. And that's the way I left it.

All my fierce left me. My body started shaking, my head started pounding like a boy just got a drum for his birthday. I fell down on my knees on the deck, hanging my hands off the railing and breathed in slow and long. Pain hit me something wicked then, rushing through my stomach to my back, my chest, my head. I stared at the black water, spiked up with foamy white, and thought about jumping in right behind Colby. But I weren't no quitter. No wolf nor bear just gives up when they get beat or hungry. You ever seen a bear jump off a cliff 'cause life handed him a few rough draws? No, you haven't. The wild keeps going till it don't have strength in its muscles and bones. The wild don't give up; it's forever and so was I.

I made my way slow back to the cargo hold. Soon as I walked in, the smell of blood and bowels came at me hard and I didn't have a chance a' stopping it. I threw up everything in my gut behind a pile a' boxes.

Felt better after that.

Found the crowbar by the door and went to the girl's crate, trying not to look at the hog man's body, unzipped and standing to attention.

'You alive in there?' I said to the box.

Heard scrambling and her hand poked out one of the holes. 'Please. Get me out of here.'

I looked quick at myself, all the blood and the purple-black bruise across my belly, thought I better warn her. Girls scare easy.

'I don't look. . .' I said and a wave a' sickness hit me from the rocking boat. 'Don't be screamin' or nothin'.'

My ribs didn't like me for it but I dug the crowbar into the join and levered up each corner a' the girl's box. I threw the lid off and saw her, dressed in frills and flowers, kneeling in the middle of the crate. She had pillows and a bottle of water. She was bought and paid for, all right.

'Any left in that?' I asked, pointing to the bottle.

She handed it to me, staring open-mouthed, and said, 'Just a few drops.'

I gulped it down, swilling it round my mouth and spat out some a' the acid and blood taste.

'Come on,' I said, 'you got to help me with him.'

She climbed slow out the box like she'd just learned to walk. Reed of a girl, arms thinner'n saplings and body to match. Light yellow hair and twinkling hazel eyes. No wonder Colby didn't want the hog man grunting on top a' her. She was a goddamn peach and worth far more to them types a' men than I was.

'God,' she said, looking at the dead man, then back to me. 'Are you all right?'

I didn't say nothing. Truth was I weren't all right. I weren't even close to all right and I had doubts I ever would be again.

I leaned up 'gainst a crate, catching my breath and she came closer. Taller'n me.

'I heard it all,' she said, voice so clean I could hear all them letters. 'I'm sorry.'

I frowned then. 'Weren't your fault.'

She had a soft smile, smile a' someone who's lived an untroubled life. 'I know. I can't believe you killed him.'

Then her face turned panic. 'James. He'll be coming back soon. We should go.'

I shook my head. 'Colby gone swimmin'.'

'Did you. . .?'

Shook my head again and said, 'He was breathin' when he went in the water.'

She opened her mouth to say something but I spoke first. 'Them pins in your dress,' I said, pointing to the ribbon round her waist. 'Give 'em here.'

She looked where I was pointing. 'These? Why?'

Damn idiot, I thought, and held open my shirt. 'Don't fancy flashin' the world my tits is why.'

She blushed up something comic and quick handed 'em over, turning round to give me a touch a' privacy.

Once I was decent, I nodded to the dead man. 'We got to get him in one a' these crates.'

Her eyes went wide and she burst out laughing.

'Ain't no joke, girl,' I said. 'You want him found while we're still on this boat?'

Her smiles turned dark. 'How do you propose we lift *that* into a crate?'

Big damn idiot. 'We ain't gonna lift him. You soft in the head or somethin'? Get that sheet.'

I nodded to one of the tarps covering a group a' boxes. She wandered over there, arms crossed over her chest and, like she didn't want to be touching anything, took that tarp 'tween finger and thumb. I watched her struggling to pull it down and to tell the truth, I didn't know right what to make of her.

'You kiddin' me?' I said and she looked at me like I was talking foreign.

'It's stuck,' she said, tugging it like she was teasing a thread out her skirts.

'Goddamn, there's more strength in a mewlin' babe just pulled out his momma than there is in all a' you.'

I went over to her and took that sheet full in both hands. Pulled it and it came away easy. I was giving it some swagger, to tell the truth. I shouldn't a' pulled it that hard. My ribs ground 'gainst each other and sent my arms and legs shaking.

'Bring it over here,' I said, blinking away the pain best I could.

'I still don't know how we're going to get him into a crate. He's a whale, we don't stand a chance of lifting him,' she said and I called her an idiot again in my head.

'Just do what I says and don't get girly 'bout it.'

She sighed through her nose and the sound of it got right into my ear. She brought the tarp over and dumped it in a heap. Soon as we put the hog in his box, I'd get as far away from this waste a' space as I could.

'What now?' she said.

I went over to the end a' her crate as it was a mite smaller'n mine and nodded her to get to the other end.

'We gonna tip it on its side,' I said, hoping my ribs would forgive me. 'Quiet-like.'

She frowned deep and looked from body to crate to tarp to me. Quick the frown lifted and a look a' surprise came over her. Goddamn light bulb went off in her head, I could see the light flashing out her eyes. Weren't nothing else in that skull a' hers to stop it.

'Clever,' she said and took hold a' the crate.

Together we laid the box down, open side in line with the dead man. The girl knew my thoughts afore I had time to tell her and she was already laying out the tarp. One end inside the box, one end up 'gainst the body.

Both a' us knelt on the same side a' him. That's when she got real girly.

'It's just a body,' I said, 'just meat and bones. Damn bastard deserved it, no question.'

Flashes of his weight on my chest hit me. Heard his breath in my ears, grunting and quick, the smell a' his slobber still on my skin. My heart was heaving and I found myself staring at the hole I cut in his gut, wishing I could cut another.

'It's not that,' the girl said. Her voice soft and sweet brought me out the dark. 'Let's be rid of him.'

She did something then that surprised me no end. She stood up and shimmied out a' her dress. Folded it nice and laid it on top another crate. She stood there in her panties and bra and I didn't know right where to look.

'What in the hell are you doin'?' I said.

'I don't want to get blood on my dress. I'll never get the stains out.'

Trapper always said an outfit ain't complete without blood-stains and he'd come back with fresh ones least once a week. I didn't say nothing 'bout it to her, just nodded and tried not to look.

She knelt back down and didn't seem squeamish 'bout touching him no more. She dug her hands into his pockets, rummaged around and pulled out a handful a' coin. She stacked it neat next to her dress and nodded to me. Together we rolled the hog onto the tarp. Next part was easier. We lifted the ends of the tarp and rolled him right into the box. He made a wet slapping sound like flogging a bag a' eels and I smiled all the way. We shoved the tarp into the box with him, covered him up best we could.

With the crowbar I prised the nails out my crate lid and took 'em over to the hog's box. One for each corner. I got the girl to hold the lid in place. Few quick hits and the hog was sealed up ready for shipping to god knew where.

'Them folks at the other end a' the lake are gonna have a shock when they open this expectin' to find you,' I said.

'I hope they choke on him,' she said and I didn't figure words that bitter could come out a face so pretty.

She spotted something hooked up on the wall and said, 'Stand over there, out the way.'

I did and she took down a hose and starting spraying the deck. The blood and shit washed away, down drains and 'tween the boards. Seemed strange, all that hurt and hate and bile, gone with just a splash a' water. It weren't perfect but it weren't quite as obvious now neither. We washed our hands and my face and my knife and she finally put her dress back on. I looked down at my hands, saw 'em shaking, saw black in 'em, like they weren't my hands no more. Colby and his fella put something dark in me, like when I drove my knife into the hog's belly, it was driving something into mine at the same time. Felt it in there, squirming, growing. Didn't feel like me no more. Tears came up in my eyes and I let them go. Let them fall down my cheeks and into my ripped-up collar. Stood there swaying and couldn't right figure where I was in the world. Was I still by that lake? Breathing in whatever poison mucked up my mind? I wanted bad to believe that none a' this had happened, that that hog man hadn't done what he done and I hadn't done what I done.

There's a feeling what comes with killing, sick and raw

and a big rush a' relief. Maybe that's why Kreagar killed all them folks, maybe he liked that feeling. Maybe he just liked the blood what comes with it.

Girl waved her hand in front my face, tried to snap me back.

'Colby's got a cabin,' I said, holding up his key, aching for a soft place to rest my ribs. 'Figure he don't need it no more.'

She nodded and held out her hand to me. 'Penelope.'

'You what?' I said. Never heard no word like that afore.

'My name,' she said, 'is Penelope.'

Wondered brief how she came by a name like that, then I took her hand.

'Elka.'

Most people ask me where I got that name but I figured she had a name strange as mine so didn't take all that much notice. The girl smiled then just said, 'Thank you, Elka, for saving me.'

She said it so serious that my cheeks flushed up red. No one ever gave me true thanks afore. I mumbled something like 'You're welcome', then took my hand back and didn't right know what to do with it.

Penelope went quiet for a minute then took a big breath and said, 'You're going to Halveston right?'

I nodded and she looked mighty relieved. It made me a mite nervous.

She smiled with one side a' her mouth, eyes gleaming with something like mischief and said, 'I have a proposition for you.'

GIRL A' LETTERS

'No way,' I said, locking the door to Colby's cabin. Cramped little room with two berths, one on top the other.

'Come on, Elka,' Penelope said, 'it's perfect. We both win.'

I lay gentle on the bottom berth. 'I don't win nothin' 'cept earache from a prissy thing who don't know shit about the wild.'

She didn't seem put off by my words, unkind as they were. 'Please, take me to Halveston and I'll do whatever you want, I'll. . . I'll help you find a claim to mine, I'll help you get a job, I'll help you, I don't know, sign mining permits, whatever you want. Please, Colby's men will be looking for me on the roads. You heard him, I'm *bought and paid for*.'

As she was talking, I heard a lot a' mentions a' paper – permits and claims. Words I didn't know. Hadn't figured on that. I knew my parents' names by speaking but not by look in letters. Figured I'd ask around for them when I got up there. Folks like mine, what must a' struck it rich by now, would be easy to find a' course but it didn't hurt to have a bit a' help.

'They keep records a' all the miners what go up there?' I asked.

'Of course, probably in the permit office.'

'And you know letters 'nough to find someone in them permits?'

I felt squirmy and hot for asking. Not reading never stopped me doing nothing afore but I weren't going hunting for deer now, I was hunting for family and people leave their tracks in words and paper.

Penelope looked at me different then. There weren't no pity in her eyes though, there was something else there, understanding maybe.

'Yes,' she said quiet, 'I know letters.'

I lay still a few minutes, she didn't say nothing and I was thankful for it. I needed thinking time.

'I'll tell you yes or no afore we dock,' I said and she opened her mouth to complain at me. 'Don't ask me again or you'll go swimmin' with Colby, understand?'

She sighed out her nose again and if I'd a' had any fight left in me, I would a' chucked her through that stupid round window right then. I closed my eyes 'gainst her and she climbed up onto the top bunk. Few minutes of fidgeting and huffing 'bout and she got settled. Never slept in a room with anyone but Trapper and my nana afore and always thought I'd never be able to. I prayed to all them gods that I wouldn't have no dreams. I told my head to shut up and forget what it saw. Told it to ignore the burning pain in my stomach. Either them gods heard me or I must a' been too dog-tired to notice 'cause I don't remember falling asleep, I only remember waking up to a big damn shock.

BACON

Smell a' bacon.

Ain't nothing in this world like it. Salt-cured, sliced thick, line a' juicy fat crisping up in the pan. Anyone what tells you they don't like bacon is either stupid or lying. Either way that ain't no one you can trust.

Penelope woke me up gentle to that smell. Soon as it hit the back a' my throat my eyes sprung open, my mouth started watering and I quick forgot all that happened the night before. Soon as I tried to sit up though, it all came back to me like a kick in the gut. My belly and sides felt like they was made a' sharp stone, digging into my good muscles deeper with every move.

'Come on,' she said, setting the plate down on a fold-down table. 'I didn't just get you breakfast,' she said and helped me sit up on the bed.

'What you talkin' 'bout?'

'You're hurt,' she said, stern all a' sudden.

'What's it to you?'

She got a bag from the floor and tipped out rolls a' white bandages, a blue shirt, and a pack a' pills.

'What's this?' I said. Didn't like the look of it, didn't have no great love for doctors and their knives and potions and I didn't do nothing to hide my upset.

'I saw James hit you with that crowbar. If he didn't break a rib or two I'd be shocked. That money I took from. . . that man's pockets. Well, here it is.'

I didn't say nothing. Girl had hawk eyes I weren't expecting.

'Can I take a look?' she said, gesturing to my shirts.

'What you plannin' on doin'?'

She smiled sweet. 'Helping.'

Figured I'd let her, she couldn't do no worse damage. Soon as she started unclipping those pins I felt sick down deep in my gut. Felt the water rising up into my ears, sound a' buttons ripping. Bit it back, breathed deep and slow and told myself it weren't him. Weren't the hog and wouldn't be never again. Wouldn't never let no man nor woman touch me like he had.

She gentle pulled open my shirt and I saw a great wave a' pity come over her face at the sight a' me.

'You should have killed James,' she said, face blank but for blazing angry eyes. First time I realised she had some years on me. I'd a' thought she was my age by the look a' her in the crate. I suppose fear takes the years off us, makes us all frightened children. She could a' been four or five years up from me, the way she looked now.

I didn't much want to see what that man had done to my body. I could feel it well enough. I set my eyes on my hands, holding onto the edge a' the top bunk while Penelope opened up packs a' bandages. New cuts and scrapes in my skin from my tussle, red lines what would turn to white and stay there for good. Tiny reminders a' all this.

Scars was memories for me, some I'd rather forget like the Reverend, but some was happy. Sliced my arm scraping a moose hide when I was young'un, left a long white line 'cross my forearm what Trapper patched up. Changed that bandage every day he did, like a daddy's supposed to. Then there was the silver burn scar on my hand, faded to almost invisible, what Missy soothed and wrapped up with a strip a' her nightgown. But that thought weren't so happy no more, knowing what truly became a' that good woman. Memories a' Trapper and Kreagar mixed up and gave me feelings like black worms in my gut. Didn't know what was real no more.

I flinched when Penelope put her hand on me and it weren't through pain. She brushed her fingers, soft like they ain't never seen a pile a' logs for splitting, across the worse part a' the bruise, right on top my ribs. I hissed like a caught viper when she found that spot and she winced right along with me.

'Sorry,' she said, pain in her voice like she was the one being prodded, 'just a little longer.'

She walked her fingers over my skin, pressed down in places, heard me swear, moved on to someplace else, heard me swear more. Went on like that for an age till she finally looked up at me.

'Two broken,' she said, shook her head.

'You a doctor or somethin'?' I said.

She didn't say nothing but her eyes said she didn't want to be asked no more questions. Penelope took up some bandage rolls and looked me right in the eye.

She said, 'This is going to hurt.'

I figured our meanings of 'hurt' were a little different.

She looked like a bramble prick would send her screaming. I didn't pay her warning no mind, just nodded at her to get it over with. She started wrapping them bandages round my waist and ribs and, damn, did that hurt.

I swore up something awful but no matter how blue my words, she didn't stop, didn't even slow the hell down.

'You remind me of my father. So tough,' she said, smiling, wrapping me up like one a' them underground pit roasts.

My head was swimming from the sting in my ribs and for once I was glad a' her speaking. It took my mind out that dark place so's I didn't see Colby's crowbar hitting me over and over and didn't see that hog man sneering.

'How's that?' I said.

'He was very practical,' she said, 'and he helped people, like you helped me. He was a good man.'

That smile a' hers dropped off.

'Where's he at?' I said.

'He's dead,' she said. 'Drowned in a poison lake.'

My hand slipped off the bunk. How many poison lakes could there be in these parts? I figured not many. I never saw another person there, 'cept for the demon. I remembered them black claws like eagle talons but now I saw them different in my head. Saw human hands 'stead of a devil's, knife in each. Horns was rucked-up hair. Black body was shadowy skin. Then it had the hog man's face. Then Kreagar's.

Then mine.

'Elka?' Soft voice came out the dark, pulled me away from all them demons.

'Elka. . .'

Opened my eyes to Penelope, look a' fierce worry on her. She'd finished bandaging me up, and I had nought but a pin holding me together.

'Where did you go?' she asked.

'I didn't go nowhere, did I?' I said, like I didn't know what she meant. Course I did. I was by that lake, no question, I was staring at that demon and I was seeing my face and my life played out on that black skin like a shadow play. I weren't saying nothing to her about it but I looked down at my ribs, felt them shored up and not going nowhere, better'n any job I could a' done with linen strips, and I figured I could give her a mite a' my time.

'Tell me 'bout this lake. Who poisoned it?'

'My father said it was during the Fall,' she said and I knew she was talking 'bout the Damn Stupid. 'One of the Soviet bombs fell but didn't explode. It made a crater, and over the years it filled up. The bomb leaked out all its radiation and chemicals into the water.'

She talked slow enough for me to hear all the words and figure 'em out, not like that shit Colby, but she weren't so slow she made me feel thick as cold molasses. Wasn't sure if she did it on purpose. I hoped not.

'It was strange, actually,' she kept going, 'it was near the road, in the middle of nowhere really, when my father said we should stop travelling for a few days. That bomb made the whole area warm and lush but the water wasn't right. He drank it constantly, he'd say "three litres a day, we must remain hydrated",' she said that in a deep voice, mock a' her daddy's no doubt.

Her meaning confused me. Maybe that water was poisoned but I drank it every day and I didn't see no bad from it for months and they sure as shit weren't there for months. Days at most, must a' been right after I left. Her story didn't right add up to ten but I let her tell it. I weren't no one to say stick to the facts.

'I didn't drink it, there was something wrong in that place.' She sighed heavy but I told her to keep going. 'Father started to get despondent, just sat there all day staring into the water. Then came the hallucinations. Then he decided that salvation was at the bottom of that lake so he dove in.'

'And he didn't come back up?' I said. She nodded so I asked, 'When'd this happen?'

Saw tears rolling down her milky cheeks and she said, 'Week or two ago. I don't remember exactly. It was stupid. He was stupid. But he said someone else has camped out here, so it must be safe.'

A felt a twinge in my chest. 'How'd you know that?'

She shook her head a bit, eyes went wide like she was trying to picture it, 'There was a shelter already built, a fire pit. It looked recently used so we stayed.'

Twinge turned into a drumbeat echoing through me. My shelter. My fire.

Shit.

Felt guilt creeping up on my back, using them bandages for footholds. Felt I should take her along to Halveston to make amends for my part in all this. But hell, I thought quick, it weren't my fault her daddy drank himself to drowning. Weren't my fault she ended up in a crate, that was her own mess, same as me. Them steps she took from lake to Colby were her path what she made for herself. I ain't in the business of blaming no one for my situations and I weren't about to take on some girl's problems as my own. I got enough. I got demons in my head and I'm sure that one by the lake, whoever the hell it really was, didn't take too kindly to having his gut slashed. I got Kreagar tracking me, hunting me, taunting me with his boot prints and blood. Lyon half a step behind that. I was one stumble away

from her six-shooter and Kreagar's knife and all them other
demons and I didn't hate no one enough to bring them
into that pile a' shit. Didn't have no time to play nice with
no one.

'That's a damn shame,' I said, voice harder than was polite.
She looked at me like she was expecting me to say something
more. She soon figured I weren't that kind a' girl.

She started flinging bandage wrappers into a plastic bag,
sighing, huffing, then stood up and said, 'Eat your breakfast
then take two of those pills.' She pointed at the pack. 'We
dock tomorrow morning.'

Then she left, slamming the door behind her. Cold bacon
was still better'n no bacon and I didn't waste no more time
clearing my plate. Full belly, I looked at them pills, the silvery
side covered in little spider writing what meant nothing to
me. Any other day I would a' chucked them out the window
in favour of what the forest could give me, but I weren't
nowhere close to no broadleaf or witch hazel. I cursed this
boat and popped out two a' them pills. Like swallowing dry
stones right off the shore and I weren't so sure they'd do
anything at all.

I opened up the round window and stuck my head out
far as my ribs would let me. Smelled a sting on the air afore
anything else. Thunderhead was coming and I sure as shit
didn't want to be on no boat when it hit. Craned my neck
round to see north. Black clouds, loaded up with rain and
hurt. I let out my breath and closed the window. I had maybe
two days afore that storm bore down and I was off this boat
in one. Long as I was in the forest and had a tree to anchor
to, I might survive it.

It was still early but pain and pills and the rocking boat
put my mind right to sleep. I lay back on my bunk and didn't

open up my eyes till night came. Penelope snored soft on
her bunk like one of them wild boar piglets snuffling up to
its momma. Sleep a' someone what lead a gentle life. Life a'
feather beds and doting parents. Life a three-square-meals
and china cups. She might a' had a few years on me, but
damn, she didn't have a day a' wild in her.

Lying in my bunk, sore and breathing stiff, I knew she'd
be wanting a decision. Take her to Halveston and she'll help
me with letters to find my folks. But Halveston was a week or
two's trek, more for staying off the roads, and I had Colby's
coin to pay someone for the reading. Penelope was sweet
and all but she was a millstone and a risk and I didn't have
no time for it. Trapper said once that people are dangerous, some fierce as wolves, some meek as deer and you only
figured which after they got close. I weren't letting myself
get close to no one. Felt sick for it, felt like a dog for it, but
I had my own mess to deal with and Penelope had hers. She
had her smarts to get her out a' scrapes and I had my knife
and that left us both in fair shape I reckoned.

That's what I told myself anyhow, and that's what got me
back to sleep.

We'd be docking in the morning and I'd be off this boat,
walking right into a thunderhead. Give me that storm over
rocking and rolling on waves, give me earth and dirt and
mud over water any day. Rain started pattering on the roof
of the boat and got hard fast. The round window streaked
and spotted and the walls shook with the wind.

This wasn't the thunderhead, no sir, this was the calm.
This was the *easing* you in and it set ice right in my heart.
That storm was talking to me, a warning like that wolf howl
when I was in the crate. The wild was helping me survive in
the world a' men and, curse me, I should a' listened closer.

Maybe all them other pieces a' darkness kept the truth out a' me. The storm was telling me what was waiting on the other side of this lake but my demons plugged my ears. Colby's words a' beauty. Hog man's ragged breathing. Kreagar's black lies. I was deaf to it all.

TOWN A' ELLERY AND BIG BETTY

Last thing Penelope said to me afore she slammed the cabin door in my face was, 'Don't take more than two of those pills at once.'

Then I heard her shoes storming down the corridor. I'd told her I wouldn't be escorting her to Halveston. Told her the road would be safest for her and she should find a nice fella to keep her safe. She didn't much take to that idea but I didn't want no travelling companion, 'specially one who probably couldn't tell a snare from a stocking.

I put on that blue shirt she got me, hid my bloody one in a cubby hole and pinned up my coat. Said to myself, the first thing I'll do in Halveston is buy some damn buttons.

I hadn't been out the cabin since I got in and I hadn't seen another soul on this boat save for Penelope. I left slow, checking every corridor, scared someone would ask me for a ticket I didn't have, and tried to figure my way off the boat. Other people were doing the same, lugging trunks and packs full a' blankets and tents. Some had pots and

plates strapped on the outside, clanking around with every
step. They didn't need half a' that in truth. I had my coat,
my knife and a bag what was almost empty. No more a' the
Reverend's cans, no more spoons, just his tinder box and a
scrap a' blanket. Didn't need nought else. I kept my head
down and my arm 'cross my ribs. I weren't in no mood to
be nudged or jostled. Found my way out onto the deck and
got myself in behind a group a' fellas all dressed about the
same as me.

The dock was much the same as the other side a' the lake,
'cept the road led north into the mountains, there was a few
more trees dotted about, and a bunch of snakes touted cart
rides, equipment and claim papers. Three dandy-dressed
men stood smoking by a pile a' crates, one watching for
someone coming down the plank, the other two watching
the cargo offload. Didn't see Penelope nowhere but tell the
truth, I weren't looking. Little part a' me hoped she'd be all
right and I'd see her up in Halveston. She'd patched me up
good and I was thankful for that. I told her as much but she
still scowled at me something rotten when I said she was on
her own.

I didn't understand it. I'd saved her, taken her out that
crate. She'd paid me back with pills and bandages. We was
square. Weren't no reason for her to be grumbling at me.

I followed the group a' same-dressed fellas off the boat
and onto the dock. Rain came down hard and I smelt the
thunderhead over the hills. My feet sure felt good on land
even if it was churned-up mud. They belonged there, that's
for sure. My body felt like it was still swaying with the waves.
Felt sicker on dirt than I did on the boat in them first few
minutes and I didn't have no choice but to walk it off.

The few buildings around the dock mostly sold gear

and food and were strung along the road like hooks on a longline. Most a' the folk in them buildings were closing the storm shutters, locking up doors, and tying down their wagons. Men with cheap suits and greasy moustaches shouted things like *ruby and gold claims just fifty bucks, millions of dollars just waiting for you* and waved about sodden bits of paper what were probably worth more'n the land they was selling, if they was selling land at all. They didn't seem to pay no mind to the thunderhead rolling in. No doubt they had rat holes they ran to at the last minute.

Years back when I told Trapper 'bout my parents, he told me stories a' the first fools' dash north. Said his daddy told him all about it, read it to him right out a book so it must a' been truth. Trapper said men and women full a' dreams and hot blood went into the mountains. They bought their gear and scraps a' land from moustached men like them crowding round the dock, thinking the whole north was so rich, so full a' that yellow metal that people didn't have no more reason to lie and swindle. Those same fools came south just a few months later, pale skin, dead eyes, no more dreams, no more blood. Course that's if they came back at all. They didn't have thunderheads back then like we do now, but the weather still killed 'em just the same. Thunderhead'll rip the shirt and skin off your back and all folks knew it. All folks had plans for when they came. This dock weren't no different.

But I weren't making no mistakes like them hundreds-a'-years-ago idiots. I weren't looking for no claim, I was looking for people even though most a' them was just as worthless 'neath the surface. I held onto the knowing that my folks were wily as me and had set themselves up on a claim full a' worth. Tell the truth, seeing all these people headed to Halveston, same idea stuck firm in their heads, I wondered

brief how much land there was to go between them. My
parents had been up there near fifteen years, they probably
had a palace by now, no doubt paying these dreamers to dig
the gold up for 'em.

'Almost there,' I said to myself. Felt my hair and shoulders soak and it was like the thunderhead was washing away
the stink a' that boat and the hog man with it.

Them fellas dressed like me broke off toward the gin
house, collars turned up 'gainst the weather, and I was left
standing stupid in the middle of the street. A cart selling gold
pans was quick battening down afore the storm, chained up
with heavy iron cables to a stand a' thick pipes what must
run deep underground.

Still no sign a' Penelope, though I told myself I wasn't
really looking for her, just keeping an eye out for unsavoury
types. Caught the eye of one of them dandies. The one who
was watching the passengers. He took a step toward me then
stopped, backed away like a wolf been told off by his alpha.

'Papers,' voice said behind me. I turned and saw that
alpha. Woman the size of a truck, all shoulders and arms
and hair like a mountain man's stuck out 'neath a black hat.
Gold badge on her chest and a worn-out red jacket what
weren't even close to fitting, all said she was the law up here.

'Papers,' she said again. 'Quick now, ain't got all day.'

She weren't even really looking at me, more like right
through me. Seen so many people up here she probably
didn't give two shits if they were legal or not. She was watching the town lock-up, board up doors and windows, bracing
itself for the storm.

But I didn't have no papers and she quick noticed I wasn't
handing her nothing. Them eyes hit mine hard and she
puffed up her chest. Another red jacket came up beside her.

'Where are your papers? Your ticket,' she said.

'Don't got no papers,' I said and it was true. 'A man paid for my passage.'

'This is the town of Ellery,' she said, grander'n the place deserved, 'and we don't accept excuses. No papers means a night in the lock-up and morning passage back south with the cargo.'

I weren't no stranger to the cargo but I didn't much fancy another two full days rolling about, feeling green. I quick scanned the place, looking for the road out, braced my legs for running and prayed my ribs would forgive me. But the big woman took a hold a' my arm and started pulling me toward one of them buildings, the one with the sign hanging out front painted with the same shape as her badge.

It happened all too quick for me to stamp and swear. She grabbed me up like I was a salmon she clawed out the river and the other red coat trotted on behind. Them dandy men took notice, squinting through the rain. They was close enough to hear what she said. Girl on her own, no papers, man paid for passage. They was expecting Colby no doubt, watching for crates they thought me and Penelope was in. Now they figured something must be wrong.

'Hey, no,' I said, 'I got my ticket paid for. You got no right.'

'Show me your ticket and you're free,' she said, bored, heard it all before.

We got close to the lock-up building, rain got harder and louder, and I saw something that made me want to run right for the hills. My face. Staring blank-eyed at me off a poster tacked up to the wall. Right next to that same poster a' Kreagar I saw in Dalston and Genesis. Ink on both was running with the weather but it was me, anyone could see that.

They know my face. Lyon knows my face. Whole world gonna know my face and put me behind the same bars as that murdering son bitch. I tried pulling away but ain't no way I was getting free a' this woman. My other hand started looking for my knife.

'Hey, hey, excuse me,' a sweet voice said and my heart both sunk and burst to see Penelope walking toward us, picking her way 'cross muddy streams in the road.

'Help you?' the other red coat said.

'You seem to have stolen my partner,' Penelope said, eyeing me hard to say shut the hell up. Her pretty white dress was soaked through, showing off her unders and her hair was flat 'gainst her head.

'Partner?' big Betty said.

'Yes,' Penelope said, holding onto a wet bit a' folded-up paper and putting on an even more dainty voice. 'Her name is Porter, we're heading north. Forgive her brashness, she's a little. . . touched,' she said, tapping the side of her head. 'She's a good worker, I need her to run the mine.'

Felt my back prickle. Wind started picking up and Betty got impatient.

The woman looked around. 'Where's your equipment?'

Penelope sighed all fake and loud and said, 'On the boat of course. Here, here's her ticket, now let her go.'

Other red coat took the paper and big Betty's grip went slack. My eyes kept flitting 'tween Betty and that poster a' me. Last thing I needed was her realising my papers was already tacked up on her jailhouse. Penelope looked at me like I was something stuck on her boot and I weren't at all sure if it was part a' her act.

Red coat opened up the papers, read out the name, 'Porter McLeish', then he gave the paper to Betty.

'I need her. I know she's got a mouth on her but come on,' Penelope said, more friendly to Betty, 'give a girl a break.'

My heart beat heavy in my ears and throat, drumming along with the rain. All them seconds they spent looking over that paper, words what meant nothing but a headache to me. These three people around me all had a magic I didn't and I sure as shit didn't enjoy feeling like that. Them words on that piece a' nothing could send me back south on that boat or could set me right on my path north. All from paper. That rubbish that rips easier'n cotton, breaks down to mush in water, bleaches out its meaning after too long in the sun. That paper right there in big Betty's meaty fingers, and the people who could make sense of it, had total power over me.

That weren't no fun.

'Seems to be in order,' big'un said slow, looked down at Penelope. Her eyelids didn't have no lashes, just creases a' skin and puffy bags 'neath her eyes. Made her look like a frog taken unawares by a heron.

But Betty weren't convinced. She squinted them bug eyes at Penelope and said, 'And where are your papers, miss?'

Pink flushed Penelope's cheeks and she opened her mouth to give some new excuse but didn't get a chance. Shout went up from the dock. Dandies stood up straight and a crane winched up a crate too heavy for the deckhands to lift.

I knew that crate. Penelope knew it better. Blood-stains covered the yellow wood. Penelope stared at me, eyes glistening with fear.

'What in the hell. . .' red coat said and tapped big Betty on the arm.

Betty growled somewhere deep in her throat and let me go like she was flinging mud off her fingers. She pushed the papers back to Penelope and said, 'Get going.'

Neither a' us needed to be told twice. Betty and the red coat strode toward the boat just as the crate was set down in a splash a' mud. I looked at Penelope, saw her panic and the devil and angel on my shoulders just shrugged and said, Elka, you don't got no choice.

'Come on then,' I said and started walking fast out a' Ellery. 'We got to get shelter.'

Penelope followed and we only looked back when we heard the splintering of wood and the screaming from the women.

'Just keep walkin',' I said and pulled Penelope along with me. I couldn't afford to have her lagging behind, ogling the crowd.

Word spread quick around Ellery but even a dead body weren't enough to tempt people out their homes when a thunderhead was coming. We kept our heads low and our stride fast and I found myself wishing to heaven we'd get to shelter afore the storm hit. Hell, I could a' wished for anything but just like almost all else in this life, you wish in one hand and shit in the other, see which fills up quickest.

THUNDER'S COMIN'

We got out the town and I quick dragged Penelope off the road and into the forest. Smell a' trees and sap and rain and leaf litter mixed up with the sting a' the coming storm filled me up and set me smiling for the first time in too long. Thunderhead was coming quick. Rain was heavy and cold, like the world was dropping rocks on us. Sky was dark and full a' fat black clouds.

Penelope couldn't take the pace. She heaved in breaths and leant up 'gainst a tree. I rested a minute on a rock, let my ribs stop screaming.

'We need to find cover. Storm's comin',' I said.

Penelope looked up at the sky like she knew what she was seeing. 'There should be a town along the road, we should. . .'

She shut up when she heard me laughing. Hurt to laugh but it didn't matter. I cursed that devil and angel on my shoulder.

'Next town you'll see is Halveston,' I said and took a little pleasure in seeing her face turn grey.

'You mean. . .?'

I set my eyes level with hers and pushed up from the rock. 'Thunderhead's comin'.'

I weren't in no mood to talk to her. I weren't in no mood to look at her. I weren't in no mood to do nothing but walk. I'd spent too long in a crate and too long on a boat. All I wanted was to find an outcrop or cave to shelter in afore the thunderhead found me.

I didn't know these woods and a chill was getting deep in my skin. It helped my aching ribs but put me in a foul mind. Penelope had nought but a lacy cotton dress and useless shoes. She walked a few steps behind me, arms across her chest, trying to hold in all the warm she could. Heard her chattering teeth following me. Heard her stumbling. She tried to speak to me once but I didn't say nothing back and she didn't try again.

Didn't complain though. Not once. She didn't say, 'I'm so cold' or 'I'm so hungry' or 'How much farther?' She just trudged on behind, look a' black storm on her face.

I quick found an overhang what was perfect for shelter. It was on the other side of a stream fattened up to raging by the rain. Penelope looked at that water, mouth open, like it was wide as the Mussa. City folk don't got a brain or eyes for the wild. They see a thing so much worse and bigger and angrier than it is. They see a skeeter taking its meal out their arm, they slap that bug with all they got and they moan for days 'bout the itch. Itches worse when you slap them. Wild folk just brush them skeeters off, gentle and kind, and don't pay no mind to a red bump here or there. We know there's worse things in the wild than an itching elbow. After all, when a grizzly's chasing you, you don't remember to scratch.

'Step where I step,' I said to Penelope and she swallowed hard. 'That water is just a sniff up from icy, you fall in you might as well not bother gettin' back out.'

'You can't be serious,' she said, as hoity-toity as I'd ever heard. 'I can't cross that.'

I kept my temper, didn't grab her hair and force her on like I wanted to, just said, 'Then die here in the thunderhead.'

She huffed out her nose, a sound what set my teeth on edge but didn't say nothing else. I took that to mean she would step where I stepped.

The stream was all white water and jagged rocks not used to the beating.

'Stay here,' I said.

Sundown was less than an hour and I felt the thunderhead in my bones. It was coming in quick, bearing down on me like a mad god what I forgot to pray to. I had to find a way across this stream what both me and Penelope could handle. Time was, I'd a' waded across no questions, just let the water hit me wherever it wanted till I got to the other side. I didn't have the strength in me to do that. The thought a' the water buffeting 'gainst my ribs and belly set me shaking. A ways upstream I found a tree what had fallen clean across the river, giving us a bridge and a death trap. I looked at it with a wily eye. Wild gave me this but it never gave nothing for free.

Rain had made the tree bark, covered here and there with moss, slick and slimy. The log had been there a while and made a kind of dam behind it. A calmer pool what we might be able to wade through. I grabbed a stick and tested the depth from the bank. Waist high, maybe a step deeper in the middle. Ran my hand over the log to see if we could

walk it but it was like stroking ice. I weren't too happy at the
thought a' being up to my nethers in that water but same I
didn't want to be falling off that log onto the rocks.

Down the bank, Penelope stood where I left her, shivering like a foal just been spat out its momma. Water kept her
attention, she weren't looking for me. Even this far away I
could see the fear in every bit a' her. Her shoulders tensed
and her eyes kept head on, flitting every few minutes left
and right. She lifted her heel. Shook her hair. I saw a deer
flicking its ears, legs like coiled springs, ready to run at a
twig snap. Neck long and slender, ripe for slicing.

'Found anything?' she shouted.

Took out my knife.

'I found something,' I called back, 'but you ain't gonna
like it.'

I used my knife to anchor into the log. Stabbed it in there
hard. Shudder of the hit sent my ribs splintering. Penelope
joined me up by the calm pool just as the first thunder crack
split the sky. My toes went cold as deep-winter ice.

'Listen to me,' I said, 'you hold onto the log. Soon as we
get to the other side you take off your dress quick-like and
start jumpin' stars.'

'I can't. . .' she said but I weren't having none of it.

I grabbed her around the shoulders and made her look
in my eyes. 'Thunderhead is coming and I know you know
what that means. We got to get to cover and if you don't
cross this river right this damn minute you gonna get swept
up in that storm and pulled apart like you's no more'n wet
cotton. You get me?'

She kept my gaze for a few seconds then nodded. 'What
about you?'

'I'll be doin' the same, don't you worry.'

I took off my coat and boots and socks and stuffed 'em into my pack. With my good arm, one what didn't have cracked ribs 'neath it, I held it up out the water.

'Stay close and move quick,' I said and dipped my toes into the river. Cold shot right through me, made my side ache. This was really going to hurt.

Behind me, Penelope hiked up her dress to her waist and took off her slipper shoes. She held them awkward in one hand while her other felt along the log. Heard her gasp when the water got to the top a' her legs.

She swore up something unholy when that water got just a few inches higher and I wondered where she heard all them words. Made me smile though. Made me think a' Trapper when he stuck a fish-hook in his thumb, cursing the heavens and all us people on the earth. I laughed all the while I cut that hook out.

I pulled the knife out the log and used it like a bear uses its claws to climb a tree. Current pulled at me and slippery rocks 'neath my feet did all they could to trip me. I dug my toes in, dug my knife in and tried to forget about the cold.

Water was deeper'n I thought, right up to my bandages. I could a' cried when that chill hit my bruises.

Penelope kept up that swearing when she got to the middle a' the stream. She hiked the dress up higher so's her flat belly was showing. I glanced over my shoulder at her, leaning heavy on the log, more than she would a' needed if she weren't holding onto her dress like that.

Thunder struck and I felt the boom in my bones.

'Faster,' I said and drove my knife into the log.

Drove it in too deep.

Pulled it out too rough.

The log rocked. One a' the stones holding it steady slipped. Sick feeling hit my stomach and I saw it all happen like it was going at half speed. Penelope's weight on the log helped it shift. I caught her eyes, wide as mine.

I hurled my pack onto the bank and lunged for her, felt my side rip fresh. She scrambled to get away from the log but it was turning in the flow, pushing her away from me.

'Elka!' she kept shouting, trying to run in the water, against the log, against the current.

Thunder crashed above us but I didn't care none for the thunderhead in that moment. All I cared for was getting that girl out.

But I couldn't get to her. The log twisted, rolled, sent Penelope under, pulled her downstream toward them sharp rocks and white water. My heart thudded and the cold stole all my air. Couldn't shout for her.

I got out that river fast I could and ran down the bank, eyes on that log. Eyes on the white spray, looking for her white dress. I kept up with the log but the river was quick and I was hurting.

'Penelope!'

Found my voice. Found my air. Blood was flowing for the running.

'Penelope!'

The log caught 'tween two rocks and I dashed into the water. Second later blonde hair burst out the spray, pale arms clung onto the bark. Heard the wood straining 'gainst the river and the rocks. Awful creaking, cracking sound.

'Penelope,' I shouted, 'let go a' the damn log!'

I got closer. Creaking sound got louder, like a drumroll reaching its peak. She weren't letting go. She pressed her face up against the log, hugging it.

'Goddamn it girl,' I raged, 'let go!'

Stubborn prissy thing she was. The river slammed into my side and set my vision blurring and spinning. The cold and pain and dog-tiredness sent dizziness right through my head. My bare feet slipped but I caught myself. Shook it away. This weren't no time for wussing out.

I grabbed Penelope's arm.

'I got you,' I said, voice loud over the roaring water. 'Let it go.'

She looked at me with wild, red eyes. Seemed to take her a minute to know me but when she did, she let the log go. We struggled out the river, had my arm around her waist, holding her up. Didn't notice my ribs. Didn't care if they didn't like my efforts.

We got out onto the bank and right away I started pulling off my clothes.

'Take off your dress, quick,' I said then noticed, with a bit a' shock, that she'd managed to hang onto her shoes. Let myself smile as the shivering set in. Noticed blood spilling down her leg and a nasty cut just south a' her knee. Wild takes its pay wherever it can.

Just then I heard a cracking sound what weren't thunder. The log split right where Penelope was hugging it and it was like a rubberband been released. The trunk shot down the river, struck a rock that sent it end over end in the air. It smashed to kindling and the river swept it all away.

Neither me nor Penelope needed to say anything. It was all right there, floating down the river.

Stripped down to our undies, skin all goosey and ice-pale, we jumped stars and ran back up to where I'd thrown my pack. I pulled everything out till I found the Reverend's tinder box.

'Find some twigs, dry ones, not ones off a tree, and a

few bigger branches,' I said, breathing smoke. Penelope didn't argue.

Thunder crashed, felt like it set the whole world shaking. All I could think was quick, quick, fire, get a fire, get your back to the wall, hunker down. Now. Do it now!

I opened up that box with shaking hands to make sure the striker and wool were dry. Breathed out my thanks that they were.

I dragged everything over to the outcrop, which, now I was closer, I saw went pretty deep into the hillside. Grabbed all the bits of twigs around and cleared a flat space inside the mouth a' the cave, out of the way of the coming rain. In nought but my undies, shivering from head to toe, teeth chattering like nosy birds, I breathed all my warmth into my hands.

Sun was dropping and the sky was black with thunder. I had one shot.

I fluffed up the wax paper, set my twigs and bits a' bracken close, and set the metal rod into the paper. Few deep breaths. Steady hands.

'Come on, Elka,' I said to myself.

I scraped the striker down the rod and sent sparks into the paper. Again and again until it caught. Flames burst up and careful as tending a fallen chick, I fed it twigs until it crackled into life. Shaking, Penelope came with kindling and thick branches what had mostly dried after the rain and I raised that fire up to roaring.

I took off my bandages to dry them along with my clothes, and tears pricked at my eyes. The cold water had taken down the swelling on my side but it was still ugly. Purple and black bruise reaching from the middle a' my belly halfway round my back. It covered so much a' me that I wondered if I'd ever get my skin back the way it was.

I cursed Colby from head to toe.

Noticed Penelope staring at me. Look a down-deep horror on her face.

'What?' I said.

'Those scars. . .' she said, meaning the Reverend's work across my back. In truth I'd forgotten 'bout them. They weren't deep, healed quick and I didn't see 'em day to day.

'Long story,' I said, smiling. 'Worth the tellin' though.'

She got comfy on a flat rock and asked me to tell it.

'They was the work of a man what got his due,' I said. 'Crazy fucker if there ever was one.'

I told her how I came upon Matthews' homestead and that fine chilli. Told her 'bout the Reverend and my thinking that I was in a safe haven with a man a' god.

'So when I woke up buck-naked in his basement, you can 'bout imagine my surprise,' I said.

Penelope laughed, first time I'd heard it, like a tinkling bell in the middle of a baying crowd.

'He cut me elbow to elbow, neck to butt,' I said, 'then. . . someone came in and slit the bastard's throat.'

'Who?'

Picture a' them legs flashed in my head, smell a' the woods in my nose, grit-tooth voice in my ears. Still couldn't right say who it was.

'Don't know,' I said, 'but I went all the way to Genesis looking to shake his hand.'

'Genesis?' she said, turned pale.

'Aye, hick town south a' that lake.'

She nodded. 'That's where I met James.'

I figured as much. 'Man's dead. Can't hurt you no more.'

But I knew dead didn't always mean gone. I still heard

the hog man's breathing, still saw his slobbering face when I closed my eyes.

The sky went black and rumbling and I felt it shake up my bones. Heard the wind thrashing the trees, heard the snapping branches and creaking trunks and I was damn glad of a rock roof over my head.

Penelope huddled closer to the fire, put her back 'gainst the wall and didn't say nothing for a while, just wrung out her hair and tried to dry it without setting light to it. She tended to the cut on her leg, wiped up the blood, tied a strip a' cloth around it.

'Is that why Magistrate Lyon is after you?' she said out a' nowhere and my heart kicked.

All the forest sounds, the river, the fire, the skittering critters and buzzing insects switched off. All I heard was my blood in my ears and the thunderhead laughing in the sky.

'James wasn't the only person I met in Genesis,' she said.

'Don't know no Lyon,' I said, gritted teeth. Hand found my knife.

'Don't get dramatic,' she said. 'We seem to be doing a dance, you and me. You save me, I save you, I save you, then you save me,' she nodded to the river.

'What about it?'

Penelope looked at me, saw the wild no doubt. 'I saw the posters of you in Ellery. I could have turned you in right there and that giant woman would have locked you up.'

I didn't say nothing. Didn't right know what to say.

'You know what I did instead?' she said. 'I cosied up to a *disgusting* man so I could steal his ticket. His name was Porter McLeish.'

I let go a' the knife but kept it close. 'I didn't ask for it. Why would you do that?'

She sighed fierce and angry. 'Because you saved my fucking life.'

Sounds a' the forest came back to me. I looked at this woman, this stranger, with new eyes. Felt a stab a' shame for thinking bad of her and lying to her not five minutes past.

'Lyon's after the person what killed her son,' I said, quiet.

Penelope lifted her eyebrows.

'The man what raised me up from a babe did it,' I said. 'Found out he was a killer from Lyon. She thinks I been helpin' him or know where he is but I don't. I don't know nothin'.'

She stayed quiet a moment, taking it all in.

'What's in Halveston?' she said.

'Real parents went up there, made their fortune out a' gold and stones.'

Penelope nodded. Sadness come over her mixed in with a look I'd seen before. Same look I saw on Colby when I told him where I was going. Look a' pity.

Thunderhead rocked the sky, wind bent the trees double and whipped out the fire like it weren't more'n a candle. Penelope shuffled up close to me, white as snow and shivering in the dark. Weren't no point in trying to get the fire going again, not till the wind died off, so I tried best I could to keep her warm.

Wind was howling worse'n dying wolves, trees was groaning and the ground shook 'neath me. Was like Mother Nature herself woke up raging, storming through the world in hobnail boots, slamming doors and smashing plates. Lightning lit up the skies so we didn't need no fire to see by and I weren't fearing no bears or wolves out tonight, they's as chicken of the thunderhead as I was.

When you're alone in the woods the thunderhead's like

the end a' the world come down right on your head. But when you're with someone what's got goodness in them, even a useless snip of a girl, it's just a storm. An awful, life-destroying bad storm but there ain't no evil or malice in it. It's just weather. Weren't never just weather with Kreagar.

Strange feeling came over me when I was huddling 'gainst the wall with Penelope by my side. Feeling a helplessness, like I was giving up all my fierce to this woman I didn't know and she would carry me the rest a' the way. Scary thing was I wanted her to. Sat 'neath that outcrop in the dark, feeling her tense up with every strike a' lightning, every boom a' thunder, I wanted to let go a' the hardness in me, the stones and grit what Kreagar and the forest had put in my bones and blood. I wanted to give it all up. Next I know I have tears on my cheeks, falling out my eyes like rain out the sky.

The cave kept us safe when hail ripped up the soil and we didn't say no more to each other that night. Weren't nothing I could think of to say. I didn't sleep, ain't no sleeping during a thunderhead, but I barely noticed.

Couple hours later when the thunderhead passed south and we figured we weren't going to get blown away, I relit the fire to chase the cold out my bones and stoked it up to blazing. Penelope took the dry bandages and started wrapping me up, tender as a momma.

I don't remember when but I closed my eyes. Can't a' been for long 'cause I woke up before the sun. Something weren't right and I felt it even in my dreams. I sat up, looked around and my heart near stopped.

Knife was gone. Penelope was gone. And I heard growling in the dark.

BIG ASK

Followed the sound a' panic. Heavy breathing, whimpering, whispered prayers to a god who weren't listening. Penelope stood at the bottom of a slope. Halfway up yellow eyes shone in the dark, caught by the firelight. She held my knife out at arm's length, in both hands.

'Penelope,' I said, quiet, and the growling got louder.

She whipped her head around. 'Elka, get back, there's something in the ferns.'

'I see that,' I said, 'it's a wolf.'

Snap of a twig behind them yellow eyes. Something told me it weren't my wolf.

I came up close behind her and said, 'Give me my knife.'

Panic makes people stupid and she weren't no exception. I put my hand over hers and prised the stag-horn handle away.

'Back to the fire. Now,' I said. 'Where there's one wolf, there's a whole damn pack and they'll be riled up after that storm.'

Penelope trembled. 'I couldn't sleep. I heard steps, I tried to wake you,' she started blabbering, 'I thought I could scare it off.'

'Back to the fire,' I said and pulled her away. Kept my eyes on them yellow ones but they didn't follow. They didn't move. Growling stopped.

Soon as we got safe behind that fire I slammed that stupid girl against the wall a' the cave and put my knife right to her throat. Firelight made her eyes look like glassy pools.

'Don't touch my knife,' I said. 'And don't go chasin' wolves in the dark.'

She nodded, shaking, wincing at the rocks in her back.

I held her eyes. Sent my meaning right into them. This weren't no game. You die in the dark.

I let her go and sat down to stoke up the fire.

'Sorry,' she said, meek and mild, and sat down beside me.

'Goddamn it,' I said, didn't even bother to hide my anger, 'don't you know nothin'?'

She stared into the flames like a child what got her hand slapped.

'There's wolves out there,' I said, 'and bears and wolverines and all kinds a' snake. *Goddamn* it, you could a' been ripped up in less time than it takes to have a piss.'

Wanted to shake her. I could a' woken up and found her pulled open like a turkey on Christmas, all kinds of gore, strips a' that pretty white dress hanging out a wolf's mouth. I seen and smelt and tasted too much blood. Felt it all around me. All I could see. Felt the splash of the hog man's blood on my chest. Felt the Reverend's hot on my back. Felt my own all over me and the lake demon's all over my hands. I closed my eyes and looked at the face, that pair a' legs. Face weren't mine, legs weren't no stranger no more. Distance from that poison water gave me a picture clear as glass and I knew it was truth. Kreagar was in that basement. Kreagar was by that lake. Kreagar was my demon and I was his angel and he was just waiting for me to fall.

'Elka,' Penelope said, 'what is it?'

My chest went tight, cut off all my air. I tried to gulp down breath but it wouldn't let me. Demon hands was round my throat. Kreagar hands, covered in blood. Gripping tighter. White spots covered my eyes, smell a' iron in my nose. Fire and flames swam like oil in water. I was falling into a black ocean. Ocean a' rotten blood.

Penelope slapped me clean across the cheek.

Shock of it sent my lungs opening up. Air got to me. Sense got to me.

'Elka,' she said and I used her voice like a rope, 'deep breaths, come on.'

I did what she said. In out. Climbed higher out the dark. The ocean disappeared and the fire came back. Penelope came back.

'You had a panic attack,' she said, like it was nothing, while I was sucking in air like it was going to run out.

'How you know so much?' I said.

She opened up the water flask and handed it to me. 'Father was a doctor.'

Said that word *Father* all flat, like she was talking about grain or brushing her hair. Nothing in it. Being a doctor it made sense that Daddy knew 'bout the poison in the lake but, being a doctor, it didn't make a stitch a' sense that he drank all that water.

I looked at her out the side a' my eye. She had more learning than I reckoned. Don't know why but it made me nervous. People with book smarts and secrets had a way about them, a way a' looking at you like you was a puzzle they need to figure out. Some would do anything to solve it, even if it meant backstabbing and cheating to win. Colby done that. His smarts and silver tongue put me in that crate. Penelope's smarts had patched me up and got me out a' Ellery. Put a speck a' fear in me to wonder what else she could do. In the wild, I could face down a bear and I could put up a good fight 'gainst a lone wolf or mountain lion but in the world a' people, I was the straggler in the herd.

I was sick of it.

'Penelope,' I said, 'will you do somethin' for me? Part a' this whole "you save me, I save you" thing we got goin'.'

'What do you want?' she asked, wary and not trying to hide it.

I felt hot in my cheeks and squirmy for needing to ask. Cursed myself for not paying more attention to my nana when I had her. I looked into the fire, couldn't bear to look at Penelope and see the pity in her eyes or worse, the laughing. I took a deep breath and told myself there was no shame in it. And if she laughed at me, well, I'd leave her in the woods for the wolves.

'Teach me letters.'

KEEPIN' TEMPERS

'Promise me,' Penelope said, nervous, 'that you won't kill me if you get something wrong.'

I frowned at her. 'Only way I'd get somethin' wrong is if you teach it wrong.'

Sun was up and we'd left the cave 'bout half hour ago. Spotted wolf tracks close to the fire but didn't say nothing in case she panicked again. Three sets, maybe four. A pack scouting party. Flutter a' something dark and cold went through me.

'I'll make sure to teach it right,' she said, edge a' fierce in her voice. I suppose learned people don't like it when their smarts is questioned by someone like me. Same as I would get ornery if she told me how to best skin a rabbit. There is things some people know and some people don't but we all got to learn sometime. We was both children to each other, no matter how many years we had 'tween us. I was learning something she'd known since she was toddling and I'd show her trapping and gutting, tricks what was second nature to a wild-raised girl.

'Halveston is 'tween them mountains,' I said, pointing through the trees to the valley. Snow still covered the mountains near to halfway down and I knew we was getting close to the top a' the world. Down in the Mussa valley snow wouldn't be even close to the ground this time a' year.

'Never seen mountains that big,' I said. 'Makes Ridgeway's hills look like skeeter bites.'

'You came from Ridgeway?' Penelope asked.

'What of it?'

'That's. . . five, six hundred miles.' She looked at me, then at my boots. 'On foot?'

'Not all of it,' I said and scuffed my boot 'gainst a tree root. 'Was in a crate for a while.'

Didn't right know what that many miles meant. Couldn't quite figure if it was not enough or too many. It'd taken me months to do it and I weren't no slowpoke.

Spring was chirping in the world and it hit me hard that I'd left my home, my Trapper, last summer, a few months shy of a whole year gone from that life. It'd been all them months since the Reverend cut up my back and Kreagar whispered in my ear, *Think on why I ain't killin' you.* A whole winter past and I didn't feel no closer to figuring why. Made me tremble, the thought a' what'd happen when I did.

'You gonna teach me to read or talk about my walking some more?' I said, red in the face and wanting to take my head off the past.

'I can't concentrate on the alphabet until I get something to eat,' she said, first hint a' whining in her voice.

Suppose I couldn't expect other folks to go without food as long as I could. All these city folk used to eating every day, they think the sky is falling down on them they have to go hungry for more'n a few hours. Penelope didn't have no fat on her, no reserves for her body to live off 'tween meals. If that was the price for beauty and the desire a' men, well hell, you can keep it. Alive and ugly is better than pretty and dead.

'All right,' I said, 'pay attention. You teach me, I teach you, that's how this is gonna work. I ain't gonna be fetching and feeding you like you're a damn child what can't do nothing for itself.'

I took a handful a' snares out the bag what I'd made her carry on account a' my ribs, and showed her how to spot a rabbit track and set a snare. Watched her close as she set them, loop the size of a fist, three fingers high off the ground, twigs and brush arranged to funnel that game right into the trap.

'Not bad,' I said when she set the last one. 'I ain't got no patience to teach you firelightin' or stand about chilly while you practise. We need wood.'

Like a trained puppy she went foraging for kindling. I had a flame up in no time and she looked at me like I was one a' them magicians with the travelling show, pulling doves out my sleeves.

'You know so much,' she said, more talking to herself than me.

'Making fire's the easiest thing in this world if you got the smarts for it.'

'We had an electric heater in our house,' she said and I said that sounded dangerous.

'It was,' she said. 'We had a fireplace but couldn't light

it. Mother's weak chest, you see,' she sighed. 'There's something about an open fire.'

I couldn't argue there. Even in the middle a' the day, sun
shining down through spring green leaves with nothing in
the world to worry over, a fire was still a comfort. A little
piece a' home all the way out in the wild.

'All these things you can do,' Penelope said, 'the way you
live, I've only read about in books. Father taught me medicine, Mother taught me piano and iambic pentameter.'

'What they used for?'

She laughed and threw some twigs on the fire, flames
ate 'em up like sugar treats. 'Nothing. I can tell you why a
fire burns, the chemical reaction. I can recite a poem about
flames dancing in a lover's eyes but that won't keep me
warm out here, will it?'

'Won't cook no rabbit neither,' I said and in truth I felt
a bit bad for her. She was deep in my world and she might
as well have been a fly on a bison's arse all the good she
was doing.

'Feel the same when I'm around people and their papers,'
I said.

Penelope looked me in the eye, smiled a little sad-like
then picked up a sturdy twig. In the dirt she drew three
lines: / and \ and a – right through the middle.

'A,' she said. Next to that she drew something what looked
like Genesis Maud's hefty cleavage on its side.

'B.'

Then a half moon. Some memory of my nana and her
chalkboard stirred deep down.

'C.'

And dozens more till she got to Z.

Then she went back to the beginning and made me

repeat them all from memory. I didn't get them all, hell, felt like there was hundreds a' them stupid squiggles. How's anyone meant to remember them all and then put 'em all together to make all them words? There's got to be hundreds a' words out there and I sure as shit didn't have room in my head for all a' them. Started feeling antsy. Started getting twitchy. What in the hell was the point?

Sixth time through them dirt letters, I'd had enough. My face was red and hot and Penelope kept telling me I wasn't paying no attention. Just concentrate, she kept saying in that whiny voice a' hers. Come on now, L M N O P, repeat it, repeat it, like I was a goddamn mockingbird. I pulled out my knife and stabbed it into the dirt right in the middle a' that O.

That shut her the hell up.

Then I stood up and stalked off to check the traps. Sure, it weren't polite behaviour but I sure as hell weren't polite. I only promised I wouldn't kill her, didn't say I wouldn't get angry with her. Didn't say she wouldn't get my boot to her jaw if she pissed me off enough, and I was getting close. Was best all round if I took myself away from her.

Found the first trap empty and still set. Nothing was coming down this run. I pulled it out, stuck it in my pocket. Next one had a scrap a' rabbit and a foot still stuck in the snare. Not much else. Some other critter, probably a wolverine, got my lunch afore I did. Cursed it but couldn't blame it. I would a' done the same.

Through the trees I caught glimpse of Penelope, sat on a stump left over from when this forest was logging land. Stumps all over the place but new trees sprung up to fill the gaps. Made this part a' the forest greener'n usual. Also meant more shrubs and groundplants around, good for cloudberries, but not this time a' year. Nana used to have me fetch buckets a' the damn things for bakeapple pie. Weren't worth the slog in my mind. Never had much time for sweet things, made my teeth ache for meat.

Penelope stared off into the forest, scratching at the cut on her leg she got from the river. Said in my head, don't be scratching at that, sticking dirty nails into your skin. No good will come of it. She was sat in a ray a' sunlight, all in white, glowing angel-like. Didn't think she looked beautiful. Didn't think she looked human. She looked like dinner, wrapped up nice like Christmas, waiting in the spotlight. I moved through the trees, taking vantage behind her like I was stalking that buck me and Trapper bagged.

Then I heard soft kicking in the undergrowth. Kicking what meant the end a' life, not the beginning. On the stump, Penelope looked like Penelope again. Some part a' my mind, right near the back, that part that sends you running from bears and tells you you're hungry, was mixed up and sent confusion back to the front a' me. I ain't never been in the woods with someone weaker'n me. I always been the beta wolf. Now I was the alpha. Alphas take what they want but my mind weren't right sure what it wanted.

Kicking snapped me out of it.

Found the rabbit in a snare, loop tight round its neck. Looked into them big black eyes and they looked right back.

'Sorry fella,' I said, soft as his kicking.

He calmed down. Knew what was coming.

It's a strange thing to take a life. Before the hog man I wouldn't a' thought twice 'bout taking this rabbit by the feet and stopping him squirming. Now I saw an animal what done nothing to deserve it. Hog man deserved it, I'll tell you that for free, but this rabbit didn't do me no harm. Wrong place, wrong time he was and nothing else. I was his hog man. I was taking things from him what he sure as hell didn't want to give.

My belly growled. Took out my knife. Everything was backwards. I was the alpha, I had to provide, but I just. . . couldn't.

I always lived by rules a' my own making. Rules what told me bad from good and kept me on the right side. Weren't sure what the right side was no more. If I killed this rabbit, would I be any better than the hog? Better'n Kreagar? Rabbit seemed to sense my questioning and kicked up a fuss. Snare tightened.

Hog man didn't have to attack me, I told myself, ugly lust and a thick bull head made him. I ain't got no bull head, I ain't got no lust, I just got to eat and this rabbit was food. That's what I said anyway but still my knife wouldn't cut the thing's head off. Didn't feel myself no more. This was a goddamn rabbit. I killed hundreds. Stewed 'em, smoked 'em, canned 'em, fried 'em up with onions and taters. Who in the hell was I that I hadn't gutted this thing yet? He was a good size, would feed us two up right nice for the evening. My head was tangled up and I couldn't free it.

'You caught one,' Penelope said from behind me. Made me jump right out my coats. Hadn't heard her. Too busy feeling sorry for myself, all this whining going on in my head. Poor rabbit, didn't do nothing, tiny fuckin' violin. What a goddamn idiot. If she'd been a bear. . . hell. Couldn't afford to be whining. Couldn't afford them hog-man memories, not out here.

Took the rabbit by the feet, loosened the snare, and broke its neck.

Felt a sick wave a' grief hit me. For a goddamn scut-tail. I held up that limp body to Penelope.

'Don't suppose you know how to skin one a' these?' I asked because I knew I couldn't do it myself.

Penelope smiled and took the dead rabbit without blinking. Other hand asked for my knife.

'Maybe you should collect some wood,' she said, soft enough that it didn't sound like an order but firm enough that I knew she meant it.

She went off by the fire while I dragged back a few thick branches what had fallen in the storm. I tended the flames and watched her working. Gentle and soft she went at that rabbit like it was a teddy bear she didn't want to rip. Prised off the skin 'stead a' pulling it. Nicked at the fur round the feet 'stead a' chopping them off. I couldn't watch.

'Stop it, stop it,' I said, shaking my head. 'It ain't a baby you're nursin' on your tit, it's dinner and we're both starvin'.'

'You asked me to skin it,' she said, 'and I've skinned a rabbit before. I know what I'm doing.'

I laughed. 'You don't know shit. Meat'll rot afore you get that skin off.'

'Show me,' she said, handed me rabbit and knife.

I took 'em both without even a twinge in my head. 'You got to gut the thing first,' I said and dipped the blade into its belly. Guts spilled out like stew slopping in a bowl. Still hot and steaming. I felt myself smiling.

'This is the liver, kidneys, heart,' I said, pulling 'em out in one handful. Penelope watched close and I saw myself, eight years old, looking at Trapper the first time he brought back a deer.

'Then you take off the feet,' I said to Penelope, laid the rabbit down on a stump, broke its lower legs, cut 'em off.

Trapper stroked the hide, dark brown and glossy, knife in the other hand and said to me, Deer is a beautiful thing, girl, you got to treat it right. Laid out on the hut's porch, he stuck the blade into the belly. Made a hollow sound like you was cutting into a plastic bottle.

'Get your thumbs,' I said, ''tween skin and skirt, the belly edges you don't want to eat, then you work it loose, quick and firm.'

Trapper got a bucket and let the guts spill out. This one's already been bled, he said, got to make sure you bleed 'em good. Got to make sure you shoot 'em calm, he said, fear spoils the meat. This one died meek, he said.

Penelope made an 'ahh' sound and nodded, looked at the rabbit close and I could tell she was remembering my words.

'Once you got the skin off the back and can see daylight 'tween fur and meat, take the head off.' I twisted the neck, sliced through the fur, and pulled it off. Penelope gasped and I smiled. Chucked the head in the bush. Ain't nothing of worth in a rabbit's head.

Trapper tied the back hooves and hung the deer on a hook. Front legs brushed on the bloody porch. This breed a' deer, he said, ain't as easy to skin.

'Then you hold onto the skin,' I said, 'and the body of the rabbit, pull 'em apart.' Heard that stretching sound like pulling tape off its roll, and the back legs popped out the fur. Then the front legs, like pulling off stubborn socks, came out all pink and shiny.

Trapper told me to watch careful as he worked his fish-gutter knife into that deer. Small knife, small cuts, don't want to damage the meat. This will feed us for months, he said, you got to respect it. Then he started tugging at the skin.

I handed the naked rabbit to Penelope. 'Got it?' I asked

and she nodded, turning it over in her hands. 'Next time we catch one, you better do it a damn sight quicker.'

Trapper had the deer skinned down the neck. Always the tricky part, this, he said, took his blade to its chin, sliced up the side of its jaw. Hold onto the head, he said, keep it still, and I did. I held on, my baby fingers dug deep and tangled round the glossy, dark fur.

Back a' my neck prickled.

'Get a hazel switch,' I said, urgent in my voice. I needed her gone, now. 'Strong, green. Thick as your finger.'

She went without question. I was alone. Felt tangles round my fingers.

Memories ain't no one's friend. They show you all the good things you had, all the good things you lost and don't let you forget all the bad shit in between. Trapper told me once that your head can protect you if something truly bad happens. It can make black spots and empty places what should be filled with horror. I figured that's what my head had done. Locked some memories behind doors, covered 'em in chains and padlocks. Goddamn pussy it was, keeping all that from me. I didn't ask it to, it didn't have no right. What good did that do anyone? I'd remember it all soon. I was already starting to. Longer I was away from Kreagar. Longer I was with Penelope. Them doors would open one day and everything come at me, like a thunderhead rolling over the mountains. Soon it would hit and nothing would be the same.

I SAID CUT IT OFF,
SHE SAID DON'T YOU DARE

Penelope put wild garlic on the rabbit, roasted it up right nice over cherry wood. I tell you, I ain't had a better meal this side a' the Mussa. My doubts and whining had gone and I knew it weren't really the rabbit I was afraid to kill.

We stayed in that clearing the rest of the day. My ribs was feeling better for the food and rest and I set some more snares for tomorrow's breakfast. I didn't notice when Penelope started limping. She said it was a blister on her foot from the wet shoes, nothing to do with the cut on her leg. That was fine, that was healing. I believed her. She was the one with the medicine smarts after all.

We didn't talk much to each other rest a' that day. I weren't in no mood for it. Kreagar's words in that basement kept repeating in me like bad chilli. *Think on why I ain't killing you,* he'd said. Them words came out a' Kreagar's mouth, not my Trapper's. That's why I didn't recognise 'em for so long. Maybe he didn't think I'd led Lyon to him on purpose, which was why he weren't killing me. But there was something else in there, some darker reason he was still on my tail. I could feel him there, somewhere just out a' sight, over that hill or behind that tree. I'd be ready for him when he came for me, you can be sure a' that. When I wasn't setting and checking snares, I practised.

I carved a pale circle into a tree what could handle it, about the height a' Kreagar's head. Held my knife by the blade and threw it at the target. Knife bounced off, stuck itself into the dirt. Same thing happened second time, third time, all the damn times.

'It's the weight,' Penelope shouted from the fire.

I scrunched my face up to a frown. 'What you know about it?'

She came over, slowly. 'The handle is too heavy for the blade.'

Back tensed like she'd said something bad a' my first-born. 'Handle's perfect. You don't know shit about knives.'

She took it off me. 'And you don't know shit about physics.'

Opened my mouth to argue but I didn't even know what the hell that was.

'You didn't make this knife to be thrown, did you?'

Shook my head.

She stuck out her finger and laid the blade on it, right up at the hilt. Then she let the knife go with her other hand. It fell right on the ground.

'What's that meant to prove?' I said.

She picked it up. 'That your handle is too heavy and the knife isn't balanced.'

I had to be able to throw it, hard and right on target. 'How do I make it right?'

'This bit,' she said, pointing to one of the two antler nubs at the base. 'Get rid of it.'

'Be easier to cut the steel,' I said, took the knife back, looked at it sad-like.

'It's up to you,' she said, 'but you'll never get it in that target the way it is. You have to change it.'

Change was one of them words I weren't too friendly with. Nana told me I had to change when she caught me skinning a rabbit. Man in Ridgeway once told me I'd never get a husband the way I was. Only person never to tell me to change was Kreagar and that's because, way he saw it, I was already just the same as him.

'Not yet,' I murmured, turned the knife over in my hands, my knife, my life. 'Don't need to do it yet.'

Spent the night 'neath a low-hanging tree. Branches touched the ground and made a natural cave. Couldn't sleep all that well on account a' Penelope. She spent the night tossing and grumbling in her sleep so we both woke up tired. I ain't no fun when I'm tired and Penelope ain't no picnic neither.

We was like wolverines fighting over a squirrel that day. We walked maybe twenty miles, sunup to near sundown, and I swear Penelope moaned the whole time. My feet hurt. I'm hungry. I'm tired. I'm cold. Whine, whine, whine. She limped more'n she had the other day I reckoned she was making it out worse than it truly was. Ain't no blister as bad as that. She didn't have no head for pain, that was for sure.

She made me carry the bag. Weight of it made my ribs smart but it weren't worth her moaning if I tried to give it back.

'Keep up,' I said, growling them words as we went up a craggy slope, 'or I'll leave you behind.'

We was coming up the foothills of them mountains. It would only get steeper, rockier, and Penelope would only moan more.

'I have to rest,' she said. 'I have to drink something, my god.'

I didn't stop, just unclipped the flask from the pack and threw it on the ground for her to pick up. Half empty already, all down her gullet since morning.

We had maybe three days left to Halveston and I prayed it wouldn't be like this the whole way. I thought horrible things that day. Thought about leaving her in the middle a' the night. Thought about finding a ravine and giving her an accident. Thought about putting hemlock in her water. Anything to shut her the hell up.

Next day I got my wish. Penelope barely said a word. She just trudged on behind me, pale and sweating with the effort, and didn't give no word a' complaint. In fact, only thing she said, after a whole morning a' walking, was to ask if we could stop for a spell in the shade. Soon as we sat down I knew something was wrong. She breathed like someone was beating on her chest, all stuttered and shallow. She rested 'gainst a trunk, hands dropped into the dirt. Ant crawled over her fingers but she didn't do nothing to shoo it away. That ant went up her wrist, circled round her arm. Red ant, biter. Nasty little itch that would be. It got to her neck before I pinched it away.

'Penelope,' I said, clicking my fingers in front a' her eyes. Big black pools they were when they should a' been pin-pricks.

'Hmm,' she said, 'are we going?'

'You ain't goin' nowhere,' I said.

She tried to scratch at her leg but couldn't reach and didn't have the energy to move none.

When I saw the bandage and her skin either side a' it, I set my jaw firm. Bandage was yellow. Skin was red and webbed with angry veins.

'Shit,' I said to myself.

I unravelled the bandage, fabric sticking to her, using pus and blood for glue.

'Goddamn, Penelope,' I said. 'Why in hell didn't you tell me about this?'

Tears came out her eyes. 'I didn't want to hold you up.'

I used water to soften up the bandage and peel it off. Cringed when I saw the state a' her leg. Cut no longer'n my thumb was wide open, white skin round the edges and red all over. It weren't bleeding but *seeping* foul-smelling yellow pus what turned my stomach. I could see her veins carrying the nasty up her leg, into her gut and chest and head.

'It's septic,' she said.

'No shit,' I said. 'Wait here.'

I took the flask and found a quick-running stream. It came straight out the mountain, straight off the snow. Cold and clean meltwater. Got back to the tree to find her poking at the wound. . . Doctor's child should a' known better.

I smacked her hand away and poured the icy water over her leg. She grabbed my arm tight, fingers like eagle claws, and screamed like a goddamn banshee.

That's when I heard rustling in the trees some ways away and remembered we was in the same woods as a wolf pack. Penelope just gave them an announcement. I didn't see nothing out there but that don't mean they couldn't see me.

I quick found a flat stone and some broadleaf and yarrow. Little bit a' water and I mashed it with a rock to paste. I got Penelope's wound as clean as I could get it and stuck the poultice right into the flesh. She screamed again but I was ready and held my hand tight over her mouth. I kept her eyes with mine.

'We ain't alone out here,' I said quiet.

Her tears fell over my hand, down my wrist. I could see she understood and I took my hand away.

Rustling in the trees got louder. Closer.

I ripped a strip a' fabric off the blue shirt, made it wet, and tied it over the poultice.

'You itch this,' I said, 'and I'll cut your fingers off.'

She nodded. Didn't argue.

She drank up the last a' the meltwater, she said it would bring down her core temperature though I weren't right sure what that meant.

We walked together now. My good arm round her waist, taking all the weight off that leg. It was slow. Too slow.

Wondered if them wolves was behind us. Wondered what they would do if one a' their pack was injured. Didn't need to wonder long. I knew it like I knew the sun would rise. They would leave the wolf behind. Pack's only as strong as the weakest and, right now, Penelope was dead weight. Rules a' the wild are there for a reason. You got to make tough choices to survive. We had wolves circling us, waiting for the moment we was weak enough. If Penelope didn't get better, we wouldn't make Halveston and the wolves would take me too if I was near her when it happened.

We made camp but I didn't sleep. I sat up, staring into the fire, watching Penelope shake and sweat as the rest a' her blood turned bad. Thought about what I was going to do. The back part a' my brain, the primitive bit, told me to leave her. You cut off a tree limb when it's about to fall, you don't wait till you're sleeping 'neath it. Front part a' my brain told me I should carry her all the way to Halveston if I had to. But I had broken ribs and she weren't light. I thought I could cut off her leg afore the rot got too high but all that blood would attract all sorts. The two parts a' my brain argued long into the dark. Stars came out, studded the sky but I weren't seeing no beauty in it no more. Three or four times in the night I thought I'd made a decision only for a few minutes later my head to say, you sure about that? And the whole argument would start again.

When I saw a pair a' yellow eyes staring at me from the other side a' the fire, that decision weren't mine no more.

HALFWAY TO NOTHIN'

I can't right imagine what Penelope must a' thought when she woke at sunup. A big damn wolf lying on top of me. Me not moving 'neath it. Soon as I'd seen that black smudge in the firelight last night I knew I'd been right. It was my Wolf howling out his warning 'bout Colby while I was on the boat. He must a' come round the edge a' the lake, over them mountains what would a' killed a man for trying to climb 'em.

Took me a good hour to explain to Penelope why I weren't dead and she weren't dead and she weren't hallucinating and I weren't crazy. All while Wolf sat beside me, looking at Penelope like she was something he hacked up after dinner and weren't at all sure what it was he ate. He was bigger'n when I left him outside Genesis, and finally I felt like my world was whole again. I ruffled up his fur, scratched him behind the ears, rubbed my thumb 'cross that black smudge and wrestled about with him in the dirt. All while Penelope stared, like a bug-eyed fish, and winced and gasped every time he showed his teeth or growled.

'Don't show no anger or fear toward him,' I said, 'and he won't rip your arms off.'

'How. . .' she said, 'how can you do that with him? He's a *wolf.*'

Wolf looked up at her then, burning in his eyes, and she pushed her back into a tree trunk.

'Way I reckon it, men killed more wolves than wolves ever killed men,' I said. 'I know who I'm more afraid of.'

Penelope was still pale, like moonlight struck her face and didn't let go. The poultice may've helped the pain but it wouldn't cure the rot growing in her blood. That would need more smarts and potions than either of us had.

'It's stopped pussin' at least,' I said while I freshened up the poultice.

Wolf looked over my shoulder. Look a' sneering on him. He weren't taking to Penelope, kept his distance like she was the cuckoo a' the pack.

'All this walking, not much food,' she said, 'my body can't fight it by itself. I need antibiotics.'

'Where'd they come from?'

Wolf gave one a' them low yelps and I scratched his neck to calm him.

'Halveston,' she said, wincing when I put a fresh dressing on her leg, 'a pharmacist.'

'Come on then,' I said and stood up, 'we got to get you there.'

One arm over my shoulder, we made our way over the final ridge 'tween us and Halveston. Wolf trotted behind. Felt like he was shaking his head at me as if to say, what the hell are you doing carrying this meatsack around? Get rid a' her, get to Halveston quicker. Couldn't expect a wolf to think much else.

Took us hours to get to the top a' the ridge 'tween the mountains. Hours were worth the view though. South I saw the lake stretching further than I could see. Town a' Ellery at the tip, barely anything from this far away. The road north was just a scratch on the land, like a scar running through the world.

North? Hell. If I thought the road was ugly, it weren't nothing compared to the land. Black clouds sat brooding in the far-far away, hanging over a landscape turned alien in the Damn Stupid. Craters and holes the size a' the Mussa valley, showing stripes a' coloured rock and fat plumes a' smoke coming from everywhere.

World up here, scarred and angry, don't give up its goods no more, least not without a tooth and nail fight. Made me sick all them trees, all them critters, what must a' died when the bombs fell. Them bombs weren't even meant to fall on our land. It was a mistake, a guiding error or some such nonsense, the old'uns said, what meant all their bombs fell at once in the wrong places. They was meant for the down south cities and places humans already wrecked, they was meant to kill people not the wild. They filled the sky with smoke and poison and turned the thunderheads feral and vicious. Old'uns said they stopped the water running and all the lights went out. They left behind a world of burnt rock and scraps a' green and no one never said sorry. I figure the wild don't think us humans deserve what it's got no more and tell you truth, I think it's right. Staring out at that land, all ripped up ragged like it weren't precious, like it weren't alive and breathing, like it was just some nothing anthill to stomp out. Hell, staring out at that near broke my heart.

Trees weren't tall and bright and needle-sharp up there. They didn't pierce the big blue like them in the Mussa. Even though it was spring, there weren't no fresh life up here. These were trees grown up in sorrow and hard soil, green was dark, trunks was twisted and stunted, and I could hear 'em weeping. Right across the mountains, right across the low plains and torn-up land, them old wailing voices carried strong on the wind. The North was raging, low and slow like only land knows how.

That's why all them folks going up for the yellow metal was fools, they lost soon as they set their compass and took a step. Sad piece a' cold grew in my chest thinking on my parents. They left with that letter writ in their heads, *millions in gold, claims are going cheap and there's a fever of excitement in the air. We'll be back rich as Midas. Tell my little girl, I love you.* Were my parents fools like the rest a' them? Maybe 'cause they was my blood the earth would give 'em half a chance. Figured the wild owed me that but right now, looking at this land, us humans owed the wild so much more.

'Are you all right?' Penelope said 'side me. Didn't realise how long I'd been staring and seething. Wolf nuzzled 'gainst my leg.

'Ain't nothing I can do for it,' I said, 'this land ain't gonna be friendly to us.'

'That's Halveston,' Penelope said. 'Gateway to fortune, they call it.'

Close to the foot a' the mountains was a town bigger'n I'd ever seen. That one road led right into it and more'n a dozen roads led out. It was like a dandelion fuzz, one stalk going right up to it, then all these other tiny spindles pointing every which way. Told me there weren't all that much north a' this place, least nowhere big enough for a road. Felt like I'd reached the end a' the world.

Halveston was sitting right on a dried-up river bed, saw

the dark line the water took from 'tween the west mountains. Wondered if one a' them Damn Stupid bombs took
out the river, turned this valley brown. Land was spiked with
tree stumps, all grey and rotting in the weather. All them
trees built Halveston and was still building it. Town like this
was spreading out like blood on snow, soon be big as Couver
City. Much as I wanted to, I couldn't hate Halveston. Felt
my parents in them streets, felt my momma buying potatoes
and dresses, felt my daddy bartering for a good price on his
bucket a' gold.

Half a day down the mountain and I would be there.
Right where my parents were. I saw huge buildings and wondered which one my momma and daddy lived in. My blood
started heating up inside me like a stewpot on a rolling boil.
They'd be so happy to see me, I thought, they'd take me up
in their arms and say, we knew you'd come, and I'd tell 'em
all my stories. Of the thunderhead and the flying table, of
the crazy Reverend, of the poison lake and sailing across the
lake in damn first-class accommodation. Not a' Kreagar or
Lyon. Not never a' them.

We'd talk right on into daylight. All I had to do was get
Penelope to the permit office.

As if that girl heard my excitement and wanted to mess
it up, her legs buckled 'neath her. She started shaking and
convulsing and spitting up white foam.

I shouted her name and held her down so she didn't
split her head open on a rock. Wolf's ears pricked and he
growled low, not out a' anger but out a' something else,
worry maybe, or suspicion.

I'd seen this afore, years ago and it was all kinds a' bad.
Farm boy in Ridgeway had these fits, they'd last for hours
and every time he woke up, a bit a' his mind didn't come

back with him. When his parents were out in the fields, the cows would low when the boy was sick and Mom and Dad would come running. Happened again and again until one day the cows didn't low. Boy was lying on the floor. None a' his mind came back. He was alive but empty. Word was his daddy took him out into the woods and left him there, couldn't bear to kill him, didn't have the money to keep him. I sure as shit didn't want Penelope to come back empty. I needed her letters. I needed her. I held her tight to me, stopping her arms from flailing and her head from ragdolling all over the rock.

Finally, she fell still. Too still. My heart went wild. She couldn't be dead. She couldn't die. Not this close. Not after all this.

'Penelope, don't you dare,' I whispered right into her hair, 'don't you leave me now.'

Felt her breath on me. Felt her heartbeat in her neck.

Wolf came up and sniffed her, like he was checking if she was dead or least waiting for her to be. There I was, holding this sick woman, full a' infection, and a nasty, wild wolf watching over us. We was some kind a' family right there. Wolf trotted off to the down slope a' the hill, turned back and barked low at me, like he was saying, if you got to keep the stray, let's get moving. Then he ran off down, saw his tail bobbing away.

Penelope weren't waking up.

Wolf came back, barked again, louder this time. His yellow eyes fixed mine but worry for the girl clouded up my mind. Felt like crying and that pissed me off. She'd got under my skin, made me care for her and now she was sick as a dog and mine to nurse. Wolf took my bag 'tween his teeth and tugged. I knew what he wanted, know his mind just as I know mine. We needed to get to Halveston. Figured a town that big would have a doctor. She weren't going to get no better lying here.

'I can't carry both,' I said and he twitched his ears at me. 'You got to pull your weight,' I said and, still holding onto Penelope, awkwardly took the pack off my back.

Despite my ribs, despite my tired and aching body, I hauled limp Penelope up. She weighed less than a yearling buck.

'You get the pack, Wolf,' I said, nodding to the beast and the bag.

Felt like he was narrowing his eyes at me. Slowly, he put his teeth round the strap, like he was doing it only 'cause I was carrying something heavier. Gave me a low growl.

'Don't be whinin',' I said, 'least you ain't got broken bones in you.'

He started half-lifting, half-dragging the bag and I didn't have the stones to tell him off. He growled most the way like a grumbling child forced to shell nuts. Every step was a cracked shell, every scrape a' the pack was another kernel in the basket.

'Didn't think you was such a grump,' I said, hefting Penelope closer to my chest. Ribs weren't happy but I told 'em to quit whining.

Louder growl out a' Wolf made me laugh but I'll tell you, a mite a' worry started nibbling at me. A wolf's instincts are sharper'n cracked flint and he weren't taking to Penelope. I suppose I couldn't blame him, parts a' her story 'bout her daddy didn't right make sense. Maybe it was Wolf being back that made me see that. She weren't telling me the whole true but right now, half-dead, she was telling me enough.

Halfway down the hill Wolf veered off to the right. I

shouted at him but he didn't even turn to growl. I called
him a thieving son bitch and bring that pack back here. He
ignored me and I quick figured if I didn't follow him, I'd
never get my bag back. Swore at him. Cursed him. My body
felt like it was going to break apart any minute, I didn't have
no time for wrong roads.

Shouldn't a' sworn or cursed him. That wolf was a
beast sent straight from heaven. When I found him he
was sitting, smug look on him, on the porch of a shelter
cabin. One of them small huts trappers and hunters and
lost idiots can use in case a' emergencies. They're dotted
all over the wild and they got a fire and wood and a bed
and maybe even a scrap a' food if you're lucky. Best of all,
they ain't locked.

'All right, Wolf,' I said, 'you ain't useless.'

Penelope started stirring, moaning in my arms, and I tell
you, the relief, the heart-swelling, damn tear-jerking, damn
wanting-to-shake-her-for-making-me-worry, all came over
me at once. Hell, I nearly dropped her.

I rushed into the cabin, felt the chill, stale air of a place
what ain't seen people all winter, and set the girl down on
the bunk. I chucked the bunk blanket, half-eaten by moths,
on the floor and afore I could turn around, Wolf had made
his home on it. I stoked up the fire in the stove and shut the
door. Place'd be toasting in no time. Night was coming. It'd
taken longer to walk here than it should a' on account of
the extra weight.

Maybe it was the warm or the flat bed, but Penelope soon
opened her eyes. She took a minute to realise she weren't in
the woods no more, then them eyes found me.

'Where am I?' she said and I sat down on the bunk next
to her. She was still ghost pale and I could feel the fever-heat

come off her body. I reckoned that fit was just the first a' many 'less we could get her to a doctor.

'Shelter cabin,' I said. 'You started fittin' on the hill.'

She sat up, winced and hissed at the movement of her leg. 'You carried me?'

Felt squirmy inside. 'You save me, I save you, that's the deal right?' I said it quiet-like, squirmy coming out in my voice.

She smiled at me and the squirmy went away.

'Is the wolf here?' she asked, face turned grave.

'He's lazin' about on the floor,' I said, 'like a damn pig in shit.'

Wolf snuffled and stretched, dug his claws into my boots.

I unwrapped Penelope's dressing. Smell a' decay and pus and iron blood hit me hard. The veins around the cut were calmer than they were afore the poultice and I figured it had slowed the poison by a day or two. The cut was nasty, though, full a' rot and skin tinged black at the edges.

'Can you walk?' I said. 'Truth this time, no more thinkin' this is goin' to get better.'

Penelope didn't answer for a minute, looked down at the mess she'd made a' herself, then shook her head. I gave her the flask and told her to keep drinking till she hit metal. Then I took the blanket out the pack and covered her up.

'I'm sorry, Elka,' she said, cradling the flask like she was praying to it.

'Don't matter none now,' I said. 'You can't walk which means you can't come with me to Halveston. Worst part is I damn sure need you to come to Halveston.'

Penelope sighed, not loud-like, not like some stroppy kid, but like someone who was feeling a sight sorry for themselves. I didn't take well to pitying yourself. It weren't worth the effort or time and it pissed people off.

'We'll hole up here,' I said, 'for the night. Talk about it again in the mornin'.'

She didn't argue, nor did Wolf, 'cept for a gentle huff when I shoved him out the middle a' the floor. I laid down beside him and listened to him breathing. Soft in outs, calm like he didn't have no care in the world. I suppose he didn't. He was warm, he was out the weather and he was with his pack, even if he didn't much like one a' the members.

Had a sick feeling in me, like before a storm. You know it's coming but you can't quite figure when. When I laid down to sleep that night, that's what I felt. Even though I was with Wolf again, thing what felt right and as it should be, and with Penelope, girl what I came to see as more'n just a waste a' space, I couldn't find no comfort. I felt an itching at my neck, kind you get when you're walking round town and keep seeing the same face no matter how many turns you take. Maybe it was being this close to Halveston and a shit-ton a' people I didn't know. Maybe it was knowing that soon as I walked into that town, I'd see myself and Kreagar in charcoal nailed to every post.

Lyon's face came into my head. All ice and glass she was, not like a real person. She mouthed something to me. Some words I couldn't make out. Words I didn't want to hear.

Woke up to cold sunlight and a snoring wolf. Lyon stayed right there behind my eyes. Wish I'd known what she was saying in my head, them words was silent but something in me said they was true.

Penelope woke up soon after me. I changed her poultice and gave her some more water. Wolf sat up, eyes like hard stone set firm on the girl. Wish I could a' known his thoughts.

What was it about her he didn't trust? She had secrets, sure, but they couldn't a' been all that worse'n mine. It nagged at me something fierce and made me look at her different.

Broad-spectrum antibiotics.

That's what she told me to get from Halveston. She had to repeat it a couple a' times, them fancy words don't take quick to my head. I told Wolf to keep an eye on her but he wouldn't stay in the hut, 'stead he sat outside the door and I couldn't argue with that. I stroked his head, knelt down in front of him and wrapped my arms around his neck.

'Don't you go nowhere,' I said right into his fur. 'I need you.'

Wolf rubbed his head 'gainst mine and I knew he'd be here when I got back. It was only when I started down the hill toward Halveston that I wondered if I would be coming back. Had me a sick feeling that Lyon was in that town, had me a sicker feeling that Kreagar was too. I told my gut that Lyon was hunting Kreagar in Martinsville, way down south. Alls I had to do was get to a doctor, find them 'biotics and get Penelope walking. Sounded easy in my head but Halveston weren't like nothing I'd ever seen afore and it was ready to chew me right up if I put little as one foot wrong. Turned out I was 'bout to put both feet, both hands, and the rest a' my whole damn body wrong.

HALVESTON

Halveston was one a' them towns what grew up quick. A Boom Town they called it, only a handful a' years old. Filled with a mix a' them what picked through mud for months and came back with nought but bleeding fingers, then there was those what found their fortune and threw it away on whisky and women, and last was them folk what preyed on both types: the claim runners, the brothel madams, the metal merchants what weighted their scales backward. Hundreds a' people all clawing for yellow metal and rocks.

Halveston was a town a' wood and rats and rust. The town had started as just one line a' timber buildings. Them buildings got joined by another line, then the gaps 'tween 'em got filled with huts and carts, then the town spread out in all directions. Hard-packed road turned to mud at the gate and people a' all kinds came out the woodwork. Men, women, Blacks, whites, Chinamen, them Latins from the far south, even some hard-faced yellow-hairs with voices thick like molasses. Heard they walked over the ice up in the far north-west, Trapper

said that's what them ruskis did in the Second Conflict, came
down on BeeCee from the top. Trapper said that place other
side a' the Bering was full a' Reds but I weren't seeing no one
a' that colour. Figured he was wrong about that so maybe I
should just forget all them things he told me 'bout people,
'cept how to kill 'em if I felt the need. Figured he'd know
right how to do that. People in Halveston was giving them
yellow-hairs a wide berth, few were shouting words I didn't
understand. Figured folk up here blamed them for the Damn
Stupid which was a fool thing to do. They ain't responsible
for them bombs same as I ain't responsible for that Ridgeway
kid whose shoes I got. Gave one a' them yellow-hairs a smile,
while them others gave them grief.

People what grew from seed up here was stained, you could
tell who was who quick as slapping a tick. Sallow cheeks and
bent spines, most a' them had one a' them hacking coughs,
some had twisted up club feet and I saw one what didn't
have no hands but was shelling nuts quicker'n I ever could.
The locals all had a look about 'em what said they was sick
but you couldn't right place the ailment. There was just a
tinge, a taint on 'em what put me on edge. You can tell a
tree got rot by the colour a' the leaves and feel a' the bark
so you don't go trusting it to hold up your cabin roof. These
people was like them trees. You could stoke a fire with 'em
all through winter but couldn't right trust 'em to keep the
rafters from crushing you while you was sleeping.

Halveston was a chilli pot boiling up. For every grey
local there was a hundred colours and sizes and I even saw
someone with tattoos like Kreagar's on half his face. I walked
'tween throngs a' dark-skins chattering in a tongue I'd never
heard. Sounded like they was rolling them words around
their mouths a few times afore sending them out. Weren't

no single word I could make out but the rhythm in it was curious. Hundred tongues found my ears; harsh spitting ones, ones like honey dripping off a comb, even a couple a' coal-black men clicking they tongues. My boots sucked and squelched in the mud, mixing in with the talk and shouting and four fellas picking fiddles, a babe screaming somewhere up ahead and hawkers screeching they wares. It all made tunes and music and sent me almost forgetting my purpose.

Halveston was a drug town. A revelry town. A town a' sins and sinners and gold and mud and cold metal-smelling air from the smelter shops. It was a town where junk was given a second chance. A yellow short bus been dug into the dirt was now growing beans and housing chickens, front end of an old Chevy been turned into a grill touting plates a' ribs and biscuits. To say I felt right at home would be something close to the truth.

I ain't never much liked people but the people a' Halveston were all passing through, either 'tween south and their claim, or 'tween life and death. There weren't no one here now, in the middle a' spring and fine days, what would still be here after winter. No one was looking at me or for me. This was a town you could disappear in easy, whether running from the law through the twisting streets or through a few well-placed coins in a judge's pocket.

I asked a woman, sodden in moonshine and more mud than skin, where I could find the doctor. Slurring, she called me sailor, told me the right direction, then said come find her after, she'd show me a fine time for a good price. I laughed when I walked away. I ain't never been mistaken for a fella afore but it gave me relief that maybe I wouldn't be recognised.

Barrow a' boots outside the doctor's office told me the

rest a' what I needed to know about this town. Dying was as much a business as living. Them boots was selling for a few bucks a pair and a kid a' seven or so was taking the coin. No one wants to walk in a dead man's shoes, that's why they so cheap. Story goes you can't take more'n five steps afore the reaper comes tapping at your shoulder. But I been wearing a dead boy's boots for years and no reaper come for me, not yet. Hell, he wouldn't want no part a' me and what I done. I'm heading straight down to the devil himself.

Seeing that barrow put all the music out my head 'cause above it, pasted up on the wall though half-covered by a poster touting toothbrushes, was my face in charcoal, right next to one a' Kreagar.

Sent shivers through me it did. Them shivers turned to icicles when I realised the paste was still wet. My eyes went up and down the street and I saw them white papers on every corner, every lamppost. I spun round and round but there I was, staring back at me, taunting me. Then them icicles went to sharp steel in my bones and I saw at the end of the next street, top a' low hill, the law office. Big, dark stone and teeming with red- and black-jacket officers scuttling about like beetles. Was like a black cloud hung over that place, made the horses tied up outside stamp and whinny. Bars on every window. A jailhouse as well as an office looming over Halveston, and nowhere I wanted to be.

Thought about cutting Penelope's leg off then just so's I could get out this town. Wolf would a' done that if one a' his pack was hurt. I stood outside the doctor's house like a crabapple hanging off a low branch. Feet wouldn't move to go in or turn away. I was easy pickings.

The barrow boy stopped his selling and I saw him duck inside the doctor's office. Didn't have time to think on why.

'Are you lost, miss?'

I spun round to a skinny man in a dark blue suit what looked like it came out a museum. Pair a' eyeglasses on a chain round his neck and a green, shiny waistcoat hugged a paunch what seemed a bit too big for the size a' him. He had a skinny moustache, waxed to neat points, black gumboots kept the mud off his trousers and he wore a tie printed with dancing birds.

'Miss? Are you lost?' he said. His voice sounded like he was holding his nose.

'I know where I am,' I said and took a few steps to block his view a' the poster.

He must a' sensed my tensing up. He shook his head and said, 'Excuse my manners, I am Stanley. Stanley Bilker.'

He held out his hand, clean and pink and too soft for a man in this part a' the world. I shook it and left crumbs a' dirt in his palm. He gave a little 'heh' sound then pulled out a gleaming white handkerchief to clean himself up.

'Now, miss,' he said, 'you look like the kind of girl who is not afraid of hard work. Am I correct?'

'I suppose,' I said and found myself wanting to get away. Something about this fella sent my blood chilling.

'Well, now, I have just the thing.' He dug into his jacket pocket and pulled out a stack a' papers, all folded up neat. 'A girl like you, clearly strong, obviously determined and a dynamite to boot, well, all you need now is a claim.'

Felt my gut sink.

'I have one here.' He rifled through the papers and pulled out one. 'Fifty dollars and you get land worth at least a million, *guaranteed.*'

'I ain't interested and I ain't got fifty bucks,' I said, backed up a step toward the doctor's but Stanley weren't giving up.

He pulled out another paper. 'Thirty dollars gets you this prime piece on the inner bend of the Kannat River,' then another paper, 'twenty-five gets you the outer bend.'

'I told you, I ain't interested.' I stepped up onto the porch a' the doctor's, towered over the little man in hope he'd get the message. Didn't want to have to pull my knife to get him to listen.

He held up his hands, both full a' claim papers, and said, 'I see, maybe it is the upfront payment that's putting you off. We have many payment plans available, you can take the inner Kannat right now, right off me, right now, no charge, not even a cent,' he held it out to me like he was giving candy to a kid, 'then come month's end, I'll visit and take twenty percent of your clean-up as payment. What could be easier? You look trustworthy, look like you could really make it up here, which is why I'd do this for you, I wouldn't do it for everybody, there are a lot of people here who won't find a nugget all season, even on land rich as mine, but you. . .'

Stanley was pattering like he was practising in front of a mirror. It didn't matter who he was talking to. I shouldn't a' been worried about him recognising me off the poster. He didn't see faces, just marks.

Heard a door open and a bell ding behind me. Stanley stopped. A tall man in a long white coat stood half out the doorway. Old round the face but sharp in the eyes, he had hair on his head same colour as the coat and a shadow a' stubble across his jaw. Jaw like a steel girder that was, square and solid to match his nose, both a' which had taken a fist or two in his time.

'Afternoon doc,' Stanley said. 'Me and the lady are just conducting a little business, sorry for the disturbance.'

'We ain't conductin' no business,' I said, sharp. 'I ain't interested in your papers.'

The doctor raised both black and white eyebrows and said, 'You heard her, Bilker, run along.'

The waxed moustache twitched and he clenched his fists around them neat papers. 'You got some nerve interrupting a sale, doc.'

I caught sight of a revolver in a holster on Stanley's hip. Blood went freezing, last place I wanted to be was in the middle of a gunfight. The doctor stepped fully out the door and both me and Stanley saw the twelve-gauge he was using as a walking stick.

'My porch isn't a market, Bilker,' he said and the salesman paled. 'Take your business, and your stink, elsewhere.'

There was more 'tween these two than just me and I weren't in no mood to find out what. Stanley shoved his papers back in his pockets and held up his hands in defeat.

'This time, doc, and only because we're in the presence of a lady.' He bowed to me and said, 'Miss, when you change your mind, I will do you a great deal.'

Then he straightened his jacket and turned, striding away in his rubber boots like a kid what's just tripped over and don't want no one to notice.

The shotgun knocked on the boards as the doctor went back in his office. 'Are you coming in or should I give you a toadstool and a fishing rod?'

'I don't like fishin',' I said, not getting the joke, and followed him.

Smell a' alcohol hit me. Not the drinking kind but the pure, clear stuff what stings up something vicious. We was in a small, square room. One wall was taken up by a glass-top counter, one was a faded-green curtain what touched the floor and the one that didn't have the front door and windows was rows and rows of jars, full a' potions and dried-up herbs, little white pills and tiny vials. Ain't never been in a doc's like this. The one in Ridgeway was a fat toad of a man and whatever he could fit in a suitcase.

'What ails you?' the doctor said, taking his spot behind the counter and laying the shotgun right on the glass. Weren't no sign a' the barrow boy.

'Ain't me,' I said, looking round wide-eyed at all them bottles and jars. 'I'm fit as one a' them bettin' horses.'

A smile crinkled up his eyes. 'Have you passed through here before? I feel we've met.'

I looked at him straight then. 'No, sir, I don't think so.'

He kept that smile and said, in a tone what meant he was really saying something else, 'I never forget a face.'

I swallowed hard then saw, through the glass counter, right 'neath the shotgun, that poster a' me and beside it, one a' Kreagar. Alcohol vapours pricked the back a' my throat and my voice came out weak.

'I ain't never been to Halveston afore,' I said and he just stared at me.

Felt my blood heating up. The door was closed. Maybe there was a back door through them curtains. Maybe I could grab that shotgun afore him.

If he caught me staring at the poster or saw the shifting panic in my muscles then he didn't let on, just asked what he could help me with.

'Friend a' mine got hurt and the cut turned rotten,' I said, keeping the tremble out my voice best I could. 'I need me some a' them broad. . . broad spendin' 'biotics.'

Them salt an' pepper eyebrows raised up again and a

silvery scar on his forehead caught the light. He scratched at his cheek and it made a sound like a steel brush on stone.

'Broad-spectrum antibiotics?'

I winced, thought I'd remembered it right after all that practising. I nodded and the doctor pulled open a drawer 'neath the counter. Few seconds a' looking and he set a small white box on the glass.

'Doxycycline,' he said. 'Two a day for a week should clear up any infection.'

I picked up the box, looked at all them jumbled-up letters, weren't even sure if they was in English.

'That everything?' he asked, kindness in his voice.

'Throw in a couple a' them bandages,' I said. Seeing how white and clean they was showed me just how rotten them others were.

He took two tight rolls from a shelf, along with a squat glass bottle. 'For sterilisation,' he said. 'That's forty-five dollars.'

My chest went tight. I ain't got forty-five bucks. I ain't got many more'n ten. I pulled out Colby's coins and held 'em in my open hand. 'I. . .' I said, hell, I didn't know what to say. 'What will this get me?'

The doctor looked at me sad-like, then held up the bandages and the bottle, took the box out my hand. 'Just these. Doxy is hard to come by these days.'

Chest went tighter. Penelope weren't going to be on her feet again with just bandages and rubbing alcohol. She needed them pills and I needed her.

'What happened to your friend?' doctor asked out a' nowhere. Could sense the decency in his voice. He weren't asking questions to get ahead or swindle me, he was asking out a' doctor's concern.

'Fell in a flood river. I pulled her right out a' there quick as I could thinking it'd be the cold what'd get her. Didn't pay no mind to no cut. More fool me.'

I weren't really paying attention to what I was saying. I was just filling time while I thought of a way.

'That's very brave of you,' he said. 'Not many people would do that.'

'It's what you do for friends, ain't it?' I said, felt my eyes going hot and prickly. I needed Penelope and it weren't just for her letters. Sure she had her secrets but, hell, we all did and mine weren't rosy. I had to find a way.

'I need them pills,' I said and my eyes went to the shotgun, felt the weight a' my knife on my belt. But that weren't the way, I told myself, that ain't no way to live. 'I can trap,' I said. 'Get nice furs for your missus. I can. . . clean up, I can work it off.'

Doctor pursed his lips and said, 'I'm sorry, I don't have need for that.'

Someone shouted hello from behind the curtain and I heard the banging a' boxes. 'Delivery,' the voice said.

The doctor looked at me curious-like, eyes scrunched up and lips moving around like he was chewing up a thought. 'I'll be back in a minute,' he said, then nodded to me.

He barely moved the curtain when he went through it and I heard him greeting the other fella.

That white box was staring right back at me. My blood was running all through me, galloping alongside my heartbeat like horses on a stampede. The devil and angel on my shoulders was arguing up a storm. One was screaming 'bout Penelope and my parents. Other was shouting 'bout rules a' living. I break them rules I ain't no better than Kreagar but, hell, I had black sins in my past already and weren't no angel could shout loud enough to blow them away.

Heard the doctor's footsteps coming back, saying his goodbyes to the delivery man.

I snatched the box and bolted for the door. Then I was outside, boots slapping in the mud. My head whipped round expecting to see a twelve-gauge following me but there weren't nothing but an open door. Should a' kept my eyes front. Should a' kept my wits sharp. Should a' hid them pills.

I ran right into the back of a man on the street. I bounced off his black coat, slipped in the mud onto my backside. The man turned around and all my air went out a' me. I knew him. I'd seen him at Kreagar's hut. I'd seen him at the Genesis hanging tree. Standing right beside Lyon.

Her lieutenant, the stocky one with a beard down to his chest, saw the open doctor's door, saw the box in my hand, saw the panic in my eyes, all in less than a second. He grabbed me up, took the box off me, and looked me straight in the face. He had to know me, my like was on every wall and post in this whole damn town. I cursed myself. I cursed that devil on my shoulder for showing me wrong. This is what I get, I told myself, this is what I get for breaking them rules. This was it, he'd drag me off to Lyon and she'd start asking questions. Questions I couldn't answer yet. Questions about Kreagar and her son. Penelope would never get her pills. I'd never see my parents.

'You got a receipt for those?' he said, sneering, voice like tumbling rocks. He knew the answer a' course.

I didn't say nothing, I couldn't. My voice was froze up in my throat. My eyes was froze up wide open. Fear put ice in me and everything went stiff. Felt like I would shatter if he let go.

'I think you need to see the doctor,' the lieutenant said and as he dragged me, I saw a shining six-shooter on his belt. I remembered that squirrel outside Kreagar's hut, shot right through the eye, and I started looking around frantic for Lyon.

But she weren't nowhere. It was just me and him and a few people who stopped to stare, including that Bilker fella a little ways down the street. Mercy was Lyon's man didn't seem to recognise me. He didn't put them charcoal faces to mine. He hadn't seen me up close in Dalston like Lyon had. But soon as he took me to the jailhouse, she'd see me and my life, and Penelope's, would be done.

The lieutenant pulled me through the doctor's door and threw me 'gainst the counter. My eyes saw the shotgun and the white coat and the doctor staring down at me, look a' confusion on his face.

The lieutenant grabbed the back of my head and pushed my face 'gainst the glass. He put the pills right next to my eye and said to the doctor, 'I caught this girl stealing, I thought you'd want to face the snipe before I take her up the hill.'

The doctor picked up the box and read the label. I braced myself. Then I noticed that the poster a' me 'neath the counter was gone.

'You left before I could write up your ticket,' the doctor said to me and picked up a pad and pen chewed up at the end.

Lyon's man looked as confused as me but I tried to keep my face turned away 'case he figured me out.

'The gank *stole* those pills,' the lieutenant snarled, grinding my head 'gainst the glass so hard I thought it would crack. 'She was seen running from this building.'

The doctor scribbled something on the pad but didn't

look up at the lawman. 'Because she has a seriously ill friend in need. She stole nothing.'

The lieutenant gaped like a fish, looked from me to the doctor and back. 'She bought these?'

Doctor nodded and ripped the page off the pad, handed it to me with the pills. 'And these,' he said, taking the rolls a' bandages and bottle a' alcohol back off the shelf, 'but you left in such a hurry, you must have forgot them. Let her go, she's done nothing wrong.'

Took the grunt a few seconds but he let me up. I kept my face toward the doctor.

The doc handed the bandages and such to me with a wide smile and a glint in his eye from the afternoon sun. My mouth went fish-like too and that paper trembled 'tween my fingers. I weren't at all sure what was happening or what I'd have to do to pay back the doctor. All I knew was I was in deep, stuck right 'tween Lyon and that shotgun with no way a' squeezing out.

Lyon's man scratched the back a' his neck. Then he looked at me and said, 'You paid for them?'

Kept my eyes on the counter, didn't want him seeing too much a' my face. I nodded.

He grunted and said his sorrys to the doctor. Then, like he'd been stunned by a slap in the face, he wandered outside, black coat disappearing 'tween all the people.

Just me and the doctor. I sighed heavy, felt squirmy in my chest, waiting for the hammer to fall right on my head. Was worse'n that time I cut too deep when I was gutting a deer and spilled all the shit and poison out into the meat. Trapper came raging at me and hung me upside down in a tree for the whole night. Said he was gonna use me to replace the doe I ruined. When he came back next morning, big ole cleaver in his hands, I felt the squirmy fear like nothing I felt afore. He just cut the rope a' course but that feeling stuck right with me. Felt it again now, in the doctor's office, but worse 'cause this time it weren't just my life hanging.

I handed back all the medicine, figured I could always cut Penelope's leg off if I needed to, though not if I was full a' pellets or behind iron. I mumbled some kind of apology, shoved it all 'cross the counter, but the doctor shoved it right back.

'Bill of sale is final,' he said. Little smile on him said more'n his words.

I opened my mouth to say what the hell you mean, what you want in return, but nothing came out. Then I opened my mouth to say thank you but it didn't seem close to enough. So I just nodded and he nodded back and that was that. I left the doctor's office with the pills, the bandages and a whole heap a' kindness what was heaviest of it all. He'd put an invisible mark on me. One what weren't going to wash off in the rain. One what couldn't be cut away or burned out. It was a piece a' bright light that sent that darkness from Colby and the hog man scurrying into a corner. I seen true kindness in that doctor, a man what carried a shotgun as a walking stick, and I'll tell you, that's like seeing the face a' god.

I tried to figure it all as I walked out a' Halveston and back to Wolf and Penelope. I tried to understand what the doctor was doing and why. Took me the whole walk. Half a day uphill. It weren't till the sun dipped and streaked red and yellow 'cross the sky that I figured it out. I saw my future in that sky like one a' them fortune tellers at the county fair. I was heading right for blood and gold. I was heading for a reckoning. I was heading for Kreagar and Lyon and whatever plan they both had for me. There weren't no escaping that, no matter how far north I ran, no matter if I found my parents or not. The sky don't lie. It don't know how. Sun is sun, rain is rain, storms is storms, and future is future. Didn't need no letters to read that. The doctor had taught me all I needed to know 'bout the rest a' my life in that one act. He was giving me a chance to do the right thing like he had. To face down Kreagar and face down my past 'stead a' running from 'em both. I just had to be brave enough to do it.

GOT ME A PLAN AN' I'M STICKIN' TO IT

I didn't tell no one 'bout the doctor or Lyon's man. Weren't sure why. I knew Penelope wouldn't judge me for it, knew Wolf wouldn't care none. I suppose I wanted to keep it just mine. That doctor, didn't even know his name, names are the last things to matter in this world after all, gave me something more'n pills and bandages.

I weren't ready to share that.

I gave Penelope the Doxy and told her how many and when. She was snow-pale and sweating rivers and weren't in no shape to be charming a permit clerk. It'd be a week afore she could walk and more'n that for the cut to heal right. That meant a week a' kicking my heels in the shelter cabin. A week a' hunting and trapping and tending fires and playing nursemaid when all I wanted was to get back to Halveston and find my parents. They were there, or least they had been once. I could feel it deep in my bones. My momma and daddy walked through them gates, Halveston mud stuck on their boots, dodging snakes like Bilker who tried to sell 'em their oil. Maybe that doctor had tended them, sold 'em pills or plasters. Maybe I'd seen 'em in the crowds already.

A jumbling little spark set itself in my stomach that week. Rolling about and turning my insides into twisting bugs. I was close. So damn close. But something in me said there was rocks 'tween me and my folks. Rocks shaped up like Lyon and Kreagar and all them things I done back when I didn't know better.

I kept thinking over what the doctor had done for me and Penelope. Sure didn't do it so's I could go to Lyon, tell her all them foul things I did and pay my penance, else he would a' let me go straight to the jailhouse with her lieutenant. He meant for me to find redemption in another way, no doubt by cleaning up the mess I brought into Halveston, like dirt I'd tracked in on my boots. Kreagar's charcoal face was staring out of Halveston same as mine and the doctor knew it. That meant Kreagar still weren't caught. Lyon's men and no doubt her too were in that town. That meant Lyon had a good reason to be here and, for all my bad, I weren't that good a reason. Kreagar was. He was following me, waiting for *something*, I still didn't know what, and Lyon was following the both of us.

I sat on a boulder and twirled the point a' my knife on the stone. Smoke rose out a' Halveston chimneys. Thought I heard fiddle music on the wind. Kreagar was down there or out in the woods stalking. It was time to stop running from both my chasers. I had me a plan. One cooked up on the boulder, staring out in the sky.

Spent day after day on that rock while Wolf paced around in the dirt. Every morning, after I'd checked the snares at dawn, after I'd tended Penelope and changed her dressing, after I'd filled up the flask from a babbling spring up the hill, I'd climb up that rock with my knife and stay till the sun went sleeping. I ground the nub of my knife handle into the stone. I didn't have no saw, no other blade; it was stag horn 'gainst rock and I'd make sure rock would win.

I weren't eating much in them few days. I didn't have no time left. I needed to get my knife into throwing shape if I stood any chance a' lifting myself out the shit I'd been swimming in for years.

My hands started bleeding on the second day a' grinding. Made me work all the harder. Pile a horn dust got bigger while the nub got smaller. I watched my knife, the only friend what had stuck with me through all this and knew me better'n anything, change into something new. Something what would give me freedom 'stead a more secrets. That knife, though clean and shining, was covered in all kinds a' blood. Blood what I had spilled. I told my knife there was only one left. One more time hot red would cover its blade.

Days started repeating themselves. Sky would go inky blue and black and I would climb down, find a spot on the floor a' the cabin and sleep. Fingers ached and burned and bled and then it would start all over again.

Wolf huffed and whined at me or growled whenever Penelope said something to me. They'd both got themselves into an uneasy truce. He weren't eating her and she weren't screaming every time he showed his whites. Felt a mite odd, sitting 'tween them two, being the only one either a' them would talk to. I never seen a wolf act like he was, not in a wild pack nor in all my months with this one. I weren't sure whether it was Wolf what was cracked and turning nasty or if it was Penelope who was nasty all along.

I was out on the boulder one a' them days, Wolf curled up at the base, when I heard him growl. Deep and fierce and my blood froze up in me. My head went racing to Lyon or Kreagar or a grizzly but it weren't none a' that.

Penelope was walking out the cabin, leaning heavy on a stick but walking. Cheeks rosy and looking more alive than dead for the first time in days. She had the flask in her free hand and I quick realised she was bringing it to me.

'Calm it, Wolf,' I said. 'You ain't got no quarrel with her.'

But he didn't stop. He stood up, bared all them teeth, flattened back his ears and raged at her. Penelope turned statue. Saw the fear in her eyes and I felt a river a' guilt run through me. I jumped off the rock, knife in one hand, and grabbed Wolf by the scruff.

He yelped and quick stopped making a fool a' himself.

There was something in Penelope what made his wild blood boil. Maybe he saw something I didn't in them golden curls and skinny legs. Couldn't tell, in that tiny moment, if Wolf was warning me off Penelope, off going to Halveston, off learning letters and dulling down that wild part a' me, or if he sensed all them secrets she had stuffed down inside her and knew I was in danger. I started remembering all them things she said about her daddy and how he ended up. How all her stories didn't quite make two and two into four. She was fives and sevens to that wolf and I wondered if his numbers weren't truer'n mine.

I looked her in the eye. Weren't sure what I was expecting to see, maybe all them secrets she's been trying to hide. But then I figured if people could see secrets so easy, I'd a' been swinging from the Genesis tree along with my saviour.

'You shouldn't be up,' I said, keeping the grumbling wolf behind me.

'I've been horizontal for nearly a week,' she said, hobbling closer. 'I'll go crazy if I have to stare at the holes in the roof another minute.'

I sniffed hard. All them late, cold nights had stuffed up my head. She held out the flask just out a' my reach so's I'd have to get closer. Wolf had muddled up my mind and for the first time I looked at her like she had secrets bad as mine.

'What's the matter?' she asked, her face cracked into worry.

Bit a' me wanted to lay out all my wonderings and see how many she picked up as true, see how many she squirmed out of with big eyes and big words. But the horn dust coated my hands and all the important parts a' me wanted to keep working, keep toiling till I had it perfect. No ma'am, I thought, we ain't doing this dance today.

I stepped forward and took the flask, took a drink a' that cold water. 'Nothin'.'

She nodded slow. Felt awkward for the first time. That's one thing I'll always remember 'bout Penelope. I never felt awkward with her till that moment. Even after that hog man did what he did and I was standing in front a' her, bloody and bare, it weren't awkward. Even hauling her out the river, stripping down to skin and talking 'bout her dead daddy, it weren't awkward. Something changed and I didn't like it one bit.

'What have you been doing out here?' she said. 'You've been a ghost this week, out at first light, back after dark.'

I held up the knife and the half-ground nub.

Her face lit up like a bank a' fireflies. She took the knife off me and stuck it on her finger like she did all them weeks ago. It swayed a bit, trembled, then slid off her finger.

'Close,' she said, then struggled down to pick it up. 'Once you're done, this will throw like a dart.'

I took the knife back and felt a little burst a' heat in my chest.

'Alls I got to do then is practise,' I said. And I would, all day till there weren't no chance a' me missing.

Penelope smiled at me and there weren't no lies in it.

Them next few days I came into the cabin afore sundown. Wolf wouldn't sleep inside no more and spent more and more a' his time out hunting or whatever it is wolves do in the woods. I'd find him asleep next morning outside the door or by the boulder. I figured he was mad at me for grabbing him and he'd forgive me soon enough. But damn, it broke my heart to see him getting further away every day. Felt like I was losing a part a' myself. But I needed to be inside that cabin with an hour or two of light left in the sky if I was going to save the rest a' me.

'I won't get mad this time. I swear it,' I said to Penelope. 'Teach me.'

Penelope sucked in air and tensed up. I could tell she weren't none too happy at the thought but she agreed all the same. I figured maybe she was paying me back for getting the 'biotics and not cutting off her leg. I didn't care none for the reason.

She prised a rusting nail out the wall and scratched all them letters in the floorboards. As she was doing each one I realised I remembered most all a' them. Fluttering rose up in my chest and burst out my face, turning me into a smiling idiot.

'A, B, C, D, E, F, goddamn G,' I said, almost hooting happy. I got all the way to T afore I stumbled.

Penelope was shocked as I was and she helped me rest a' the way to Z.

'There's hope for you yet,' she said, smiling and I knew, deep down, she was right.

FOUND BONES

Penelope's leg cleared up enough for her to walk without a stick and 'bout the same time I got my knife to balance perfect on her finger. I'd last seen Wolf the night afore and I felt sick about it when there weren't no sign a' him in the morning. Soon as we was ready to get moving again, I didn't want to. I wanted to wait till Wolf forgave me and came back, but I knew that weren't close to happening till Penelope were nought but a memory.

I never figured I'd have to choose 'tween them and I sure as shit never thought I'd choose her.

I learned the letters for my name and for Wolf, tree, buck, and Lyon. She said over the next few days we'd move up to five, six and seven letters, then tenses and sentences. I felt a snowflake a' fear in my gut at all that learning I had in front of me but I didn't have no time to think on it long.

Penelope was fit enough to make the trip to Halveston, although she was fretting over her hair and dress and shoes. I told her Halveston people weren't going to look twice at a bit a' mud on you. Fact was they'd probably look three times at you and follow you down the street if you didn't have no mud at all. Once we got to Halveston it'd be a quick visit to the permit office then I'd be knocking on my parents' door. I didn't know they faces but I knew they'd be smiling when they saw me. They'd go big and rosy and they'd hug me and hug me and kiss me and hold me and they wouldn't never let go.

I tell you, that snowflake in my gut turned into a blizzard the first step Penelope and me took down the hill to Halveston. Penelope was slower'n usual but she didn't complain and I kept close in case she fell. The clouds turned grey and fat and started spitting out their rain when we got to the gates.

'They might not be in town,' Penelope said, keeping her voice low and her back straight around all them people. 'Your parents, I mean.'

There couldn't be many more people in BeeCee what weren't here or in Dalston or Ridgeway and there weren't nothing north but wild. They were here. They had to be.

I didn't say nothing 'bout it to Penelope. Just nodded when she looked at me like I didn't hear her.

Halveston was a different place with a pretty face next to me. All them men what didn't even see me first time round were whistling and barking at Penelope. All the sour-faced women looked at her like she was a temptress come to steal their husbands. A woman like Penelope in a town like this, damn, that's like ice water in a drought. Everyone wants a sip and no one wants to share. Her white dress was a shade a' brown now but it didn't matter none. Them men saw bare shoulders and offered their jackets. They saw a bandage round her leg and offered to carry her to the damn moon and back. Then there was I, bulked out in coats, heaving around a pack, shorter'n the skinny goddess beside me. Hell, I may as well have been a mule for all the smiles and eyewinks I got.

'This place. . .' Penelope said, all breathy, looking all around like the town was magical. 'It's just so. . . *alive.*'

'You won't be long you walk around lookin' like a damn simpleton chasin' a balloon,' I said. 'This town ain't friendly, don't you ever think it is.'

Rain was getting harder the deeper into Halveston we got. The mud was thickening up to bad gravy and folks was putting on hats or scuttling into the saloon bars and card dens. Penelope's slippers what had survived the flood river got sucked off her feet with every step. When it happened the third time she swore up a storm, pulled off the other shoe and threw 'em both in the mud.

'It's good for the skin,' she muttered when her feet turned black.

I just laughed. For all her learning, for all her pretty face and china-white skin, she was walking through a frontier town barefoot. Weren't nothing high and proud about that.

'Good day, miss,' came a voice I recognised, all weedy and up the nose.

I was ready to tell him to go hang but I quick figured out he weren't talking to me.

'Good afternoon, sir,' said Penelope, smiling like a cat at that snake, Bilker.

Slimy shit didn't even know I was there.

'A woman as fine as yourself shouldn't be out in this downpour,' he said, hat on his head keeping off the rain, 'especially without proper attire. Please, I would be happy to show you the finest boutique in Halveston. Your man here can wait outside under the awning. I will be happy to help negotiate the cost, I have many friends in town who would be more than willing to give a discount to a beautiful lady. If you need a room for the night for yourself, I know a place with clean sheets. Maybe you and I can have a drink while your man finds other occupations.'

Penelope raised up both her eyebrows, then laughed. Not her real laugh, I knew that one, this was a laugh that said, you just said exactly the wrong thing, sir.

'Oh dear,' she said, seeing right through him, 'I fear you have misunderstood. My friend here is no man and, as I see it, neither are you.' Stanley bristled, moustache twitching, but Penelope kept going. 'I know you, sir, your type is found in every corner of this wretched country.' Stanley tried to interrupt but Penelope weren't having none of it. 'You *slither*, from person to person. I'd bet handsomely that you also sell claim papers. I'd bet more those claims are worth less than the wood pulp they're made of. Do you prise coin from dead men's hands? Or do you steal it from the living by trading on their dreams?'

Stanley puffed out his cheeks and started blabbing something that no one was paying no attention to. People around had stopped to listen and I could see, even in the rain, Stanley's cheeks turn red.

Penelope stepped closer to him and spoke louder so all them around could hear. 'Do you know why you do this? Well, do you? You're the type of man who cannot work honestly because your. . .' she nodded her head toward his manhood '. . .anatomy is severely underdeveloped.'

Laughs bubbled up from 'neath the overhang of a general store.

'Miss. . .' Stanley hissed, soft like his voice had been cut right out a' him.

I stood there, grinning wide. Then Stanley looked at me finally, recognised me, and I saw his eyes go big like fishbowls.

'You. . .' he said, turning all his anger on me.

Folks all around was laughing and jostling each other, crowd got bigger as news spread.

'Sir,' Penelope said, stern, and snapped his attention back to her, 'I do not require your services.'

Stanley looked at all the faces a' Halveston. All a' them faces smug smiling, waiting to see what he would do next. Shame is a dangerous gift to give a man like Bilker. Men like Bilker ain't got no compass guiding they actions and when you give that kind a' man a gun, you'd best be careful what you say next.

Penelope looked him right in the eye and said, 'You can go now.'

Waxed moustache trembled on his face and his hand was itching to pull out that revolver. My hand found my knife and he caught onto that. I was close enough to him to drive that blade into his gut afore he could even touch his gun.

He figured it. He was a swindler but he weren't stupid. Stanley held up both his hands and gave a bow to Penelope.

'Well done, woman,' he spat. 'I shan't bother you or your *dog* again.' Then he backed away a few steps and said, 'But Halveston is a small town. I'm sure we will cross paths again very soon.'

He pushed his way out the crowd, nearly knocking over a fella as he tried to get away.

I let all my laughter out and put my arm round Penelope's shoulders. 'Hell, girl! You may as well have cut off his pecker and given it him on a damn silver platter.'

She smiled. 'I don't think they make platters that small.'

'He won't be forgettin' that anytime soon,' I said, then realised what that meant. 'We made ourselves an enemy. Halveston's just got a lot smaller.'

The gathering a' people started to break up but one woman, done up 'gainst the rain in a heavy purple coat with gold buttons and not so much as a speck a' mud on her, came close to Penelope and shook her hand.

'I've been wanting to say that to him for years,' the woman said. She had a strange accent what Penelope told me later was pure-blood French, though I weren't sure what part a' BeeCee that was close to and I didn't care none to ask.

The woman held onto Penelope's hand and said, 'Stanley has friends in low places. Keep your eyes open.'

Penelope nodded but it weren't in fear of that little snipe, it was out a' knowing something the French woman didn't. 'My friend and I have taken care of men far worse, but I appreciate your concern, Miss. . .?'

The woman took her hand back. 'Madame. Delacroix. Amandine Delacroix.'

Penelope's body tensed up like she just been dipped in ice water.

'*Enchanté*,' Penelope said 'tween clenched teeth.

They stared at each other for a minute or two. Penelope all wide-eyed and stiff, Delacroix all knowing and amused. Penelope knew her, or least her name, but she ain't never mentioned it to me. Just another a' them secrets she got stored away in that pretty head a' hers.

Penelope and Delacroix started talking quick in a tongue I didn't have no clue over. The woman had lines round her eyes and a hard-set jaw, raven-black hair done up loose with pins, spilling out round her face. That hair could a' been down to her shoulders or down to her knees. Just like the rest a' her, I couldn't be right sure what I was seeing. Older'n me and Penelope put together. She weren't skinny but weren't padded out neither. She looked like someone out of my nana's magazines, glossy, like she had too much colour in her. She had money and she weren't afraid to show it in a town like this. Woman like that didn't take no shit from no one and Penelope knew it. I weren't at all sure what was happening 'cept that I was getting bored and my parents weren't going to find themselves.

''Scuse me,' I said, louder'n what was strictly polite, 'we got some place to be and I ain't gettin' any drier standing out here.'

Delacroix weren't too pleased with the interruption. She stopped talking, then licked all her teeth 'neath her lips. I watched the bulge a' her tongue swirl round them gums and felt a mite a' sickness in my gut.

'*Pardon, mademoiselle,*' she said and I weren't at all sure I liked what she called me.

Penelope was paler'n when she was sickest.

Delacroix's eyes lingered on me a beat longer'n they should have. Out the corner of my eye I saw all them posters a' me and Kreagar and I cursed Penelope for drawing attention to us.

'Do we have an understanding?' the woman asked her.

Penelope, stiff-like and reluctant, nodded. Delacroix smiled and said her oh-rev-wah's to us both. I watched her walk away, though it weren't like any walk I'd ever seen. That coat hugged her body and she near glided over that mud, a purple hourglass full a' sand and secrets. A group a' men were waiting for her. I squinted at them through the rain and saw their dandy clothes. Dandy men in Halveston. Dandy men what I'd seen before.

'We're goin',' I said and grabbed Penelope's arm. She weren't arguing and let herself be dragged.

It was early afternoon but there was a darkness in Halveston that made it feel like midnight. No sun high in the sky, just black clouds full a' rain, and a town full a' danger. That woman had made Penelope tense and quiet but after I made a joke 'bout her bare feet, she loosened up.

Even though they was on every post, Penelope only pointed out my poster once and that was to say they didn't get my hair right. I kept it short but the poster had it down to my collar.

'Shave it off and nobody will recognise you,' she said.

I was tempted but then I figured my parents wouldn't take too kindly to some skin-headed girl claiming to be their daughter turning up unannounced.

We asked for directions to the permit office. Other side a' town. Small brick building 'tween a brothel what used a rusting airplane wing for a sign, and an eating house with red plastic chairs outside. Made sense, I thought, you buy yourself a claim, then go get fed and celebrate with a girl or boy what can't say no. This town was full a' traps made to separate coin from purse.

'So you gonna tell me?' I asked as we walked.

Penelope didn't look at me. 'Tell you what?'

'Don't play dumb shit with me,' I said. 'You know what.'

Penelope wiped wet hair off her forehead. 'Bought and paid for, remember.'

'Wouldn't a' figured it'd be a woman what bought you.'

I don't know why but I took her hand then and held it tight. Them days on that boat, in them crates, were best forgotten.

'What you agree with her?' I asked.

Penelope sighed. 'That I'd pay her back before the end of the month or I work off the debt on my back.'

'How much?'

She laughed, all bitter-like. 'Too much.'

I squeezed her hand and an idea popped right into my head. All smiles, I said, 'Hell, my parents must be rich as sin, all these years up here, they'll give that Delacroix woman a damn truckload a' gold if I ask them to.'

'Elka. . .' Penelope said but I weren't listening.

'All we got to do is find them. You'll be free a' that debt afore mornin'.'

'I don't—'

'You save me, I save you, remember,' I said and she smiled, sad. 'Pick up the pace and we can give her the coin afore sundown.'

'All right,' she said but she didn't sound certain.

I was so giddy with it all I didn't hear the tone, didn't hear her true meaning, didn't hear the warning. But damn, my parents were here, I felt it. And we was going to find them today.

The permit clerk was a thin man in an open-collared shirt. He was squirrelly with a beard what only seemed to grow on his neck and chin. Rest a' his face was baby-smooth. He could a' been forty but that skin made him look no more'n twenty.

'Help you?' he said when we walked in. No one else was there but the office was laid out like it had room for two dozen. The clerk had a desk with two chairs in front of it what we sat in. Behind him was rows and rows a' metal cabinets and stacks a' paper.

'We're looking to find some folks who leased a claim a

while back,' Penelope said. All them nerves she had after meeting Delacroix was gone.

Clerk sighed. 'Can't help you. We don't give out that kind of information.'

Penelope looked like her daddy died all over again. Pain painted up her face and she shuffled closer to the desk.

'Please, it's very important, we have to find them.'

'Rules are rules,' he said but not as firm.

'Oh,' Penelope said with a smile, 'couldn't you bend the rules just this once? My friend is looking for her parents.'

Clerk sighed again but Penelope's smile was gold to a penniless miner.

'I'd be really, *really* grateful if you could help us out,' she said, fluttering them eyelashes.

'Well. . .' Clerk said and Penelope knew she had him, 'I can't give you the information but if you found it yourself. . .'

Penelope smiled along with him, understanding just what he was saying. 'I'd love to slip behind there and rifle through your papers,' she said.

I groaned but I saw hearts spring up in that clerk's eyes. Weren't the only thing springing up neither.

Clerk nodded feverish-like and said, 'I'll go dig out the claim papers. They're right at the back. . . where we won't be disturbed.'

Then he dashed off 'tween them metal cabinets. I turned quick to Penelope and said, quiet, 'You ain't gonna do what I think you're gonna do, are you?'

She frowned at me and said, 'What do you take me for? I want you to make yourself scarce, go get something to eat or something. Leave me the pack and your knife, you know, just in case.'

'I ain't leavin' you alone with him.'

Penelope put her hands on my shoulders. 'I can handle him. Just tell me your parents' names and leave me the knife.'

'I ain't happy about this,' I said.

Penelope smiled then kissed me on the cheek. 'Trust me.'

I did. Hang me for it but I did trust that girl. I told her the names and the year they went, all words what was burned into my head from my momma's letter. I gave Penelope the knife what she put at the top a' the pack. Knife on its own raises questions. Knife in a bag ain't looked at twice.

'You coming?' shouted the clerk. 'There's a huge stack of papers here for you.'

I groaned again. 'Kick him hard in the nethers he tries anything.'

'I will.'

Then I left her in that office and never asked what happened 'tween them metal cabinets. Rain was coming down hard now and the town had turned ghost. No one in the streets, shutters locked up 'gainst the wind. The rain was a mercy. It made my face in them posters run into a black smudge. First time I felt I could walk about that town safe, though it weren't no pleasure. My boots were good boots but they was having a hell of a time in that mud. Penelope in her bare feet didn't stand a chance.

Lucky thing I knew where was selling boots cheap and I had more'n enough coin for a pair. I picked my way through town to the doctor's office and his barrow. Figured the bad luck of wearing dead man's boots was worth the risk.

Doctor was sat on his porch, shotgun 'cross his lap. Barrow was right next to him, piled high.

'Didn't think I'd see you again,' he said, though it weren't a friendly greeting.

He was in shadow, didn't get up, didn't seem in no mood for visitors.

'In need a' some boots,' I said.

'You've got boots.'

'For my friend, what cut her leg. She's better now thanks to you,' I said. I was looking round for the boy who was taking the coin but he weren't nowhere. I pulled out a few dollars. 'I got money for 'em.'

'I don't want your money,' he said, something dark in his tone.

I spotted a pair at the top a' the pile what looked about the right size. Probably a young lad's, not all that worn out neither.

'What you want then?' I said and got close enough to snatch them boots if I needed.

Doctor saw what I was thinking like I was shouting it out loud. He slid the barrel of the shotgun 'tween the tied laces and lifted up that pair a' boots.

'Him,' he said, voice cracking. 'I want my son back.'

My heart sunk down to my feet. His lad had sold the shoes.

'What happened to him?' I asked.

The doctor looked at them shoes with red eyes I could see even through the shadows. 'He was found two days ago in the woods. His. . . legs were gone,' tears rolled fat and free down his cheeks, 'they were cut off like he was jointed. We found,' he almost couldn't get the words out, 'we found a fire. There were. . . there were bones.'

He dropped the shoes and broke down, sobbing into his white sleeve. Burning bile rose up in me. Rain soaked me to the skin but I couldn't feel it. I was all burning raging hating darkness. I told myself it couldn't be. Couldn't be him.

'Did your boy have his hair?' I asked. I had to be sure.

The doctor looked up at me, confused, like I was talking in tongues. 'How do you know about that?'

Goddamn him. Kreagar killed the boy but the bears and wolves found him afore the law did, took the meat right off his bones. Every bit a' rage I had boiled up inside me. I saw everything Kreagar had done in that doctor's eyes and I cursed myself for bringing hell down on him. Kreagar followed me right to this good man's door.

'I. . .' I said, trying to pick out all the right words but there weren't no right words. There'd never be right words again. 'I'll find the man what did this. I swear it. I'll find him and I'll kill him. Ten times over, I'll kill him.'

He looked me with iron in his eyes. 'How'd you know him?'

'Don't matter how.'

Doctor stood up. 'You brought this monster to my door and it doesn't matter?'

I shook my head, sent raindrops flinging. 'He's been hunting me all winter.'

He sneered. 'Wish he'd caught you. Wish he'd killed you instead of my boy. My beautiful boy.'

A deep-down sorrow surged up in me and turned the world black. 'So do I,' I said. 'And he still might, 'less I get him first. I'll do my damnedest to get him first for what he done. I swear it up and down.'

The doctor reached down and picked up the shoes. He flung 'em at me, all the fight gone right out a' him, and said, 'I hope your friend knows what you are. God help her.'

I caught the boots. Weren't no need for a thank you. This good, kind man was far beyond thank you. He was broken and it was me what broke him. Kreagar may have held the knife but I was his hand. I always was.

I held them boots close to my chest and I ran. Ran through

them streets till they all started looking the same. The rain weren't showing no signs a' stopping and the day was fading into night. I found my way to a whisky den, the doctor's words and his tears ringing in my ears. I needed to drown him out. I was seeing all them things what I done, might a' done, could a' done. Seeing what Kreagar done when he was Trapper and I was blind. I saw it all laid out in front a' me like the Mussa valley from the top a' the ridge. All them memories tried to force their way back into my head. Felt like it would kill me stone dead if I let them.

They found bones. Doctor's voice was hot in my ears. I needed something hotter.

'Three fingers,' I said to the bartender and pointed to a bottle behind the bar.

He poured me a drink and took my money.

Firewater burned my throat and sent white-hot spikes into my gut.

Colby's dollars, those what had paid for my body, got me two more glasses and change. That was enough.

Kreagar's words stuck in my head like porcupine spines. *Think on why I ain't killin' you.*

I took another drink and the spikes dulled.

I was never the type a' person to hide my truth at the bottom of a bottle but I weren't near close to strong enough to face it right then. Seeing that doctor, kindest man I ever met, gutted and bleeding because a' me, was more'n I could take.

I just weren't that strong and it was ice-clear that I never was. I had to clear the devil and angel off my shoulders. I had to throw the weight a' all this off my back.

I stumbled out the bar and saw right what I needed to do. The jailhouse, lit up in the dark, stood watch at the top a' the hill. Its eyes right on me. I started walking toward it, through the empty streets, feet sloshing in the mud. Toward Lyon and all them questions she would ask me. Toward a jail cell and a life a' chains. I'd tell her everything I knew 'bout Kreagar and she'd catch up. At least I wouldn't be running no more, I said to myself. At least it would finally be over.

Hand grabbed mine, excited voice said in my ear, 'Elka, I found them.'

I spun round to Penelope, legs covered in mud from running, hair and dress soaked from the rain. I didn't right understand what she'd said. My blood was thick with drink and fear and I couldn't a' told you my name if you whispered it in my ear.

I looked back at the jailhouse then back to Penelope, saw her through cloudy eyes. Couldn't think a' nothing else to do so I handed her the boots. She took them without paying them no mind.

'Did you hear me?' she said, then pulled me round to look her in the eye. 'I found your parents.'

ROAD TO TUCKET

Sat in a quiet corner of a poky gin joint called Pershing's Rest, I made Penelope repeat them words over and over again. The rotgut got to my head and I was ready to walk up to Lyon and damn near bend over. I couldn't do that. Not with Penelope riding on my back. She needed my folks' money much as I did. I weren't going to let her work off that debt, a debt what weren't truly hers, being the pleasure a' men like the hog.

I told her, in my slurring words, that I was sorry for even thinking a' leaving her. She weren't sure what I was talking about but she told me it was all right, she told me she understood and she put her arms around me, held me tight.

Shit, I ain't never been drunk afore and I didn't choose the best water for the first time. Halveston bartenders cut their whisky with paint thinner and chilli peppers, ain't no wonder I couldn't see straight. Ain't no wonder I was ready to give up my life because Kreagar killed some kid I didn't know. Kreagar killed a lot a' folk.

'Your parents,' Penelope said, clicking her fingers front a' my face to get me to pay attention. 'I wouldn't have believed it if I hadn't seen the documents myself. They bought a remote claim just outside Tucket about fifteen years ago. No death record for either of them so chances are they're still up there.'

'Where in the hell is Tucket?' I said.

'About fifty miles north-west.'

'Fifty miles. . .' I said and planted my face in my hands. Four days' walk, less if I was on my own and didn't stop to eat. 'Son bitch. . . goddamn son of a bitch.'

'Elka—'

'I thought I was done. I thought they was here and I could. . . I could stop runnin', stop fightin'.' All my tears came out my eyes.

'What are you running from?' Penelope asked.

'Him,' I slammed my fists on the table, 'him, him, him. That goddamn murderin' bastard, Kreagar Hallet. He ain't never gonna stop till he finds me. Till he kills me n'all.'

'The man who raised you,' Penelope said like she was putting all the pieces together, 'and the one who murdered Lyon's son?'

'He killed a boy in town not two days ago.'

'That spotty clerk told me,' Penelope said, shaking her head, 'he said there were. . .' she looked me sideways in the eye like she weren't at all sure how I was going to react '. . . strange circumstances, with the boy's legs.'

'Bears and wolves take their dinner wherever they can,' I said.

Penelope gave me one a' her looks what I couldn't figure. Something like confusion, something like pity. She opened her mouth to say something more but must a' thought better of it. Weren't nothing else to say. Kreagar killed a boy, no doubt like he'd done god knows how many times afore. Animals picked at what was left. That's that. Just bad luck on the part a' the boy what meant a full belly for a beast. Ain't nothing else to it.

Penelope looked down at the table, started scratching at the wood grain like she couldn't bring herself to look me in the eye. Then she said in a quiet voice, 'Do you think he's in town?'

'He'll be close. Wherever I am, he ain't far,' I said and she looked up at me, all the strange look gone out her face, replaced with pure worry. Whether that was for me or for her own skin, I weren't sure.

'He's out there,' I said, 'in the wild, tauntin' me. He's breathin' down my damn neck waiting for me to. . . shit, I don't even know.'

Penelope put her hand over my fist. 'Then we go to Tucket. We get the hell out of here.'

I looked up into her eyes and, as swimming as mine were, they seen her straight. She had just as much reason to want out a' Halveston as I did. Way I saw it, we didn't have no choice.

'You and me, Elka,' she said. 'Lyon will find Hallet, Delacroix won't find us and if she does. . . well, maybe your parents can help. We'll be rid of them all.'

The fog a' drink was lifting off me like a winter blanket put away for the summer. I turned my fist round and put my fingers 'tween Penelope's.

'Rid of 'em all,' I said.

Outside, the rain was easing and night was thick and black. Penelope talked us into a back room a' Pershing's and I was mighty pleased to see there was a bolt on the inside a' the door. We both lay down that night on a single cot, 'neath the same blanket. I weren't sure if it was the drink or the company but I slept sound and woke up at dawn with a head 'bout ready to split open. Penelope said she ain't got no sympathy for me and made me wash my face in a horse trough before she'd give me time a' day.

Penelope flirted her way to a good coat and, along with that lad's boots, she finally looked like a stiff wind wouldn't blow her over. I'd spent most all a' Colby's coins, what Penelope gave me a look what could melt stone for, but we had enough left over for a breakfast a' corned beef hash and a side a' chilli beans to share 'tween us. Tell you truth, Penelope ate most all of it. When she weren't picking at roast squirrels on a stick, that girl could eat. My belly weren't feeling at all right and I left it mostly empty the rest a' the day.

We didn't go back to the shelter cabin. Weren't no point. We'd cleared it out when we came to Halveston and there weren't no Wolf waiting there for me. Penelope had got herself a map from the clerk and marked out my parents' claim in thick pencil so when we left that town, we left it with a firm idea a' where we was going. Truth of it was, it sure felt good to have a line on a map to follow 'stead a' just my wits and gut.

'You better catch us some rabbits tonight,' Penelope said when we was walking north through Halveston.

I mumbled that I would and felt sore for spending all them coins. Sore in pride and sore in my head. Halveston was waking up. Hawkers shouted all round me, every word cutting through my ears and ringing round my skull like dynamite through rock. Every step was sloshing up my insides, making my mouth fill up with water and stinging bile. If this was drinking. . . shit. Told Penelope over and

over not to let me go near a bottle again. Tenth time I said
it she told me to shut up or she'd smash one over my head.

On our way out a' Halveston I spotted the weasel man,
Bilker, and gave him a smug nod. He stood there looking
like he had a fish-hook stuck in his lip. I weren't afraid a'
him coming after us no more. We wouldn't be even close
to Halveston when he finally got his tail out from 'tween
his legs.

We didn't stay long on the road out a' town. I don't like
roads, they invite trouble and questions. Half mile outside
the town limits we hiked up into the forest. The line to Tucket
steered us west enough to keep clear a' the Damn Stupid
craters and torn-up land in the far North. There could be
a mountain a' gold up there ripe for picking but it weren't
worth it. I didn't ever want to see that ravage again. Didn't
want to hear the land moaning, crying out its sorrows on
the wind. I knew it was there and that was enough. Figured
I might go there one day, pay my respects, say sorry for all
them human ills but now weren't the time. I needed life
around me. Penelope and my folks and my wolf. I needed
the trees and critters and berries and bracken. The quiet
and calm of things what weren't changing or falling down
around my ears.

This was a forest a' pure beauty. We was too far north
now for the lodgepole pines but black and white spruce and
some a' them alpine firs covered everything. Moss crawled
up rocks and strangling ivy tightened round trunks. Forest
was thick and the air hung round in a mist most a' the day.
Smelled a' softness and warm and like them first days a'
spring, even this far into summer. This forest was alive, I felt
it in every bit a' me. Exciting chatter a' squirrels and crickets,
tracks and trails a' deer and moose, no sign a' man's heavy

hand. It was one a' them forests what you can hear breathe in and out and what seems to curl round you in the night.

Penelope didn't seem to pay much mind to the forest. I reckon all she saw was trees and more trees and I thought, that's a damn shame. With the dead boy's boots on her feet, she mostly kept up and we made good time that morning. My head cleared up and my gut stopped shaking by 'bout midday. Penelope must a' noticed me perking up 'cause she started talking for the first time.

Didn't much like what she started talking about.

'What was he like?' she said and my insides went twisty.

'Who?' But I knew.

'Hallet,' she said. 'He raised you, and you had no idea what. . . what he was?'

'He's a man,' I said, stepping over a lichen-bloomed rock. 'I always knew that.'

Penelope huffed a bit then creased up her forehead. 'A man couldn't do what he did. He's a monster.'

I laughed. 'Ain't no monster. Monsters ain't real 'cept in kids' imaginations, under the beds, in the closets. We live in a world a' men and there ain't no good come out of tellin' them they monsters. Makes 'em think they ain't done nothin' wrong, that it's their nature and they can't do nothin' to change that. Callin' 'em a monster makes 'em somethin' different from the rest of us but they ain't. They just men, flesh and bone and blood. Bad'uns, truth, but men all the same. What Colby did to us was worse than bad but that don't make him a monster. He chose what he did same as I choose to snare a rabbit for eatin'. Am I a monster?'

Penelope shook her head.

'Then he ain't neither. He's just a bastard. Nothin' a man can do can make him stop bein' a man.'

Penelope didn't say nothing more right away, she kept that frown on her head and didn't look at me. Maybe I shouldn't a' brought up Colby, maybe it was too raw to be talking a' him in the same breath as Kreagar.

'What was Hallet like, as a man?' she asked me.

Tell you the truth I hadn't thought about who Kreagar was afore he was Kreagar in months. That man what I knew, Trapper, he was dead. Had his throat slit by Kreagar's charcoal face in Dalston and by Lyon's icy words and by me knowing they was truer'n anything. I ain't never talked about him, not to no one.

'I called him Trapper,' I said, picking each word careful out my head. 'He found me in the woods when I was seven. I stole a piece a' jerky off his porch, see, and he chased me with a shotgun. Damn though, that jerky was worth it. Ain't never had the like outside that hut. Afore him I was with my nana, her cooking was boiled beef and dirt compared to Trapper's.'

Penelope half smiled at me. Figured she didn't like me speaking well of a man like Kreagar. But I carried on anyway.

'He taught me things,' I said, remembering all them lessons with a tiny heart swell. 'How to hunt, trap, find rabbit runs for snares. Taught me what plants I could eat and what would kill me stone dead. All them things what have kept us alive and fed out here the last few weeks are 'cause a' him. Can't be forgettin' that just 'cause he done awful things to other people. He always taught me in a way what I understood, no matter how old I was.'

'He sounds. . . nice,' she said, though I felt her pain to say it.

'He had a temper on him somethin' rotten a' course,' I said, then pulled up my sleeve and showed her a line a' little white scars on my forearm. 'Got them when I set off a marten trap by mistake. He prised it off me then made me sleep outside for three nights for ruinin' his trap. He said no critter gonna come close to a trap what's stunk all up with human blood. Might as well throw the damn thing in the river.'

'He and my father sound like kindred spirits,' Penelope said, sad but smiling.

I helped her over top of a sharp-edged boulder, one a' them what got kicked up by the Damn Stupid and hadn't had time to get softened by the wind and rain. They was all over this forest and made the walking slower'n I would a' liked.

'You don't say much 'bout him.'

'There isn't much to say. He's dead.'

'I figure that's when there's the most to say. Ain't no one arguin' with you.'

Penelope didn't say nothing for a quarter mile. She just stared at them boots and kept her footing.

'He liked books,' she said, 'and newspapers, magazines, everything written. He and his father kept everything from before the Fall. I grew up reading about a lost world.'

'Can't a' been much worse than this one.'

'My father told me it was a cold war at first, nothing happened, no one died. Then it just *happened*. They attacked or we did, I don't think anyone knows for sure anymore. Bombs started falling, people thought the world would be changed,' she said, keeping pace with me. 'There was so much tension, so much paranoia, neighbours turning on neighbours, rich on poor. So when the war broke out, it was like the dam finally broke. It lasted years, killed god knows how many people, tore the world apart. Even heard some people in White Top call it the Cleanse. When it was over, it was a new start but nobody won.'

Her voice turned sour and her face twisted up to match. 'The world didn't change. There is still murder, still rape and fighting. We fucked it up,' she said. 'We had this chance, this clean slate, and we just carried on the same as we always have.'

I knew what she was talking 'bout, knew why she was sore over it. I seen all them evils a' this world first-hand and they done damage to me I don't even know about yet.

'I suppose it ain't what's different now that's more fearful,' I said, 'it's what stayed the same. I grown up from a seed in this world, don't know no other. I lived each day like I weren't gonna get no food nor water. Every day I did was a good day. I can't expect more'n that. In truth, girl like me can't expect much a' this life and I never have. You got to live in the here-now, not the back-then. Else you'll send yourself mad.'

'Is that why you didn't see what Hallet was doing? You didn't add up all the pieces from *back-then* and figure it out. Ever think you could have stopped him killing?'

She'd turned fierce on me, taken her own hurting and made it my fault. I didn't like it one bit.

'You want to be careful with what you say next,' I said, turning my voice hard as flint. 'I like you, Penelope, but you make out like I killed them women and that kid along with him and we're done. That French woman and all them hog men can have you.'

Penelope flinched and sighed heavy like all the air and fierce went out a' her at once.

'I'm sorry,' she said, 'I don't think that, I didn't mean that. I just wish. . .' She stopped short a' actually saying anything 'bout herself.

Instead she said, 'I suppose even those closest to us can be strangers.'

Way she said it told me she knew that all too well.

'Your daddy?' I asked.

She nodded. Didn't say more and I didn't ask more. I figured she'd tell me 'bout him when we was far enough away from him and his memory that she weren't afraid no more. That could be Tucket, hell, that could be the moon for all I knew, but I weren't going to push. I wouldn't have no one pushing me so I couldn't right expect the same a' her.

'I like to think, Elka, that if you'd known,' she said slow, 'that you would have turned him in.'

I liked to think that too, but in truth, I ain't sure if I would. Trapper was the only family I had and it was like a knife in my chest to leave that. I could a' turned him in, told Lyon that hell yes I knew him and he was in a hut ten miles off the dirt track out a' Ridgeway. I should a'. Then the doctor's boy would still be breathing.

But hell, if I followed that road a' thought, I wouldn't a' run from Lyon, wouldn't a' ended up in Colby's crate what meant I wouldn't a' found Penelope. She'd be in Delacroix's cat house right now if I'd turned him in. Ain't no changing it and I wouldn't, knowing what I know now.

'Can't be livin' in the back-then,' I said, ''cause it'll damn near break your heart.'

Penelope smiled and said, 'I grew up in a house obsessed with the past. It's hard to let go.'

'By the sounds of it you and your daddy lived a damn fine life down south,' I said, stopping at the edge of a stream to fill up the flask.

'Few years after Mother died, Father became sick of

treating White Top's rich,' she said, crouching down to splash her face. 'He said they were the ones that caused all the heartache of the world and he felt as if, by setting their broken bones or curing their children's sore throats, he was just as bad. So he dragged me up here to administer to the miners. That's where he was needed most, he said.'

'Somethin' true awful must a' happened 'tween there and that lake,' I said, taking a long drink from the flask. I weren't expecting her to tell me and she didn't.

'We should speed up,' she said, smiling all stiff at me.

I laughed to myself and she saw it. We was playing a game, me and her, and hell if it wasn't a little bit fun. I ain't never cared 'bout another person and what they been through in their lives but Penelope had me snared up like a rabbit first time out its hole. First time I saw her I thought this girl ain't going to last the night. But, strike me, she did and she kept lasting and kept surviving and I ain't never met no one like that. First time I think in all my life, what must have been close to eighteen years by then, I didn't want to be alone in the wild. Strange feeling that I ain't never felt with no one else. Penelope got under my skin, dug them long nails in, and weren't going nowhere.

We didn't talk much more that day. Couple a' times Penelope pointed out a mushroom or plant fat with berries and asked if we could eat 'em. Only if she wanted to be toes up afore sunup, I said, but found her a few cloudberries sweet as honey what stopped her moaning for a few hours.

Hour or two afore sundown, we found a spot to camp. I left Penelope the Reverend's tinder box and quick told her how to get a fire going. Then I headed off into the woods to set snares. They was a long shot, we weren't going to be there long past dawn, but I figured it couldn't hurt to set 'em. Dusk was coming what meant the deer would be on the move. Found me a trail and quick set my last two heavy snares into spring traps. Set a few simple snares round rabbit runs then picked my way back to camp.

Penelope sat there, grin spread wide across her face, all lit up by roaring firelight.

'Look!' she said, voice all squealy.

My eyes caught the tinder box. She'd used most all the wax paper when I would a' done it with a piece the size a' my fingernail. Year ago I would a' tore her down for that, wasting tinder ain't nothing to be proud of, but right then, I didn't care one stitch. She could a' used the straps off the pack to light that fire and I still would a' been happy for her.

'Shit,' I said, sitting down and warming up my hands. 'Soon as you catch your first rabbit, you ain't gonna need me no more.'

She laughed, that ringing bell sound what meant it was true, then put her long arm round my shoulders, pulled me close and kissed me hard on the side a' the head.

'Sorry my dear, but you're stuck with me,' she said and let me go, fat smile still on her face.

'Shit,' I mumbled and she punched me in the arm. Girl could hit harder'n I thought.

Full a' surprises she was.

'I figure we walked just shy a' thirty miles,' I said. 'This pace, we'll be in Tucket afore sundown tomorrow.'

Penelope turned serious. 'Do you want to go straight to your parents' claim?'

Strange squirmy feeling set itself in my belly. 'Don't know,' I said. 'What. . . what would you do?'

She took a long breath. I could see them thoughts churning up 'neath that blonde hair. 'I would. . . I would get to

Tucket tomorrow, find a room, then approach them in daylight.'

I nodded along with her.

Then I heard a *snap* out in the trees and the tell-tale thudding on dirt. I sprang up, pulled my knife out my belt and told Penelope to stay put, keep the fire high. She knew better'n to argue or ask questions now.

I dashed off into the forest, heart right up in my mouth I was so excited. Found my trap and in the last light a' the spring day, I saw a small, pale brown shape struggling. I came up on it slow. It was young and small, but more'n enough for me and Penelope. We'd be feasting tonight. I got closer, through a stand a' cottonwood trees. It weren't moving quite right for a deer, maybe it was lame or its blood-line way back was affected by the Damn Stupid bombs. Still good eating on it though.

I hadn't had deer since that last buck I shot with Trapper near a year ago. First time he let me pull the trigger. That feeling, that rush a' heat and excitement, came back to me now. All them deer I skinned and gutted with him didn't feel like this one. They was bigger, hide smoother, hair that little bit longer.

The deer saw me and froze. I put my knife in my belt and put my hands out to it, giving all the *shh* noises I could. Step by step I came up on it, then when I was close enough—

'Hey! Get away from him!' Man came screaming out the trees.

I fell backward, pulled out my knife and held it out ready to cut.

The man, black-skinned and with a brace a' rabbits slung over his shoulder, held his hands up.

'Please,' he said, voice gone soft, 'please, my son.'

In the dying light, I looked again at what was caught in my snare. I scrambled backward, till my back smacked 'gainst a tree and I couldn't go no further. Blood pounded in my ears and cut out any sound. Weren't a deer. Weren't a deer. Weren't a buck or a doe or a yearling.

It was a boy and he was crying.

The man knelt down and freed the boy's leg from my snare. The kid stood up and clung onto his daddy.

'I'm sorry, I'm sorry, I'm sorry,' I breathed them words in and out of me and I stared hard at that child, fluffy black hair on him, 'I didn't see, I couldn't see.'

The man looked at me with a deep frown on his face. 'No harm done,' he said and he said it kind and I didn't right believe the tone.

'He should know better than to go wandering off,' the man said, smiling and stroking the boy's hair.

'Mark,' the man said, held out a hand to me, 'Thompson. This is Josh. Is that your fire back there?'

Penelope. My gut froze.

'I saw the light,' he said, warm in his voice but the rest a' him was shaking. 'I'll trade you a rabbit for some heat tonight.'

He grinned and it was one a' them real grins. I didn't have no fear for the fella right then but the boy caught in my snare had shook me up something awful and there weren't no way I was letting my guard down around them two. Not now, not never.

THAT THOMPSON BOY

Penelope sprung up when she saw me leading the Thompson fella to the fire. She grabbed up a thick log and held it ready to bring down on his head. Then she saw the boy, clinging to his daddy's shirttail. I told her I caught us dinner and laughed. She dropped the log onto the fire and looked at the pair a' them wary. You got to have a hell of a good reason to be out in a forest this far up the world. They weren't dressed for it neither. The man's shirt, green once, was ripped up and muddy, with blood-stains from them two rabbits. The boy had on a T-shirt in much the same state. No coat. No pack.

'We's tradin' fire for a full belly,' I said by way of explanation.

'Elka,' Penelope said quiet to me, eyeing Mark, 'are you sure?'

I thought a second on what I could a' done to that boy and said, 'Damn sure.'

Penelope nodded, pushed past me to hold out her hand to Mark. 'I'm Penelope. Are you going to give us any trouble?'

She weren't smiling. Weren't joking.

'You'll get no trouble from us,' he said, solemn like he was praying, and held his boy close. 'I hope you'll do me and my son the same courtesy.'

Penelope caught my eye, saw me nod. 'Well all right then.' She smiled and winked at the boy. 'Hungry?'

She took them rabbits off Mark's shoulder and took my knife off me. We all sat round the fire and her and Mark each skinned a rabbit while me and the boy stayed quiet.

Mark and Penelope was chatting like they was long-lost lovers and I ain't never seen her so at ease.

'My sister lives in Tucket,' he said, 'I'm to work in her lumberyard.'

Me and Penelope looked at each other with a smile. Mark was so skinny he looked like the rumble of a circular saw would shake him to splinters.

I didn't hear much a' what they was saying, just kept my eyes and wits sharp. All this noise, all this light and smell a' rabbit could bring bears. Most though, I kept my eyes on Mark. He had thick black stubble on his face and eyes what looked like they hadn't seen sleep in days. Figured he was only five or so years older'n Penelope, them lines on his face was hard-living, not long-living.

'You two travelling on your own?' he said, sticking one a' them rabbits on the stick over the fire.

Neither a' us said anything.

'What happened to you both?' Penelope said, taking the questioning away from us.

Man put his hand on the boy's back. 'Josh and I were

on the road from Halveston. We were attacked. They took everything.'

'Roads is for damn fools,' I said, shaking my head at him.

'You're not wrong about that,' he said. 'I'll be sticking to the woods from now on.'

The fella had kind eyes and wouldn't let his son more'n six inches away from him. Felt my muscles relaxing. Conversation went stale and quiet then so Mark turned his attention on me.

'Funny name that,' Mark said, 'Elka. I've never heard it before.'

I smiled and pulled one a' the rabbits off the fire. 'My momma said my daddy found me out in the forest one day, just a baby wailin' in the trees. It was only when he wrapped me up in elk hide that I shut the hell up and fell right to sleep. My momma said what's why they called me Elka, 'stead a' Elk, on account a' me bein' a girl.'

Penelope laughed. She ain't never asked 'bout my name so she ain't never heard its tale.

'Is that true?' she said.

'Course it's true,' I said, smiling. 'You think I'd lie about somethin' as important as my own name?'

The boy giggled then quick went quiet when we noticed.

'Very glad to meet you, Elka,' Mark said. 'And you, Penelope.'

I figured it was the fire but Penelope's cheeks bloomed red and she gave that man a smile the like a' which I ain't never seen on that face a' hers. That smile came right through her eyes.

Mark and his boy stripped that rabbit clean to the bone. I felt bad for the kid and his rumbling belly, so's I gave him my share a' the catch. Mark looked at me smiling and him and

Penelope chatted 'bout things I didn't care for. I watched the boy scratch patterns in the ground with a stick. Night was heavy on us all and the cold was creeping close to our little circle a' warm.

'You can both sleep close to the fire,' I said when the chatting quieted and the boy was close to falling asleep 'gainst his daddy's arm. 'But you even breathe in the wrong direction and that son'll be the only one you'll ever have,' I pointed my knife to his nethers and he shuffled backward, 'you get me?'

He nodded frantic and said, 'Yes ma'am, I get you. Nothing will happen, I swear it. You saved my son, I owe you.'

I nearly killed your son, I thought but didn't say nothing.

'Goodnight, Mark,' Penelope said, smiling soft, then stood up with me and we both moved a few steps further from the fire. We lay down side by side and I put myself and my knife 'tween her and him.

'They're good people,' Penelope said right in my ear so they couldn't hear. 'You could be nicer.'

'All people are good till they ain't no more,' I said. 'Now shut up and go to sleep.'

Heard her sigh and heard the man whisper calming words to his boy. I turned onto my side so I could keep my eye on them. Mark sat up 'gainst a tree with the boy nestled up comfy by his side. Mop a' black hair resting on his daddy's belly. Mark saw me looking and gave me a smile and a nod. Then he closed his eyes, rested his head back 'gainst the tree and tried to find sleep. Maybe he was a good sort. Ain't never seen a man take care a' his kid like that.

Trapper once gave me the warmer blanket when we was on a two-day hunt. Said I didn't have no meat on me yet, least not enough to keep the chill out. That weren't Kreagar doing that. Kreagar wouldn't a' given me shit. He'd a' let me freeze if it meant he didn't. Trapper was the man I called Daddy when he weren't close enough to hear. Kreagar was the man I wanted to kill. They was two men in my head what just happened to have the same face. I had made peace with that. It was the only part a' my past what I could make peace with. Everything else was a fog stuck 'tween my ears. But hell, that fog was clearing quick and for the first time I had an idea a' what I'd see on the other side.

I stayed awake all night. I watched the moon through the trees start on one side a' the sky and end on the other. Mark and his boy didn't stir. Nor did Penelope. I woke her up afore dawn, gentle and quiet.

'We got to move,' I said. 'Afore they wake up.'

'What? Why?' she said, all blurry from sleep.

'You know why. We fed 'em, we kept 'em warm, we can't be babysittin'.'

She sat up, looked 'tween me and them, still sleeping 'gainst that tree. I thought she'd argue with me, talk about 'moral duty' and 'he's just a kid' but she didn't do none a' that.

Instead she said, 'You're right.' Then got up, silent as a snake sliding through grass.

We collected all our things and crept away without waking them. I felt a mite a' guilt 'bout leaving them but Penelope laid out three branches into a big ole arrow and scratched the word *Tucket* in the ground.

'I won't leave them to get lost,' she said and I didn't say nothing about it.

Once we got far enough away, and the sun was just starting to pull itself up the sky, I said, 'What made you think they was good people?'

'Just a feeling. Instinct.'

'You trust that?'

'Yes,' she said, firm, 'I just don't always follow it. Like with James. My instinct said he was trouble but he was just so charming. I won't make that mistake again.'

I laughed. 'My gut don't know shit when it comes to people. It told me every word out a' Colby was god's truth. It didn't say nothin' about Kreagar neither.'

Penelope laughed too and told me to stick to the forest.

'Only time my gut been right about someone is when it told me to get away from Lyon, far and fast and don't be lookin' back.'

'She's relentless,' Penelope said, shaking her head. 'I heard she started off as a sheriff a few towns west of White Top. There was a shooting in a gambling den and a kid who was washing dishes got killed. She didn't know the boy from Adam but she tracked the shooter all the way to Couver City, found him in a rail station. Rumour was she tied the man to the back of her horse and dragged him the whole way back to White Top.'

I swallowed back stinging bile and asked her if the fella lived. Couldn't keep the tremble out my voice.

'After a three-day ride? I heard that when they untied him and rolled him onto his back, there wasn't a scrap of skin left on him. You could see his skull, ribs, pelvis, all the way down to his feet. His bones had deep scratches from the road, they guessed he died early on the first day. She told everyone exactly what she did. The dead boy's parents called her a hero.'

Tremble moved into my hands, into my fingers. I held the filed-down handle of my knife.

'She was made Magistrate soon after that,' Penelope said.

'She won't stop until she has Hallet. Who knows what she'll do to him for murdering her own son?' Then she shivered, though it weren't cold. 'God help him, because he's the only one who can.'

GOOD FOLK A' TUCKET

We got to Tucket close to sundown. Both a' us weary and hungry and without so much as a penny 'tween us for room or board. Penelope's story 'bout Lyon was playing out in my head over and over. I saw that shooter's skull, scraped clean a' flesh, laughing at me.

Kreagar done the bad to Lyon's son but she figured I knew about it, helped him maybe, knew where the poor kid's body was. There weren't no way I was going to convince her otherwise 'less my plan, my damn fine plan what I'd ground my knife handle down for, worked. Shit, it had to work 'cause there weren't no way I was running for the rest a' my life. In truth, I didn't know how much further I could go, there weren't all that much land left 'tween me and the great blue. I was living on borrowed luck and there was only so many times it would get me out a' scrapes. Figured my chances were just about used up.

At least here, in Tucket, I'd bought me some time. It was barely a town but first thing I saw was there weren't no charcoal pictures a' me or Kreagar on posts and walls. Long arm a' Lyon hadn't got this far north yet, but it wouldn't take long – couple a' months, weeks maybe. Them feelings and fears 'bout her and Kreagar got pushed back in my head and a bigger worry came smashing 'tween my ears.

My parents. After so many years, so many miles, so many people 'tween there and here, I found it hard to believe they could be so close. This was the top a' the world, a handful a' buildings smack in the middle a' Nothing and Nowhere. All the smarts said they was here. The words from my momma's letter said they went through Halveston. Permit office said they went to Tucket. Weren't no death notices for 'em. All I knew led me here but, hell, my gut was churning and saying don't be so foolish, Elka, you ain't that lucky.

Saw a few people wandering about Tucket. My momma could be that woman sweeping her porch. My daddy could be that fella pushing a barrow. I didn't even know what they looked like.

Tucket weren't big. It was a curve of a town, following the path of a narrow river. The lumberyard Mark talked 'bout sat sprawling and low on the other side of the water. Clunky wooden bridge joined up the two halves a' the town. Heard the chug a' the generator and the buzzing of a saw cutting beautiful spruces down to planks. Made my stomach turn but I suppose most people expect a roof over they heads. Ain't going to get a roof just by wishing for it.

Rest a' Tucket was a group a' small wooden shacks and one a' everything. One general store. One claim office. One gold buyer. One boarding house. One drinking hole. All fitted with heavy storm shutters and public shelters in case a' thunderheads. The only people round were more mud and shame than men. They sat quiet on stoops and doorways, hats pulled down on sleeping faces outside the bar, sense a' loss and disappointment weighed heavy on that town, pushing it down deep in the mud.

Course not all folks wore their melancholy so open. Few men – women too – were strutting round like roosters showing off their combs. As Penelope and me trudged through the town, we saw them roosters all had one thing in common. Every one a' them carried a mason jar full a shining golden flakes. Out in the open, proud as a stag just got his sixteenth point. Had me a feeling that all them folks sobbing into a finger a' whisky used to have jars just like 'em.

'What they do with it?' I asked Penelope. 'That yella' stuff. Who's buyin' it?'

Penelope spotted a rooster and her jar and figured out my meaning. 'I'm not sure. But I heard some of the southern cities have pretty much rebuilt themselves. They'll want jewellery.'

Felt a fish-hook in my lip at mention a' jewellery. 'All this diggin' and toilin' for a couple a' shiny trinkets?'

'Shiny trinkets and frivolous spending make people forget what world they're living in. Why do you think it's so valuable?'

I huffed. Seemed a fool way to spend your coins but if it made my parents richer'n god then I suppose I couldn't much complain. Though looking 'bout this town, it didn't look like anyone was rich, not really. Doubt was heavy on my shoulders and I didn't like it, not one bit.

Night was coming up quick and it brought with it a breath a' cold what told a' the coming winter. This far north we had maybe a month and half afore the first snow, less if it was one a' them years with a sting in its tail. Some years snow comes right when you're having your midsummer cookout. Sometimes it won't come till you're putting up the streamers for Christmas. Ain't no way of knowing for certain, you just got to listen to the wind, feel it on your skin, hear what it's telling you. This wind was telling me don't get too comfy, Elka girl, you got a long, dark night ahead a' you.

'We ain't got no coin,' I said. 'We sleepin' in the woods?'

Penelope smiled at me and told me to follow her. Her sharp eyes had picked out something I'd missed and that put me right on edge. I weren't used to the back foot. It weren't no fun place, but after all this, I figured Penelope knew what she was doing.

But she damn well didn't.

We was walking to the bridge over the river. On the other side, at the lumberyard, I saw a reunion 'tween a man and a woman. Mark and the boy had made it to Tucket in 'bout the same time as us and he was there, hugging what I figured must be his sister.

I grabbed Penelope's arm and said, 'Not a chance. We ain't stayin' with them.'

'Why not?'

I pulled her back, out the middle a' the road.

'Too dangerous,' I said and I weren't meaning for us.

'Don't be ridiculous. They're good people.' Penelope had a frown on her what could curdle cream. She yanked her arm free a' me.

'Exactly. They're fine people,' I said, hissing out my words, 'and I don't want them to come to a bad end.'

'What are you talking about?' Penelope asked, looking at me like I was one a' them loons right out their cage.

I pulled her in close so no one around could hear. 'If that man and his boy help us out, help *me* out, that's enough

to put 'em in harm's way if they ain't already.' Penelope
tried to interrupt me but I weren't having it. 'That doctor in
Halveston, he helped me, he was the kindest soul I met this
side a' Couver City. Kreagar knew it, don't ask me how but
he did, and now that doctor's son is dead. All 'cause a' me.
I ain't havin' no more blood on my hands.'

Penelope relaxed, her face broke into sympathy. 'That
was a coincidence. A horrible, terrible coincidence, but you
can't blame yourself. Hallet isn't here, is he? He's down in
Halveston.'

I shook my head, felt my fear boiling up to rage. 'Kreagar
is *everywhere*. He's a hunter, a damn fine one, you ain't gonna
see him till he wants you to and by then he's already lined
up his shot. He's here. I can feel it.'

'Elka,' Penelope said, put both her hands on my arms,
'calm down. He's not here. He's not watching us and if he
is, that boy has got his family around him to protect him.
Nothing is going to happen to them but I'd really, *really* like
to sleep under a roof tonight.'

I looked her in the eye, saw pleading, saw dog-tiredness,
saw a kind a' certainty I didn't have. Them eyes was telling
me to trust her. Wolf would a' growled and said no, ma'am.
Suddenly felt an aching in my chest for that beast. He had
it simple: a forest, a saddle a' rabbit, that was all he needed
and time was it was all I needed. I looked over my shoulder
at the lumberyard, lamps burning in the low light, voices
shouting happy tidings carrying on the air, across that calm
river. Penelope was saying to me, though not using her
words, that her and me belonged with people, not sleeping
in the dirt. Wolf didn't like people, that was plain, and few
months ago nor did I, but I had me a cloud in my head.

In truth, I didn't know right what to do.

And I chose wrong.

I nodded to Penelope and walked half a step behind her across that bridge. Stood half a step behind her when we came up on the lumberyard. Mark and his sister stood outside a pair a' big barn doors, painted red once but faded to blood-brown. His face lit up the dusk when he saw us coming.

The boy was by the barn. He chucked sawdust in the air and ran about 'neath the flurry. Motes a' pale yellow, flakes a' wood what had been spruce and alder and cherry and oak, covered his hair, turning it from black to white, like he had the sun rising behind him, lighting him up. He was smiling wide and laughing. Nothing like the boy I met in the woods. That made it all the worse. My stomach swirled and churned like an eddy in a high river. Stuck in one place, trying to force itself out a' the corner and sail down the stream free as wind. I watched that boy spinning like a sycamore seed 'neath that sawdust as Penelope talked her way into the Thompsons' house. I felt like my insides was turning to stone. Felt like I was cracking up and splitting down the middle.

The Thompson sister was saying my name. Tore my eyes off the boy and looked at her. Smooth brown skin and black hair cut down to her scalp. Arms what had felt true work, hauling lumber no doubt, and a scar along her chin too perfect to be from a milling accident.

Her name was Josie and she said I was welcome at her table anytime. I shook her hand. Rough as mine and strong. She was taller'n me but only by a hair. I liked her and I didn't make no bones about it.

'Thank you,' I said and smiled true, a bit a' relief in me that the boy had a woman with arms like that to look out for him. 'Penelope been wantin' a proper roof over her head for weeks.'

'We have plenty of space,' Josie said, voice like sunburn and smoke. 'You got Mark here to work on time and that's worthy of a master suite.'

She nudged her brother but his face twinged like the joke weren't funny. Penelope was smiling at Mark like they was back in the woods, all twinkles in her eyes and I felt a mite squirmy being so close to 'em. Stomach sank at the thought a' making talk with 'em all evening.

Josie led us all round the barn and mill yard to a small house sitting out on its own in the middle of a field. I knew it was a field, 'stead a' just *land*, on account a' the fence. I don't like fences. They're like teeth sprouting out from the earth, sharp and open, a trap waiting to spring. You ring your patch with teeth and you make a mouth what's going to swallow you up. A fence is a way a' showing the world what exactly you got claim to. In my head that just makes it all the more easy to take away.

The house was one with stairs up the middle, a second floor and bedrooms off all sides. It was the biggest house I ever been in and was made mostly out a' stone. Felt old inside, maybe even made afore the Damn Stupid. Carpet on the floor worn down to threads. Cracks running through plaster walls. Paintings in frames hung skewed. Place smelt a' woodsmoke and barbecue sauce and the long hallway carried the sound a' clattering pots from the kitchen. More people. More people Kreagar could choose.

Josie's husband, pale as chalk and hair colour a' that sawdust, came jogging down the hall, smiling and wiping his hands on a cloth. Jethro. Josie and Jethro. They had music in their names and music in the way they moved, grabbing each

other, kissing cheeks, hands shaking mine and Penelope's
and Mark's, all without pause. Jethro was a coiled-up spring
where Josie was water. He jittered, she flowed.

Much as I tried to keep myself cold to them, they had
something in them what warmed me up, melted my ice. I
cursed 'em for it later, when the snow came and the world
went to shit. But right then, I was happy for the fire and the
food and the company. Six a' us sat round a scratched-up
wooden table in the middle a' the kitchen, Jethro stirred
pots, served up plates a' ribs and piles a' potatoes and
greens. I ate like it was my last meal and it sure felt like it
was. Sat next to the boy, seeing his eyes light up, shoving fists
a' mash in his mouth. Didn't know it then, what was going
to happen. Not like I know it now. But my body, my wits, was
telling me something.

Demon settled in my gut, took up a home there, put
himself up a fence. What I owed to Penelope stopped me
from running out that door. I stayed quiet most the night,
kept my eyes down. Soon Josie stopped trying to talk to
me, soon the boy fell asleep 'gainst my arm. They laughed.
I didn't.

Mark and Penelope asked each other question after
question – why you got that bandage on your leg, where
you travelling from, White Top? Beautiful town. I watched
them, turned toward each other in their chairs, paying no
mind to no one else at the table. Josie and Jethro had eyes
on Penelope too, you couldn't help it. She was a beauty no
doubt and she made everyone laugh and smile and forget.
Even the boy seemed to like her. It was like I was looking in
from outside. It was normal and human and they was having
fun and I realised how happy I was for Penelope that she got
to speak to someone other'n me.

Night drew in and Penelope and me shared a room. It had two narrow beds either side of a small table and no matter how soft that mattress, how heavy that blanket, I couldn't find no comfort. Couldn't close my eyes for seeing Kreagar. Saw him walk through the door. Saw him climb through the window. Saw him standing on my bed, scrap a' hair and blood in his fist. Brown hair. Boy hair.

No sir, I couldn't find no comfort.

Penelope slept like she ain't got no secrets. A thunderhead wouldn't a' woken her 'less it threw her up in the sky. She opened her eyes to watery dawn and smiled at me, asked me how I slept.

'Nervous?' she said, still wrapped up in the blanket.

'What I got to be nervous 'bout?' But I knew. I knew exactly.

'When did you last see them?' she asked.

She sat up and rubbed her head, her hair stuck out all over like a squirrel tail.

I shrugged. Didn't know when I last seen 'em. In truth, I didn't remember ever seeing 'em. Felt like this was a goose chase when the goose already went south for winter.

'You don't have to come,' I said. 'You can stay here and make house with these folks.'

Penelope raised her eyebrows at me, set her jaw hard, and told me to shut up and get dressed.

'We're leaving after breakfast,' she said.

And we did. Breakfast a' fried eggs and thick bacon. We left with promises to come back and see them all soon. Penelope left Mark with a smile and a kiss on the cheek. Left the boy with the same. I ain't the kissing type.

Walking helped my nerves. When you're walking, you ain't really anywhere. I could walk forever, keeping moving, keeping going. You ain't got to make conversation. You ain't got to explain yourself. Penelope read the map, kept us going straight. I walked out a' Tucket with a rock in my chest. Sharp and cold and pressing right down on the core a' me. I saw Kreagar in every man we passed by, saw him 'tween the trees when we got up into the woods, saw him staring out at me from still water. Figured it was only a matter of time afore one a' them phantoms was real. He was getting closer to me or maybe I was getting closer to figuring out his words, figuring out why he didn't kill me on the Reverend's table.

I was. Them doors in my head was rattling 'gainst their chains.

My parents would help, they'd protect me, they'd forgive me. That's what parents do, ain't it?

'We're close,' Penelope said. 'That ridge up there, it's this one on the map. The claim should be just the other side. If we follow the river, we'll be there in an hour.'

This close, my gut started twisting. I'd always imagined my folks would run at me, arms open, cheering they joy at seeing the daughter they left behind, throwing up gold like confetti. Didn't cross my mind the truth of it. This far north the cold don't just freeze you. It don't just crack your skin and stop your heart. It turns you to ice on the inside. People up here were hard as the ground, they say howdy with a rifle, and there ain't no reason my parents wouldn't be the same, if they was there at all.

MY PARENTS

The Tin River claim, what my parents owned, sat on the inside bend a' the river. The water made the land into a pocket, the ridge behind it acting like a natural barrier to the weather. Penelope said the river was a shoot a' the Yukon, come wending its way 'cross the land, leaving gold like a trail. A log cabin sat square in the middle a' the flat land, just out a' flood reach. Spruce and fir grew up tall and strong behind the cabin, rising up onto the ridge some ways. There weren't no other shack or road or person in sight and after the few months I'd had, it was a goddamn paradise.

Penelope nudged me, smiling, and opened her mouth to call out but I grabbed her arm.

'Not yet,' I said.

Something weren't right.

A wooden sluice box sat quiet and dry on the grass, moss growing up its side. A handful a' green plastic pans, some broke, some covered in black mould, was strewn about all over the place. A water pump was rusting near the bank. The hole they'd dug in the land, running along the length a' the river bend, was more a meadow now. Summer wildflowers grew up in clumps, covered up forgotten pipes and shovels.

No one stirred inside the cabin.

Only sounds on the claim was birds tweeting in the trees, the rushing a' the river, rustling a' rabbits and small critters preparing for winter. Sound a' my heart. Sound a' Penelope breathing.

I started walking to the cabin. You can't never be sure in these parts. My momma or daddy could a' seen us coming, could be waiting behind the door with twin barrels a' buck shot. I stepped up onto the porch, heart beating right in my mouth.

'Momma?' I said, loud enough to get through the door. 'Daddy?'

Expected one a' them to throw open the door, wrap me up in they arms and say, my girl, we could a' shot you!

But they didn't.

Door weren't even closed. It was getting on for noon but there was only darkness in that cabin. I looked behind me. Eyes found Penelope standing a ways back, arms crossed over her chest, deep creases a' worry in her forehead.

'Ain't no one here,' I shouted. 'Looks like there ain't been no one here for least a year.'

Penelope dropped her arms and started walking to me. Halfway she stopped. Strange look passed over her face.

I didn't pay it no mind at first, 'stead I pushed open the door. Smell a' dust and damp hit me. Saw holes in the roof right off, a branch in there clogging out the light. Single room, bed on one side covered with a sheet hanging from the ceiling like a canopy. Black iron wood burner sat in the middle a' the room, chimney twisted and useless. Pile a' logs. Pots and pans. Window looked out onto the river, not that you'd know it for all the grime. Place looked like a hungry bear been through it and found not much a' anything, 'cept maybe whatever was under that sheet.

Penelope called me from somewhere outside.

I found her behind the cabin, staring down at a scrap a' earth.

'What's that?' I said.

She turned around and stepped to the side. She weren't staring at a scrap a' earth. She was staring at the wooden cross stuck in it.

'It says Phillip,' she said. 'Your father.'

Twinges ran through me. Short, sharp pains in my hands and feet and head.

'You said they was alive,' I said, all quiet.

'I said there was no death record.'

Next to the grave was a half-dug pit. A grave what didn't get filled.

'Only one a' them,' I said. 'Maybe Momma's still living, off with a new man in Halveston or some such place.'

I weren't convincing no one, least of all me. Thought a' that sheet over the bed and my toes went cold.

I went back in the cabin and stood beside that bed, Penelope with me.

'Want me to do it?' she said and I said yes.

Slow, she lifted up the sheet. Saw the feet first. Grey and withered. Then the rest a' her. Dried out like tinder. Dead lips pulled back over her teeth made it look like she was screaming at the world. 'Tween her hands, them hands what wrote my letter, lying on her chest, was a shovel, still caked with dirt. She must a' buried her man then came in here to sleep and just not woken up. Surprised the bears didn't find her.

'Hi Momma,' I whispered.

I didn't realise I was shaking all over till Penelope put her hand on my arm. Then around my shoulders. Then pulled me into a hug. I ain't much for hugging on a normal day but this weren't no normal day. I held onto Penelope like I was holding onto life. I must a' cried but I don't remember now. Everything came crashing down on top a' me. All them hopes I had of a loving family, arms round me, telling me them three *I love you* words what no one ever had.

'I'm sorry,' I said into her collar.

'What for?'

'There ain't no gold to pay that French woman.'

'It's OK,' she whispered, 'I'll be OK.'

I buried my momma next to my daddy. Penelope made a cross and carved her name on it.

Muriel.

Made me wonder brief what my name was. That weren't something I'd thought about, not in my whole life, till I saw that wood marked. I wondered what would be written on my cross. Elka weren't the name these folk gave me or what my nana called me but everyone who knew my real name was dead. Weren't no one left to know me as what these folk intended, weren't no one left to ask. I was dead now what meant no one was going to help me.

'Should we make death records for them?' I asked Penelope when we drove that cross into the dirt.

She stood quiet for a while, looked all round the claim, at the river and the sluices.

'Not yet,' she said then went inside the cabin.

I stayed outside. Weren't no way I was going back in there yet.

My parents was dead. People what I didn't know from a shit in the woods. They was all I had this last year. They was all I was shooting for.

Now what? What was left for me now 'cept a killer on my tail and the law closing in round my neck? What was left? I turned away from them graves and the people what slept in them and went down to the riverbank.

Tin River was pure wild. I watched a pair a' deer, a doe and her young, snipping shoots on the other side a' the water. A big cow moose walked slow and steady far to the east. The smell of it was more a drug than all the whisky in Halveston, fresh and crisp and full a' truth. Ain't no lies out in the wild, 'cept what people take with 'em. Ain't no disappointments. Things are what they are. Pine trees smell a' pine. Bright red berries are warning you not to eat 'em. Bear won't try to kill you 'less they think you're trying first.

I kicked the rusted-up pump, sent a rain a' brown flakes into the grass. It didn't look in too bad shape, though I didn't know shit about machines. I can build a smokehouse in an afternoon with a knife and a handful a' nails but ask me to clean an oil filter and you might as well throw that engine off a cliff all the good I'd do.

Heard Penelope in the cabin, clattering about, throwing junk out the door. Huffing and wiping her forehead.

'Find a broom,' she shouted in a tone what weren't friendly.

If she hadn't found one, there weren't one in that tiny cabin.

I went into the trees, found a nice straight sapling and

some bracken. Ten minutes later I went into the hut and asked her what needed sweeping.

'We should make this place habitable,' she said, took the broom off me. 'Can you climb onto the roof, try to dislodge that branch?'

I felt like my arms and legs was made a' metal. Everything was slow and difficult. Every time I caught a glimpse a' them graves the weight got heavier. Felt like it was pushing on the inside a' me. Trying to get out a' the breaks in my skin. My nose was full a' the smell of it. My mouth wanted to shout it. My eyes wanted to cry it. My ears wanted to block it all out.

But I couldn't break. There weren't no sense to it. Night would come soon and bitter cold would come with it. Ain't no time for grieving in the wild. I weren't going to be the next person to die in that cabin and nor was Penelope. I got up on the roof and started chopping limbs off the branch to free it.

There was some good to it, I suppose. With my momma and daddy dead, they didn't have to know what I'd turned into. They'd remember me as that pretty baby they left in Ridgeway. Maybe they died thinking I'd turned into a school teacher or married a kind fella. They'd never know about Kreagar and all them things we did. They wouldn't get Lyon knocking on their door.

That was a mercy right there.

I hoped they died thinking good a' me, if they thought 'bout me at all.

I sawed off that last limb with the teeth on the back a' my blade and hauled the branch out the roof, threw it on the ground. The hole weren't that bad.

I could fix it. I could fix it all.

Penelope tidied up the inside a' the cabin, swept out all

the dry leaves and dust. I used the sides a' the sluice boxes
– least the planks what weren't rotten – to fix the roof and
by sundown we had ourselves a mostly closed-up cabin.
Together we straightened the chimney pipe and she set a
roaring blaze going in the stove.

We burned them sheets.

Sat on stools, not a crumb to eat, we kept that fire hot as
the cold crept in.

'What do we do?' I asked.

My head was full a' buzzing flies and my eyes kept seeing
my momma's dried-out feet.

'Nothing tonight,' Penelope said.

Her face was pale, even in firelight, and blank. For the
first time, I didn't have a clue what she was thinking and it
didn't look like she was close to telling me.

'Are you all right?' she asked me, after a few minutes
a' quiet.

'Will be, soon,' I said. 'You?'

She looked at me. Her eyes were red and I weren't sure if
it was from the fire or dust or something worse.

'We're safe here for now,' she said, felt like she was choos-
ing her words careful. 'Officially, your parents are still alive,
which means they still own the claim.'

'What if people find out they dead?'

'Then the claim goes to the highest bidder and we don't
have two coins to rub together.'

'And we don't have nowhere to go,' I said, finishing up
her words.

We'd been at Tin River less'n a day but I liked it. It was
quiet, away from people, away from danger. Felt like I was
back at Trapper's hut. I could hunt here. I could build
A-frames to stretch deer hide and trade it in Tucket for

steel traps and maybe a shotgun 'case a' bears. I could build a smokehouse and make some a' that jerky what me and Trapper made. Penelope could tend the hut, help clean the kills, keep the fire lit. Maybe we could even find a few flakes a' gold.

'How do we stay here?' I said. 'I want to stay here.'

Penelope breathed in deep, figured all the options.

'We lie. Then we mine this place down to the last flake to pay off Delacroix, if she ever finds us.'

Felt like laughing.

'I don't know shit 'bout gettin' metal out the dirt. And what you mean we lie?'

'Your parents will have claim papers somewhere.'

She explained the whole process a' *bequeathing* a claim to a relative or friend and in truth I weren't paying no attention. I didn't understand most of it and I trusted she needed this place more'n I did so weren't 'bout to lie. Long and short a' it was, we find the claim papers, fake some signatures, then go back to Tucket and file the papers with the clerk. She said if we found gold afore we did all this, that gold was worth 'bout as much as gravel out the river.

We found the claim papers the next day, hidden 'neath a loose floorboard. Also found a mason jar near half full a' nuggets the size a' my fingernails. No dust. No flakes. Goddamn chunks.

Penelope gave a whoop a' joy at seeing it. She said we could buy new sluice boxes, fix the pump, maybe buy a wooden rocker and some new shovels. I said we'd need a rifle too, in case a' bears.

'How you know so much 'bout minin'?' I asked.

Penelope was practising my daddy's mark on a bit a'

paper. After a few tries she got it as close as if it was his ghost guiding her hand.

'When my father said we'd be travelling north to the mining towns, I started researching. I read half a dozen books and articles about it, and about the most common injuries and illnesses the miners get. To better treat them.'

'Damn good job you did else we'd be up shit creek right 'bout now,' I said.

'At least we know there's gold here,' she said, nodding at that jar on the table. That yellow metal gleamed and twinkled in the sunlight, felt like it was putting me under a spell. I just wanted to touch it, wanted to hold it close and wanted to show what I found to anyone I saw. Here, look, this is mine and I'm a goddamn god walking now.

'Why don't we just buy the claim with all this?' I said.

'Why give it up when we don't have to?' Penelope said, smiling, and I couldn't much argue with that.

'Is Elka short for something?' she said, pen over a dotted line. 'I'll need to put a full name.'

'Put yours,' I said and her forehead crumpled up like the paper.

'Why?'

'My parents didn't name me Elka. Kreagar did. What means he'll know I'm here. What means Lyon will too. Put yours.'

Penelope looked at me close. Sunlight came bright through the window, lit up that gold, lit up her eyes and her hair the same colour. She ain't never looked prettier.

I'll always remember her like that.

'You know what you're doing right?' she said. 'You realise what you're giving me?'

I shrugged. 'A pile a' dirt. A falling-down cabin.'

'A home,' she said. 'A piece of the world to call mine.'

'I'd like to hope I can stay long as I want, too,' I said, smiling, showing off all my teeth.

Turns out that weren't all that long.

'TWEEN A RABID WOLF
AND A RAVINE

Penelope went to file them papers with the clerk in Tucket the next day. She said they looked at her funny but stamped 'em all the same. Signatures matched and it was such a remote claim what hadn't posted any gold finds in the last few years, they didn't much care who dug it. No fuss. Claim was hers and weren't no one what could take it away. It was easy, she said, easier'n she ever thought it would be.

That made me nervous.

She didn't take none a' them nuggets with her but she didn't come back to Tin River that afternoon empty-handed neither. She had an official, *bona-fide* claim permit and another piece a' paper, folded in half, what she gave to me. Look a' death on her face.

I unfolded the paper and it was like looking in a charcoal mirror.

'Shit,' I said.

'They're all over Tucket. They weren't there yesterday. And that isn't the worst of it,' she said, breathing heavy, pacing all round the room. 'Delacroix's men,' she said, voice going up high, scraping her hands through her hair, 'the ones she had with her in Halveston. Far too well-dressed for a place like Tucket.'

My face was all over and there was people in that town what had seen it. Delacroix's dandies had seen it too. And them nice Thompson folks.

Penelope must a' seen where my thoughts were headed. She put out her hand and said, sneering look on her face, 'Before you accuse Mark and Josie of turning you in, I went to see them.'

'They seen this?'

'I asked them not to say anything, told them you were a victim, not a criminal. They'll stay quiet.'

I hissed out all my air. 'Ain't no tellin' for how long.'

I crushed up that paper and threw it on the floor. It rolled, then started to unravel. My face twisted and grew and stared at me.

'I didn't tell them where we were, if that's what you're worried about,' Penelope said.

I didn't care none for her tone. 'Course I'm worried. This my life you got in your hands.'

She turned on me something fierce. 'And what about my life? Huh? If those men find me I'll end up chained to a bed, fucked by strangers until I die from it. They followed us to Tucket, Elka, so much for covering our tracks. I thought you knew what you were doing.'

Time was I'd a' slammed her up against the wall, thrown her clean out the door but not now. I seen the fear in her, same as I'd see it in a trapped rabbit. They're meek and mild till you back 'em into a corner, threaten their life. I had me a mite more patience these days but it wouldn't last forever.

'Your life *is* my life, you goddamn idiot.' I stood up and came up close to her, tried to keep my voice calm. 'We's tied up together now. We got to get rid a' Delacroix. We got to get rid a' Lyon and Kreagar. Shit, Kreagar finds me, he finds you and he won't think twice on guttin' you like a trout. Ain't no way I'm lettin' that happen and I got a goddamn plan for that. A plan what's either gonna free me or kill me.' I stopped, voice cracked at them last words.

She looked down, kicked her feet on the boards.

'I just didn't count on a damn madam wanting you,' I muttered. Then a thought hit my head. 'Why does she? How'd you know who she was?'

Penelope's jaw clenched up like a duck's arse underwater. She took a breath and something in her changed, a bit a' relaxing, a brick fell out a' wall somewhere.

She said, 'I was sold to her, don't you remember?'

She weren't kidding 'bout bought and paid for. Pity for the girl welled up in me. I had a taste a' what it felt like to be traded for coin and it weren't something I liked to think on.

'Course I remember that. I figured that's how she knew you, but how'd you know her?'

'I overheard her name, her voice, when the. . .' she went all bitter, '*sale*, was made.'

'You ain't never said who sold you.'

She huffed all her air out her nose and said, 'It doesn't matter now.'

'Horse shit it don't matter. Course it does. I ought a' find that snake and make me a damn belt out of it.'

But she weren't budging. I tried to get it out of her but she quick shut up like a clam and didn't say nothing for a while. I was mad at her for that. She put me in the middle a' Delacroix and her dandies and weren't giving me no good reason as to why. I walked circles round that room with iron in my head, hot and pressing on my eyes, causing a world a' pain.

The whole world was coming in on us, all sides, all spikes and crushing and slicing and wanting a piece of us both. We'd had two days a' quiet. Two days a' peace after I buried my momma. We washed in the river. We watched the dusk colours paint up the sky. I caught a salmon out the river, full a' eggs and ready to spawn, and I don't have no time for fish. Except there. In Tin River I had time and I had stomach for fish and for company and, shit, I didn't even realise when I started crying. I just wanted calm. I wanted to be free of it all.

I went out the cabin and shouted my rage. Shouted it into the wild. Cursed the French woman. Cursed Lyon. Cursed Kreagar. Cursed all them folks what was stopping us from having a life.

Took me till next morning to calm down. I spent most a' that night throwing my knife, practising my aim, driving that blade deep as I could into the tree trunk. Penelope gave up trying to get me to come inside at sundown.

I couldn't be living with all the knives ready at my back. I had to rid myself of at least one a' them.

Hour or so after sunup, I pulled my blade out the tree the hundredth time and something clicked in my head. Back in the cabin, Penelope was already awake and stoking up the fire for a brew.

'Reckon that in that jar is enough to pay off Delacroix?' I said.

'Probably, but then we won't have anything left for the equipment.'

'Ain't no guarantee we'd find anythin' else in that dirt. We could spend it all and have nothin' to give her,'

I said, rubbing my face like I could make it change 'neath my hands.

Penelope went quiet. We didn't have many choices. We'd found us a piece a' paradise and even though that mark on that claim paper weren't my daddy's, rubber stamp and the law said this place was ours now.

'We're stuck smack 'tween a rabid wolf and a damn dead drop ravine,' I said, 'and we only got a month or so afore winter comes and locks up the ground.'

Look on Penelope's face said she knew it. I thought 'bout how I'd get myself out that situation. I could jump off the edge a' that ravine but there weren't no guarantee I'd be alive at the bottom, weren't no guarantee that wolf wouldn't jump after me and keep chasing. I ain't got no time to build a bridge. I ain't got no weapon left to fight it. All I got is to get the attention a' something worse than the wolf and hope I can slip away when they're clawing at each other.

'Lyon,' I said.

Penelope looked up at me from beside the burner. 'What about her?'

'I can't imagine what that French woman does is on the right side a' the law.'

Penelope raised her eyebrows. 'Very much not.'

'Lyon's all about the right side a' the law and I got somethin' she wants.'

'What? You're not going to turn yourself in? Elka, you can't,' she said, firm as rock. She stood up, put herself 'tween me and the door.

'Don't go spittin' glass, girl, I ain't got no plans to end up in one a' her cells.'

Instead a' pointing at me, she crossed her arms and said, 'What then?'

'You ever heard that phrase, catch two rabbits with one snare?'

Penelope frowned, opened her mouth to say something then changed her mind. 'Stead she said, 'I've heard a version of it.'

'I figured a way a' skinnin' both them rabbits.'

That frown got deeper. 'What do you have that she wants?'

I took a long breath to give me time to find the words. I weren't at all sure what Penelope was going to say.

'I know where her son is buried,' I said and her eyes went bug-wide.

'How do you know that?' she said and I heard a quaking in her voice.

Could tell she didn't really want to know the answer but I had to tell it. It was one a' them locked rooms in my head and I was ready to turn the key.

'I dug the grave.'

TWO RABBITS

Penelope helped me write the note on the back a' my wanted poster. Every few minutes she asked if I was sure 'bout this, if I knew what I was doing. She was different. Like we'd built a bridge 'tween us in all these months and I'd just knocked out one a' the supports. Bridge was still there, still holding, and you could just 'bout walk across it but it weren't wholly stable. Weren't wholly safe. I figured it was a shock, what I done to that boy. But at the time, I weren't at all sure what I was doing. I didn't see a boy when I threw dirt on them bones and flesh and skin. I saw an animal. Didn't realise the only animal was the shirtless, bloody man holding the knife.

'I'm sure,' I said. 'Two rabbits. One snare.'

'And if it doesn't work?'

'Then you can give Delacroix that gold and hope that Mark fella is as sweet on you as you are on him,' I said and winked.

Her cheeks bloomed red and the bridge got a little steadier.

'Read it to me,' I said.

Penelope took a deep breath and coughed dust out her throat.

'Magistrate Lyon, you've been looking for me a long time, and with good reason. I know where your son is and I will tell you if you do something for me first. In Halveston lives a woman named Amandine Delacroix. With a man who goes by the name of James Colby, they kidnap young girls and traffic them in crates via the Ellery ferry boat. Stop her and I will tell you where your boy is. Once she is in jail where she belongs, post official notice outside the Tucket general store.

'I didn't sign it,' she said.

'Good,' I said. Felt sick down deep in my gut.

'How does this kill two rabbits?'

'Delacroix goes to jail and Lyon goes all the way back down south to Ridgeway. Ain't no way she's trustin' that to her lieutenants. She'll be wantin' to see what's left a' her boy face to face.'

'What is left?'

Bones, I thought, but didn't say nothing. We'd have a few weeks if this worked. And then winter would come down fierce on this country, making travel north near impossible. I felt the cold in the air, like Death himself breathing over my shoulder, just waiting for me to step wrong. Two rabbits gone. One big damn bear left and he weren't going down without a fight.

Dead a' night I went back to Tucket. The town was dark, not so much as a torch burning in a window. By starlight and a sliver a' moon, I found the general store and the board they used for town announcements. I pinned the note up there, right 'tween posters a' me and Kreagar.

I weren't the praying type but I said a few words then to the great spirit. To whatever god it was looking over me. I said I was sorry for what I done and I said I'd make it right, if this worked, I'd make it right. Wolves howled in the forests, far away in the mountains. Their voices carried on the still night, and I figured that was sign enough my words been heard.

I walked out a' Tucket without that weight in me. First time I had hope that me and Penelope would make it through all this. Tin River was a three-hour trek and I might as well a' been skipping, all that happy bursting out my feet.

But all the scheming and fear and closeness to humans and time in towns had dulled my wild. Didn't even cross my head that someone else in Tucket was awake that time a' night. Didn't cross my head that they was looking 'specially for me. A year ago I would a' run circles on my way back to the hut to throw off tailers but I didn't that night. I walked a crow line to Tin River and I was followed the whole damn way.

SNAKES

I woke up next morning with a feeling a' lightness all through me. Sun was spilling in through the window and Penelope was snoring soft and sweet on the bed. I'd slept sound on the floor, better on hard wood than on feathers and fluff. Nuthatches and warblers made music in the trees outside and there weren't more'n a breath a' wind to disturb them.

I snuck out quiet so's not to wake Penelope, and went down to the river. Mist laid low over the water and the marsh and meadow on the far side. Sense a' deep-down calm in the world. Weren't no sound but for the birds and trickling water. I washed my face in the river and went out into the woods to the west a' the cabin. I'd set up the last couple a' snares I had a few miles into the trees and went to check for breakfast.

Felt like home in them woods. Felt like I'd been a part of 'em since birth and before. My kin had worked this land and my blood was buried with 'em in the ground. In Trapper's hut it took me years to feel more'n just a visiting nuisance. The way a' Tin River weren't the way a' Trapper. It weren't his house, his rules, it was mine and Penelope's and we was making it work.

Two a' the snares weren't touched but one caught a rabbit on the neck, killed it afore I even got to it. Now normal times you want a rabbit to still be kicking when you find it. Otherwise ain't no telling when it died and rotting meat ain't no one's idea of a good morning. But this little fella was still warm and in the cold north, that mean he was fresh as if I killed him myself. I cut him free afore the blood attracted worse.

Then I heard the scream.

Then I heard my name in that scream.

I ran.

That rabbit bounced around in my hand but I weren't letting it go. Ain't no sense in wasting food when that girl could a' just had a bad dream.

But shit, I ran like I had a whole wolf pack on my tail. Felt them in the trees, running alongside me. They jumped over logs and brush with me. They leapt a patch a' bog and caught me on the other side when I stumbled. Them wolves weren't chasing me, they was guiding me. They was my rush and panic. They was my heart and soul and teeth and claws.

I burst out the woods. Cabin right ahead. I didn't hear no screaming no more. Wolves howled and gnashed at the tree line. Their growling voices said protect your pack. Protect your territory.

I pulled my knife. Slowed down.

Couldn't see nothing through the window. Penelope liked to keep a sheet over it at night, keep out the moonlight. Cursed her for it then. I set the rabbit down gentle on the porch.

Creak a' one of the loose boards inside.

The running heated me up. Sweat came out my hands, my knife grip went slick. My heart thundered all through me and all the sounds what weren't me and what weren't out that cabin switched off. No more birds. No more river.

I moved round the outside a' the cabin, straining my ears 'gainst my own breathing.

The cross on my momma's grave was crooked. I'd put it in straight. Footprints what weren't mine or Penelope's was pressed like stamps into the dirt. 'Bout the size I wore, maybe a half bigger. I let out my breath.

Not Kreagar.

Wiped my hands on my trousers, tightened up my grip on my knife.

No horses nowhere what meant it probably weren't Lyon.

I got right up close to the back a' the cabin.

Heavy footsteps. Man's footsteps. Pacing all round the room. Penelope's voice came through the log wall.

'No right,' she said, fierce but wary. 'You've got no damn right.'

The reply was muffled and lost in the moss 'tween the logs.

Thundering in my chest turned to hammer blows and drumbeats. Man was in there with Penelope and I had to get him out, just like getting a bear out his cave. You got to wake him up and lure him out with promise a' food or threat a' danger. Figured I'd meet this fella with the latter.

I went back to the tree line, sat myself down low, them wolves all round me, adding loud to my voice. Wished right then for a rifle to knock this fella down soon as he stepped outside.

'Penelope, get that fire going,' I shouted.

No answer. No door opening.

'Damn it woman, you not awake yet?'

Nothing.

I sidled up closer, out the protection a' the trees and shouted her again.

Curtain twitched but the door still didn't open.

There weren't no other way in that cabin. If they didn't come out, I'd have to go in and one a' them rules a' the wild is you sure as hell don't go walking into a bear cave, 'specially when you know damn well the bear's at home.

'Penelope,' I shouted, halfway 'tween trees and cabin. 'Wake up, girl.'

'Elka,' she called from inside. Not panic and screaming. 'Elka, that you?'

'Course it's me you damn fool, who else it gonna be?' I kept my voice calm and natural-like.

Nothing for a few seconds. Then, 'Come in here, would you, I have to talk to you.'

Weren't nothing natural 'bout her voice. Even if I didn't know some fella was in there with her, I'd a' known something weren't right. I didn't want to play games no more.

'He got a gun?' I shouted as I came up close to the porch and where I left that rabbit. I looked at that limp rag a' fur. Had to cook it soon else it would spoil and my belly was rumbling for meat.

'Yes,' Penelope said through the walls.

I put my knife in the side a' my belt, 'neath my coats and out a' sight.

'I left my knife inside,' I said. 'I ain't armed.'

'Then come on in, my dear,' said the man and the door opened a crack.

My heart flipped and I felt like I'd been gut-punched. I knew that voice. Weedy. Through the nose.

'Morning Bilker,' I said, pushed the door open the rest a' the way and stepped inside.

Puny little six-shooter in his hand. Weren't even pointing it. Penelope sat on the bed, tears down her face but I saw quick it weren't from Bilker dropping by for breakfast. Purple welt was coming up on her cheek. Tears were pain not fear.

Good girl, I thought and nodded to her.

'Elka,' he said, snitch a' tremble in him. 'So pleased to see you ladies again, though I didn't expect to find you on my new claim.'

'What you talking about? This place ain't yours,' I said.

He smiled, like a weasel. 'Yes it is. I sold this claim fifteen years ago. The owners I see are sadly no longer with us.'

'And?' I said.

'The claim reverts to the seller upon the death of the owners.'

'They signed over this place to us, check with Tucket, it's ours,' I said.

Bilker nodded, licked his ratty moustache and used his pop-gun like a pointing finger. 'Yes. Yes, that's what Glen down at the office said. He said that Phillip's signature is on that bequeathment.'

Then he clicked his tongue and waved that gun around. I caught Penelope's eye. She looked like she knew just what he was talking 'bout.

'*Except*,' he said quickly, 'it looks like Phillip has been dead a rather long time and his dear wife is freshly buried. Maybe even freshly killed by you two thieves.'

My heart near stopped.

'Once I feed all this back to Glen, we're old friends you see, he'll void that bequeathment and this choice piece of land will be mine. Again.'

He smiled a row a' brown-streaked teeth. Chewing 'bacco and sin turned him to rot inside and I could see it all. Saw maggots squirming in his gut. Saw roaches crawling round his face and out his eyes. Saw hissing snakes sliding through his hair and round his arms and legs. He was a weedy devil stood before us trying to take my home away.

'You don't know what you're talkin' 'bout, Bilker,' I said. Moved myself 'tween him and Penelope. 'This place is ours and you're trespassin'.'

He raised his gun right up to my face but I weren't blinking.

'Get off my property,' he said, 'or I will kill you both. There isn't a jury in this land that would hang me for it.'

'*Except,*' Penelope said, standing up, 'everyone in Halveston saw us humiliate you. You have a pretty good reason to want revenge on us and considering this is, legally, my claim, what do you think that jury would say? You followed two young women into the wilderness and shot them, for what?'

His moustache twitched and his gun hand started shaking.

'Don't look good for you, Bilker,' I said.

He laughed a hissing, nasal laugh. 'It won't matter. I just wanted to come here and give you both fair warning. I'm not an unreasonable man, ladies, so I'll give you until the end of the day. I'll be back with red coats.'

He walked backward toward the door. Penelope stepped forward.

'Stanley, wait,' she said, voice turned all kind. 'Can't we work something out? A cut of all we find?'

He puffed out his narrow chest and looked Penelope head to toe, lingering his eyes round the middle a' her.

'Women aren't good for mining,' he said, licking his moustache again.

Penelope put her hand on my shoulder and pushed me gentle aside. 'How about something else then?' she said, soft, and I wanted to be sick.

He sniffed. Only a few steps from the door. Then he sneered with all his face, look a' pure disgust on him.

'Typical *whore*.' He spat at her feet.

White heat ran through me and I charged right at him. Felt the shock wave a' the gun going off but didn't hear the shot. I slammed his hand 'gainst the wall till he screamed and dropped it. In the scuffle it got kicked into the middle a' the room. Bilker weren't as weak as he looked. He pushed me back and cracked his knuckles on my cheek. He threw himself at me, knocked me to the ground. I twisted, couldn't reach my knife. His hands was round my throat and he was panting and red-faced and squealing like a damn pig.

'Stop,' Penelope screamed.

Bilker looked up. I looked up. She pointed that gun right at his face.

The coward in him came back. 'Don't do anything stupid.'

'Get off her,' she said and he scrambled off me, hands up in the air in surrender. I got quick to my feet and spat a glob a' blood on the boards.

'You OK?' she asked me, not taking her eyes off him.

'Ain't no foul. Man hits like my nana.'

'I'm not stupid you know, I didn't come here alone,' he said and I weren't sure I believed him. I didn't see no other footprints and I didn't hear no one in the trees.

'You look pretty alone,' Penelope said, then raised that gun level with his eyes. 'This is my land.'

'Yes ma'am, it is, it is, and you can keep it,' he said, shaking.

Penelope weren't shaking.

'I must have made a mistake,' he said, blabbering them words. 'This isn't my claim, never was. I got the wrong place.'

'Yes you did,' she said, finger firm on that trigger. Had a horrible sinking in my gut that she was going to shoot him. She was going to kill him. He weren't no threat, not now his balls been cut off.

'Get the hell out of here,' I said, 'and don't you dare come back.'

Penelope nodded.

Bilker shuffled back to the door, flung it wide and backed out. Penelope moved to the doorway. He had his hands up, stumbling backward down the steps, out onto the grass.

'We're good? Right? We're good?' he kept saying as he got further.

'We will be,' Penelope muttered and pulled the trigger.

Blood sprayed the ground. Bilker dropped like a stone in a river and I couldn't right believe what just happened. I stood there like an idiot, ears ringing, heart pounding.

I looked at Penelope. Gun still pointed. Hand steady.

'I'm not a whore,' she said quiet so's I barely heard.

I prised the gun out her hand and went outside.

Bilker was still breathing but not for long. Shot through the chest. Blood turning the dirt black. He choked and sputtered red all over his face then fell still. Eyes open and staring up to the sky.

But he'd been telling the truth. He weren't alone. A shout a' surprise came out the woods to the south and the sound a' snapping bracken and running feet. Too far away to chase. Too far to shoot.

I dropped down to my knees. Gun in my hand what Bilker's friend had seen. All my breath left me, ringing in my ears turned to blaring like all the birds were screeching at once, all out of tune and with not a beat a' rhythm 'tween 'em.

This was the end. Red coats would be coming and soon. Least they'd take me away, least they'd think I done it. Penelope would be free. Part a' me wanted it all to be over. That fella would bring the law here and we'd be done with it. I was tired, right down to my marrow, that I figured, hell, let them come. Hurry the hell up.

Penelope stood in the doorway, blank face like what she just done was nothing. I ain't never seen her like that. Bilker weren't no threat, not to our lives, maybe to that cabin, this scrap a' land, but not our lives. Killing for anything but that ain't right, no matter what way you spin it.

'I'll start the fire,' Penelope said and picked up the rabbit from the porch.

I closed Bilker's bug eyes. I couldn't right say I was sorry the snake was dead but that didn't matter none.

I didn't go back inside, even when I smelt the char a' rabbit and felt my stomach ache for it. 'Stead I dug a shallow grave some ways away from the hut. Dragged Bilker to it and rolled him in. He tumbled into the dirt like chunks a' brisket into a pot. I covered him up and dumped the broken sluice boxes and branches over the grave to hide it. When I was done, getting on mid-afternoon, the only thing left a' him was a trail a' blood in the grass. Bugs and critters would soon lap that up.

I stood outside, kicking the ground. Didn't know what to do with myself. Didn't know who that girl was in the cabin no more. She'd pulled that trigger without blinking like she was stoking a fire or tying up her hair. I turned the gun over in my hands. Silver handle with a worn rosewood inlay. Scrolling and etching round the barrel. More a decoration than a weapon. More for show, for inspiring fear in people than giving them a real reason for it. Bilker weren't a good man and he threatened to take our land off us but he weren't going to kill us.

I slumped down onto the ground and rested my arms on my knees, gun in my hands.

'He would have taken this from us,' came Penelope's voice from the cabin. She stood on the porch, then, when I didn't tell her to go hang, she came and sat beside me.

'We lost it anyway,' I said. 'He weren't lying 'bout not coming on his own.'

'Doesn't matter. He came onto this land with a gun, intending to kill us. It was self-defence.'

I laughed but it weren't funny. 'Self-defence to shoot a man reaching for the sky?'

'What do you mean?' she said. 'He was reaching for a second gun when I shot him.'

I shook my head but didn't say nothing else.

She sighed. 'Sometimes you have to do bad things to keep what's yours.'

I stood up and brushed off my trousers. 'I know,' I said and walked away, toward the trees.

She called for me but I didn't turn round. I needed some time away, in the quiet a' the woods. Felt like I was losing myself. We all done bad things. Ain't no man or woman alive what can say different but I didn't want that to be the way a' my life, not no more. Kreagar done terrible, awful, sinful things with me standing right beside him, but I was trying damn hard to make it right. At least, I was trying damn hard not to repeat my past.

I walked through them woods till sundown turned the sky to deep yellow and red. My path laid out afore me. Blood

and gold and here I was, covered in 'em both. I sat beside
the river, staring east across the wide, flat meadow.

A young deer with just nubs for antlers picked his way
across, nibbling here and there on summer shoots. Ain't
nothing more calming. I couldn't hear nothing but the
dusk bugs chirping and the river. This was life. This was my
true life. Ain't no one could take that away from me. Then
I figured it. That cabin, that land and paper and rubber
stamp, that was Penelope's true life. She weren't a wild thing,
happy with the wind knotting up her hair, happy sleeping on
a bed a' holly and ferns, picking off ticks like they's nought
but sticky burs. She needed a bed and a blanket and a lock
on her door. Bilker wanted to take that off her and he cut
her deep with words while he was doing it. If he'd tried to
take the wild off me, I would a' shot him too.

I watched that deer till the dark fell and moonlight lit
him up. But it weren't a deer no more.

A boy stood right out in the middle a' the meadow.
Blond. Pale.

Screaming.

A rifle shot rang out in the dark and my eyes sprang open.

I was leaning up against a tree 'side the river. Dawn was
crowning and I was shivering up something awful. Winter
was close and I was a fool falling asleep outside, on the
ground. I shook away the picture a' that boy, whoever he
was, and made my way back to the cabin. Got there an hour
or so past dawn. Smoke curled out the pipe and the rising
sun turned the beaten brown wood to rich red-gold.

I went straight in and set myself down by the fire. Penelope
didn't say nothing, just sat on the bed, flicking through a
book. Soon as feeling came back into my hands and face, I
said to Penelope, 'I get it.'

'Get what?'

'I get you,' I said. 'I get your thinking 'bout Bilker. If the law comes here then we'll deal with it. Ain't no sense in wringing our hands in worry. Law comes, it comes. If Bilker's friend tripped up running and got eaten by a bear, well then, that's that. I ain't wasting time frettin'.'

She smiled, tension went out a' her and she said, 'Did you catch breakfast?'

'Hell, woman! You ate yesterday. Damn, you expect food every day?'

She threw the book at me, gentle-like, and laughed.

'I found this when you were sulking,' she said and reached under the bed.

A rifle. Old and worn, not been fired in more'n a year.

'Where'd you get that?'

'Under the floor,' she said. 'I dropped a hair pin between the boards. I've only got two left so I prised it up.'

'Gold and guns 'neath this floor,' I said. 'Wonder what else my folks been hiding.'

I spent the rest a' that day outside in the light, working to free the rifle a' rust. Penelope sat on the porch reading that book. Some story a' love 'tween a girl and two fellas. The girl sounded like a empty-headed fool and Penelope said I weren't wrong but the fellas weren't no better.

We didn't have no vegetables growing nowhere and it was too late in the season for planting. I needed to get the rifle clean and firing quick and bag us a moose. Enough to keep us in meat all winter. Though that meant at least two days out in the wild tracking and I weren't at all pleased with the idea a' leaving Penelope on her own. We figured we'd use some a' that gold for a sack a' taters and some onions. A bag a' rice maybe. Penelope said she'd learn how to fish and pull a few salmon out that river afore they spawned and turned rotten. We planned how to make the cabin safe and warm for winter. My folks had got themselves a tidy stockpile a' wood and I said I'd add to it best I could. We'd make up some bear-proof shutters and dig a cold store 'neath the cabin. Said we'd start pulling gold at first melt.

Felt damn good to plan it all. Felt better to start chopping logs and hauling dirt but a deep-down part a' me said I was an idiot. A kid what was dreaming, 'stead of a grown-up what knew better. Weren't no chance Bilker's friend got ate by a bear. Weren't no chance he didn't run back to Tucket and find Lyon and tell her right where we was. All that worry and fret was gnawing inside me like a beaver on a spruce. Soon them teeth would gnaw right through and I'd fall apart but till then I wouldn't let it show. Penelope was happy and I kept the worry buried deep for the both of our sakes. Even though that sky was clear, a black cloud hung low over our claim. I was just waiting for that cloud to turn into a storm and rip our lives clean in half.

SILVER IN THE WATER

It weren't safe for me to go to Tucket. It weren't like Halveston, big enough to get lost in. In Tucket you could spit one side to the other. My face was all over it and Bilker's friend, whoever he was, had seen me, not Penelope. Tell you the truth, I was glad of it. I'd had enough of people and towns. Tin River suited me just fine. Over the next few weeks we got deep into fall and Penelope made her first trip to Tucket since we posted the note to Lyon. Came back that evening smiling, Delacroix's men weren't in town no more what meant she weren't being looked for no more. Her trips to Tucket – to Mark – got a whole lot more frequent.

I got the cabin ready best I could, dug the larder, piled up the wood, even made myself a straight up-and-down smoke-house – all that was missing was its hat. Only thing we was having trouble with was the food. My snares were coming up cold and we didn't have no bullets for the rifle. Cold was crisping up the air and hunger was barking at our backs.

Snow started crawling down the mountains and we woke up more'n once to frost on our window.

Penelope, on her trips to town, would get Mark to carry sacks halfway into the woods and dump them 'neath a twisted oak. Once they'd said their cooing goodbyes and he was out a' sight, I'd pick up the sacks and take 'em rest a' the way home. Taters, carrots, even a bag a' cabbages. People in Tucket and all round were preparing for winter and stocking up their larders so wouldn't part with their food for nothing. That jar a' gold went low quick but we got rounds for the rifle, a great wad a' zip bags, and a nice fishing rod and net off a lady what broke her arm and couldn't use it no more.

Penelope said the posters a' me were either blown off by the wind or torn down by folk what were tired a' seeing my ugly mug, and no one put up no fresh ones. She said too that the note I left for Lyon was gone but nothing else been put up yet and there weren't hide nor hair a' any a' them dandy men.

'You watch, I'll fill up that larder in a day,' she said, smiling when she came back with that fishing pole.

'I'll believe that when I ain't died a' hunger halfway through winter.'

Penelope was useless with that rod. She landed maybe one out a' every ten bites she got and that one was a two-bite tiddler. All I heard all day was her shouting she had a fish on then cursing she'd lost it.

'Mark and Josie said the salmon would be running up this river in a few days, maybe a week. She said they can run late in the year in these parts but we have to be quick, they come and go in a day or two,' Penelope said, throwing the pole on the bank. 'We can pick them out with the net instead of wasting time with this thing. We just have to be careful of bears.'

Them few days went by and I had so much to be doing round the claim that I near forgot about Bilker and keeping an eye out for the salmon. Figured if the law was going to come down on us, it would a' happened by now. Maybe his friend really did trip and hit his head and was now gurgling away in a bear's belly. Maybe Bilker just didn't pay him enough to care.

One morning I was shoring up the sides a' the larder with poles and laying a board down on the floor to keep the bugs out when Penelope gave a whooping and shouted at me to bring the knife. I ran outside and damn near fell over when I saw it.

The river was full and raging with silver. The salmon thrashed about, squeezing over and under each other trying to move 'gainst the current. I ain't never seen nothing like it. A ways up the river I saw a momma bear flinging fish to two cubs sat patient on the bank. So easy and quick-like she was flicking ants off a mound. That bear didn't even know we was there and, 'sides, there was plenty for the both a' us. Bears are good like that. In times a' plenty there ain't no sense in fighting for the sake of it. Humans could learn something from 'em. Only fight when you got no choice.

Penelope jumped up and down on the bank, grin like a new moon on her face. She was shouting at me to hurry and I didn't need to be told twice. I waded into the water and, on account a' me being stronger and salmon being all muscle, swapped knife for net. I dumped fish after fish out onto the bank and Penelope made quick work a' cutting out their gills and stopping 'em wriggling.

'Hot damn,' I shouted over the splashing and rushing, 'this is the way to fish!'

'Keep going!'

We got near fifty pounds a' salmon and Penelope cut 'em all down to fillets. She wrapped 'em up in them plastic bags and we put 'em down in the larder 'neath the cabin. Winter was half a breath away and that larder was near freezing. The river still ran with them fish and we sat out and watched 'em. That night we made a fire outside and roasted up one a' the salmon whole. It spilled all its bright orange eggs and we scooped 'em up with spoons.

'I could get used to this,' Penelope said, mouth full and popping with roe.

Close to that fire, smell a' woodsmoke and barbecue salmon, I felt just the same. Penelope and me talked and laughed 'bout things I don't remember now. We talked until the fire turned cold and we didn't have no more wood close to hand to feed it. Slept sound that night, above a proper food store what, once I got us a moose, would last us all winter.

Woke up next morning to Penelope prodding me. 'Come with me to Tucket today.'

'Why?'

'Mark and Josie have been asking after you. There are only so many excuses I can give.'

'Tell 'em I'm dead.'

'They've met you, they wouldn't believe it.'

I smiled and figured they was smarter than they looked.

'What is it about that Mark fella that gets you so wound up?'

She shrugged, all coy-like. 'He's nice. He's kind and so many men in this world aren't. He's also got work and money, and just as many men in this world don't. He's a good prospect.'

I weren't at all sure if those was reasons for being sweet on someone but I figured Penelope knew more 'bout that than me.

'Come on, please,' she said. 'You've been out here for weeks and haven't seen anyone else. It's not healthy.'

'You and I got two meanin's for healthy.'

'You keep saying we need proper wood for the shutters and roof of the smokehouse,' she said, sounding like she was leading me down a path. She was. Josie had a damn lumberyard.

Shit.

'Fine,' I said, 'but we ain't staying the night.'

Penelope's voice went all high-pitched and she shook my shoulder near out the socket.

'And none a' that!'

We got to Tucket afore noon. It was quieter'n last time. A lot a' folks had packed up and gone south for winter and I couldn't blame 'em. Winter in Ridgeway was bad enough and these northern folk said us southerners had hot beds and soft heads all year round.

We went straight to the Thompsons. Mark came running out the door a' the mill when he saw us coming over the bridge.

'Penny!' he shouted, waving and his boy came running behind him.

'Penny?' I said quiet to her afore he reached us.

She told me to hush and greeted Mark with a hug and a kiss on the cheek. Did the same with the boy.

Mark then turned on me and wrapped me up in a hug what I weren't too pleased about. He weren't all skin and bone no more, Jethro's cooking fattened him up nice. Over Mark's shoulder I caught Penelope's eye and shook my head. She tried not to laugh.

'So good to see you, Elka,' Mark said. The boy stayed behind his legs like he'd forgotten he'd fallen asleep on me last time I seen him.

'And you,' I said, trying to sound like I meant it.

'Josie around?' Penelope asked. 'Elka needs some wood.'

'Aye, she's just inside,' Mark said and called her. 'She won't take your money but if you cut the wood yourself you can have it.'

I raised up my eyebrows. 'You got one a' them circle saws?' He nodded.

I ain't never used one but I seen 'em and figured they'd be fun. 'I'd be happy to.'

'We're about to break for lunch,' he said. 'Join us?'

Josie came out and hollered Penelope's name. Saw someone else moving about in the barn and figured it was one a' the mill hands. Didn't think nothing of it.

'Elka,' Josie said in that voice a' hers, like hot honey dripping into your ear.

She came right up to me and kissed me on both cheeks. I done told you before I ain't the kissing type and along with that hug from Mark I wanted to kick Penelope for making me come here.

Penelope winced at me, like she was waiting for me to throw a tantrum and run away but I didn't. Human rules say you ain't allowed to do that.

'Nice to see you 'gain,' I said, and Penelope relaxed. 'Fella here says you can give us some wood if I cut it myself.'

Josie smiled out one side a' her mouth and looked at Mark. 'Did he?'

Mark studied his shoes. 'I did, yeah.'

Josie took in a long breath and said, all breezy-like, 'Well then, I suppose we can spare a few planks.'

Then she gave her brother a look what said that wood was coming out his pay packet, and said to us, 'Hungry?'

Just like last time, Jethro was cooking up a feast. He hugged me when he saw me too. The only one a' this family what didn't was the little boy clinging to his daddy's legs. That made him my favourite and I gave an inside smile when he was sat next to me at the table. Mark made puppy eyes at Penelope, and she made 'em right back at him but I weren't sure no more if hers were real or just 'cause he was a good *prospect*. Didn't think I'd ever understand Penelope all the way through.

'All set for winter?' Josie asked me then spooned green beans on my plate.

I took a chunk a' corn bread from the heap in the middle of the table and said, 'Most done, 'cept the shutters and smokehouse roof, what we need your wood for.'

'Elka's dug us a larder and made a woodpile big enough for three winters,' Penelope said, grinning, and I felt my cheeks go hot.

I'd been thinking long about my hunting trip and I didn't have much time left afore the snow shut me out. 'I need to get us a moose or caribou but I ain't happy 'bout leaving Penelope all alone in that cabin, middle a' nowhere with all them bears and wolves.'

Penelope frowned at me and said, 'You never mentioned anything.'

'I don't tell you everything, *Penny*,' I said, winking at her. 'I was wonderin' if you good folk would mind taking her in for a few days?'

Mark's face near exploded with happy. Even the boy perked up and said her name a few times, smacking his spoon 'gainst the table like a drumbeat.

'Of course, that'd be wonderful,' Mark said then looked at Josie and faltered. 'If it's OK with you and Jethro.'

The husband and wife exchanged a look and Josie said, a little like she'd been bullied into it, 'We'd be proud to have you.'

'Elka, are you sure about this?' Penelope said.

'It'd make me feel a whole lot better 'bout a huntin' trip if you was here.'

Mark banged his fist on the table and a square a' corn bread toppled off the heap, got caught by the boy and turned quick to crumbs.

'Settled!' he said and put his hand over Penelope's.

'That's very kind,' Penelope said, blush coming up on her cheeks like she'd flipped a switch. 'Thank you, Josie, I won't be a bother.'

'It'll be nice to have a lady round the house,' Jethro said, nudging his wife, 'instead of this old hen. Pen, promise you won't come in covered in sawdust.'

Penelope smiled, said she wouldn't, and the smiles and laughing went on from there.

I figured I could deal with these folks every now and then, 'specially if Jethro kept his cooking this fine. Maybe it would be good for me to have people in my life after so long with just me and Kreagar, then just me and Penelope. Humans is meant to be together, so they say, that's why we make towns and cities. Wondered brief if I was going 'gainst my nature by staying out in the wild, or wanting to at least. Then I figured too many people together had made the Damn Stupid so I weren't at all sure.

We finished up the meal and while Penelope helped Mark with the dishes and clearing, Josie took me out to the lumberyard.

'Really going to hunt a moose on your own?' she said.

'Why not? I shot plenty in my time.'

'Won't you have trouble getting it back?'

'No, ma'am, I got myself a ways a' doing it that served me fine so far.' And I did. Simple really, a sled, with wheels if necessary. I'd learned to haul meat on my lonesome from the age a' twelve.

'If you say so,' Josie said and pushed open the doors into the barn.

Sound a' saws running off generators and smell a' hot wood hit me. The barn, huge and square, was full a' machines and stacks a' smooth, even planks. A giant pile a' sawdust sat in the far corner and I just wanted to jump into it and throw it all around like it was a snowdrift.

Whoever was in the barn when we arrived weren't here no more. Figured a worker on lunch break same as Mark. Josie showed me to a pile a' die-straight, perfect round tree trunks, long as I'd ever seen. Beautiful white spruce, shame to shave it down to planks but I got to have me some storm shutters.

Afore Josie did anything, she turned on me and said, hard voice, 'I saw those posters of you.'

My throat dried up.

'Should I be worried?' she said.

'No ma'am,' I said but I was lying. They should be worried, though not a' me.

'I built a good life here for me and mine and no matter how sweet you and your friend are, if anything threatens my family, I'll turn you and Pen into sawdust. You get me?'

I nodded. 'I get you just fine.'

She held my eyes a moment longer, made sure I looked like I was speaking true.

'Help me lift this,' Josie said and took one end a' the top log. That was that, no more said 'bout it.

We rolled the log onto the saw bench and lined up the end with the blade.

'Hold it and push once I turn it on,' Josie said, nodded to me. 'This will cut inch-thick boards.'

'Sounds right,' I said and braced myself 'gainst the log.

Josie fired up the machine and I damn near went deaf. It was simple work and made my arms ache in that good way what meant you had used 'em right. Josie helped me cut the first log but after that she just watched.

'This girl,' she said, loud above all the roaring, 'Penelope, what's her story?'

'What you mean?' I said, paying more attention to the wood than her.

'She a good sort?'

I looked up at Josie then I got her meaning. She had a look a' concern on her. 'My baby brother, he's a head-over-heels type, you know?'

I cut the last plank out that log and switched off the machine to make sure she heard all I had to say.

'Penelope's best sort there is,' I said, meeting Josie right in them brown eyes a' hers. 'Saved my life more'n I can count and didn't ask for nothing from me. Could a' screwed me over a hundred times but she's got one a' them pure hearts. Your brother'd never do better in this life.'

Josie, hard woman that she was, kept my gaze a bit longer, seemed she was in the habit a' that. She must a' seen what she wanted 'cause her face broke into a wide, white-tooth smile.

'Thank you,' she said, nodding and turned the machine back on.

I cut four more logs and she said that was enough, told me we could take as many planks as we needed from the pile what had been treated and dried on the other side a' the barn. She said that she made me cut 'em so she wouldn't have to pay her hands to replace the stock. I told her fair enough and we figured the best way to get them to Tin River. Weren't no roads for a cart so we settled on floating 'em up river. I ain't never been much good on the water, last time it was in a crate, but I didn't much fancy carrying 'em one by one through the woods.

Josie and I went back in the house and found Jethro and the young boy in the kitchen and Mark and Penelope nowhere.

Panic poured over me like rain but before I could say nothing, Jethro held out his hand and said, 'They went for a walk, you know, as young lovers do.'

Then he grinned wide and Josie rolled her eyes.

Not sure why but I had a question in me what just needed to come out. 'What happened to the boy's momma? She gonna cause trouble for Penelope if she finds out 'bout them?'

Josie looked at the boy, then me, then took up a cloth and started drying a plate what weren't wet. 'Childbirth got her. No trouble.'

Part a' me was relieved that Penelope weren't going to get some jilted wife coming raging at her. Other part of me was sad for the boy. Growing up without a momma weren't fun and I knew it just as well. Felt a pang in me for the momma I lost, the loving arms I'd never have.

I washed up and sat down at the table, opposite the boy.

He stared at me with button eyes and I felt myself smiling along with him. He had a pencil in his fist and was drawing pictures on faded newsprint.

'What's that you drawin'?' I said.

He lifted his hand and turned the paper round to me. Then he jabbed a finger down. 'That's our house,' he said, 'that's Daddy,' pointed to a rough circle next to the square, no arms no legs just a blob, 'and Auntie JoJo,' another circle, this one with a scratch a' hair on top. Then he pointed to Jethro, himself and Penelope and even I was there, a scratch on the corner a' the page. There was one left, a filled-in black circle near the top a' the house.

'What's that?' I said.

The boy went quiet, scared almost, then said, 'That's the boogeyman. Looks through my window.'

Josie shook her head. 'He has nightmares.'

Boy stabbed his pencil into the circle and started scratching deep grooves into the paper. 'He's real, JoJo, he has black lines all over his face.'

My insides turned to ice.

Josie huffed and grabbed the paper off him, screwed it up in her hands. 'He's seen those posters around town and now he thinks there are monsters under his bed.'

The boy started wailing for his drawing then, when he figured he weren't getting it back, his bottom lip wobbled and fat tears came rolling out his eyes. Josie told him to stop being a nuisance, Jethro tried to quiet him, but the boy weren't having none of it. He ran from the room and I heard his footsteps and bawling all the way upstairs.

My head kept going back to the black circle. Was it just nightmares on account a' him seeing them posters? Or was Kreagar right here, outside this house, marking that boy for his own? I thought 'bout telling them to leave, right now, pack up, go south like everyone else. But sat there at that kitchen table while Jethro gave Josie a look what said she was being mean Aunt JoJo, I couldn't say a word. If I told them what I knew, who I was, who goddamn Kreagar Hallet was, then all this would be lost to me, maybe to Penelope too. I knew that Penelope would stick by my side but I couldn't take her away from Mark, not when they was just getting acquainted. If my plan, my damn fine plan, didn't work then she'd need him more'n ever, even if it weren't true love.

I told myself it was just nightmares. That boy was young and Tucket was half a step into the wild. Him and his daddy been attacked on the road up here, caught in a snare, that was enough to crack up a young'un. Them charcoal posters just gave all that fear a face.

'Friend of mine has a skiff you can use for the wood,' Josie said, raising her chin toward the door like I'd caused the kid's fit and they wanted me gone.

'Much obliged,' I said.

The river running just outside Tucket joined up with another branch what would take me and the wood right back to the claim. I met up with Penelope at the boat, all red-faced and giggling with Mark, and I said she'd be best staying here. Winter was close and I didn't have much time left to bag a moose.

She didn't argue long, nor did Mark, and Josie, who was helping me load the wood, shrugged and said all right then.

'Three days,' I said, 'four top. I'll come back here and fetch you when I'm done.'

Penelope gave me a hug and said good luck, shoot us a moose. Josie rolled her eyes right back in her head and

Mark thanked me for giving him time with Penelope. Felt a mite sorry for Mark then but I didn't let it show.

The man whose boat it was was a jolly round fella with a white beard tight to his cheeks. We said our goodbyes and good lucks and such and sped up the river, dragging a dozen planks and a saw, and a bag a' nails what I borrowed off Josie. The fella helped me unload at Tin River, hauled them planks out onto the grass to dry off, and then turned the boat around and went on his way with a hat tip and a wave.

It was all so rosy. Sun was on me and warming up the edges, all the folks in Tucket had been smiling and helpful and it made me sick in my gut. I kept seeing that little boy and the fear what struck his face when I asked what that black circle was, kept thinking what was going to happen to him. But hell, he had his family around him and even Kreagar would have to work hard to get the best a' Josie.

I quick laid out all the wood to catch the last few hours a' sun and packed a bag. Knife in my belt. Rifle slung over my shoulder and rounds in my pocket. It was getting close to sundown when I set out but that didn't matter none. Cold ain't no enemy when you can make a fire easy as I can. I'd seen moose out on the other side a' the river, crossing the meadow north-west to south-east. Figured on going up the world 'stead a' down.

Felt myself a little burst a' excitement in my chest, growing up my neck and putting a smile right on my face. I was out here, on my own, no other person near and I had me a hunting rifle. I checked on the smokehouse and figured four planks on the top would make a fine roof and 'bout the same for the door. That'd take me two hours when I got back and I prayed hard I'd have meat for smoking. Had me a powerful urge for some jerky, mouth went watery at the thought, and as I shut up the cabin and walked out into the woods, I set my head remembering all that jerky I made and ate with Trapper. We tried a hundred different dry rubs, different wood for the smoke, different age a' meat. Took us 'bout a year but we figured the best recipe for each animal and, damn, the one we had for pig was hand to god the best I ever tasted.

My head went through all the weights and measures a' salt and sugar and spices what would go on the moose I'd be shooting. My belly gurgled and rumbled all the way into the wild and I was happy as a dog chewing on a T-bone.

Shame I'm a goddamn idiot.

The safety on this old rifle didn't work and safety weren't my friend. One time when I was fourteen I'd tripped up, fallen hard, and my gun had gone off right beside me. That bullet cut a chunk out a tree right next to my head. Since then I ain't never walked with a loaded gun, 'specially one with a busted safety, so's on that hunting trip I didn't have a round in the chamber ready.

I'd spent a day walking only to spot a cow moose, perfect damn size, perfect damn place, munching on grass like nothing else in this world existed.

That's when I found out my coat had a damn hole in the pocket and I'd dropped every single one a' my damn bullets all over the damn Yukon.

I watched that moose wander off all calm-like and I tried my damnedest to hold in all my raging. But hell, I just ended up laughing. All that song and dance I made a' putting Penelope with Mark and keeping her safe. Well, she'd just have to stay there a day or two longer while I went back to get more bullets, or least find some a' the ones I dropped.

I walked back 'tween the trees, breathing in all the fresh, cold air a' the North afore I got back to the cabin. Bullets, hunting, and my plan, my damn fine plan what was going to free me a' Kreagar and Lyon, went straight to hell, when, in the new dawn light, I saw three horses tied up outside my front door.

HOWDY, NEIGHBOUR

I weren't in no mood for stalking then. I knew right away who was inside my house and what they wanted. In truth, I almost turned right around and ran right back into the forest.

But then I remembered Kreagar. All his evil was still free in this world. He'd keep on killing till he was behind iron or 'neath the dirt and Lyon weren't smart enough to catch him on her own or she would a' done it already.

I strode right up to the cabin, useless rifle resting in my arms. Felt my knife in my belt.

'Magistrate Lyon,' I shouted and quick the door flung open.

Saw her silver six-shooter first, pointed right at me. Then my eyes found hers. I hadn't seen her since Genesis and not up close since Dalston, more'n a year ago. She looked so much older. Her neat blonde hair weren't so neat, her hand weren't so steady.

She came out and her two lieutenants came out behind her, guns up.

I didn't move, didn't raise my hands, didn't drop my rifle though she told me to.

'Good to see you again, Elka, is it?' she said and that ice-cold voice put a chill through me. Suddenly thought what in the hell am I doing? This woman shot a squirrel 'tween the eyes, burnt my home to the ground and has been chasing me for more'n a year, and I just invited her in for a goddamn nightcap.

Shit. All that cocksure feeling went right out a' me and I told myself I should a' run for it when I had the chance.

Lyon must a' sensed that shift in me. Her hand went steady as bedrock.

'All this time you been chasing me,' I said, trying to keep my voice calm. 'What you want?'

Lyon held out her free hand to that stocky man what near arrested me in Halveston and he gave her a piece a' paper. She held it up.

'You know Kreagar Hallet,' she said and I recognised the note me and Penelope left in Tucket. 'I knew you did, when I first saw you in Dalston.'

'That French woman in jail?'

Lyon shook her head. 'No, Ms Delacroix is not in jail.'

Shit.

'Then you ain't getting nothing from me,' I said.

Lyon came further out the cabin, stepped down onto the dirt, and signalled to the stocky fella. The other one, skinny and young, stayed quiet. The stocky one came at me with another piece a' paper in his fist. It was out of a newspaper and was most all words. I recognised a few but couldn't make no sense of it. There was a picture though and that said it all.

'Amandine Delacroix was hanged in Genesis last week,' Lyon said and my throat went dry as sand. The picture showed a smart-dressed woman hanging three feet off the ground, unmistakably Delacroix, and two men swinging beside her. Them dandy fellas.

First thought that went through me was Penelope. She was free of all that business and I couldn't help but smile.

'Appreciate it,' I said and shoved that paper in my pocket. The young fella didn't have his gun drawn and the stocky one had it hanging by his side. I could run. Trees weren't far. But Lyon'd shoot me afore I got ten yards. Not in the back. In the knees, in the arms. She didn't want me dead. Not just yet.

'Where is my son?' she said and I saw her finger itching to squeeze that trigger.

I figured a deal's a deal and gave her the place as best I could remember it.

'Ride back to town, send three men south to check,' she said to the stocky fella.

Cold water filled up my gut. 'You ain't going yourself?'

She shook her head slow but her eyes didn't move off me. That unsettled me right to my core.

'Hallet is here so I will be here.'

Didn't think a' that, did I? Pure, deep-down fear ran through me.

The two men mounted their horses, exchanged a few words with their boss what I couldn't hear over my pumping heart, then rode off. Me and Lyon was alone and there weren't no one close enough to hear a gunshot.

Soon as the horses were out of sight and hearing, she holstered her piece. Wished I had a bullet then so's I could a' taken the shot, ridding myself a' her right then, but I figured she could probably draw and shoot me clean through the eye afore I even raised my rifle.

'What now then?' I said, scuffing my boot in the dirt.

Lyon sat on my porch, rested her elbows on her knees and stared up at me. In truth, I didn't know what in the hell was happening. Felt like I did with that doctor afore he gave me them pills but I figured there weren't no way I'd get that lucky twice.

'What now, Elka, indeed,' she said and she sounded tired.

'How'd you find me?' I said.

'Stanley Bilker, name sound familiar?' she said and my eyes went to the pile a' junk on top a' his grave. 'Your girl-friend caused quite the stir in Halveston which wasn't too clever. Stanley recognised you from the poster and he, as you probably noticed, is not a man who takes humiliation well.'

I couldn't argue with that.

Lyon kept talking. 'He came to me, saying he'd seen you. He and one of my men followed you here and, strangely, Mr Bilker never made it back. You wouldn't know anything about that would you, Elka?'

I winced. Heard that shot all over again. Realised I was standing on the patch where he bled out.

'Maybe a bear got him,' I said.

'Maybe.'

The openness in her was unnerving, like she was calming a pig afore slitting its throat.

'My man said you killed him, tried to get me to come out here and arrest you on the spot,' she said and I wanted to shout, hell I did, Penelope pulled that trigger.

'But I was too busy with Delacroix and her whore house,' Lyon said. 'The world is better off without a man like Bilker, but still, it's against the law and I uphold the law.'

I swallowed down a gulp a' grit. 'You arresting me, Magistrate?'

She bowed her head. Strand a' blonde hair fell down over her eyes. They was weary eyes, tired a' living, tired a' crying.

'Give me a reason not to,' she said.

This was it. It weren't quite how my damn fine plan was meant to happen but I didn't have no choice.

'I'll give you Kreagar,' I said and she looked up at me, them tired eyes blazing.

Then she laughed. Horrible sound, it was. All the humour gone right out a' her and a sound like sand rubbing on glass taken its place. Right then, like the gods was hearing me, the sky went dark with clouds. To the north, the thunderhead rumbled to life.

'How are you going to do that?' Lyon said.

I shook my head. 'Ain't that easy. If I give him to you, you leave me alone. You take down all them posters a' me, you stop lookin' for me. I give you Kreagar, I'm dead to you. Get it?'

She stood up, quicker'n I expected. I jumped back, gripped my rifle. She looked at me strange, like she'd got some kind a' meaning out my words what I didn't intend.

'You helped him, didn't you?' she said and tremors went through me.

'I don't know what. . .' But she put her hand on her gun.

'Do you know what he did?' she said, stepped closer but didn't draw. 'Did you help him cut them up?'

Flashes went through my head.

Deer lying on the gutting table turned to women, to Missy, turned back to deer. Pelts stretched on A-frames blinked out, fur turned to pink skin. Skulls and bones changed shape in my head. I thought a' that blond boy I seen in my dream, standing, screaming in the meadow.

I shook it all away. Near shook my head clean off. 'I didn't know.'

But I'd known it all along, down in the dark heart a' me. The place a' locked rooms and lost keys. But all them doors was flying open now. All but one.

Lyon ran at me, grabbed my arms, made me look her right in the eye. I let her. I didn't have no energy in me to fight her. Them doors were sucking me into their darkness, sucking me back through time to all them days in the woods with that man what I called Daddy.

She shook me and shouted. 'Did you eat them too?'

Then I turned cold on the inside. I saw myself cutting strips a' meat, hanging up rows and rows a' them in the smokehouse.

Best jerky I ever had.

JUST LIKE HIM

Lyon gave me a flask a' water to sip and sat beside me on the porch. I stared at the pool a' my sick in the grass.

'How long were you with him?' she asked.

'I was seven when he found me in the woods.'

She weren't exactly motherly but she had changed in them few minutes. Some a' that ice in her melted and I think she believed me that I didn't know.

We sat quiet for a while and I watched the clouds roll in slow from the north. Tint to them spoke a' snow.

Finally Lyon said with a sigh, 'Give me Hallet and you and me are done. I won't pursue you.'

I looked at her, felt a mite a' warmth coming off that porcelain. 'What 'bout Bilker?'

She squinted up at the sun. 'He was trespassing.'

I took that to mean she wouldn't think no more 'bout it and for the first time in more'n a year, I could taste real true freedom.

We didn't discuss details, there weren't all that many. I just told her to stay in Tucket, keep that six-shooter loaded and the horses saddled.

'Be ready,' I said, ''cause Kreagar ain't gonna come easy.'

In truth, I hadn't a damn clue where to start. He was a ghost in these woods, same as me, and wouldn't be found till he wanted to be. I told Lyon as much and she said she'd wait, as long as it took.

There was a desperation in her, I saw it plain. Same kind a' thing that fella in the rail station must a' seen afore she tied him to the back a' her horse. Seen that desperation afore, in my dream by the river, that blond boy. Same eyes. Same hair. Kreagar right there with his rifle aimed.

Felt sick again but kept it down.

'You remind me of him,' she said and I looked at her frowning. 'My son, I mean. He was always in the woods. Covered in dirt and bringing home insects in jars.' She paused, smiled, then said, 'He brought home a rabbit once, tiny thing he'd shot with an air rifle. So proud of himself. He stood there in the kitchen saying Mom, Mom, I got us dinner.'

Then she laughed, not that bitter sound, but one full a' sorrow. 'I cooked it, like he asked, then he took one bite, turned up his nose and spat it all over my clean table! He said he was sorry for killing it because he didn't like the taste. Then he sat at the table, stern face on him, and thought about what he'd done. He gave that rabbit full funeral honours and vowed never to kill an animal again, unless it was a cow of course, because he said he liked beef.'

I smiled. 'Good kid you had.'

That word, 'had', might as well a' been a knife in her. Everything changed 'bout her then. She stood up like she'd been caught out being friendly and said, all the authority back in her, 'Get me Hallet. Alive.'

Then she got on her horse in one quick move and said, 'Soon.'

She went to turn the horse then stopped and said, 'Oh, and Elka, if you try to run before Hallet is mine,' she pointed right at me with the leather strap, 'I'll take that pretty blonde friend of yours to Genesis instead.'

She didn't wait for me to answer. She shouted 'Yah!' at the horse and dug her heels into the poor beast. He set off at a gallop and was off the claim and in the trees in a blink. Then I was on my own and my chest went tight and panicked and I couldn't right figure what in the hell had just happened.

She could a', should a' killed me but something, maybe some piece a' pity in her gut stayed her hand. My life been given to me and there was only one reason for it. Kreagar was the only thing standing 'tween me and the rest a' my life. Lyon been turned in my head from cold, hard lawkeeper to a mother wanting revenge.

Course I couldn't blame her.

I sat there for longer'n I knew. Dark was coming and I didn't notice Penelope till she was ten feet from the porch. She waved, called my name. A swell a' pure shame near drowned me and I broke down, fat blubbering tears coming out a' my eyes. I couldn't stop 'em, couldn't wipe 'em away fast enough.

Penelope ran to me, concern all over her face and knelt down in front a' me, her hands on my shoulders.

'What happened?' she asked. 'Elka? What is it?'

But I couldn't speak. All I could do was hang my head and let it all come flowing out. Dam was burst. Doors was open. Weren't no stopping it.

'What you doing here?' was 'bout all I could say.

'I needed a change of clothes,' she said. 'What are you doing back here so soon? What about the moose?'

I just shook my head. Shame cut the tongue right out my head.

I let Penelope lead me inside. She sat me down on the bed and I curled up like a baby 'neath the blanket. I was shivering and sobbing and felt sick all over again. Penelope kept asking me what was wrong, what happened but I kept shaking my head. Soon she gave up asking and just sat beside me, stroking my hair, cooing and shh'ing me like a kid what had a nightmare.

I had had a nightmare. Ten years a' nightmare and I was just remembering the details. Reliving it like I'd just woken up. Kreagar was that demon by the lake, horns and claws coming at me in the dark, laughing at me like he knew all along what I done. And he did, course he did. I remembered his face after he told me my nana was dead, bite a' jerky in my mouth.

'You like that?' he'd said. I did. I did like it. That was why he kept me. I knew it now. 'Cause I liked the flavour of his life.

Nana. . . I opened my eyes wide. That bloody sack, full a' pig what he'd got from town, what he made me cut up. *Found your nana.*

I ran outside, emptied out my stomach all over again. Fresh, hot hate boiled up in me, seared my insides, turned my heart to scar tissue.

Penelope came rushing out behind me.

Thunder cracked to the north and clouds hid the moon and stars. Only light was from a candle in the cabin window.

I stood up straight, pulled in cold air, faced out into the darkness.

'I'm all right now,' I said, didn't turn around to Penelope. 'I'm all right.'

'Are you sure? What happened? Did you get a moose?'

I'd forgotten all 'bout the hunt. Didn't feel like admitting I'd lost all the bullets so I just shook my head again.

She asked me more questions, said things I don't remember now, mostly words full a' worry and curious. The more I heard her voice, the more relaxed I got. The more I felt like me again.

I know now what I did in that hut with Kreagar, at least most of it. I got to live with it. And I will. But Penelope don't got to know. I couldn't take the look a' horror on that pretty face. That bridge we built 'tween us would be smashed to splinters and that weren't something I'd do, not now, not ever.

'Did you catch anything else?'

I turned round and smiled at her. 'Could say that. I'll tell you all 'bout it,' I said and, back in the cabin, in the warm, low light beside that wood burner, I did. I told her 'bout Lyon and Delacroix and the damn fine plan and overhead, a storm rolled in.

SNOW IN TIN RIVER

Penelope read every word a' that newspaper what said
Delacroix was dead. Read it twice, three times, more'n that
over the next few days, even nailed it up on the wall. Told
me she couldn't believe it. Told me she couldn't believe
leaving that note in Tucket worked. Told me she couldn't
believe everything was going so damn well.

But for me, the shit was just beginning. I had no idea
how I was going to catch Kreagar and get free a' Lyon and
I weren't afraid to admit it. Trapper taught me everything I
knew, there weren't no way I could think of to get him on
the back foot. Kreagar didn't have no back foot. All this time
I'd had this damn fine plan that I would catch him and turn
him in but it was all hot air. Never figured I'd actually have
to do it. Lyon was meant to catch him. Lyon and all that
Law she had on her side were meant to do my job for me.
In truth, I hadn't given half a' thought to how I'd go 'bout
it. The down-deep details a' the thing. And now, when my
bluff been shouted in my face, when it true mattered and I

was the only one what could find him, catch him, maybe kill him, I was coming up empty.

'I don't know where to even start,' I said, 'he could be anywhere or nowhere. He could be dead in a ditch in Halveston for all I know.'

Penelope half smiled at me. 'You'll find him.'

Easy for her to say. Her demon was slayed, hanging off a tree by her neck. Mine was roaming the woods, hungry and without no hint a' good in him.

The storm what started further north a few days ago was coming in slow, weren't bad though, weren't no thunderhead at least. Every time I thought it would hit, it stayed that little bit out a' reach, kept its insides to itself. It would come, a' course, right when I didn't want it to. I spent more'n more time on my own, climbing trees, doing this and that, I only went in the cabin when chores needed doing. Every day I was in that place, fixing up the smokehouse though I didn't have nothing to smoke in it, and making the shutters for the window, I kept my eyes on the forest, searching for a flash a' grey fur. I kept my ears open for any growl, any sound a' padding feet. I missed Wolf something awful in them days. Not sure why then after so long without him, maybe 'cause he was wild and I was just remembering I was too.

Weren't no sign a' course. I had me human work to take care of and there ain't much a wild thing hates more'n human work. I'd most finished the shutters and smokehouse and I thought 'bout going on another hunt afore winter set in proper. We'd need the meat and we'd spent near half my parents' gold in supplies to get us this far. Weren't no one in Tucket this time a' year what would part with a moose haunch.

Penelope took a trip into town to see her sweetheart and I found myself at a loss a' what to do. I'd tended the fire. I'd checked and reset my snares and I'd washed my smalls and set 'em to dry near the burner. In just my shirt and slacks, I went outside with my knife and picked a tree. Scratched a target into the bark and stepped back ten foot. I aimed and threw the knife. It slammed into the wood 'bout six inches south a' the circle. Threw it again and it glanced off the tree and stuck deep into the dirt.

When I picked up my knife I told myself this was how I'd have to do it, when the time came. This was what would bring down Kreagar. I couldn't shoot him, the rifle was too heavy and bulky 'case I needed to run and if he got it off me, hell, he was a crack shot and I'd get no more'n five steps. I couldn't get in close with my blade, he was stronger'n me times ten, I wouldn't stand a chance. But he couldn't throw a knife on target even if he was chucking it in a bucket. That was where I'd get him. A talent I'd made myself, a skill I'd trained, what he didn't have no idea of. Only way to slay a demon was to do what he weren't expecting. A hit to the leg would cripple him but a hit to the heart would kill him. Lyon said she wanted him breathing but I wanted him dead. It was the only way I'd be sure. If he was dead, so was my secret and I could throw away that last key to that last door in my head.

I threw the knife at the tree with that knowledge sat square at the front a' my head. The blade stuck deep into the middle a' the target. Gave that wooden thud what sent birds to wing in the meadow. Saw Kreagar pinned to that tree, right through the tattoos on his chest, bleeding out his mouth and nose, choking out his last. I pulled the knife out, let him slump.

I was starting to understand what he meant in the Reverend's basement a whole year ago. I was figuring out why he didn't kill me. I was figuring out what plan he had for me and I didn't like it one bit.

I practised all day, till my arm ached and I couldn't see the tree for darkness. Penelope didn't come back that night and I didn't expect her to. She was seeing more'n more a' Mark and always came back to the cabin smiling and talking 'bout how well he was doing at the lumberyard, how Josie was thinking of raising his wages, how he was thinking of heading back to Halveston after winter for a better job, better prospects, she said.

'He's asked me to live with him,' Penelope said, fingering a rip in her denims. 'Even Josie said it was OK, can you believe it?'

'Course I can,' I said, 'you's family to them folk.'

Then I remembered that little boy's drawing, that black circle. 'How's the kid doin'?' I said. 'Still havin' nightmares?'

'Josh? They've gotten worse. He doesn't sleep much now.'

'Josie said it was him bein' foolish on account a' him seein' the posters a' Kreagar round town.'

'I didn't want to tell you. . .' she started saying then got all quiet.

'Tell me what?'

She kept on at that rip in her trousers.

'Tell me what, Penelope?'

'In case you did something stupid. . .'

'Tell me what, goddamn it?' I stood up and stamped hard on the boards.

'He was spotted,' she said. 'Kreagar. About a mile outside Tucket.'

My heart went hard and Penelope carried on.

'A pair of hunters checking their trapline found a fire and spotted a man running through the trees. The man, they said, had black marks all over his face. When they saw the poster, they said it was uncanny. He's here, Elka.'

I sat back down slow. I'd had a feeling Kreagar was in Tucket but didn't right believe it. It weren't solid. It weren't concrete. But now. Hell, now I didn't have no choice but to honour my bargain with Lyon. There weren't no other way. I looked out into the trees, into the wild, and wanted to run but Lyon's words kept repeating in me like rotten meat. *I'll take that pretty blonde friend of yours to Genesis instead.*

This time last year, when I was walking away from my burning home, I'd a' said shit, what do I care 'bout some prissy southern girl? Hang her twice if you want. Now I looked at Penelope, thought a' her picture in the newspaper, swinging from the tree, and near reached out and hugged her. There weren't no question a' me leaving.

Next day I went to Tucket and I found the site where them hunters said they saw Kreagar. All was left was a black scorch in the dirt and a few heavy tracks leading north what meant he probably went south. Them tracks disappeared like someone had taken a wet cloth to a chalkboard. Just like Trapper always done when he was hunting. I weren't going to find him like this, 'specially once winter hit. He never did his killing in winter, said the snow told tales. He went to ground and slept most a' the days like a plump grizzly in his cave. I'd have to lure him out and that meant putting his favourite treat on show.

But I didn't know if I had it in me to do that no more. Year ago, maybe. Two year ago, ain't no question. I couldn't figure how a person could change so much in such a short time. Maybe I weren't as wild and heartless as I thought I was. But then again, maybe I was just as rotten as Kreagar for even considering what I was about to do.

Back at Tin River, I lay awake while Penelope slept and thought all 'bout how I'd have to do it, all the to's and fro's, backs and forths. I didn't like it, what I'd have to do, but way I saw it there weren't no other option. It'd be safe a' course, but it weren't a good thing to do. Took me most a' the night, till it was pitch outside and the chill was coming through the walls. That chill went right into my bones and woke up the devil and angel on my shoulders. One said no then the other said hell no but they weren't changing my mind. Not now. Not when so many lives was riding on it, mine n'all. By the time I figured it all, the snow started falling and I was right out a' time.

A DIAMOND, WAS I?

Woke up to white. Two foot a' snow covered Tin River and turned down the volume a' the world. Snow did that, made everything feel calm and distant. Made me calm and distant. Penelope lit the burner with shivering hands and her breath came smoky out her mouth. I'd slept a few minutes here and there and I had about me a feeling a' numbness what weren't the cold. I kept running it through my mind. Was it worth it? Could I risk it?

I sat on the porch outside the cabin, boots soaking in the chill and wet a' snow. I pinched up flakes 'tween my fingers and watched 'em melt to nothing. Thought it strange how the snow could turn the world on its head then just disappear like it weren't never there. When the ice melted in the spring, sometimes it left behind bodies what got caught out and froze. Nobody would find 'em for months, oftentimes longer. Made me sad to think a' them out there, tired come the night and thinking they'd just sit and take a snooze. Never woke up. Never knew what hit 'em. Winter was the beast of the world. The great demon what locked up the rivers and stole away the food, turned the days to night and killed old folks in they sleep. I'd all but missed last winter, stuck by that poison lake, but this far north, I'd have no chance of escaping it again.

'Aren't you freezing?' Penelope said behind me.

I shook my head but didn't say nothing. My thoughts were in the dark, in the heavy marsh a' shame and I couldn't wade myself out. Wondered brief if I ever would.

'Can you believe this snow, it's so beautiful,' she said but like she weren't expecting an answer, then she didn't speak for a while. I felt her eyes on me, heating up twin spots on my back.

'What?' I said, flicking snow with a twig.

'You're different. These last few days.'

'What you know of it?' I said, meaner'n I should a'.

Penelope's hide was thick to my words now and she didn't go raging at me. I blew a stream a' smoke out into the air. Penelope sat down next to me, shoulder to shoulder. Felt her warmth through the layers a' coat and fur and felt sick by it. She nudged me but I looked to the other side a' me, away from her. Was all I could do not to weep and shout my sorries.

Felt her shivering and she got in a bit closer to me. All I kept thinking was, you don't know nothing 'bout me, you'd hate me if you knew. Thought a' her hating me was worse'n anything right then. It'd happen soon, when she figured it all, but till then I could hold onto her like clutching a rope over a crevasse. Weren't no way I could climb back up it, didn't have no strength, way was blocked by a ledge a' rock, but I could hold on a bit longer. Just a few more days.

'When's it good,' I said, blinking at the sun, 'to do somethin' bad?'

Saw a puff a' her breath but couldn't look at her face.

Took her a while to say something, when she did her voice weren't light with talk a' twinkling snow. 'When you have no other choice.'

Tone of it made me turn.

'Ain't we always got a choice?'

'Not always. When it's your life or theirs.'

Thought brief she was talking 'bout Bilker but there was something in her face, stony white like a smooth wall built up to keep out wolves, that said otherwise.

'Your daddy?' I said and she met my eyes. She looked like she was 'bout to deny it, 'bout to try to bluff her way clear.

We was beyond that.

'He sold me. To Delacroix.' She sniffed up the cold, then smiled. 'But you already knew that.'

'Had me a feelin'. Why'd he do it?'

'Morphine habit and no money to pay for it. We were at the lake and I overheard him one evening talking to a French woman in a clearing between the lake and the road.' Her voice turned bitter. 'It was strange because there was no one else out there, you know, I hadn't seen anyone else for days and days. That's what made me listen. They agreed a price and Delacroix said she'd send men to collect me in the morning. My father. . . god. . . he said he got the better deal.' She shook her head then kept on. 'I was so *angry* at him. He was meant to protect me, not throw me to the dogs for a fix. I let my anger get the better of me. I waited until he was addled, dragged him to the lake and swam him out to the middle of it. He couldn't swim, you see. When I got to Genesis and met Colby, I was too messed up to realise what he was doing or that he was Delacroix's man. I was on my own for the first time, he was there and he offered to take

me to the ferry boat. He was kind and handsome, you know
how it goes.'

'Why'd you lie 'bout it?' I said.

'It's not that easy to admit to murder.'

Wanted to say, I know. Damn it, I know. The face a' that
hog man, turned slack when my knife stuck his throat,
still came to me when I shut my eyes. Still felt his breath. I
murdered him but he weren't the one locked in my head.
He weren't the one. But my mouth wouldn't make the
sound. My throat wouldn't give it breath. You can't admit
to someone else what you're too damn afraid to admit to
yourself. We was all allowed secrets and me and Penelope
had figured that 'tween us a long time ago.

'I trust you, Elka,' she said, so tender I put my arm round
her.

Then she leant her head on my shoulder and said, 'Are
you going to do something bad?'

Felt heat in my eyes, like sparks come straight out a fire.
I already done something bad. So many bad things. What
was one more? I didn't answer her 'cause in them moments,
them quiet, still, perfect white moments outside our cabin,
on our land, with nought but each other and a fire in the
grate, I couldn't tell her a lie.

In my head, lying now would be the worst thing I could
do. Better to tell her nothing than a lie.

She felt me tense up, felt my chest go tight 'neath her
head. She sat up, took my hand and said, 'What you did
with Kreagar. . . it doesn't matter now. You're not the same
person. You're not him.'

My chin started trembling. 'How'd you know?'

'Kreagar wouldn't have pulled me out of that crate. Or
out of that river. Would he?'

He would a' pulled her out just to kill her himself later.
I said no.

'Underneath all the grime,' she said, smearing a spot a'
dirt on my cheek with her finger, 'you're a diamond, Elka,
clear and tough and priceless.'

'But you don't *know*. . .' I said, in no more'n a whisper.
That heat in my eyes burned, everything went flickery and
blurred up with tears.

'I know enough,' she said, but she said it in a strange way.
That same way she said it to me 'bout her daddy. I hadn't
told her 'bout the. . . what Lyon made me remember. The
way she was looking at me, mix a' humouring and pity, same
way she looked at me back in Halveston when we found out
'bout the doctor's boy and his poor legs, that same look what
said she knew what Kreagar done and she knew what I done.

My tears dried up. All the snow cooled down that heat
and she nodded to me, slowly, reading all them thoughts
right off my face.

Right then all I wanted was to get the hell away. Shame
ran all through me like the whole Yukon River was rushing
in my veins. I stood up, stumbled off the porch and into the
snow, messed up all that perfect white, just like I'd messed
up everything else.

'Elka.' Penelope stood up too but I couldn't look at her,
not now, not ever never again, no sir. 'Elka, it's OK,' she
kept saying, but it weren't. Course it weren't. She'd figured
it. All this time at Tin River thinking I'd got free of it, that I
could live a real proper true life after all that I done. It was
all horse shit and I was a goddamn fool for thinking otherwise. Penelope knew what Kreagar done to the doctor's boy,
shit, everyone did. She put all the twos together and got
four and got me. She'd snuck in them doors a' mine when

I wasn't watching and part a' me, that dark part, wanted to slap her clean 'cross that pretty cheek for the betraying of it. That's what it was, after all, betraying. Knowing something 'bout me that I didn't even proper know myself. Damn her she *knew*. Anger and rage gritted up my teeth, seized up all my muscles, made everything in me hard and jagged and stabbing. I shook all over, hot was back in my eyes.

I tried to hold it all in, keep all the heat from spilling over and melting the world. I dug my teeth into my lip so hard I tasted blood. Made my stomach tighten up.

I spat on the snow. Great smear a' red almost sizzling. That was it. I seen it right there in that tiny little picture and everything came clear and calm. Blood on snow was my mark on the world. It was a horror at first, made people look and question and for a time worry 'bout how it got there. It'd never be more than a freak thing to stare at and quick shuffle away. But then, come spring, it'd be gone, melted, everyone would forget it was ever there, no matter how bad it was, no matter how shocking.

'I'm goin' huntin',' I said and pushed past her into the cabin. Couldn't look at her. I grabbed my knife and hat and stormed back outside. She tried grabbing me but I shook her off. She tried talking to me but I ignored her. I was hurting right down deep, worse'n Kreagar ever hurt me. There was once pureness 'tween me and Penelope what me and Kreagar never had. We'd both come out a' them crates with new lives but now she rubbed blood and shit in that. Weren't her fault, course it weren't, but it felt like it in my raging head. She should a' damn well said something. She knew the rotten core a' me and my shame and that was too much. Hell, I couldn't make peace with what I done, I sure as shit couldn't make peace with someone I cared for knowing 'bout it too. Why didn't it matter to her? Why didn't she go running from me, screaming? Why was she still here?

Then I figured it and it was the one thing what kept me from throwing my fist to her face. She ain't been in all the doors in my head. There was still that one there, locked up with padlocks and chains and bolts slammed home. If she'd opened that one, if she knew what was in there, she'd be out that cabin quicker'n you could spit, calling out for Lyon and her iron bars.

Penelope shouted my name, shouted it loud and raw till she was all but screaming. Shocked birds out their nests, sent critters fleeing. Heard tears in her voice, heard confusion and anger and all kinds a' things what I couldn't, didn't want to, make sense of. Broke my black heart to hear it. When I got to the trees, I paused brief, there weren't no going back after this, after I left this place what we'd made into some kind a' home. Penelope seen me stop, figured she knew why. I turned round, looked at her, standing there wrapped up to a bundle in coats and a blanket, holding something up over her head. She shouted and her voice carried crisp right to my ear.

I'd forgot the rifle, how was I going to shoot moose without a rifle? Felt my knife on my belt, stroked my thumb over that worn-down nub on the handle and turned away, started out into the trees.

I didn't need no rifle no more, did I?

I weren't hunting moose.

THERE HE IS

I circled wide round the claim so's Penelope wouldn't figure on where I went and made my way through the trees. Snow was tough going and soaked my boots and trouser legs with chill. I liked winter for the quiet, the feeling a' curling up next to the fire, knowing you got chores but thinking, hell, I can't go hunting in six foot a' snow, then curling up all the tighter. Hated winter for the wet, water goddamn everywhere, getting in all the things it shouldn't. But you got to take the good with the rotten.

Heard a noise somewhere behind me. A crunch a' hard snow. Either it was a fat pine cone falling or someone walking in step with me made a mistake.

I stayed still. Listened. Scanned them trees for puffs a' breath.

Nothing. Not a whisper.

Pine cone, I thought. Or a squirrel what froze in the night and couldn't hold on no more. I put it down to nature and carried on.

I got to Tucket near noon. Stuck to the tree line, out a' sight a' any folks what might be out in the snow. Josie's lumberyard was running and smoke and steam came out the top a' the barn. I quick stopped into the jailhouse where Lyon said she'd be and left a message with some freckled lad in a hand-me-down uniform. Be ready, I said, bring guns. Turns out I was expected and that set my heart going rough and ragged.

'She left you this,' the lad said and took out something from 'neath the counter, wrapped in brown cloth. A red tube 'bout a foot long with a plastic cap.

'What is it?'

He looked at me bored and dull in the face, like he'd just woke up. 'Flare. She said pull the cap when, you know, you're ready or whatever.'

'What's it do?' I said, turning it over, sniffing it.

He yawned and shrugged and I was sick a' him quick. Left without another word and put the flare in my pocket. Made me a mite nervous. Lyon weren't here but she was prepared. I weren't. Not one bit. Made it all real and that set my belly churning up. Hands shook and I said to 'em to calm down, it was just the cold. Told myself to put on a merry face and dredge up the friendlies.

The kid had to believe me.

Kreagar was close, I could feel him in the hairs on my neck and smell his stink on the wind. I knew him better'n I knew myself, that's for sure. Kreagar didn't have no secrets from me no more, he'd laid all his bloody cards on the table while I still had a king lost in my coats. He'd be in these trees, waiting like one a' them fish what's a rock till a guppy comes along then *snap*. Laughing in the trees would be his ripples in the water. Clumsy footsteps in the snow would be his ridges in the sand. He would follow them, no question.

I got close to the Thompsons'. Saw Josie come out the house and head to the barn, wiping her face like she'd just got her fill a' Jethro's cooking. Could see Jethro through the window at the back a' the house, cleaning up in the kitchen. Spotted Mark in the barn, in a string vest despite the cold, hauling logs onto the cutting table. Gentle and strong and a good father he was and I almost ran back to Lyon and told her no, ma'am, I can't give you Kreagar.

Almost.

'Stead I went through the trees, round the barn and house till I was on the far side. Then I saw the boy. Playing in the snow, making angels and throwing handfuls at the boards a' the house. I didn't see no kid then. I saw that curly black hair as pelt. Saw them pudgy arms as bait. I told myself I'd keep the boy safe, no doubt, he was just there for play, just long enough for Kreagar to show himself.

I'd gone to that house with a single thought in my head, one path I could walk down but that path went twisting and forked and broken and I lost my way quick. I didn't mean for it to happen the way it did. That I got to tell you right now, though I won't make much difference no more. What's that saying 'bout the road to hell and good intentions? I was running down that damn road, barefoot and full a' regret. But shit, I couldn't hate what I was 'bout to do too much, figured it'd lead Lyon right to Kreagar and stop god knows how many more killings. That ain't a bad thing, is it? Them thoughts were what damned me to the pit without no hope a' salvation. Right then, in the real, deep, primal part a' me, I didn't think I was doing nothing wrong.

After all, I thought in them moments afore I said my hellos to the boy and all them moments afore when I was making up this plan a' mine, this awful, horrible, terrible plan, that sometimes you got to tie up a kicking rabbit to lure in a wolf. The human in me figured the rabbit would wriggle free in them last seconds or I'd shoot the wolf afore it sunk its teeth. Wild part a' me knew it was easier to catch a wolf what had a full belly.

Then I stopped dead, full a' shock and disbelieving.

That was Kreagar thinking. They was Kreagar words in my head. They weren't mine, weren't me. No not more.

Knowing that, feeling that black poison in me, like oil swimming on water, my legs went from 'neath me and my knees hit the snow. I wanted to slap myself, kick myself, rip my goddamn brain out a' my head for even coming up with the idea, rip my heart out for believing it was *right*. My guts wanted to heave up them thoughts and spill 'em, hot and steaming, on the snow. I wouldn't do it. Couldn't do it. No sir. Whatever I was, however bad I was, I weren't Kreagar. No sir. I weren't him. His rules a' living weren't mine and I wouldn't look at human life like he did, as nothing more'n meat. That boy weren't bait. That boy weren't a deer or a rabbit or a thing to hunt. He was snow-pure and sweet as his uncle's apple pie.

Soon as I'd figured that, a weight came off my back and the world, the trees, the snow, the boy, they were clear and bright and I was too. I was going to catch Kreagar but I weren't 'bout to use a boy to do it. That'd make me no better'n him. I'd track him myself and find him myself and I'd sure as shit kill him myself. That'd make it all the sweeter. Catching him using all them smarts Trapper taught me would be the sting in the tail that bastard deserved. He'd know it too, that his own stupid self, using me for arms and legs, damned him.

I smiled, my face aching with the cold, and felt a surging a' triumph and freedom what I ain't never felt afore. Kreagar was going to pay for what he done and I was here to collect.

Felt me a strong urging to go say goodbye to the boy. Then I'd go into the woods and I wouldn't come out without Kreagar's head in a sack or Lyon's hand patting me on the shoulder. That boy was grace and good and all them things what I weren't. I caught him in a snare all them months back and I weren't 'bout to put him in another trap.

I came out the trees at the back a' the house, out a' view a' the barn and the kitchen windows. The boy didn't run from me, he weren't afraid or quiet like he was round his daddy. I thought he might've, like he'd a' known what was in my head a few minutes ago, but he smiled when he saw me, waved and said make a snowman, Elka. That set my heart in my throat and I felt like I was choking. Made parting all the worse. Figured I could have a few moments. Few little memories I could take with me.

I dug my hands into the snow and piled it high up with him, patted it down into something like a ball. He threw a lump a' snow at me what hit square in my chest. Shock a' the cold in my collar made me gasp and I looked at him like thunder.

But he just laughed. Giggled. Threw another.

I ain't never played in the snow afore. Snow was a toil to get through, it weren't for fun or frolic. I laughed with him, giggling like a damn idiot. I threw a snowball at him and it hit him square in his chest, not hard-like, but it was a fine hit. He cried out all loud and flopped down in the snow, saying I'd killed him. Then he went still and all my muscles froze up, like I was seeing a picture a' what might a' been.

Then. 'Elka?'

I spun round, saw Penelope done up all in heavy coats, sprinkling a' snow in her hair and my heart near stopped.

The boy saw her a second later, pure joy lit up his face. He sprang up, shouted out 'Penny' and ran to her, hugged her round the legs.

Penelope hugged him back and looked at me like I ain't never seen her look at me. I don't even know what it was in her eyes. Confusion? Disappointment? Horror? I couldn't speak to ask. My last words to her were 'bout hunting and then she finds me here, boy lying still, playing dead at my feet. Felt sick for it.

She went to say something but then a hearty voice interrupted. Mark, coming round the corner a' the house. Saying hello to me and what you doing here and Josh is having a great time.

Suddenly they was a family. The boy was telling his dad 'bout the snowman what was in truth just a lopsided lump. Here's his eyes. Here's his shoulders. Here's his legs.

'I was on a walk,' I said, all but jibbering, though no one was paying me no attention, save Penelope.

'Elka,' she said, sharp and cold, 'don't you have to get on? Moose won't hunt themselves after all.'

Tears pricked hot in my eyes and I nodded. Mark looked at me, smiling and happy that I'd kept his boy busy for a spell. I said sure, yeah, course I do.

'See you later, at the cabin,' Penelope said, snow reflecting white in her eyes, turning 'em into mirrors and making her look like she got a barrier up where there ain't never been one afore.

I nodded, felt like I'd been slapped right in the face, stunned out a' myself. I looked at the boy and smiled.

'Bye, Josh,' I said, then I knelt down 'side him and

whispered close, 'you ain't gotta be afraid a' the man no more. I'm gonna get him and you gonna be sleeping safe tonight.'

I looked up at Penelope and that frown in her eyes. She didn't know what I said but when the boy hugged me, wrapped his short, skinny arms round my neck, her frown softened up.

I walked away without another word. I felt Penelope's eyes heavy on my back while I was going. Wondered what she was thinking, but in truth, I already knew it. That bridge we'd built 'tween us, that one what was wobbling already, I'd just gone and dug out the foundations. I'd sat the whole damn thing on quicksand and it weren't going to be long afore it swallowed up us both.

I got to the tree line, only looked back once to see the boy with his snowman and Penelope and Mark talking close by but not paying all that much attention 'cept to each other.

That's when I heard another a' them crunches. Saw a shadow shift out the corner of my eye. My head muddled. Guilt throbbed through me like venom from a snake bite and I didn't pay no mind to another fallen pine cone. Another dead squirrel.

I stalked off into the forest, direction Penelope said them fellas seen Kreagar. I had to start somewhere. Snow fell off the branches and slumped on the ground, covering up all my tracks, making the world like it was afore I messed it up.

Felt the flare in my pocket. Wondered brief if I could go back to Lyon, open up that locked door in my head, and let her do whatever she wanted with me.

But that wouldn't rid this world a' murdering, kid-killing Kreagar Hallet.

The fog in me cleared up so's I could just see 'cross to the other side a' all this.

I was the only one who stood a chance a' bringing punishment down on Kreagar, stopping him from taking more lives. Hour ago I'd a' baited that trap with a boy, what I knew would bring him running like a starving man to a cookout. But I stopped myself, afore I did the bad and that was what mattered. The look in Penelope's eyes was all that bad reflected back at me and it showed me what could a' been if I'd turned to the dark 'stead a' the light. I thanked her for it, in my head. I'd never say it to her out loud, that'd be admitting all my wrongs and that'd kill us both.

I'd figure another way a' getting Kreagar. I'd have to and quick, afore the winter sent him sleeping.

After all this time and heartache, trudging through the snow round the outside a' Tucket, I didn't count on Kreagar making it so damn easy for me.

FOR THE WOLVES

I'd been in the forest, moving slow and steady, for I didn't know how long, thinking on my sins, shivering, when I heard a shout. Sharp yelp it was, back toward the Thompson house. My shivering stopped and afore I could tell my feet, they was running. Didn't take me long to get back to their land when I seen a shadow dart 'tween trees ahead of me. Shadow carrying something heavy. I knew what that bundle was even at that distance. I knew what the yelp was. I knew it all.

Kreagar had the boy. I'd told him I'd keep him safe. Anger rose up in me like a belch, burning up my insides.

It was Kreagar's legs I saw in the Reverend's basement. It was him all them months ago by the poison lake, that demon what I cut, though I couldn't be sure at the time. I'd gone a year without laying certain eye on him. But now, my head was clear, the sun was bright on snow and there he was, Kreagar goddamn Hallet, wearing my daddy's face. Couldn't right tell if he'd seen me too but he might a' heard me running.

I wrapped my fingers round my knife and pulled it free. My heart thudded so hard in my chest I thought it would shake the snow off all the trees.

They weren't pine cones falling, I thought, they was his footsteps, his shadow, following me right from Tin River. Right to the Thompsons' back door.

I followed his tracks and caught sight a' him again. Too far to catch. Too far to throw my knife for fear a' hitting the boy. Josh was flung over one shoulder, not moving but smoky breath came out his mouth. Still alive. I still had time. My heart was thundering worse'n any storm, worse'n the sound them Damn Stupid bombs must a' made. My heartbeat must a' shook the world 'cause right then, heavy snow started falling, covering up all them tracks.

Kreagar's arms filled out the shirt he was in, and it was just a shirt, untucked, flapping over jeans soaked to the knee. No coat. No hat. He looked like he'd stepped right out a' summer and got caught by the weather. He slowed up to climb over a fallen log, icy with snow, and I saw them tattoos. Them black marks I took for dirt when I first saw him all them years ago. Stripes and swirls going out from his eyes and mouth, fang-like marks going down his chin, same both sides a' his face like he had a mirror along his nose. Them patterns no doubt meant something to him but what, shit, he'd never tell me, no matter how many times I nagged. Them tattoos went all down his chest and most way down his arms, mixing in with the wiry black hair. When I was just a babe, I thought a' him as covered head to heel in spiders.

Smoke streamed out his nose and his free hand made a tight fist by his side. I ducked quick behind a fat alder tree and watched him climb over the log, awkward-like with that load over his shoulder but he wouldn't put him down. His

mouth was stretched into some kind a' smile and it made
me sick and fearful to see it. All 'cause I seen it before. Too
many times. When we had a fresh deer on the gutting table,
when he'd come back bloody from his wolf hunts.

Kreagar got himself over that log and was gone, running,
lumbering like a bear with a salmon 'tween his teeth.

In truth, I couldn't make no sense a' my thoughts or
feelings right then. I was stuck behind that alder. I didn't
know nothing. I couldn't a' given you a straight answer if
you'd asked me my name or what I had for breakfast. It
was a muddle and all I remember, with any true clearness,
was the steps that got me A to B, the throw what caught me
a murderer.

All my instincts came right to the front a' my head and
took control a' my arms and legs. I weren't human no more
in them woods. I was wild. My blood was coursing. My heat
rising. All my senses fizzled and I climbed up the alder, ran
along a branch, moved in them trees like I'd been born off
the ground. I followed Kreagar through the treetops but he
was quick and moving branch to branch was slow. He was
getting further ahead a' me, I was losing sight and had only
my hearing as a guide.

We was far away from Tucket now, too far to hear shouting or cries out for the boy, tracks been covered up and
them town folk didn't have a chance a' finding us. The snow
was falling fat flakes on the world, silencing everything what
weren't me or Kreagar's crunching footsteps.

I careful and quickstepped across branches, trying to
keep 'em in eye. Panic rushed through me quick and hard
as a dam breaking. My hands were shaking, sending tremble
up my arms, down my legs. I raced 'cross a gap too big and
jumped onto icy lichen covering the oak branch 'neath

my feet. I slipped soon as my foot touched it and fell right out the tree, landed on my back in white powder. Didn't hurt. Fresh snow's a pillow. But it cost me time and a mite a' pride. Far ahead, right at the limit I could see 'tween the falling flakes, Kreagar and the quiet bulk over his shoulder vanished behind a snowbank.

'No no no no,' I said over and over, smoky breath puffing, scrambling up to my feet.

Despite the weather, Kreagar's deep tracks was easy to follow, easy to see. He wanted me to find him. He wanted me to see it.

But when I got to that snowbank, feet sinking deep in the cold, I saw two sets of tracks. One straight down the hill, one veering left. Weren't no telling which to follow. Devil set me a trap and I didn't have no clue how he did it. All this fresh snow should a' covered up anything more'n ten minute old. It didn't make no sense. None of it made a lick a' sense. Fear for the boy burned up in me so hot it could a' melted the world. Panic and anger and hate, all of it. That boy was meant to be safe and back in his home with his daddy and Penelope.

Everything was bubbling up in me and clouding up my head. I followed one set a' Kreagar's boot prints, then turned back and followed the other. I couldn't think in straight lines. The boy was going to die if I didn't figure it. That darling little fella, that curly black hair, them smiles he had. I saw that pencil scratch a' me on his drawing. Part a' his family. Part of a pack and I was 'bout to lose him.

I swore up something fierce. Turned myself round and round and round till I heard it. The sound what broke the whole damn world.

No more'n a second of a scream. Cut short. Life cut short.

I honed in on that sound. Ran like it was my life being taken, like the hounds a' hell were snapping at my heels. I dodged 'tween trees, kept my breathing quiet as I could. Didn't hear no other sound. No kicking a' young legs. No crying out.

There's a thing that happens in the forest when life is snuffed out afore it's meant to. There's a silence that comes down on everything like a blanket. Happens for a mite when you take a rabbit out the snare, break its neck. There's a deeper silence when you take out your blade or pull the trigger on a moose or deer. Deepest silence for a child.

The forest was weeping blood and so was I.

I was too late.

I caught a flash a' metal in the trees. A knife twisting, changing grip. Felt that knife right in my heart, slicing cold. My legs buckled up 'neath me. I fell down onto my hands and knees and wanted more'n anything to scream all that pain, all that guilt, right out into the winter air.

But that wouldn't do that boy no good. Dying on my knees wouldn't honour no memory a' him.

My tears sizzled on the snow.

My fists clenched white.

My head set firm.

'Goddamn you,' I whispered, 'goddamn you Kreagar Hallet.'

I clambered up in a tree and moved through them branches. Not that far ahead, I saw Kreagar in a clearing ringed with thick brush. I didn't see nothing else, maybe my head wouldn't let my eyes take it in, like it didn't all them times Kreagar brought home a pig.

I didn't see the boy. All I saw was Kreagar and a world turned red. My heart, my whole *being*, was broken up like someone took a hammer to thin ice. You can't put ice back together. Even killing Kreagar wouldn't put me back together now.

He breathed out smoke and I saw in him a thick line a' evil, black and festering.

That son bitch snatched the boy's life, like he was just borrowing it to begin with. I closed my eyes. I wished to high heaven, to all that's holy and good in this world, that time would turn back so's I could a' saved that boy even if it would a' lost me the devil. It would a' been worth it. I would a' saved that boy and chased Kreagar all the way to the top a' the world if I could.

But that decision been made for me now and I hated them heavens for it. I got there too late, too damn late, useless as a damn toothpick 'gainst a raging river. I cursed myself every which way till I didn't have no more words for myself. Only way I had even a sliver of a chance to pull my soul or spirit or whatever I got in me out a' the clutches a' the devil was to send that devil back to the pit.

That boy what I'd built a snowman with not an hour ago, all that life he had bundled up inside him was let out, like a tyre letting out air.

How easy it was for Kreagar to take living away. Easy as a garter snake swallowing a mouse. It's always easy to kill what ain't you. Easy for a bear to kill a salmon, easy for a wolf to take a caribou calf. Ain't easy for a bear to kill a bear or a wolf to kill a wolf or a man to kill a man. Kreagar couldn't a' been a man, not down deep. He was something else. Some new type a' animal.

I was back at Trapper's hut with Lyon 'bout to burn it down. Felt now like I did then. That my little bubble was burst. That all them things I thought I knew as true weren't nothing even close. Some a' them chains over my last door slipped off.

I lost Mark his son.

Josie and Jethro their nephew.

I didn't even want to think 'bout what I lost Penelope.

I was frozen. Couldn't lift my arm to throw the knife. Couldn't open my mouth to shout my sorrows. What was the point in me? What in the hell was I going to do 'gainst Kreagar fucking Hallet?

From the middle a' the clearing, he paced ten strides north, then, with just his hands, started digging in the snow. Got himself a shallow hole then took something wrapped up in his shirt, something else my eyes wouldn't let me see, and buried it like a goddamn squirrel buries nuts. He was making a larder. One final fucking insult. My stomach heaved and churned and it took all I had to keep it down. Here's your boy, they'd say when the body was found, but he ain't whole. The rest a' him's just sitting there, few feet away, and you ain't never getting that back.

One thought hit me harder'n anything, felt like it would knock me out the tree, push me into the snow till all I saw was white and cold. I couldn't save him. I was too slow. My stump legs couldn't get through the snow fast as Kreagar's.

I could a' shouted.

I could a' roared at him through the forest, made him turn and come at me 'stead a' that boy.

But down-deep, pure primal fear, covered up with dumb hunter's logic, stopped me. If I shout he'll bolt. If I scream his name, he'll disappear into the woods for the rest a' winter.

Bullshit.

It was boot-quaking fear and nothing else. If I shouted,

he'd turn them evil eyes and that snarling rage right on me and he'd kill me no question. Damn coward I was. All the rest a' my days, I saw the Thompson boy's face behind my eyes and I'd have to live with it.

I don't remember when the snow stopped but I remember when I stopped crying. I saw Kreagar's face, head on, spattered with red, smoke coming out his mouth like some demon climbed straight out a' hell. And shit, he looked happier'n I ever saw him. He looked like he was finally at peace with the world and that ain't something I ever thought 'bout. I never got to ask him why but in that look I thought I figured it out. Kreagar's got something in him that's snapped, some bit deep inside that's broke or missing. Doing this, maybe that fixes that break, patches up the crack for a spell. I suppose it's a choice, ain't it? Live all your life broken or take moments a' wholeness where you can, no matter what that means. This is a world a' hurt and shit and blood and bullets. This is a world where a strong arm is a' more value than a strong mind. The Damn Stupid changed up all the people a' this country, changed up coin to mean not much, changed up cities, changed up the law, it made murderers a' all us what's left. I'd killed a man to survive, maybe Kreagar had too, to survive inside his own head. What kind a' person was I to judge him? To take his life like he weren't nothing more than a trapped wolverine? Hundred times over I'd said I'd kill him but something stopped me throwing that knife and dropping him dead like he deserved. Now I faced him, now I saw what he was behind all that blood and bile, and I pitied it. I damn well pitied him. Killing him weren't my job. It was Lyon's. She'd lost a son to his rifle and she deserved the pleasure a' seeing the light leave his eyes.

Kreagar left the clearing, breathing heavy off into the forest. I set the flare burning right in the middle a' all the blood, and followed. Didn't take long to get ahead a' him. I figured his path quick.

'You're a long way from home, Kreagar,' I said, oak branch 'tween my knees. I kept all the fury and tears out my voice. Couldn't show him weakness, not now not ever.

He stopped, bared them teeth a' his, and looked all round for me.

'Who's that talkin' at me out in the trees?' he shouted, blood dripping off that knife and the scrap a' hair and skin I now seen hanging off his belt.

'Saw what you did to that boy,' I said, couldn't say his name, heart tightened and didn't want to beat no more, 'saw where you put him. See his curly hair on your belt.'

'That you, Elka girl? That my Elka playing squirrel in the trees?' he shouted.

Hearing him say my name, the name what he gave me and a year ago was the only one who ever spoke it, sent a yearning through me for them days. Them simple days a' hunting and chopping wood and tending the hut. Them simple days what turned to shit with one trip to Dalston.

'I ain't yours,' I said, wondered brief if he could hear the sad in my voice. 'Never was, never gonna be.'

I took out my knife. Weighted right nice for throwing.

Soon he started threatening me, saying all the nasty things he would do to me if he caught me, but he wouldn't never catch me. I was a ghost in them trees. He'd killed something in me when he took the Thompson boy and I'd be his spectre now, haunting him for what little life he had left. He leaned 'gainst a cottonwood tree right in front a' me.

I stood up on the branch. Weren't no slipping now. I raised up my knife and set my sight right on his heart. One hit on target and that'd be the end a' Kreagar Hallet. I gripped the blade 'tween my fingers. Tightened up all my muscles.

I thought 'bout building the snowman with the boy. Thought 'bout Mark thanking me for keeping his son busy and laughing. Rage ate through me like fire through paper.

I threw my knife right on target. Through that soft spot in his shoulder. Heard the wood-thud what said the blade went right into the tree. He howled and shouted and tried to pull the knife out but he was a coward for pain. Them barbs cut deep. Deep into his flesh like he'd cut so many others.

'I'm gonna find you! I'm gonna kill you slow, Elka!' he roared, sending birds out their nests.

I let out something like a laugh. There he was, murdering, kid-killing Kreagar Hallet. The man what was a ghost to me this last year who I never thought I'd see again. I'd built him up in my head as some kind a' god what I couldn't touch but when I looked at him, he was just a man, bleeding out his shoulder. A broken man, what needed justice and a place where he couldn't hurt no one else.

'Magistrate Lyon's gonna find you first,' I said. I cast my eye back to the clearing and saw plumes a' red smoke showing the way. 'Told her where you is and where the boy is too. She'll see what you did to him. She's been hunting you a long time, across mountains she's gone, looking for you.'

That shut him up. Colour drained right out of him and he tried on the friendly with me but we was far past friendly. Sound a' horses carried on the breeze.

I weren't in no mood to see Lyon again and she'd spot me quick in these trees. Felt sore for losing my knife. I honed it and shaped it and kept it sharp till the time was right and it caught me a killer.

Maybe it was me moving, not caring no more if he saw me but Kreagar started shouting.

'Elka, Elka, there you is,' he said, fierce. 'How's them cuts on your back? Healed up right nice?'

'No thanks to you,' I said.

He hissed 'gainst the cold. 'You figured it yet? You figured why I didn't kill you all them chances I had? When you was a babe, with that crazy Rev, by that lake, in Halveston, in your Tin River claim.'

I didn't answer, I couldn't because I had figured it. I remembered all them words he spoke in that basement. I knew exactly why he hadn't killed me all them times he could. He wanted me to choose his life, his path. He wanted me to come back to him by choice because, in his head, we was just the same. In his head, I was a murderer, a killer, and I had the same *tastes* as him. I was his successor.

He laughed, all wheezing and full a' spit and blood, like he'd heard my thoughts.

'You got yourself a pretty girlfriend,' he said. 'Bet she'd be sticky-sweet roasted up right nice.'

Then I got angry and all them words I been saving up came out a' me.

'You're sick, Kreagar. Sick in the damn head and I ain't a stitch like you. I fucking loved you. You were my daddy and you. . . you a killer. You're Kreagar fuckin' Hallet. You ain't my Trapper. The man what. . . did that. . . to the Thompson boy and all them others deserves to swing and you will. Lyon ain't gonna show you no mercy for what you done.'

Them horses got closer. Heard voices now. Weren't no mistaking Lyon. Cries went up. They must a' found the boy.

Kreagar heard it too. All the fight left him and he hissed out pain as smoke on the air.

'Does that bitch know?' he said. 'She know who pulled the trigger what shot her boy?'

Them locks on that last door burst open. Alls I had to do was turn the handle.

'You did,' I said, but my voice was all tremble.

He laughed, spouting smoke into the air like a bull charging. 'You been walking my wolf road all your life, Elka girl, clawing and biting right on my heels, begging for scraps and teaching and I gave 'em both. I gave you everything you'd ever need to walk right alongside me. You and me Elka, we's twin flames, remember. Even if I ain't living no more, you ain't never gonna be rid of me.'

'Lyon'll get rid a' you. Lyon'll break your damn neck. I ain't no twin a' yours. We's mud and sky, river and rock. We ain't the same.'

He bared his teeth and showed off the beast in him. 'Just you wait and see, girlie, just you wait.'

Saw movement in the trees.

He smiled and the door creaked open.

'You better run, Elka girl,' he said, keeping that smile on him. My heart thundered in me like a whole herd a' horses.

He weren't even trying to pull that knife out no more.

He said it again. Run. Go on. Get going.

He didn't say goodbye, didn't say see you soon, didn't say sorry. Kreagar weren't one for sorry.

A shout came through the trees, 'There!' then the horses started running fresh. They found the trail and it was time for me to go.

Kreagar, grinning, waved.

THE LONGEST WINTER

I went back to Tin River. Penelope weren't there a' course. I couldn't face going back to Tucket, seeing all them people crying and screaming, blaming me. Tin River was quiet, covered in fresh snow. Soon as I got there, got in the cabin, I broke. I collapsed on the floor, shaking all over, and let out all the rage and sad and fear in me. I shouted at the world for not letting me save him, cursed heaven and hell for making me promise to, making me break my word. I beat the floorboards with my fists until my blood stained the wood.

Then I heard the rumble in the north.

Out the window I saw the thunderhead roll in. Bigger and blacker and faster than any I'd ever seen. I didn't have time for weeping and screaming, the world didn't care. It swept down the mountains like it was swallowing up the world. It's what I imagined it was like when them Damn Stupid bombs fell. Like the world was ending for real. That storm was so big I couldn't imagine there would ever be an end to it. Figured that was my punishment. It weren't Lyon going to hang me, it was the wild what was going to take payment.

I didn't have none a' them storm shutters on the cabin, just wood ones, and they wouldn't last long. Only hope I had a' living through it was the larder. I levered up the floor-boards, hunkered down with the zip bags a' salmon and pulled the boards back.

Then it hit. Like a charging bear slammed right into my chest.

Deafening and crashing and shaking up everything. It weren't like no thunderhead I ever lived through. Doubted there'd be a cabin left when it passed over.

Don't know how long it raging up above me. Could a' been days. I sat 'neath my cabin, in the dark, freezing cold, while the rest a' the world was pulled down around me.

I noticed the quiet. That meant I was still alive at least. But I had a fear in me 'bout what I'd find when I went outside.

I climbed out a' that larder, my bones creaking and feeling like they would snap for the cold. It was just 'bout daylight but I could barely see it for the snow. I was buried. The whole cabin was under ten foot a' whiteout. One a' my windows was broke and the snow poured in. The thunder-head had put me in a prison cell, that's for sure and I deserved it. This was me now, till I could dig myself out. If I ever could.

It was over, weren't it?

Lyon had her man and he'd swing in Genesis. Penelope had her man, whatever was left a' him. And me? Shit, I didn't need or want no man. I had my walls. Had my quiet. Hell, ain't nothing more quiet than snow. Had the rest a' my rotten life to figure what had happened in them first eighteen years and forget it.

I couldn't light the fire so I ate one a' them sides a' salmon raw. Almost threw it back up. Penelope didn't come back that night, nor the next. I bet that storm tore up Tucket something awful. I wondered brief how she was doing, what she was doing, if she was happy out there. Then I told myself I was stupid. There weren't no happy in Tucket for that family. There was grief and anger and I was the cause a' all that. No matter how you want to spin it, I led Kreagar here. Right to their front door. I said it would happen, first day we set foot in Tucket, I said so. Cursed Penelope for thinking otherwise. Wolf weren't warning me off Penelope in that shelter cabin. She weren't the dangerous one. I was and he was trying to tell her, make her run and get shot a' me. I weren't built for human company. I bring a rain a' shit and blood down on anyone I come near.

Just like Kreagar.

I'd had a fear in me since the Reverend's table that I'd turn right into him, I'd be the new beast a' the woods, hunting them what didn't stand no chance. He killed the doctor's boy and Mark's to show me what I done to Lyon's. He was laughing in the trees while I was screaming. He'd been waiting for me to figure his way was my way and I was him all through. Just what he wanted a' me. I thought I'd taken that last step into the dark afore I got to the Thompson house, afore I played in the snow with the boy and promised to keep him safe. But I heard them words in my head then and they was Kreagar's. Just 'cause I was raised by that man and had done terrible things in his name, didn't mean I would become him. I always said I walked my own path, found my own track in this world, and the sound a' them words, right in that moment, reminded me a' that.

Least I had that. Least I hadn't become him. Not yet anyways. That gave me a mite a' solace while I was trapped in snow and sorrow.

I spent them days after Kreagar and the boy tense and waiting, slow digging my way out the cabin window. Every sound what hit my ears was muffled and hard to place and I thought it was horses. Hooves kicking up dirt, boots crunching on snow. Coming for me for what I done. That door in my head was wide open. Kreagar kicked it in for me and ushered me inside with a big sweep a' his arm. *She know who pulled the trigger?*

Only one person what weren't me knew for sure what happened that day back in the Mussa valley. That man was sitting in a jail cell or already hanging off the Genesis tree. Felt like I was just the same, every day waiting for the snap a' the rope round my neck.

When I finally dug myself out, I quick realised the thunderhead brought full-blown winter with it. The cold came harsh and fast to Tin River and Tucket. That storm had dropped double, maybe three times the amount a' snow what was normal. It cut off every path to Tucket, sealed up Tin River and me with it. Even Lyon and her long-legged horses couldn't wade through this. This weren't just a snow flurry what settles the ground. This was the long, dark night, the few hours a' sunlight a day till the world turns again, and it brought more and more snowstorms, heaping white on white, bending the trees, sending all the critters into their dens to starve.

Penelope never came back a' course. I ate every other day and with just me out there, the salmon we caught and the rest a' the supplies we'd got was enough to get me through to spring.

I didn't see no other person that whole winter while I

cleared the snow round the cabin and fixed up all the bits
what the thunderhead broke. It was like I was cracking rocks
in a quarry with chains round my feet, trying to do something worthwhile as my penance. Board up the window, split
the boulder. Shore up the porch, haul the rubble. Maybe I
was rebuilding a life. Every nail in a loose roof tile was a step
closer to redemption.

I was miserable and rightly so. It was lonely and cold and
I craved company worse'n I ever craved food or water. Never
thought I'd say that in truth. Always thought I wanted the
lonesome life. People is trouble. Folk have darkness in them
what the wild don't and that scared me silly. Kreagar had
that dark, so did Penelope for what she did to Bilker and
her daddy, what meant I did too. It weren't a dark that the
light could disappear and it took me all them winter months
to figure that.

I boiled snow for water and set traps when I could for
fur and meat but I didn't hold much hope to catching anything. Didn't deserve it. The wild agreed and my traps came
up empty or sprung by a pigeon. Pigeons make good eating
but in them months food was ash on my tongue, stone in my
stomach. When I slept it was like someone in my head was
flicking on a projector in a picture house, showing me all
them memories, all them decisions I made and dark times
I'd got through. The Reverend's knife dragged over my back
all over again. The hog man breathed over me, bore down
on my chest. The dear Thompson boy lay in that forest a'
blood, and me, just minutes too late to save him. That blond
boy in the meadow, screaming, then the gunshot waking
me up sweating and crying. Suppose that's what guilt and
fear do to you, turn all your memories into devils scratching
inside your head.

More'n once I thought 'bout cutting a hole in that river ice and lowering myself into the pull a' the water. I'd die a' the cold or drowning but it only mattered that I'd be dead. Thought 'bout just walking into the snow, no coat, no boots, no hope. Thought 'bout using the rifle or anything to make it all stop. All them memories was beating down my door, wanting a piece a' me. Every night when I closed my eyes I saw the Thompson boy drawing at his table, smiling and showing me as part a' his family. I saw Missy, that poor woman what I brought right to Kreagar, who showed me tenderness by bandaging up my burned hand. I saw Kreagar and Trapper and my momma and daddy and Lyon and Penelope, all shaming me and sneering down at me.

Only one fleeting moment that winter gave me any kind a' hope for a life beyond all this. One morning I was clearing a fresh fall a' snow off the roof. It was getting too heavy for the wood to support and I didn't fancy fixing it all over again. I sloughed off a chunk a' the powder and watched it fall with a crump on the ground. Then I saw it. Across the river, near the trees on the other side a' the meadow, a wolf padded silent through the drifts. Ain't no telling if it was my Wolf, but it could a' been and that was enough. The wolf disappeared and I didn't see it again in them eight months a' winter.

When the sun came back and the snow started melting, I felt that stone in me start to crumble. Spring was all 'bout new life a' course and maybe I'd be allowed one. A fresh start.

One day, the snow most melted and cabin 'bout fixed, I was chopping wood when Penelope came back to Tin River.

THERE SHE IS

I dropped my axe and stared.

'Hello,' she said.

'Hello,' I said back.

She had dark rings 'neath her eyes and she looked thinner'n the last time I saw her. Outside the Thompson house. An hour afore Kreagar killed the boy. Felt like another life.

We went inside the cabin and I stoked up the fire and set a kettle boiling. We sat quiet for a while and I felt squirmy inside, her just being here. Didn't right know what to say.

'What have you been doing all winter?' she asked me, staring round the cabin at the empty salmon bags, papers and pencil on the table.

I shrugged. 'This and that.'

My voice sounded strange inside my head. Croaky and weak. Then I figured why. It ain't been used in months.

Penelope picked up a piece a' paper and looked at all them crooked letters.

'You've been practising?' she asked.

'Sometimes. Don't think I got it right.'

She put the paper down. Didn't look at me. Then she took out something from her pack, wrapped in cloth, and handed it to me. I knew the weight of it right away. I threw off the cloth and felt like smiling.

'My knife?' The one I last saw stuck in Kreagar's shoulder.

I hadn't thought a' much else this winter. Kreagar. Blood. Guilt. They did a dance in my head all them months. All that changed was who was leading the waltz.

'Lyon gave it to me,' Penelope said. 'I didn't feel right keeping it.'

Felt like I was seeing a friend again, holding that blade, wiped clean a' all the things it'd done. I murmured my thanks.

'How you been?' I said.

'How do you think?' she said, on the edge a' spite.

'If you came here to fight just get started, I got wood to chop.'

Penelope said nothing for a minute, was like she was trying to gather up all them thoughts, calm herself down enough to say what she truly wanted to say. She dug into her pocket, handed me a piece a' newspaper.

Spidery black writing and a photograph. Kreagar. I knew them tattoos, no matter how bad the picture. He weren't swinging from a tree. He was sitting in front of a stone wall, arms tied behind his back. Black spots what weren't tattoos on his chest.

'They shot him,' Penelope said. 'Lyon called it execution by firing squad, but she was the only one with a gun.'

My hands started shaking. 'When?'

'A week after. . . you know.'

Before winter. All these months, he'd been dead the whole time. His body was frozen in the ground. I didn't know right how to feel 'bout that. I suppose I'd sentenced him to that myself when I set that flare, when I threw my knife. But it didn't stop me from feeling like I'd lost Trapper all over again. My true daddy, the one what I shared blood with, was outside this cabin, turning to bones and dust in the ground, along with my momma, and I didn't know them from strangers in the street. But the man what raised me and saved my life that night in the woods when I was seven, the man what taught me to hunt and trap and set fires and smoke, the one what patched me up when my knife slipped and what stayed by my bedside that winter I had a weak chest. That man was dead now and so was the demon inside him. He'd found peace at the end of Lyon's six-shooter and the world was that bit brighter for it.

'I'm sorry,' I said to Penelope and I meant it.

'Lyon told me something when I went to see her, after it all calmed down,' she said.

My insides went cold.

'She said Kreagar told her what happened to her son and she said he was very convincing.'

Turned to ice.

'What he say?' I asked. But I knew, course I knew. It weren't hidden from me no more, that door was off its hinges, turning to kindling in my mind.

She just looked at me, waiting for me to tell her.

I nodded, felt heat in my face. 'He said I did it, didn't he?'

Penelope looked down at her feet.

'She comin' for me now the snow's most melted?' I asked.

'I think so.'

Right then I'd a' let her. She could drag me back to Tucket and shoot me dead too for all I cared. All that mattered to me right then was Penelope and what she thought a' me.

'Did you kill her son?' she asked and her tone said she'd been wanting to ask that forever.

My eyes prickled. 'Yes.'

'Oh god, Elka. . .' she said, put her hand over her mouth. The horror in her eyes was enough to set my tears falling free.

'I didn't know. . .' I said, and I didn't. 'My head made doors and locked all them memories behind. The things Kreagar did to them women, with the. . . the eatin'. . . I ate it too and, hell. . . I liked it. I feel sick for it now. I didn't know. I didn't know till I got away from him. I didn't *see* like I do now.'

Getting out them words was like pulling spines out a' bear's paw. It weren't easy, it hurt like hell and wouldn't stop bleeding, but it had to be done.

'We was hunting, he pointed out a young buck,' I said. Penelope closed her eyes but I needed to get it all out, suck all that poison out a' me. 'Sandy-coloured thing, lighter fur than most other deer. It was the first time he let me shoot with him. I was excited, like he finally trusted me. I lined up the shot with him next to me. The buck was just standing there, lookin' at a butterfly or somethin'. Then I pulled the trigger. He was so proud a' me.'

'That wasn't a deer, Elka,' Penelope whispered, horror all through her voice.

'Was to me. Then. There ain't no excusin' it, I know that and I'll take my punishment, but I swear up and down I didn't know what I was doin'. Kreagar didn't kill kids. He never did. Until the doctor's son in Halveston. Was me who shot Lyon's son. I did it and that bastard son bitch Kreagar's been showing me what I done all up and down this country. He's been throwing my sins in my face and them boys were the price. I got to live with that every damn day same as I got to live with not being able to save Josh. I was too late, Penelope, too goddamn slow running after, too. . . I don't know, I couldn't save him.'

She looked me right in the eye then. Felt her gaze in me, searching round for lies she weren't going to find. She must a' decided 'cause she got up, walked over to me and hugged me tight to her. I froze a second then relaxed into her, wrapped my arms round her and cried it all out. I ain't never cried so much as I had done in that cabin, for my dead parents, for myself, for the boy, for Kreagar, now for what I was 'bout to lose.

'You have to go,' Penelope said, kissing me on top a' the head.

'What?' I said, pulled apart from her.

'Lyon will kill you. You have to go.'

'I deserve it,' I said.

She shook her head. 'No you don't. Kreagar did.' Then she knelt down in front a' me and put her hand on my cheek. 'Remember what I said? You're a diamond, Elka. Underneath it all. Nothing can change that. I don't want to see your picture in the newspaper.'

I frowned deep then and tried to figure all her words into some kind a' order what made sense. 'You. . . you don't hate me?'

She smiled, sad then, and her eyes started glistening. 'Of course I don't.'

'But. . .' She knew all I done. Every bit of it. She's got to hate me. 'What about the Thompson boy?'

She tensed up then and I feared I'd undone all that mending. 'Kreagar killed him and you warned me that he would, all those months ago when we first got to Tucket. You knew bad things would happen and I didn't listen. I did as much as you in getting Josh into those woods but you're the one who caught Kreagar. I can't hate you for that. Neither can Mark or Josie or Jethro.'

I'd most forgotten 'bout them over the winter. Them names brought sunshine pictures back into my head and it made me hurt all the more.

I shook my head. 'I deserve Lyon's firin' squad for what I done. Three boys is dead 'cause a' me. I killed one and I couldn't save the others.'

Maybe if I'd figured earlier what I done to Lyon's boy I could a' saved Josh, or the doctor's son. Maybe god or the wild or something up there would a' let me save him if I admitted to myself what I done, took my punishment when I first seen Lyon in Dalston. But I didn't, I didn't know what I seen back then and I made the same mistake twice. Them gods were saying, Elka girl, you ain't taking no responsibility for what you done so we're gonna make you and you gonna see the truth of it.

'I deserve to hang,' I said.

'No you don't, no you don't.' Then she leaned close, put her forehead on mine and said words what I never thought I'd hear from no one. 'Much as I want to slap you some-times, I still bloody love you, all right? I love you, Elka.'

I didn't bother to stop the tears. After all this time, this journey up the world, I finally heard them words spoken to me by someone what meant it. All this time searching for my momma and daddy to get that and it was Penelope all along. I played them words over and over and I stamped them on my brain, over every blood-stained, evil memory I had. *I love you, Elka. I love you, Elka.* I grabbed Penelope and I hugged her so tight I didn't never want to let her go.

Then she said something else what made me tighten up that grip till she couldn't get no breath in her.

'And I forgive you, for everything.'

Was that enough? Was this one person's forgiveness and love enough for all my sins? Then I decided that it weren't the number a' people whose forgiveness mattered. It was who that one person was. Penelope was enough. Just her was enough for me and always would be. She was my redemption and my salvation. I always figured a sweet apple ain't never going to grow on a sour apple tree but maybe I had more sugar in me than I thought. If this peach of a woman, with all her smarts, thought I was good down deep then maybe I was.

'You have to go,' she said and I said OK.

Penelope left not long after that. She hugged me and she cried and thanked me over and over for pulling her out that crate last spring. She told me I was the best friend she ever had and to take care a' myself out there. We both knew I weren't coming back. We both knew we weren't going to see each other again. All that I had left in Tucket was grief and a bullet with my name on it. I waited till I couldn't see Penelope no more, till she was through the trees and gone round a hill, then I packed a bag.

I figured I'd go west, see what was 'cross the BeeCee border, maybe get there for winter and walk 'cross that frozen ocean like them yellow-haired folk in Halveston. I had me a tinder box and my knife. It was a good knife what had caught me a murderer. I used to think I didn't need much more'n that in this life but I was wrong. I needed company, a friend, and my heart ached for Penelope. That was my real punishment, my prison sentence, not getting to see my friend again. Weren't no worse Lyon could do to me than that.

When I walked away from Tin River and the graves of a family I never knew 'cept for some old words in a letter, I left invisible footsteps in the moss. First step was light and carried with it Penelope's forgiveness, them words a' love she spoke so stern and fierce to me in the home we made for ourselves. The home we built weren't just wood and nails and dirt, no sir, it was life. We was both running from black sins and secrets when we stumbled into each other but together, we built something damn great. One a' my footsteps carried them days with her and that one kept on a true heading. The other footstep, well that one were so light, that one tried to pull me off the compass any chance it could. That one stained the moss with blood, heavy with Kreagar's promise to me. *Just you wait and see, girlie, just you wait.* It carried the seed a' possibility that he'd been right all along. I was a second from becoming him on that snowy day in Tucket. I saw the boy as bait, not as a creature a' human worth, just like Kreagar seen all them people he killed. Long as I was in them woods, there weren't no one I could hurt.

But that down-deep wild side a' me had the potential to do what Kreagar done and think how he thought. There weren't no way a' knowing that I wouldn't. Maybe one day I'd take the wrong path. I just had to keep the bright light burning to chase off the dark. I had 'em both with me every step I took away from Tin River, into the wild, into the nowhere and nothing.

Whatever god it was looking down on me must a' taken pity, heard my revelation, or figured I'd suffered enough in my short life, 'cause on the sixth day out a' Tin River, I found tracks only one wild beast could make and on the seventh day I heard him howling.

ACKNOWLEDGEMENTS

They say it takes a village to raise a child. Well, it takes a whole country to publish a novel. This book will pass through dozens of hands before it reaches the reader. It will be edited, marketed, publicised, formatted, proofread, designed, printed, bound, distributed, stacked on shelves, mailed out and finally, read. Thank you to everyone involved at every stage, you're all rock stars.

Thank you to my agent, Euan Thorneycroft, and the whole team at AM Heath. You saw what I wanted to achieve with this story and helped me get there. Elka and I are much stronger for your guidance.

Huge thanks to my editor Sarah Hodgson and the whole team at HarperCollins and Borough Press, also to Julian Pavia at Crown, my editor across the pond, your advice, patience, and enthusiasm have been invaluable.

Thank you to my mum for inspiring me and attacking (constructively, of course) the writing efforts of ten-year-old me with a red pen. I may have cried and stamped my feet but hell, I wouldn't be writing these acknowledgements without your belief that I could do better. Thank you.

Lastly, to my wife, Neen, my rock, my critic, my counsellor, my whole damn world, thank you.